"Readers will enjoy this emotional exploration of a soldier's journey as he returns home to his family's farm after fighting a war in the Pacific. This story examines not only the traumatic impact on his own psyche but on the lives of all who love him most. With alternating points of view, Tromp weaves a complex historical tale incorporating love, suspense, hurt, and healing—all the elements that keep the pages turning."

—Julie Cantrell, *New York Times* and *USA Today* best-selling author of *Perennials*

"Oh my! What a story! *Shadows in the Mind's Eye* is a stunner of a debut novel. Sam and Annie's love is beautifully rendered, Sam's combat fatigue (what we now call PTSD) is compassionately portrayed, and Janyre Tromp's writing effortlessly captures the Southern voice. And the last half of the book is one dangerous, breathtaking twist after another, as Sam's worst nightmares come to pass. A compelling look at a town struggling to find its soul and a wounded couple struggling to reclaim their love. Not to be missed."

—Sarah Sundin, ECPA best-selling and award-winning author of *Until Leaves Fall in Paris* and *When Twilight Breaks*

"An achingly poignant tale of rediscovering love and trust between wounded hearts. Love, forgiveness, and danger weave together in Tromp's emotional tale where the greatest of battles are fought in the mind. Beautiful in description with complex characters, readers will not forget this emotional journey."

—J'nell Ciesielski, best-selling author of *The Socialite*

"Stunning and compelling, Janyre Tromp's *Shadows in the Mind's Eye* kept me turning pages, with a cast of true-to-life characters, pitch-perfect narrative, and a plot that will keep the reader wondering what is true (and what is imagined). Intense and full of heart, Tromp delivers a fresh voice in the world of fiction."

—Susie Finkbeiner, author of *The Nature of Small Birds* and the Pearl Spence series

"With twists and turns as unexpected as an Arkansas thunderstorm, Tromp brilliantly explores the things war can change and the important things it can't."

—Lynne Gentry, *USA Today* best-selling author of *Lethal Outbreak*

"A hair-raising, mind-bending psychological thriller, *Shadows in the Mind's Eye* by Janyre Tromp deftly explores a marriage torn asunder by war. Is a marriage worth fighting for when you cannot see the people your husband is fighting, or when you even become the one he is fighting? Tromp's nuanced empathy elevates this story to another level and blurs the line between villain and hero, causing readers to ponder the lengths they would go to to protect themselves, even against ones they love."

—Jolina Petersheim, best-selling author of *How the Light Gets In*

"*Shadows in the Mind's Eye* is an intense, beautifully written novel about secrets and sacrifice. A story about poignant trauma and truth potent enough to heal a broken family. A fabulous debut!"

—Melanie Dobson, award-winning author of *The Winter Rose* and *Catching the Wind*

"With pitch-perfect dialect, lyrical prose, and homespun wisdom, Tromp delivers a slow boiling mystery that dares to ask the deepest questions about faith, love, suffering, evil, and hope."

—Elizabeth Musser, award-winning author of *The Promised Land*

"Tromp's debut novel is the perfect blend of historical fiction and psychological thriller. *Shadows in the Mind's Eye* hooked me early on and kept me enthralled until the very end. The story is complex and offers readers a glimpse into the toll that trauma can take on a marriage. A story of war, of heartache, of love and healing, this novel will appeal to a broad swath of readers. Tromp is a new author to watch!"

—Kelli Stuart, award-winning author of *The Fabulous Freaks of Monsieur Beaumont* and the upcoming release, *The Master Craftsman*

SHADOWS
in the
MIND'S EYE

a novel

JANYRE TROMP

KREGEL
PUBLICATIONS

Shadows in the Mind's Eye: A Novel
© 2022 by Janyre Tromp

Published by Kregel Publications, a division of Kregel Inc., 2450 Oak Industrial Dr. NE, Grand Rapids, MI 49505. www.kregel.com.

This is a work of fiction. All incidents and dialogue, and all characters with the exception of some well-known historical and public figures, are products of the author's imagination and are not to be construed as real. Where real-life historical figures and public figures appear, many of the situations, incidents, and dialogues concerning those persons are entirely fictional and are not intended to depict actual events or to change the entirely fictional nature of the work. In all other respects, any resemblance to persons living or dead is entirely coincidental.

Published in association with William K. Jensen Literary Agency, 119 Bampton Court, Eugene, Oregon 97404.

Scripture quotations are from the King James Version.

Library of Congress Cataloging-in-Publication Data
Names: Tromp, Janyre, author.
Title: Shadows in the mind's eye : a novel / Janyre Tromp.
Description: Grand Rapids, MI : Kregel Publications, [2022]
Subjects: LCGFT: Christian fiction. | Novels.
Classification: LCC PS3620.R668 S53 2022 (print) | LCC PS3620.R668 (ebook) | DDC 813/.6--dc23/eng/20211022
LC record available at https://lccn.loc.gov/2021051656
LC ebook record available at https://lccn.loc.gov/2021051657

ISBN 978-0-8254-4739-6, print
ISBN 978-0-8254-7794-2, epub
ISBN 978-0-8254-6945-9, Kindle

Printed in the United States of America
22 23 24 25 26 27 28 29 30 31 / 5 4 3 2 1

To Grandma and Bobpa,
thank you for your sacrifices
and the real but beautiful pattern
for marriage you left behind.

And to my own hubby, Chris,
thank you for working with me to make our own
beautiful framework for our kids.
Love you more.

*"For Satan himself is transformed
into an angel of light."*

—The apostle Paul
in his second letter to the Corinthians

CHAPTER
One

—SAM—

Darkness had long ago swallowed the Greyhound bus moving down the road so slow that it might as well have been going backward. It took every ounce of my control not to elbow the driver out of the way and stomp on the gas pedal. After all, the war was over, and every man here was ready to get home to his kinfolk. I wasn't no exception.

I scrunched my eyes shut and choked back another cough, the burn crawling down my throat and making me gag. Tugging my wool peacoat tighter over my shoulders, I hoped the major next to me hadn't noticed my flushed cheeks when we boarded. Last thing I needed was some officer ordering me off the bus and into an infirmary.

"You all right, soldier?"

I bristled, habit forcing my body ramrod straight. "Sailor."

"What?"

"I was a coxswain for a Higgins boat."

He stared at me like I was spouting Greek.

"A pilot for amphibious beach landings?"

When he still didn't show sign of understanding, I shifted the blanket so's my navy uniform showed. "I'm a sailor," I said, adding "sir" at the last second. No sense getting court-martialed for disrespecting an officer, even if he was army.

"Right." The man shifted. "No offense intended, but you don't look so good . . . sailor."

"I'm just fine, sir."

All I wanted was to get home and wrap my arms around Charlotte Anne and my sweet baby girl, then sleep for the next week with nobody pokin', proddin', or askin' me how I felt. The Lord as my witness, I swore I'd never leave our orchard and Hot Springs again.

"There's a hospital in Malvern. Maybe you oughta—"

"I reckon I'll take that under advisement, sir." Although I'd tried to make my voice respectful, it came out with a shade more lip than I, or my Ma for that matter, would've liked.

"Don't want you bringing home cholera or anything." He chuckled, then rubbed a hand over his mouth as if he realized how ridiculous he'd sounded and wanted to stuff the words back in.

We'd all been quarantined on the way home long enough that I was sure my backside had grown moss. The U.S. military had seen fit to be sure the only thing I brought home was a mild case of malaria and a smidgen of lead hidden in my shoulder . . . although they didn't know about the Japanese saber buried under the ratty underwear in my pack. That was my souvenir—a reminder of what happens to somebody who shoots a man in the back.

"Thank you kindly, sir. I'm just anxious to get home to my little girl."

The man smiled, and I relaxed.

"I got me a son." He pulled out a stack of photographs—a sturdy toddler, a wife, an older gentleman with grease smudged on his cheek—and I *mm-hmmed* in all the right places, least as much as was fittin' for a perfect stranger. It was almost like I'd returned to the person I was before going to war three years back. I traced the image of the little boy with my finger, registering that the major hadn't likely met his son yet, just like I hadn't met my little Rosemary.

Lights flashed off in the distance, igniting my memory, and the boy's picture slipped from my fingers and fluttered to the floor. My breath came in snatches, my mind desperately telling my heart to slow, that there wasn't nothing dangerous here.

"Just lightning." The major was studying me. "Makes me a mite nervous too."

I clenched my fingers around the dress gloves in my lap. Even with the thunder, a body would think the hum of tires on the road and no threat of Japanese Zeroes strafing us would help me settle, maybe even fall asleep in two hops of a grasshopper. But I was pretty sure I'd left behind whatever hop I used to have on some island in the Pacific—squashed by the military regimen and then ground down by the Japanese for good measure.

The major leaned over and retrieved his photo. I noticed his perfectly manicured hand as he brushed off a bit of dust before slipping his boy's smiling face into a pocket of his immaculate uniform, no frayed edges in sight. Wasn't no way this man had been anywhere near the front. I rolled my head from shoulder to shoulder. Some folks have all the luck.

I could near feel Ma reach out and swat my head for such disrespect. *Samuel Robert Mattas, I taught you better than this.*

Sorry, Ma. Maybe you could intervene with the Almighty upstairs and—

"So where you headed?" The major watched me like a body might watch a dog foaming and growling. More than a little annoyance skimmed over a healthy dose of fear. Lord Almighty, I'd turned into a mangy cur.

"I know you mean well, sir. But I'm trying to sleep. It's been a long time since . . ." Since what, I wasn't sure. Since I'd been safe enough to sleep without waking to panic coursing through me? Since I'd been home? Since I'd had a normal conversation with a stranger without near biting his head off?

At least he'd served. It was all those 4-Fers who got themselves out of the war, lyin' back and takin' it easy that deserved my wrath. Well, maybe not all of them. Certainly not Doc. He'd paid mighty with the polio. Wouldn't wish that on nobody, least of all my best friend.

Thunder rumbled in the distance, and I closed my mind against the devil clawing at me. I was home, in Arkansas. My Annie and Rosie were waiting for me on the farm. Ma too. No landing run, no artillery, no Japs waiting to light up anything that moved in the waves.

Just a storm.

"I'm headed over to Crows." The man was still chattering while sweat tickled my spine. Somebody somewhere must've told him talking set a man at ease. Must never have met a mountain man.

Just a storm.

I held my breath, the growls creeping closer, seeking a target . . . the world pulsing, vibrating with the sound . . . the smell of fire crawling across the Arkansas plains . . . the green of the seat in front of me surging like the algae-crusted lakes we'd drunk from in the Pacific . . . the sickness roiling in my belly . . .

"My folks live up there." The major's voice echoed from deep under the water. "Pop says he held a job for me in the factory over in Little Rock. Don't know if I'll be able to take being on the floor, but . . ."

Up front someone flicked on a light, and a face jumped up to my window—hooded eyes, searching, hunting. I lurched to my feet, cracking my head against the ceiling of the bus as I tried to push the major to safety. He latched onto my arm, dragging me under, and I yanked away, panting. Didn't he know we needed to run?

"There's somebody out there." I pulled on his elbow, desperately searching for an escape route through the sea of seats.

What were they thinking letting a bus full of unarmed men meander down a highway with the headlights un-blacked? It was suicide to sit in a target all lit up like a Christmas tree.

"Ain't no one out there." The major held his hands out in front of him like he was surrendering to me, pleading like I was about to shoot him dead.

I glanced behind me to prove him wrong and saw my reflection ghosted on the glass. Ears sticking out of dark, messy curls. Eye sockets bruised by exhaustion. More lines than a twenty-seven-year-old man should've earned. Other than the whir of its tires on the road, the bus was silent, and everybody watched me. When the whispers started, I leaned over the major and said sorry before yanking the cord to alert the driver someone needed to get off the bus. I grabbed my blanket along with my peacoat, cap, and gloves before stumbling down the aisle, staggering between the seats.

Wasn't no way I would let them all stare at me the rest of the way to the Hot Springs transportation depot. Maybe a hike would bring me to my senses. A body could hope.

I forced the bus's door open nearly before we stopped, and waited, bouncing on the balls of my feet while the driver opened the storage locker and wrestled my pack to the side of the road.

"You sure you want out here, son? Ain't nothin' here but trees and coyotes."

I nodded at the old man scratching the bare scalp under his driver's cap.

"I know the folks who live on the other side of that hill."

I tried to sound convincing despite the blank void stretching in every direction. Electricity may have been strung up in Little Rock, but FDR's New Deal hadn't lit up half of Arkansas yet.

The driver sniffed at me, seeming to smell the lie, before shrugging and pulling himself back onto the bus.

"I been in worse than this," I called. But seeing as the door was already closed, I don't know who I was trying to convince.

The bus eased away, picking up speed until its red taillights disappeared around a bend.

Behind me an owl hooted, and I squinted into the distance.

Now I'd gone and done it. I had no idea where I was. Somewhere past Malvern, I supposed. Only chirping insects and the curling of ominous clouds eating away at the stars greeted me.

I shivered at the creeping cold of night and pulled a scrap of oiled blanket over my head and coat. The month of May on the Arkansas plain used to feel mighty warm compared to the frosty air of my mountain home. One more thing the Pacific had changed in me.

"Best get movin'."

One thing the last three years had taught me was how to move quick and keep going—no matter what.

Wish I could've blamed someone else for the chilled wet seeping through me, but the fault landed square on my shoulders. The good Lord knew I didn't always think things through. I had a history of it . . . especially when it came to Charlotte Anne, my Annie. Even back the first time we met, I must've been crazy on account of what I did. Ma near lost her mind when I came struggling through the door of our farmhouse kitchen with a half-froze girl in my arms that Saturday afternoon. With Doc home sick again, I'd been on my own as I dragged her out from under the ice on the pond halfway down our mountain. And I did what I always did when I didn't know what to do. I went and found Ma.

"The Judge's princess, no less." Despite her sputtering, Ma had bustled Charlotte Anne into my sister Mary's flannel nightgown and robe faster than two shakes of a rabbit's tail, me still standing in the kitchen dripping wet while they went over to the living side of the house, my own sopping jacket and boots on the floor next to Charlotte Anne's. My brother and sister watched the whole thing with wide eyes. When Ma brought Charlotte Anne back, she told her to sit herself down while she got her some soup. Then she seemed to notice the rest of us gaping in the door. "Peter, your pa's out huntin'. You take the horse and run down to the Judge's place and let the help know Charlotte Anne come up to play with Mary so's they can tell the missus where she is. Tell them I'll have her home by dinner. But don't you let on that Sam brought her. You hear?"

That's when I knew I was in trouble. Ma had never countenanced even the whitest of lies. But she knew there wasn't nobody—let alone a riffraff farmer boy—supposed to get close to Charlotte Anne lessen the Judge decreed it. Course, the Judge never once sat behind a courtroom desk in a black robe decreein' nothin'. The reason folks called Roswell Layfette "the Judge" was on account of the fact that he was judge, jury, and executioner for none other than the Right Honorable

Mayor McLaughlin and his gangster buddy from Manhattan, Owney "The Killer" Madden.

The Judge would make Ma's paddle look like a party game if'n he found out what I done. Wouldn't matter that I hadn't asked Charlotte Anne to follow me onto the ice. I'd get blamed for putting her in danger all the same. I was four years older than her nine and knew better. Somehow I'd surely bewitched her with my dark, devil looks. It wouldn't matter what the reality was. The Judge would find a reason to make me regret near killing myself to save his daughter.

I hightailed it 'cross the breezeway to the bedroom us kids slept in, then put on my only other shirt and pants. When I hurried back to the kitchen and started loading Charlotte Anne's dress into the washbasin, I guess I was hoping to wash away the guilt of what I'd risked. Or maybe I was just trying to make up for my complete stupidity.

Ma near dropped the soup pot. "Thank you kindly for your help, Sam, but I think you need some warming up too. Go sit, now."

At the time I thought Ma was shocked I was willing to help. But now I know she didn't trust me to wash Charlotte Anne's dress. She was already covering for me bringing the girl home like she was a lost puppy. Wasn't no good way to explain how a frilly dress got mangled by a boy.

Don't rightly think Annie had any idea how near death she'd come. Especially since that little girl, always lookin' sour in church, was happy as a mouse with a bite of cheese in Ma's kitchen. She was "cute as a button," Ma said. And what with her blond hair drying in ringlets, even a boy my age could agree with that. Seemed like she belonged in the fairy tales I read to my sister and brother—a beautiful princess brought back to life by her rescuing prince.

Despite the fact Ma had called me a dimwitted fool for hauling her up the mountain, she told me later she was glad I'd brought Annie to our house. The girls were inseparable after that. "They're good for each other," Ma had said.

I don't know why Mrs. Layfette kept letting Annie come to our place, especially when Annie had sneaked off to the pond that day to skate. She weren't one to countenance a dirty farm. Maybe it was Ma's friendliness with her and Mary's painfully polite nature. But I think Mrs. Layfette knew what was going to happen even then.

———————

Under the late afternoon sun, the forest near glowed in golden light. After walking most of the night and all day, I trudged up the dirt road, past the pond, energy flowing through me even as the elevation stole my breath. Annie would laugh for certain at me huffing and puffing my way up our road. It was steeper than I remembered and more treacherous on account of the fact that the logs in the corduroy roads covering all the deep gullies and ruts were rotting through. It was in desperate need of fixin'. And if the path to the homestead was in such a state, I was afraid to see the condition of the farmhouse.

When I stepped onto the last of the corduroy roads before the farm, a log crumbled under my feet. I tipped, spinning my arms frantic to catch my balance, my pack slipping off before I tumbled pell-mell on the half-rotted logs behind me, staring at the sky. My shoulder ached under the bandages as I pushed myself up and brushed the debris from my palms. So much for being presentable. I might as well have rolled with pigs. At least my peacoat protected most of my uniform. I could shuck it and not look too much like a vagrant.

I sidestepped the broken log and turned onto the little pocked lane to our house.

Up yonder a spot of sky opened up beyond the forest—the farm clearing. If I'd had more left in me, I would've run. But my feet wouldn't cooperate, and my body held me at a steady, military march. I rounded the last corner, and our peach trees spread out before me, rising from the dip in the land pointing toward the mountains on the other side. Up on our hill, the sorting shed stood like a lone sentry, looming over the farm below. The sun slipped behind a cloud and doused the light over the orchard, the tortured limbs of the peach trees reaching for the sky. Weeds had straggled up between the trunks—a sign that Annie was having trouble keeping up. But the shed appeared in good order and rows of beets were laid out neat and proper, the greens slightly purple and strong. Both were signs that my girls and Ma at least had something to eat.

As I wandered through the rows of trees with tiny peaches clinging to the branches, I found myself praying and hoping. Everything I'd read said that folks on the home front were doing fine, but part of me wondered if that was as much a lie as the magazines saying us soldiers were right as rain in April—a fairy tale sold to everyone on account of that's what they wanted to hear. But stories always seem to stop at the happy moment; they never tell the rest of the story.

I touched the row of medals on my chest, tempted to pull them off and leave them in the mud along with the memories. But the magazines also said our wives would want to see them. I wasn't sure of that, but one of the ladies at the last base confirmed it and told me the best gift I could give my Annie was to talk to her. 'Bout what, I wasn't sure.

I trudged up the hillside squinting at the house we'd worked so hard to resurrect from years of relentless mountain weather. The roof bowed in like an old swayback horse too tired to hold up much of anything anymore. Signs of poor mending jobs were everywhere. Mismatched wood tiles sat patched over the roof, and more than a few warped boards speckled the porch that stretched the length of the dogtrot house connecting the living side, the kitchen, and the covered breezeway in between. Good night, what a mess I'd left for Annie.

The yard was empty. No Rosie playing or running to greet me. I forced away the memories of abandoned huts in bombed-out villages. Repeated the refrain I'd repeated then—whatever had happened there could not happen here. Would not happen here. My girls were safe, snugged in the mountains and watched over by family.

"Annie?"

I wandered through the equally empty kitchen, my footsteps pounding in the silence like distant mortar shells. The pantry door was open, and I poked my head in, despairing at the near-bare shelves. The fire was out in the stove, and dirty dishes soaked in stone-cold water. There was a time when Charlotte Anne would have never left dishes out like this. There wasn't no dust on the countertop, though. That meant they'd been here recently.

"Annie?" I called again, this time through the breezeway. The creak of the porch swing was the only response.

I pushed through the door to the living side of the house. Mending overflowed from a basket next to the rocker, where my hand floated over the headrest. I knew my Annie had sat here night after night with Rosie, and a familiar aching to hold them both spread through me again.

In our bedroom, dust particles floated through the slanted beam of sunlight laid across our mussed bed. I smoothed the quilt before wandering through the curtain to the other bedroom. A tiny dress hung from a peg on the wall, and a slate and books sat stacked on the table. I picked up the cornhusk doll left on the bed and hugged her to my chest.

Then I trudged down the porch steps and across the yard to the small granny cabin that my papaw built for his folks when he married and that Ma now makes her home. The door creaked as I opened it, but Ma's sitting room was hunkered down all quiet—like it was locked in a time vault exactly as I'd left it, right down to the crocheted doilies on the worn chair and davenport. Silence dragged me to the bedroom in the back, where the curtains drifted and curled in the light. The neatness should have been comfort, but it rankled.

Where were my girls and Ma?

I loped to the barn hoping to find some clue, ignoring the pigs in their pen. When I pulled open the heavy barn doors, the cow jerked her head up, still chewing her cud. The horse and wagon were gone. My heart picked up pace as my imagination galloped down a path.

Charlotte Anne was a mighty beautiful woman, and even her daddy couldn't protect her up here in the mountains. Any sort of man might come and do as he pleased, especially given how the Hot Springs law turned a blind eye to pursuits most of the country would call illegal. Alongside the gambling came the mobsters, money laundering, drugs, women . . . I pounded a fist on the wooden post, demanding that my mind slow down and work proper. The Judge wouldn't be round to help—Annie would never let him—but Doc would. Ma would. There surely would've been signs of trouble if'n someone had tried to take advantage of my Annie.

More'n likely they were in town. I stood sagging in the horse's stall, the tired going all the way into my bones. I'd imagined my girls leaping into my arms the minute I got back, everybody laughing—and then maybe eating some fried chicken before snuggling with Annie. After that, as irrational as the dream was, I'd sleep and sleep, just like I'd been hoping to. Nothing had prepared me for an empty home and me near panicking over my family being in town.

"Well," I said to the cow, turning a useless circle. "No reason to keep standing here." But where to go? My own bed sounded like a bit of heaven. But I didn't want Annie stumbling onto a filthy, near stranger asleep there. It'd give her a fright for sure.

"Guess I'll bunk with you, Elsie." I shut myself in against the chill, then shucked off my muddy peacoat and shoved it and my pack into a corner. When I clambered up to the loft, I nestled into the hay under a horse blanket and lay listening to the wind whistle through the crack in the enormous, barn doors. Elsie shuffled in her stalls beneath my perch. If I closed my eyes, I might almost make believe I was back when we were first married and fixing up the house—Annie curled into me. It had been years since my arms had been full. I pulled a bundle of hay into my chest.

We'd be normal soon. Rosie would run out from the breezeway to greet me after chores, little blond curls bouncing with each step. I'd swing her into the air and not let her go for as long as she'd let me. And Charlotte Anne. My Annie. Beautiful as ever, coming out to the porch so's not to miss it, hair highlighted golden against the afternoon sun. There wasn't anything to stop it from happening now.

My eyes drifted closed and then snapped open. Fell shut . . .

CHAPTER
Two

—ANNIE—

The buckboard bench creaked underneath me—a strident voice scraping and dissonant against the soft jingle of Buttercup's harness and the low rumble of Doc's Buick in front of me. A lavender blanket of dusk hung over the road winding into the mountains.

My little Rosemary was snuggled in the wagon bed beside her uncle Peter. Both were sound asleep with warm bricks at their toes and a layer of wool blankets over their bodies. Even in May, the nighttime temperatures in Arkansas's Ouachita Mountains are cold enough to nip your fingers, especially up in the gorge. I buttoned up my knit sweater. It was a bit big on me, but it was warm. And I'd let down my hair from its usual bun, shielding my neck from the chill.

Peter's one good arm draped over my little girl, protecting her from any real or imagined attack just like he had the entire time he'd been back from the war. Next to them Dovie May slumped against the side of the wagon, snoring slightly, a bit of straw sticking out of her neatly coifed silver hair.

I was mighty glad Sam's ma had consented to going to town with us. Not only had she been a huge help in picking out supplies for Sam's return, but the fresh air had pinked her cheeks and she'd entertained Rosie with her laughter. It was almost like the old Dovie May was there—strong and healthy.

A mist from the earlier storm hung in the air and made me wish I was burrowed under a blanket too. I should've asked Doc to handle the wagon up the switchbacks to the farm so I didn't have to. But as usual, I was more worried about not fueling the gossips than what was best. Folks were gonna talk, and it weren't worth a hill of beans to try and stop them.

Mama would come right out of her grave and smack me upside the head for disrespecting the neighbors if she could. But she couldn't, and Sam was the one who'd asked Doc to check in on me in the first place. Wasn't nobody could argue with that . . . even Daddy. It made sense, after all. Doc and my Sam had been two peas in a pod ever since they were knee-high. Two boys traipsing all over town and the springs. Hardly anything came between those two. Only the polio that got to Doc . . . and me. Oh, they'd never had a row over my attentions or nothin'. Doc knew I loved Sam, and that was that. But then with Sam away, Doc got so's he'd . . .

The wagon bumped over the logs in a corduroy road, and I clung to the reins as the wheels slipped around finding slim purchase. I concentrated on Buttercup's palomino rump, trusting her to follow the Buick and not to veer off the narrow, winding road into the yawning mountain chasm. It'd be my luck to have Sam come home and find us dead on the bottom of the ravine.

My heart sped, and a smile swept through my whole body. Sam.

Doc had brought the telegram up a few days back. My Sam was coming home soon. Peter had been so excited his brother had made it across the ocean safely that he'd come out of his stoic self and done a jig with me.

Only reason I didn't camp out at the transportation depot was on account of Rosie . . . well, that and Daddy would have never stood for it. The Judge's daughter don't show weakness, even if she don't belong to him anymore.

By the time we reached the house, the sun had found its hiding place, and the moon hung curved in the sky, smiling down at everybody. A few stars poked through the gray clouds, and I wondered if the sun ever got lonely up there all by himself. The moon had the stars, and the stars had each other, but who'd the sun have? Nobody liked doing everything by themselves. But, I supposed, the sun was stronger for having to light the whole sky by his lonesome.

Wish it worked that way for people. Before Peter came home, I'd done near everything by myself for three years and didn't feel any stronger for it. I glanced back and frowned at the boxes wedged in between everybody. I'd finally accepted help from Daddy to fill the empty pantry, but I wasn't sure I wanted to know what it would cost me.

While Doc parked his auto on the far side of the corral, I slithered out of the wagon seat the best I could without waking the three in the back. I wanted to get Rosie snuggled in bed before Doc found reason to be in the empty house with me alone. Not that anything would happen, mind. It was just awkward, me having a family and him almost a brother and yet not quite.

I slid my girl out from under Peter's arm and scooted to the back of the wagon. Doc appeared lugging a flashlight and near scared me silly enough to drop Rosie. But his arm snapped out and steadied me against his chest, his blue-sky eyes catching mine before softening. His breath warmed my cheek as he shifted, his expression asking if he could help. I leaned away, one hand on the floor of the wagon, the other under Rosie as I shook my head, stretching a fake, sunshiny-bright smile across my lips. I could do this. Had to do this.

Hefting my daughter, I carried her to her bedroom, then snuggled her into her straw tick and tucked a coarse blanket under her chin. My girl's head of frizz made me sigh, and I touched a stray blond curl that had escaped her braids.

When was the last time I did Rosie's hair up nice? Mama'd never let me go anywhere without taking care with my stubborn blond curls and dressing me up right proud. Was I doing right by my girl, not taking more of Daddy's help? Or was it bad enough that I'd let Doc talk me into accepting those boxes? Of course, without them, our cupboards would be empty. Wouldn't do to let Rosie starve when help was available, especially when it meant Dovie May and Peter could keep the meager stores Doc gave us.

A rasping crept into Rosie's breathing, snatching my thoughts back. She was struggling a touch for air, and fear climbed up my throat. What if one of these times Doc's medicine didn't help? What if I had to stand by and watch as she gasped for breath and died?

Doc said it wasn't likely. But still, it niggled . . . especially since I couldn't give her another treatment tonight. A mustard rub on her chest might help. She'd probably sleep better with it, but if I woke her now, I'd never get her back to sleep. I took a steadying breath. Doc knew what he was doing. He took care of my daughter almost like she was his own.

Rosie shifted, and her wheezing cleared. Blessed silence.

I braced myself against the wall as the fear drained from my body, leaving behind a desperate, dry exhaustion. My own bed was on the other side of the curtain separating my room from hers, and it called to me like a siren's song. But animals needed caring. Peter had done most of the morning chores before we left, and I couldn't ask him to do my work for me again tonight—especially since I still wasn't sure if he was back at the Mattas farm by choice or on account of what the war had stolen from him. I couldn't afford to let my neediness drive him away.

'Sides, it wasn't his responsibility. It was mine. And the Mattas farm wouldn't take care of itself. It didn't care none that I was a city girl born and raised—and mostly alone to boot. I was a grown woman doing what generations of women had done before in times of desperation. I was taking care of what needed taking care of, not depending on anybody who could leave when times got hard.

I heard rustling outside and hurried out to help.

A neat pile of boxes already sat in the breezeway outside the kitchen door, and I gave them wide berth like they were a pack of dogs that might be friendly but could also be hunting their next meal. Doc stood in the yard holding the reins of the horse, waiting on me.

Always there, waiting on me.

"Peter took Dovie May to the cabin," he said. "Told him I'd help you finish up here so's he could settle in his ma without worrying none."

My skin pricked, and I smoothed my dress sleeves.

"You cold?" Doc led the horse toward me, his arm outstretched like we were at some ball and he was asking for a dance. Wasn't no party here.

"I'm fine." I turned, rubbing the cold stiffness out of my own arms, just like I'd done ever since Sam left.

A kitten streaked through the grass between me and the barn, circling me and mewing for scraps. Rosie's Bailey baby. I squatted and scratched his mostly white fur, sending him into contented purrs. As I fed him a tiny bit of fried chicken from my pocket, Doc sighed, then limped to the barn. The squeak and thump of his leg brace played a disjointed rhythm with Buttercup's harness until they stopped at the barn doors. No doubt waiting for me again.

Sometimes I wished he'd just keep moving.

Bailey's whiskers flared in delight as his pink tongue licked off every last bit of oil from his lips. I stood, shaking my head at his little face squinting up at me, hoping for more. He was fatter than any of the other barn cats for a reason.

"You tell the rest of them felines they can have scraps if they start being nice to my girl."

Bailey rubbed himself against my leg, weaving in and out of my steps, ears flicking left and right before trotting off to explore the grasses for who knows what.

Doc hefted the barn doors open. Not that I needed him to, but Sam had built them to resist storms and certainly didn't plan on me fighting them. Oh, I wasn't some fragile thing, mind. But I was downright grateful not to wrestle the things tonight, even though Doc seemed to struggle as much as I might.

Soon my Sam would be home, and I wouldn't have to choose between tussling with things and asking for a favor. He'd help with the farm and Rosie and his ma. He'd stay for good, and he'd do what Peter couldn't. I wouldn't have to wonder if I had the strength to do something.

Once inside the barn, I lit the lantern hanging on the wall just inside the door. Doc unhitched Buttercup from the wagon, and then I led her to her stall before slipping the bridle up over her ears and easing the bit from her mouth. Free of the metal bar, she smacked her lips and snuffled my cheek, expecting *her* treat. Apparently, I gave out far too many goodies to the animals round here.

I rubbed her forelock, and she nudged my pocket with her velvet nose, soft as the velvet Christmas dresses Daddy used to buy me to wear—until he stopped.

Buttercup nibbled on the fabric of my dress searching for an invisible treat. She knew where I hid bits of apple and carrot . . . when I had enough to share.

"Hey now," I said, laughing. "Ruining my dress ain't the way to get me to give you something." I pushed her away and then hoisted the collar from her neck.

Doc rubbed Buttercup's neck with slow, strong strokes, and the horse near rolled up in ecstasy. But when he patted her for a final goodbye, the mare's head snapped up, and she skittered sideways, ramming into me before bolting out the door.

"You sure got a way with mares." I was joking, but Doc frowned at me like I'd meant it all kinds of ways other than what the words really meant.

He straightened his bowler and brushed Buttercup's hair from his suit coat. "I'll go find her." He heaved the doors shut, closing me in with the warmth held by the barn.

As his limping steps disappeared, I hefted the harness onto its hook, wishing it was a mite lower. At least Peter had mucked the stalls. I picked up the bridle and reached to hang it.

A scramble in the haymow sent bits of straw raining down on me. The movement was too large to be any of the barn cats, and my fingers tightened around the leather reins, my rapid heartbeat loud in the silence.

The sound of a footstep on the planks above shattered my frozen stance, and I spun and backed toward the doors, my mind bouncing between escaping or protecting my girl. My foot caught on a rough spot, and I stumbled, falling in a scrambling heap.

Everything was silent. Even Elsie stood still as death in her stall.

Shivers crept down my spine. The devil himself had come out of the mountain, casting a cloud over everything. Peter had warned me that he'd caught a few drifters up on the farm.

Elsie kicked against the wall, and a scream clogged in my throat as I stumbled into the nearby grain store, searching desperately for a weapon. The cow lowed at me, rolling her big brown eyes like she wondered who'd let the crazy woman into the barn. The metal grain scoop wasn't going to do much, but I held it in front of me nonetheless. Least it might protect me until I crossed the barn to get my shotgun out of the wagon.

"Who's up there?"

My voice was run over by fear. Wasn't sure even the cow could hear me. I'd read about blood-crazed men coming home from the war. We'd asked them to be killers over there, and some were having trouble giving it up. But as the calm, chirping cricket chorus started back up, the stories of those men not quite right and doing terrible, twisted things began to evaporate.

I'd near convinced myself I'd dreamed it all when a man-shaped figure peered over the ledge. I recovered my voice, the scream ripping through the air as I dropped the grain scoop, ran for the shotgun, and stood in the shadows between the intruder and my sleeping daughter.

"Best stay where you are. I got a gun." My shaking hands belied the confidence in my voice.

The man's answer was muffled by his stumbling descent. Though I followed his movements with the barrel of the gun, I wouldn't shoot him even if I'd thought to load the durn thing. Last thing I wanted was the law sniffing around the farm because I'd killed some drifter. Sure as the sun rises in the east they'd find something, and then Daddy would swoop in to smother me with his saving.

"We don't have much food to share." My voice sounded like an unsteady girl's, cracking in the middle, but the footsteps stopped. "We'll feed you, then you best be on your way."

I shifted my sweaty grip on the shotgun. I could do whatever was necessary. *Think of Rosie.*

"Come on out." My command echoed into the rafters.

The man stepped forward, the meager light behind him casting strange shadows across his body. His tattered uniform hung on him, and a row of medals glinted from the chest that had no doubt once been broad and strong. The poor man.

The tip of the gun dipped.

I heard a match strike and fizz, watched it sacrifice its light to the lantern by Elsie's stall. The chest of the man leapt into color, and he brushed at the splotches of mud across his navy trousers. A gold wedding band caught the light, and I was so mesmerized by the meaning that I nearly missed him speaking.

"Annie?" He stepped toward me, squinting into the flickering light. "Annie?"

That voice.

The shotgun clattered to the ground. I gasped for air, my fingers fluttering to my lips, praying I wasn't dreaming. But then his arms were around me, his breath against my hair, my neck. Desperate. Lost. His body, skinnier than I ever thought possible, yet real, wrapped around mine. *Please, God. Real.*

His stubbly beard pricked my fingertips while his fingers explored my face, his calluses scratching my skin, anchoring me. He pressed my head into his chest, and his heart pounded against my hand, beating in rhythm with my own. The dovetail fit of our bodies—nearly forgotten, but precious and right.

My Sam was home.

I took a half-step back, brushing at my day-rumpled dress, wondering how he saw me, wishing I'd had time to change. Least I wasn't in my blue jeans or overalls. I choked back a laugh, imagining him mistaking me for Rosie the Riveter. He wiped a tear from my cheek, and then he sketched the trail of the others down my neck, my skin burning under his touch.

"Are you real?" he whispered, echoing my own question. I'd thought for sure I'd be a widow at twenty-three. Took more than a telegram about a homecoming to make me believe, I guess.

My fingers ran up his arm, over his muscles and bone, the line of medals, exploring for the injury I knew was there somewhere. He winced as I reached his right shoulder.

"I'm supposed to be wearing a sling, but it gets in my way." I heard the smirk in his voice. He never did let much slow him down. He lifted my hand to his lips, his breath warming my fingers before he kissed my palm. Life shifted back, and I took the first real breath I'd had in three long years.

Sam was home. And everything would be all right.

CHAPTER
Three

—SAM—

I absently twirled a length of Annie's hair as her long fingers trailed up my chest until her arms surrounded my neck in soft strength. I'd been half convinced I was dreaming, afraid to speak for fear I might break the spell and find myself back on the cold warship. But the silky blond strands with bits of straw proved she wasn't a dream.

My Annie. I'd forgotten the smell of lavender on her skin, the steady warmth of her against me. I kissed her forehead, tears running down my face, melting away the burden I'd carried ever since stepping into this uniform. I spun her in a circle, her feet lifted from the ground, and she squealed in delight. Was the best thing I'd ever heard in my life.

Home. I was home.

"I ain't never, ever leaving again."

Charlotte Anne snuggled into my chest. "I'm holding you to that."

I laughed until a cough caught me up, and I doubled over to get rid of the catch.

"Sam?" Annie leaned over me, panic tinting her voice, but I waved her back.

"I'm okay. It's just a cold."

"I'll make you some soup, then."

She moved to leave, but I drew her in not wanting to let her go just yet. "I'll be fine with whatever you got left over. Don't need to do more work on account of me. 'Sides, I got myself a nice long nap, and I'm near right as rain again."

She hesitated a moment, worrying her lower lip with her teeth. Lord Almighty.

"You keep doing that, and we ain't going to get to the house anytime soon."

Her eyes snapped to mine, and she playfully slapped my arm like she had when I was just her best friend's older brother who'd gotten too flirtatious. I leaned over her, my mouth by her ear. "I'm serious."

She shivered and stood on her tiptoes to whisper, "I missed you."

"And yet you nearly killed me."

"You know better than to scare me half to death." She said it with enough sass for me to know she was just fine.

I kissed her cheek, my heart racing at the smoothness there. There wasn't nothing soft like this on a warship. "I didn't mean to. It was strange to be in the house all by my lonesome, and I knew you'd die of fright if'n you found a man in your bed when you weren't expecting it."

"Especially one dirtier than a pig."

I stood back in mock offense. "I knew you wouldn't hurt nobody."

Annie stiffened, and I smoothed my thumb over her lips. I'd forgotten how soft her heart was. "I'm sorry, Annie. I didn't mean it that way. It's just you've always been the kindest person I ever knew. I'm proud of you for taking care of everything for so long."

She leaned into me, her head on my shoulder, and I relaxed into her, my lips reclaiming hers. I was home, and Annie was safe. Wasn't nothing in the world I needed more.

The barn doors swung all the way open and slammed into the wall. Annie jumped, whirling in my arms as a man came skidding to a halt inside the barn, swinging a shovel, gasping, hair wild.

"I ain't afraid to use this," he hollered, and my mind skidded sideways. Wasn't no drifter going to hurt my family. I spun Annie away and dove for the shotgun, pivoting up in a smooth movement I'd learned by necessity. I loaded it and cocked it, ready to shoot.

Annie screamed, her words muffled behind a stall door.

I shifted, searching for an open shot. But Annie lunged in front of me, her hands out, placating both of us, her voice drowned out by the blood rushing to my ears. The man dropped the tip of the shovel, and I took the opportunity to swing the gun's stock into his gut, sending him sputtering to the ground. Annie didn't know a man would lull his opponent into a false sense of safety before he struck.

Just as I raised the gun's barrel to knock him out cold, Annie flung herself into me, nearly keeling me over.

"Hey!" Another man's shout pierced through the roaring in my head, and I shot wildly toward him. The horse he was dragging reared and bolted out of the barn, and the man lurched out of the way. He tumbled into the hay bales piled at the entrance. I lifted the gun again, but the man disappeared completely behind the bales.

Annie grasped my arm, screaming. I nearly shook her off until her words registered.

"It's Doc!"

I froze. My mind replayed the scene, recollecting the distinct limp of the second man who'd come into the barn. The fear and surprise.

"Doc? My God, Doc. I—" Lord Almighty, I'd nearly killed my best friend.

"You always were a hothead." Doc's blond head popped above the feed, grinning. But his voice shook, his movements low and purposeful like he was approaching a wild animal. Doc limped to the center of the barn, then stooped to pull the first man to his feet. The stranger stood with one foot squarely in front of the other, rubbing his belly with his right hand. He seemed to be pained, but he was clearly using that as an excuse to center his mass. He was more than used to a fight.

Doc settled a hand on the other man's arm, steadying him like he might an attack dog. "Didn't mean to catch you off guard, Sam." Doc sized us both up, shaking his head. "I know you haven't always gotten along, but I never figured you'd go and try to kill your own brother."

"Peter?"

I studied the figure in front of me. Dressed in homespun shirt and trousers, he was near my height, strong without being heavy. Dark curls so wild he reminded me of a hermit preparing to protect his territory. I squinted at him, and around the wariness I saw the serious brown eyes of my younger brother. Folks had always taken us for twins. Did I look as savage?

Then I caught the glint of a blunt metal hook where Peter's left hand oughta been. My lungs near collapsed. I dropped the shotgun and stumbled away from what I'd done.

Peter snapped straight as the marine I knew him to be. He'd been protecting my Annie, and I'd nearly killed him. My stomach lurched as I realized she'd been trying to tell me as much—and that her fear wasn't on account of the men coming into the barn but because she was afraid of me. Could this get any worse?

"Mama?"

Annie gasped, and I spun toward the open doorway. A tiny angel stood behind Doc, clinging to his neatly pressed pant leg with one hand, a store-bought doll in the other, eyes wide with fear and maybe a little curiosity. A halo of blond curls sprung from her long braids as she peered at me—the man who was supposed to be her protector.

"Rosemary?" My voice was barely above a whisper. If the devil heard my desire, my soul-deep ache, he might come and snatch it away.

Annie touched Doc's arm like she was telling him it would be okay before scooping up our girl and snuggling Rosie's head into the curve of her neck. My daughter peeked at me before burying her face in her mama's hair.

"Hi there, baby girl," I cooed, choking back the clatter of emotions. I took a slow step toward my girls, aching to touch my baby, to hold her. Did she smell of baby powder and heaven?

Annie studied me like I might go plumb crazy again at any moment. Her sweater had slipped off her bare shoulder, revealing the bloom of a bruise. Fear stole up my throat. Had I done that?

I stood lame and useless. Peter shifted like he might intervene again. And I agreed that he should. A daddy and husband should know what to do for his girls when they were scared, and he most definitely should not be the cause of their fear to begin with.

Rosie's blue eyes peeked at me through her mama's hair. Then she turned to Peter, stretching her arms to him. Pity pulled my brother's brows down.

I lifted my chin, agony burning a trail to my core. By rights I should be the one who comforted her, but these men were what my little girl knew.

A white kitten snaked his way out from Elsie's stall, exploring the sudden quiet. Peter's face lit as he snatched up the kitty.

"Hey, sweet girl. Why don't you show him your Bailey baby?"

He held out the kitty as an offering. Rosie considered me, then Peter, then me again. One little hand rubbed down the skirt of her dress before jamming her thumb into her mouth. A small angel flying in on the silver moonlight.

Peter nodded at me, smiling, a wordless truce passing between us. I lifted the kitty in my square hands, juggling him a bit so he'd be comfortable and so I'd avoid his razor-sharp claws. Wouldn't do to drop him. "This your baby? He's awful handsome."

Rosie grinned around her thumb, reaching out to pet Bailey, Annie now holding the doll. I sank to the barn floor, my eyes on my child's mother, pleading for her trust.

Peter smoothed his hand over my daughter's hair, and I longed to know the feel of it. "We just caught him off guard. He ain't going to hurt nobody."

Annie's chin nudged at our daughter's head. "Sweet pea, this is your daddy." She shuddered a breath and set Rosie next to me.

A band of lantern light caught the strawberry in my girl's blond hair, a lighter version of her mama's. I released the kitty into Rosie's embrace, and my fingers trailed her arm, her hair. My girl. She was real. A blessing sent from heaven to cover the nightmares, the fear. For her I could be anything, do anything. I was her knight, and nothing would separate me from her again.

Through the open barn doors, I watched Doc limp into the house behind Annie, one hand on her back. With the other he carried the gun I'd almost shot him with.

Rosie climbed into my lap, not caring about the dirt on my legs.

I swept her and Bailey into my arms with a whoop, my girl's laughter revealing her trust as I stood.

Peter pushed away from the wall and tapped me on the back with the hook, softer and less sharp than I'd expected. "I'll go find Buttercup and put her in the stall for ya. Then I'll see if Ma's still awake."

I studied him for a moment as he disappeared into the night. I was grateful for his help, but I wondered why he'd come home. Before the war, he'd followed me to the Judge's world. Then, unlike me, he'd stayed there, saying he didn't want the life of a farmer. Losing a hand certainly wouldn't make farming easier. Maybe he finally saw how much we needed him. But it would be just like the Judge to sidle back into his daughter's life in such a backhanded way.

I followed the worn path from the barn to the house. Doc leaned on the kitchen doorframe and grinned as I lumbered over to him. "It's good to have you home. Your ma's good company, but we sure missed you at Sunday dinners. I'm about as interesting as a lazy lump on a log."

"You 'bout look like one too," I retorted, reversing the way things usually went. No one ever accused Doc of being lazy—he'd aimed to be a doctor like his father ever since I could remember and worked harder than a workhorse for it. Then he'd returned to practice in Hot Springs just a year before the draft got me and Peter. But being lazy was one of Ma's favorite accusations of me, and Doc had never let Ma's comment go without casting aspersions on my generally untidy appearance. I had to throw it back at him sometimes.

I settled into a kitchen chair, bouncing Rosie on my lap while Doc lugged a box from the breezeway into the pantry, grimacing with every step.

"Durned leg is getting more pesky by the day." He rubbed his thigh before pulling a silver case from his pocket, then swallowing a pill. "An aspirin a day will hopefully keep the doctor away."

I smiled at his attempted joke, but it didn't make up for wishing I hadn't likely caused my friend more pain.

Doc eased himself onto a chair outside the pantry and opened boxes while Annie put some food stores away. As they maneuvered around each other, their voices blurred into a low hum like a well-functioning machine.

Rosie chattered on about the corn, the peaches, and the kitty, but when she got to the boxes of presents from her papaw, the Judge, I nearly jumped from my seat.

Annie stopped cold, fear creeping into her expression, her hand searching behind her for Doc.

I studied my best friend. What was going on here?

Doc lifted his chin. "We did the best we could, but . . ." He gestured at Rosie.

And then I saw it too. Felt her ribs protruding, saw the circles under her eyes, torn dress far too small. What kind of man let his daughter starve on account of his own pride?

I rubbed at the ache in my head. I'd seen firsthand how the Judge collected debts. That was the reason I'd stopped toting messages and drugs and who knows what else for Mr. Madden. But it wouldn't do to second-guess the folks here. "You done right." For Rosie, I would accept help. But I wouldn't watch the tally of what we owed grow. I'd repay my father-in-law and make sure we never had to rely on his generosity again. The sooner the better so's we didn't have to find out what strings he'd attached.

Rosie squirmed in my arms, and I smiled at her, hoping she wouldn't see the falseness lurking.

"Well, my beautiful princess, how 'bout you and I go find ourselves a storybook?"

As if it were that easy to restore life as it should be, I scooped up our little girl—kitty, doll, and all—intending to take her to the living side of the house.

I felt Doc and Annie watching as I juggled to free a hand so I could open the door. My skin pricked, but despite my sudden unease, I buried my face in Rosie's middle and blew, and her giggles rose. Better than any music I'd ever heard.

The giggles fell just as we were stepping into the breezeway.

"You going to be okay, Annie?" Doc's whisper near slapped my face. "I don't want to scare you, but . . ." I turned in time to see him step closer to my wife, then brush his fingers across the bruise on her shoulder. The bruise I'd caused. I stiffened, but something in me wanted to hear what else Doc had to say. "The doctors up at the Army-Navy Hospital have told me stories about the men coming home. If you need help—"

"He'll be fine." Annie's voice cracked.

"It's not him I'm worried about."

I knew Doc was just concerned about Annie, but he wasn't supposed to be the hero of her fairy tale. Question was, was I up to it? I'd hurt my wife and nearly killed my own brother and best friend. Was I any better than the Judge?

"How about you all come down to Hot Springs on Saturday, and I'll treat you to dinner?" Doc said this loud enough that I knew he meant for me to hear.

"You don't have to—" I started as I stepped back into the kitchen. I knew how much that dinner would cost, and I already owed Doc a debt bigger than I could repay.

I stopped talking when I saw Annie's face lit up. "Peter won't mind taking care of things so's we could go."

I'd just got home, and all's I wanted to do was hunker down for the next year. I was sure Annie would understand if I told her, but . . .

"You all could even stay over and go to church like your ma's been wanting." The twinkle in Doc's eye told me he knew I couldn't say no to Annie *and* Ma.

I nodded, wondering why the mention of church hadn't dampened Annie's enthusiasm. I could turn a blind eye to the fork-tongued folk who darkened the church doors, but I didn't reckon Annie had been back since her ma's funeral.

Before I could ask, Rosie grasped my face between her palms and forced my attention to her. "Story."

"Now that I can do." I winked at Annie, determination squashing my questions. "You leave the mess in the kitchen. I'll help you clean and unpack later."

"I'll see that Doc's got a place to sleep at your ma's, then milk Elsie." I opened my mouth to say I'd do that chore, but she was already halfway out the door, her hair swaying. I pictured her dancing like we used to when this was Ma's kitchen. The thought of holding her in my arms made my fingertips burn, but I had some work to do to repair what I'd done . . . what the war had done to me.

Peter came in and turned sideways to allow Annie past, his gaze dropping in respect. He piled an armload of packages on the kitchen table, then turned to see me watching him.

"Ma didn't tell me you were home. What brought you back?" I smiled, hoping it'd take the sting out of the words—and cover my real question. *Why aren't you with the Judge?*

"Same as you. Just trying to find my footing again." He considered his rough knuckles, then me. "Men like you piloted me into the beaches and kept me safe as they could. They were some of the bravest men I knew in the war. 'Cause of them, I walked away with only a few bits of Japanese lead rattlin' around in me. Ain't none of it damaged overly vital parts." Peter grinned, revealing a mightily chipped front tooth. "Except maybe this." He held up the metal hook, opening and closing the pinchers, showboatin' his custom hand.

I swallowed hard as I lowered Rosie and her kitten to the floor. "Ma didn't tell me 'bout that neither."

"She didn't know 'til Doc told her about it. Then she insisted on taking me in after the hospital kicked me out, saying I was good as new and had all the training I needed to get by. Didn't have nowhere else to go." Peter shrugged. "Ma and I are good for each other, anyway. Her mind's sharp as a whip, and betwixt us we got a whole body to do the chores and whatnot."

"Then I believe I owe you my thanks . . . and my apology."

Peter studied me for a moment, a wry smile inching up his face. "Don't let Doc worry you none. He wasn't over there, so he don't know what it's like. The nightmares and such will pass more'n likely. And if they don't, I heard tell it's good to talk about it with someone who does know."

No one wanted to hear my bellyaching, but I wasn't going to argue with a man I'd nearly killed when he was just helping my family. A man who seemed to still be able to do most anything. Just not everything, no matter how that hook operated.

Rosie held up her dolly for Peter, and he maneuvered himself to the floor so's he was level with her.

"She sure is a pretty doll, and she's smart just like you. I bet if you introduce her to your daddy, he'll play games with you both." His hook gently pulled on one of my daughter's braids before looking at me square. "And sometimes it just takes finding your purpose." He'd returned to the previous conversation, and his meaning was clear. It was up to me to make sure my girls came before my nightmares.

Peter stood, then hesitated in the doorway. "Ma is asleep, but I'm sure she'd love to see you. You want me to—"

"I'll see her tomorrow. I'm near asleep myself."

Peter nodded, then slipped out into the night.

I relaxed on the sagging davenport, my baby girl cuddled on my lap as I sang about the Arkansas Traveler fiddling away while his rooftop leaked. He was story and song bound into one entertaining package. I oughta know. Pa used to do this very thing with me.

He'd been gone near eleven years, and I still felt a flicker of shame knowing how he'd have felt about Peter and me leaving Ma and Mary alone on the farm with only the one farmhand they could afford. Ma wouldn't countenance our hiring men for her with the dirty money we earned from the Judge, but somehow she kept the place going. Least Mary'd found a good husband in that farmhand.

As I bounced my daughter around on my knees, she set to giggling again. It was the prettiest sound I ever heard, and I couldn't help but join in. The boys in my crew would've near died of embarrassment doing such a thing . . . though they probably wouldn't be able to resist my girl either.

Annie breezed into the room, dropping the bar across the door. The thud echoed hard and permanent. When had she started bolting them in? Had the riffraff from town made their way up the mountain? Someone worse? I held back the barrage of questions, knowing the last thing she needed was me pestering her on my first night home.

But she must've caught my look, 'cause she shrugged and said, "It's a habit now. Peter asked me to start using it after he saw some drifters out on the road. Didn't figure it was a difficult thing to do if it set his mind at ease. 'Sides, I sleep better knowing Rosie can't get out once I'm in for the night."

I nodded and launched back into the Traveler as she hung the shotgun next to the door, then collapsed in the rocking chair, rubbing her arms. She was taller than I'd remembered, or maybe it was that her dress brushed her knees rather than her ankles. And Lord, she was so skinny—near half-starved, elbows and cheekbones sharp. She had never let on how much she must have been struggling.

How much had she let Doc help like I'd asked? And the Judge? My voice faltered in the song. Annie frowned at me, concern wrinkling her brow.

I plastered on a grin, then jumped up and pulled Annie into a goofy, bow-legged jig while Rosie bounced in rhythm on the davenport.

"Me turn. Me turn." Rosie lifted her arms, and a huge yawn escaped her pink lips.

"I think it's time for a bedtime story." I winked at Annie, then lifted my tiny daughter into my arms, trying not to think about how many bedtime stories I'd already missed.

I nestled Rosie into her bed, then lay next to her while Annie stood leaning against the doorframe. I'd give near anything to have her nestle on the other side of our girl, but I knew too well why she didn't. I'd let my nightmares devour my good sense, and now I needed to prove I hadn't turned into my wife's nightmarish daddy.

My arm draped across Rosie, and she nuzzled her nose to mine.

"Story," she demanded when she was sure she had my attention. The good Lord knows she could melt the iciest of hearts.

"Which do you want?"

Rosie rolled over, then snatched a book from the shelf above her bed and thrust it at me. It was a fairy tale about a selfish prince who'd been turned into a horrible beast and was stuck in his beautiful castle all alone.

I growled the man's frustration at having no one to love or to love him back. And I near cried as I told the story of the beautiful girl who rescued her father from the monster by trading her freedom for her daddy's. I ran my fingers through my hair so much like the beast's shaggy mane, my last military cut long gone. How would my girl fall asleep with such an image stuck in her mind? How would I?

"It gets better." Annie grinned. "I promise you won't have nightmares."

It took me a moment to realize she hadn't read my mind but was poking fun at my childhood fears. "That was one time!" I huffed in mock defense, hoping she'd continue the playful banter.

"Still afraid of Frankenstein's monster?" She stuck her arms out straight in front of her like the dreaded creature and moaned. If she only knew. There wasn't nothing good about a cobbled-together semi-human. I forced away the image, determined to play along.

"Mary should've never told you that story." All the way up 'til she married and moved away, my sister was forever tattling on me and never missed an opportunity to embarrass me in front of her best friend.

Annie made amends by settling the lantern on the table, snatching the book, then lying next to us, reading about the ugly beast saving the girl and somehow, someway, them saving each other. The words *and they lived happily ever after* unrolled across the last page, my girls saying the words in unison. If only it were as easy as that.

"We'll get there," Annie whispered. It was part question, but her smile said she wasn't going nowhere while we figured it out. How had I ever got so lucky?

She kissed the top of Rosie's curls, then rolled off the bed. "I'm going back to the kitchen. I won't be long. Just don't want to leave those dishes."

I slipped out from under my sleeping girl and tucked her blanket in tighter. Then after watching her chest rise and fall a minute longer, I blew out the lantern's flame. My girls had changed so much. Annie sent me photographs, but they'd showed only her and Rosie's matching hairdos caught in pins and shy smiles squinting into the sun. They couldn't capture everything that truly mattered.

Annie still had a fragile center that made me ache to protect her. But somehow she'd grown into a towering oak—strong, yet able to dance with the wind. I had a feeling even her mother would've been proud.

And little Rosie's blond curls escaping the stumps of her braids was more adorable than I'd imagined. Not to mention the devious little spark that mirrored Mary's. I'd bet most anything that she also had my sister's curious streak that begged to be let out and roam the mountainside creeks and forests.

I closed the door to the bedrooms. Annie had done well with her. If only I could give them more than a pantry filled by the Judge, dresses stitched from the scraps of other folks' clothes, and a protector who might be more akin to the beast than a hero.

The living room was thick with dark and cold. I stooped to light the woodstove but found nothing but a few scraps of wood. I leaned my forehead against the cold metal vent. I still wanted to sleep for a week, but I didn't want Peter and Doc to have to help out so much when I was home. I'd bring in more wood in the morning, even if I had to split it first.

I pushed to my feet and bumped into the little table next to the rocking chair. A photo frame clattered to the floor facedown. I hesitated, then bent to pick it up. Cupped in my hand, the photo of Annie and me showed us standing in front of the train, her belly just starting to round all full of baby, me leaving. A stranger had captured the moment with my old Brownie. A parade of strangers after that watching my wife say goodbye, turn, then ride the train, then the bus. The distance between us growing and growing.

I'd missed the birth of my first child—stolen by the war, which had taken so much from me. I'd do anything to keep my girls safe, but I wished it could've been different. If I could roll back time, I'd find a way to stay home, make myself necessary to the war effort here, take the coward's way out so I could be a real husband and father.

I set the frame on the table, then slipped across the breezeway into the kitchen.

Arms elbow deep in dishwater, Annie's body moved in time to her whispered tune. I licked my lips, watching her hips sway, skirt a-twirling around her knees. Why did I feel like a naughty schoolboy?

A scrap of the song caught my ears, and I grinned. My woman couldn't sing worth anything. Play a mean piano? Yes. Carry a tune? No. Still, in that moment, I thought she rivaled Ella Fitzgerald herself.

"My word, you are beautiful."

Annie whipped around, and the bubbles clinging to her fingertips flung across the floor. The momentary fear in her eyes near broke my heart. After we were married, it had taken a year before she stopped jumping at everything, expecting her daddy to come after us and drag her home. I was different from the Judge, though, and Annie'd always only looked at me like I'd set the moon in the sky. But now . . .

Doc's whispered words echoed in my head, and I wondered if I really might become like the men he'd described, if my nightmares would leak into my life and make me dangerous to my family—no matter how hard I tried.

I started to back away. Maybe it would be better to give her space, time.

"I'm glad you're home." Annie's words stopped my feet.

"I'm sorry for overreacting earlier, Annie. I'm grateful Doc and Peter were here for you."

She rubbed her hands dry on her apron, then turned back and leaned over the counter, her shoulder blades sticking sharp through her dress.

"I'll make it right somehow." I spoke to her back.

"Peter says I should've seen him when he first came back. If he don't hold it against you, then I surely can't."

"I don't ever want you to be afraid again."

Her shoulders raised and lowered with a deep breath. "You should eat something. I've got—"

"No. I just want to talk."

She turned to pour two mugs of coffee, then set them on the table.

"I ain't the Judge." I said the words slow so's she could really hear them, to convince her that her prince hadn't turned into some horrible, barely human creature.

Her eyes darted from my photo standing at the end of the table, then up at me like she'd compared the two and found the real me lacking. She'd heard it all before—that a man who'd hurt his wife wouldn't do it again—though not from me. Slowly she laid the photo flat before lifting a tray from the counter.

"You done good here, Annie." I eased the tray from her and set it on the table. "I can tell the fields have been tended, and Rosie is amazing."

She stood stiff like she was reliving life with the Judge, near lifeless and trapped in a pretty cage.

"What were you singing earlier?" I playfully nudged her to show that I was echoing Mary teasing her about singing in church. Her cheeks colored, and a small smile wobbled on her lips, proving Ma right. Sometimes laughter is the best medicine.

I grinned, then placed a quick kiss on Annie's forehead as I pulled her into my arms. I wanted so much more, but I needed to earn my place as her husband again. There wasn't no way I wanted to cause her fear again.

CHAPTER
Four

—A N N I E—

Sam had caught me dreaming. I couldn't help letting my husband's storytelling voice lull me into a fairy tale of my own making.

Before I knew it, he had his arms around me, and I'd forgotten to hide. It was exactly like I remembered. Sam humming Bing Crosby in my ear and us moving like the good Lord Himself had stitched us together. Sam's broad hand engulfed mine, and it felt safe and protected there.

But the bruises on my body from him pushing me away and the ringing in my ears from the gunshot sent my heart pounding against my rib cage, trying to run free. Was I just like Mama? Excusing a man on account of his empty sorries?

Sam twirled me away, then gathered me back in. But he must've caught the question in me, 'cause he stopped dancing and stepped back. He was giving me space to reorder my thoughts, something Daddy never seemed able to do. He'd just push and push until I gave in and told him what he wanted to know out of pure exasperation.

My breath came in shallow gasps, part from the dancing and part on account of not knowing what to do with myself.

"Sit with me?" Sam motioned to the table.

Grateful for someone else taking charge, I pulled my sweater back over my shoulder, then sank into the chair next to Sam. My chair, where I used to sit and touch his picture. Talk to him.

I glanced at my husband's brown eyes through lowered lashes. Here I could clearly see the streaks of green, the laugh lines, all the things I loved and missed. Why was it easier to talk to his photograph than to the man in the flesh?

"I don't remember the last time I had real coffee." Sam's finger circled the rim of his mug. "Last time I smelled it . . ." His jaw clenched, and I knew he was fighting the war. "Some Japs holed up in an old mission schoolhouse. Didn't even know we were bunked upstairs. Four of us spent a couple of hours huddled in a corner waitin' for them to come up and corner us. The coffee smelled amazing, but, lands, their food smelled horrible. Like fish rot in a pan."

His eyes focused on me, and he flinched, surprise flitting across his face like he hadn't realized he was talking out loud. "I missed home-cooked meals. The thought of it always made me homesick."

"We didn't know you were coming home."

Sam stiffened, and my mind scrambled to figure what I'd said wrong. "I mean, we didn't know you were coming home *today*. That's why we didn't meet you at the transportation depot. I had a whole plan of what we'd do. I'd fry you up chicken with cornbread. I mean, we knew you were injured but not how or when or just how long it'd be 'til you got here. Maybe we didn't get another telegram on account of . . . Well, it don't really matter none. Peter and I got it figured out, and then we needed fencing for the garden . . . and then Daddy . . ." I halted my rambling, my fingers twisting my dress.

Sam frowned, and I splayed my fingers on my thighs. *Ladies do not fidget.* I nearly glanced behind me to find Mama and her displeasure. Better her than Daddy.

"What happened?" Sam brushed a wisp of hair from my cheek.

I folded my hands into fists, trying to remember what Rosie'd told him. What she hadn't.

Sam fiddled with the handle on his mug, then caught himself, seeming to decide something. "You ain't been eating much, have you?"

"I—"

"You can't help nobody if'n you don't take care of yourself."

I stiffened. "And let Rosie go hungry? I'm doing the best I can." And I didn't need anybody telling me how to do what needed doing, even if I did look like a bag of bones.

"Of course. You're right. Didn't mean to poke the bees' nest." Sam rubbed a hand over his jaw, the rasping confirming he needed a shave, the dullness in his eyes showing how little sleep he'd had.

My lands, he'd been home only a few hours, and here I was picking a fight.

"Maybe we should just head to bed." His voice was careful, quiet, hopeful. He slipped his hand over mine, and his fingers bumped over my knuckles. "I missed you."

I thought again about the ladies' magazine articles I'd read about the men coming home. Operation Magic Carpet, they'd called it. I'd hoped they would give me ideas about how to welcome Sam home in style. I never would've guessed I'd need a sprinkle of fairy dust just to get me to move from our kitchen table to our bedroom.

What was wrong with me? This was the man who'd rescued me. Reached right through a hole in the ice, dragged me out of a watery grave, and watched over me ever since.

Sam scrubbed a frustrated hand through his hair, but his smile said he wasn't angry. So I ignored the fear roaring through me. He'd watched men die, I reminded myself. It was bound to change a body. I could look past all that and be his wife. Couldn't I?

Don't know how I managed, but I followed Sam's broad shoulders and loose-hipped stride to the living quarters and our side of the curtain. He shrugged out of his uniform jacket and hung it on a peg next to my blue work dress.

I was more nervous than I'd been on my wedding day. Less sure of myself than ever.

After removing his shoes, then pulling back the quilt, Sam sat on the edge of the bed, his leg jiggling until he noticed me staring at it. He'd always been the most steady person I knew.

"Don't know if you were ever so beautiful."

A blush rose up my neck, and I rubbed at the wrinkles in my dress.

"They wouldn't let me call you." He reached forward and stopped my fidgeting. "And I'd sent you my last paycheck. Didn't think I'd need it to get home. I would've done most anything to hear your voice."

I sat on the bed next to him, the sinking of the mattress tipping me against his side.

"Was it awful?"

Sam stiffened, his jaw working a minute.

"They didn't have much for the pain on the boat home. Some crazy sentry got all trigger-happy and shot me the day before I was scheduled to leave. If'n the ranking officers knew, they wouldn't have let me get on the boat." I imagined my Sam writhing on the ground, bunkmate running for a medic and swearing him to secrecy. Sam biting on a stick while the medic dug out one bullet, then another, and deciding to leave the last. All to get back to me.

"I was drunk as anybody down on Central Avenue." He grinned.

Drunk?

I pushed the panic down. This was Sam. Not Daddy. Sam laid on the bed, his eyelids already closing, his words slurring. "I'm just so tired, Annie. I don't want to talk about the rest right now. I don't think I'll ever sleep enough."

His breathing evened out, his mouth hanging open a mite. All that worry and he'd fallen asleep. I should go do laundry while I had the opportunity—or at least put the rest of Daddy's provisions away. I started to pull the quilt over Sam, but instead I studied the man who'd come home from the war. He'd gained a new scar across his forehead, and I was fairly sure his nose had been broken and set poorly. I smiled. More'n likely he'd complain about his already large nose getting even more character. Part of a bandage peeked from under his collar, and my fingers touched its edge. If this was the worst of it, everything would be okay.

One thing I know for certain is that memory's a slippery thing. It changes and morphs, solidifying only at the insistence of the most powerful things. It gets so that no one's ever quite sure what actually happened. As I stood from the bed, I already wondered what had really happened in the barn. If it weren't for my bruises, I wouldn't believe Sam had thrown me into the stall door or near killed Doc and Peter.

Three years of worry broke, and every tear I'd held in threatened to spill. Not wanting to wake Sam or Rosie, I lurched into our living room, then sank into the rocking chair and cried wretched, hard sobs.

Yet even as I wept, my relief was whisked away, and I jolted around, catching hold of myself only to fall into a deep well. My head ached, and I felt like I might vomit.

I gasped for air. *Pull yourself together!* Even when Mama'd caught Daddy with another woman, she didn't fall apart. She just loaded us and our possessions up—including her enormous Victrola—and drove to Dovie May's, staring ahead so hard a body'd think she might turn to salt if she'd turned for a last glimpse.

A heavy, cold gloom shrouded our old house. Wishing I'd brought in enough wood to light the stove, I blew into one hand and then the other, the breeze dragging tendrils of my hair across the silver picture frame on the little table by the chair. I couldn't see the image in the dark. I wasn't that crazy. But I had it memorized all the same.

The woman's hair was sleek, pulled tight into twin rolls on either side of her head. Her arms reached up and over a slender man dressed in a navy uniform, a white sailor's hat squashed between his arm and side.

The man's forehead leaned onto hers. Noses not quite touching. Lips divided by a sliver of air. In a few moments, that sliver would expand so big they'd feel near devoured by it.

It was their last kiss. Their last goodbye, deep and reckless with fear and loss and abandonment.

Under the grainy gray of her jacket curled a tiny secret, a girl—our girl. Just big enough to make her mama's belly swell a mite. According to some, a gift from the god of war—something to remember him by. But the weight of caring for that other life eventually weighed that woman down and awoke the devils inside her. Perhaps it was a curse after all.

The train was in the background, belching smoke, bursting with men hanging out of windows. Women, old men, children all stood forlorn, bereft.

Most of the men didn't come home.

My fingers trailed over the picture frame. There was something comforting about sitting in the darkness. A place to lose yourself, to hide.

We'd reversed the picture already. Sam had come *home*, and I'd leapt into his arms with a desperate kiss. His strong embrace reassuring me that he knew where to go and how to save us. But then . . . then . . . What was the truth? The Sam of my memory? Or the scarred man who'd been to war? Was his smile and laughter all a promise that would never find its way into reality?

I was terrified he was just as lost as I was. One thing I knew for sure, he was no longer the teenager who'd rescued the Judge's princess from Gerald Pitner at school and protected her from the whispers surrounding her mama's death. No longer the young man who'd whisked her away from a father she no longer knew, for a happily ever after.

The house breathed in the wind. Maybe folks were right. Maybe all Daddy'd done meant we were cursed, haunted. There was more than enough evidence for it. I rubbed a hand across the scar on my leg, smoothing away the memories of twice being trapped under the water.

Shame washed over me. Wallowing wasn't gonna help nobody. Most definitely not me. There wasn't a devil roaming the earth that would convince me to take the easy way out.

I pushed out of the chair. Things still needed unpacking in the kitchen. I'd do that so's I didn't have to do it tomorrow.

I hesitated at the door. I'd have to go out through the open breezeway to get to the kitchen. Outside, the frogs carried on as usual, peeping away without a care in the world, all accompanied by a chorus of crickets. It's the country's way of saying everything is just fine.

I pulled the door open, listening to the rhythm. A hiccup in the sound made me suck in my breath. I stood, silent, watching through the slit opening. Anybody that knows anything about the woods knows the critters will warn you if somebody's a-coming.

The trees across the way scratched at the stars, trying to yank down the moon as they swayed away from the wind. The chirping started again, creatures telling me all was well. But living on the mountain gives a body an odd sense. And my senses were making my ears tingle. Tall grasses stirred over by the barn, and I eased back to hoist the gun from its place on the wall. Wasn't no bear or big cat gonna take my pigs or chickens.

I sighted along the long barrel, waiting for whatever was there to show itself. The thicket shivered a moment, and out popped a cat. A little white kitty tumbling with an orange cat playfully springing about.

"Bailey!" My half-laugh and half-exasperated exclamation sent the tiger-striped kitten dashing away under the pigpen fence, but Bailey trotted up the steps like he had it all planned.

"Darn cat. You about got your head shot off."

Everything had gotten me all riled, and I'd need to settle myself if I was going to find my way back to normal. I shut the door to the living half of the house, then crossed the open breezeway toward the kitchen. Sweat trickled down my spine, and I shook my head. Don't know what I thought might be out there.

Bailey was sniffing at a package on the steps leading from the porch out into the yard. Frowning, I shooed him away and picked up the box, turning it and wiping away cobwebs that had stuck to it from the porch rail. It looked like one of the boxes of Rosie's medicine, but I'd already stowed hers away in the kitchen. I opened the box and found a vial filled with powder resting in a bit of cotton. Doc must have accidentally dropped it. Hopefully, it wasn't for a patient who desperately needed it. I settled it on the porch swing so's he could see it next time he was through, then slid into the kitchen.

My footsteps echoed in the cave-like room. Sam's kin had built the backside of the kitchen into the corner of the hillside. It was a brilliant way to keep things cooler in the summer and warmer in the winter, but being underground sure did make a body jittery sometimes. For a moment, I wished I'd let Daddy bribe President Roosevelt's Rural Electric Administration to run wires up the mountain. But Sam would've cut down each and every pole if he found out we'd gotten the lines on account of Daddy's influence, and I might've joined him.

I lit a lantern before carefully adding a bit of kindling to the banked coals in the stove. As the wood crackled on the fire, cheery light seeped into the room, softening the gloom. Down in Hot Springs, folks had electricity and running water, but they also had

Mayor McLaughlin and Daddy. And there ain't nothing that could make me want to live there—even the ghosts that whispered across the pond and stole Mama couldn't chase me from the safe haven of Sam's family farm.

A few armloads of boxes and bags still sat neatly outside the pantry. I knelt on the floor, opening a box, then stacking the cans on the shelves. I hummed to myself, wishing I still had Mama's Victrola. There wasn't nothing like Mozart's Sonata in C to get a girl moving. The happy interaction between the piano and violin always reminded me of playing with Sam's sister. Round and round we'd run 'til we flopped on the floor or ground, wherever we were. Lord Almighty, if Mama had ever found out . . . But she hadn't.

I hadn't seen Mary in I don't know how long, and I missed her something fierce.

I pulled open another box, and snuggled right on top was a bag labeled *Sugar*. I cradled the tiny thing like it was near as precious as my Rosie. The smell of sweetness floated up, and I could almost taste the desserts I'd make with it. Last time I'd had something sugary sweet, I was on the East Coast saying goodbye to Sam. We'd shared a slice of chocolate cake with strawberries nestled into the icing. Don't know that I tasted a bite, though.

I closed my eyes against more tears and tucked the bag away. Seems I wasn't going to get much of anything done tonight without crying all over it. I might as well go to bed. Crying never helped nobody solve nothing. Tomorrow we'd start over.

I shut the box lid, then extinguished the flame in the lantern, banked the coals in the stove, and tiptoed back to my bedroom after setting the bar across the living room door. I didn't even bother pulling on my nightgown before I collapsed next to Sam. Closing my mind against my wild imaginings, I curled against him, the warmth of his body persuading me to sleep. Wasn't nothing here that could hurt me none. The good Lord would protect us, and I would do whatever it took to prevent history from repeating itself. Sam wasn't the Judge, and I wasn't Mama.

CHAPTER
Five

— S A M —

I woke, disoriented, to sunlight pouring through the window and a shuffling on the other side of the curtain. I felt like I'd endured a million amphib landings in the night—my stomach rolling with the waves, muscles aching from holding in the fear, and head pounding from analyzing the murky gloom for snipers, coral heads, and shifting currents. Though I was still in my dress blues, I was home and in my own bed. For the first time in a long while, I let myself relax.

A thud filtered through the curtain, and I rolled over in anticipation of Rosie peeking out from her room. I could live my whole life working to make that girl laugh.

A hoarse meow followed, and my head fell back to the bed. Definitely Rosie's favorite. The kitten sauntered under the curtain, his tail catching it and pulling it forward before letting it swing back into place.

Bailey jumped onto the bed, pausing a moment to inspect me before rubbing his nose against my cheek. His fur stuck to my beard, and I sneezed. Annie sighed, and her arm dropped over my hip. I leaned into her softness.

"Morning," she whispered, her voice still husky with sleep. I rolled over, smiling at the wildness in her hair as she stretched like the cat. There wasn't a speck of fear in her expression.

Reminded me of our first days on the mountain, alone together in this house . . . when we'd forgotten most everything. I grinned at the memory and nudged the cat off the bed. Something more interesting was awake now.

Annie's cheeks flushed, and she ran her palm across my beard, seeming to contemplate it like it held all the mystery in the world.

"Do you think I should shave it?"

She hesitated, processing the change in subject. Her touch trailed down my neck, making my mouth go dry. When she reached the edge of my shirt, her eyes snapped up to mine.

"I don't mind." She scooted up, her mouth hovering by my ear. "You look like a right proper mountain man."

"Want to see how a real mountain man greets his wife?" I snatched her wrist, and she squealed, eyes twinkling like she expected a rough kiss on the mouth. Instead, I spread her hand across mine and kissed the tip of each of her fingers. She stilled, her breath going shallow.

But wasn't no way I was going to do anything that might frighten my wife after the scare I gave her yesterday.

A tear rolled down her cheek, and I wiped it away.

"I'll love you forever, Annie."

She nodded, then pressed her lips to my cheek and hovered there a moment, her breath an angel's kiss clearing away the last webs of troubled dreams. I wrapped my arms around her and pulled her in, my body a shield to protect her from the hurts of the past. I might not be perfect, but I'd die for my wife, and I wanted her to know it.

Another thud sounded from the other room, accompanied by a little squeal. Rosie for sure this time. I groaned and then laughed at how a body switched desires so quickly.

"Welcome to life with a little one," Annie whispered.

I flopped on the bed, taking deep breaths, grinning at my own overplayed drama. Annie snorted and nestled into my side. I hadn't realized until that moment how much I missed the sound of her happiness. Annie kissed my cheek again, then peeked at me and winked. Maybe we could start over today.

Rosie poked her head around the curtain, her doll hanging by the head from the crook of my girl's thin arm.

I patted the bed next to me. "There's room for both of you."

Rosie landed with one leap. I lifted her in the air above me, dipping and swerving her like she was an airplane. She grinned, holding her arms out stiff, playing along. Joy crackled between us, bubbling up and filling all the gaps and cracks.

I snuggled Rosie between Annie and me, tracing the curls that burst out of her braids. "So tell me. What's your dolly's name, Miss Rosie girl?"

Rosie's fingers gripped the doll's thin, fraying hair.

"Rachel."

I forced myself to keep my expression steady, to not go back to the day we'd found Annie's ma under the water.

"She was my meemaw." Rosie eyed the ceiling like it held some kind of secret. "Mama says she watches me from heaven." Rosie's gaze dropped to me, studying me, turning my face back and forth in her hands, her fingers tracing the outline of my beard. She tugged on it once and then frowned.

"Mama says you're Daddy, but my daddy don't have no beard."

"Well, I guess you'll have to help me shave it off after your mama rustles us up some breakfast. We're going to need it if'n we're going to get those peach trees ready for harvest. Wouldn't do to lose them to sun scald, now would it?"

I scooped her up and set her on her feet. We were walking hand in hand to the door when I stopped and squatted next to my girl. "You do like peaches, don't ya?" Like peaches might be the secret to world peace.

Rosie nodded solemnly.

"Well, then I know you're my girl. All my girls like peaches." I winked at Annie over our daughter's head. My girls. I sure did like the sound of that.

I near tripped over the crazy cat and collected him in my arms on our way out the door, making a mental note to check for entry holes. Last thing we needed was an open doorway for whatever critters wanted access to our house. I dropped Bailey outside in the breezeway, then opened the door to the kitchen. Rosie giggled as I bowed and swept my arm out for my girls to enter.

"Why, thank you, kind sir." Annie bobbed a curtsy worthy of all those fancy ballrooms she used to frequent and entered our kitchen like she was the princess of the world. Well, she was in my world, anyway.

Annie bent to start the stove, and I cleared my throat. That was my job again now that I was home. She shrugged—half like she was guilty and half like she was relieved—and turned the spigot to fill the pot with water from the rain barrel on the roof.

I mounded the coals, piled in some kindling, and blew. The coals pulsed red and orange 'til the wood caught. Then I loaded in a few of the remaining split logs. Despite the work that went into starting it, I wouldn't trade the happy glow for the convenience of the gas furnace we'd had in the barracks.

Annie floated through the kitchen getting breakfast ready, turning and bending like she was on the dance floor. She frowned at the ingredients and then grinned with inspiration, dropping things into a pot and setting it on the stove. Apparently, my ma had taught Annie a thing or two since I'd been gone.

"I'll go take care of the animals while you get breakfast on."

Annie stopped in mid-turn, realization lighting her face. She didn't have to do it all alone no more.

A to-do list filtered through my mind—see Ma, care for the animals, split some wood, fix the logs in the road, check the garden, the fencing, the peach trees . . . I could save the world if'n Annie needed me to.

I turned to Rosie sitting pretty as you please at the table, and I wiggled my eyebrows at her. She puzzled at me for a moment until I beckoned her to me. She slipped out of the chair and wiggled her brows experimentally. "I help Daddy?"

When I nodded, she snatched the bin of kitchen scraps and toddled to me. Wasn't much in the pail, but it weighted her lopsided all the same.

At the porch steps, Rosie shoved the bucket at me, then skipped out to the pigpen. Once we got there, I handed her back the bucket, and she dumped the slop into the trough. The two sows, already growing with piglets, gobbled everything and rooted around for more. I poured them some corn, wishing it could be more. Maybe we could go out to the meadow and find some chicory root to hold the animals until we could harvest all them beets. Pa and I had used the root for feed more than once before he died, and it'd be less expensive than buying more corn.

The to-do list kept growing, and the weight of it threatened to pull me under. Maybe we could make gathering the chicory an outing. Pa and Ma made near everything a game. I imagined us all in the meadow, everybody happily tired from digging. Ma, Rosie, and Annie picking flowers. Peter, Doc, and me talking about the price of feed or the latest baseball star coming to town for the healing waters. Or maybe we'd chase each other through the game trails like we used to and teach Rosie to climb the maple trees on the ridge. Wasn't nobody faster climbing a tree than Annie. I reckon her mama would've had an attack if'n she'd seen us swinging around the trees like squirrels.

It might only be in my imagination, but there was hope in the thoughts. Hope that somewhere was a place I might find joy and light again.

Giggles and scuffling feet echoed in the barn, and I cocked my head listening. How'd she get in there? I hauled open the big barn doors.

"You can't find me." Rosie's little singsong voice begged for a game. Hide-and-seek never got old for me as a kid neither. Even before I adjusted to the dimness in the barn, I saw Rosie's bare foot sticking out from behind a hay bale. For sure and for certain, that child had slipped in through the pigs' door. And I couldn't help smiling. Wasn't no hope more real than my girl.

"Well, wherever did my little Rosie go?" I pretended confusion. "Maybe she's over here in the bottom of the grain bin." I crept to the bin much like a cartoon villain in the funny pages would, then snatched off the lid and exclaimed, "Ah-ha!" I peered over my shoulder, and her head ducked behind the bale.

After dipping out a can full of grain, I "searched" the chicken coop, then the haymow and the cow trough.

"Daddy, come find me." Rosie's tone told me she was growing

impatient, and I knew I needed to find her right quick or risk a tantrum.

As if on cue, the little white cat popped up from the hay bale. "Bailey. Where are you hiding Rosie?" I picked him up, peeking over the bale. "Why, there you are."

The cat in my arms meowed pitifully. My, wasn't he a helpful kitty? "Look, Rosie. Bailey's thirsty. How about we get him some milk?"

I carried the kitten in one arm and the milking pail in the other. I'd sacrifice a mite of milk to the cat just to make my Rosie happy.

Before my girl or I could get bored, we were done with chores. I flew her up the porch steps, and we burst through the kitchen door to find Annie, Doc, and Peter sitting at the table, suddenly quiet. I forced myself to smile, but my skin crawled, wondering what they'd been talking about so seriously.

Annie popped up from her seat like her backside might'a been burning and pulled the kettle off the stove. "There's warm water here for y'all to wash up." But instead of looking at me, Annie stared at her feet, nibbling on her fingernail. I stood like a hunted animal; even Rosie sensed the threat and shifted behind me.

Annie peeked at me from under her lashes, and I smiled, hoping she'd see that she didn't need to be afraid. Her lips turned up at the edges, and the light climbed to her eyes. She, at least, was on my side.

Ignoring everybody watching me, I held Rosie between my arms and rubbed her pudgy fingers with soap, rinsing away the bits of straw, dirt, and cat fur. I sang her Ma's silly song about dirty fingers swimming through rainbow bubbles. Before I could dry her hands, she smacked them together, splattering me with water. Annie inhaled sharply and jumped forward, her frown saying she had discipline on her mind. But I blew raspberries on Rosie's neck in retaliation, then kissed the top of her head before setting her down.

"What were y'all talking about?" I leaned back against the counter, looking Doc square in the eyes, then Peter. Ma always said the best way to get rid of the stink was to figure out where it was coming from and get it out in the open.

Peter eyed Doc, then me, a little guilt hovering around the edges of him. "Just wondering how you're doing."

Doc was sitting in my chair, so I sat next to Rosie, then shrugged at Peter and crossed my eyes at my daughter to make her giggle. "I think I'm doing mighty good. Wouldn't you say?" I gestured to my girl.

Peter shot Doc a triumphant flick of his eyebrow and then turned to me. "Seeing as we got more people to feed, we were planning on makin' the garden a mite bigger. I have the chicken wire. All we need's the posts. I didn't have quite enough cash to buy any. And"—he held up his hook—"I ain't so good at felling trees at the moment."

"Well, that's something I can do, sure as shooting."

Peter smirked and bumped me with the wood and metal hand like he'd won some kind of argument. "I already got the trees picked out."

I grinned at my brother and teetered back in the chair like he'd actually hurt me, when instead excitement for what we could do together made me itch to get started. Even though we might not always see things the same way, I was mighty thankful he was here. But Peter had always been good at tucking truth behind side steps, which left me questioning what they'd been talking about and who'd done the disagreeing.

"So," I started to ask again, "what else were you all talk—"

Annie pushed off the counter where she'd been leaning, startling me into silence. I watched as she scooped something from the stovetop into bowls for each one of us, them set them out with a flourish.

As everyone else dug into their breakfast, I hesitated, wondering if I'd managed to uncover the stink. But I let it drop, not wanting to crush the hope in Annie.

I picked up my spoon determined to like whatever Annie had concocted. But oh. My heart kicked a wild beat. Corn mush had always been my favorite—'til the chef on the carrier took to making it every time we headed out for an insertion on a Japanese-held beach.

I lowered the spoon into the bowl, then pressed my palms on the table's surface, trying not to think of all the men who'd eaten this as their last meal. Their screams echoed through time. Terror crushed me, sucking me down. Determination dragging me through the crash of waves. The shout of marines diving into the fog of battle. The beach clogged with debris. Staring eyes half buried in the muck of the monsoon. A blackened hand reaching out—no body attached—to plead for help. An empty helmet with a hole the size of a fist in the back.

Not just any helmet.

Rabbit's.

"You all right?" Doc's voice sounded hollow, like he was calling from afar off.

I nodded, holding in my gasps. "Just not hungry."

I shot to my feet, and my chair clattered behind me. I snatched at it before it could fall, then near sprinted out the door and into the yard. Mud sucked at my boots, and I swallowed back the bile. I'd thrown myself across my engineer's body, pulling him back into our Higgins boat, holding bits of his skull against his head as blood slipped out, soaking the skim of sand in the bottom of the boat, the surf sucking away the red, then returning it only to pull it out again.

You're safe. On the farm.

The trees waved in agreement, and the lurching in my stomach settled. I heaved in great gulps of fresh air, washing away the memory of Rabbit's blood crusting on my fingers as I desperately tried to save the rest of the crew and a few surviving marines while the sea swamped our boat.

Footsteps fell behind me, and I spun. Annie stood on the porch plucking at the flaking paint on the rail, her shoulders caved in like they carried the whole world. She was why I had fought through the waves. She was the reason I'd refused to die on some godforsaken island. But I couldn't do nothing right.

"I'm sorry, Annie." I climbed the stairs and captured her hands in my own.

"I thought you liked corn mush." Tears coated her words. "I was trying to make a better start."

I pulled her into me, knowing I was the cause of those tears. "I do . . . I did." I sighed. "Things happened . . . and I—"

She laid a hand on my cheek, hushing my stutters.

"I don't know how to explain." She deserved more, but hang it all, I didn't know how to say it without the words stabbing right through Annie. There wouldn't be no taking back the stories once they was out. And there wasn't nothing in me that wanted those memories staining our farm.

My wife rubbed my cheek with her thumb, the rhythm reassuring as a lullaby.

"It's all right. Your ma told me there'd be things you couldn't talk about right away. Said Peter and your pa were the same way when they got home. It'll come. If you'd go help Dovie May make her way over here, I'm sure she'll eat some and Peter and Doc will polish off what you didn't finish. I'll fry you up some eggs. The chickens have been laying like they knew you was coming home."

The cheerfulness in her voice battled with defeat. I wished there was a way to reverse time, to find a different way. But I didn't know any other way, and I feared we'd always end up here.

"Lord knows you're too good for me, Annie. I'll just take a slice of bread, if'n that's all right with you, and I'll be right as rain 'til lunch."

Annie shifted her weight, and the porch creaked under us. "Anything else I shouldn't go fixing?"

My stomach flipped. Last thing I wanted was to cause her trouble. "I think I might've eaten enough orange marmalade to last a man a lifetime. Lessen someone else has a hankering for it."

"Marmalade?" She grinned, studying me like she was weighing my request. It wasn't something I ever recalled eating before I left home. "I don't know if I can give that up without something in exchange."

Exchange?

Her lips lifted in a smirk as she pushed onto her tiptoes, her mouth hovered in front of mine, brows lifted in flirtatious question, fingertips electrifying my neck as she drew me into her.

"Mama?" Rosie's voice pierced the pounding in my ears. Annie jumped, and I staggered forward, my body magnetized to hers.

"I'll be there in a minute, sweet pea," she said, her breath brushing my lips, her eyes coming back to mine. "I guess I'll take payment in full later." She sighed and winked, then spun round toward Rosie.

Good Lord, if that's what life is like without marmalade, I don't rightly think I need marmalade in my life ever again.

—ANNIE—

I couldn't wipe the grin from my face. Who cared if Sam didn't care for corn mush no more? I twirled as I walked into the house, humming a snippet of a Chopin trill and turn. Truth be told, I never liked corn mush either. And better yet, he'd been the old Sam, not wanting to be a bother to nobody. This was going to work. We could figure it out.

Rosie trotted into the kitchen, letting the door smack closed in front of me. I sighed, reached for the handle, and then screeched a bit when Peter yanked the door open. He pulled up before he plowed me over, but I could near see the smoke coming from his ears.

"I'm going to see what Sam's thinking for the day. Seeing as it's *his* farm and all." Peter threw the last sentence over his shoulder as he stalked through the breezeway, then down the porch steps muttering just loud enough for me to hear. "Can't take no more of that nonsense."

Rosie's giggles lofted from the kitchen, and I frowned at Peter's back. What was that all about? Don't remember Peter ever spewing his temper at anyone other than Sam. Maybe Sam coming home had stirred up memories for him again.

"Don't let him bother you. Change isn't easy for everybody." Doc slumped on the floor helping Rosie dress a paper doll as she inhaled her medicine through the pipe of a tiny clay pot. He launched back into Rosie's favorite story about the little doll going on an adventure in the woods with the squirrels and birds. He wasn't near as good a storyteller as Sam, but he did try . . . and he'd convinced Rosie to take her treatment. And so quickly. She must've come to get me on account of not wanting to sit long enough to breathe in all the medicine. Had she given Peter trouble, then Doc stepped in? Peter never did like being shown up by anybody.

I eased the kitchen door closed, praying I wouldn't break whatever spell Doc had put on my daughter.

"How'd you get her to do that without so much as an argument?"

Doc kept his eyes on Rosie, but he shrugged a slim shoulder. "I'm a doctor. I got all kinds of ways."

I emptied the mush from Sam's bowl into the pot, then moved it to the back of the stove. Sam would bring Dovie May over for her breakfast presently, and I wanted her portion to be warm.

As I watched Doc with my daughter, I wondered what it had been like for him to leave home and go to the university. It was the first time he'd been without Sam. Except for a few holidays, Doc was gone for six years. He always said he wanted to be a doctor, like his daddy was. In fact, he earned the nickname Doc by practicing his doctoring on anybody who would let him. But I thought he'd find himself a wife at school and we'd never hear from him again excepting the occasional card.

Stepping around the pair on the floor to clear the rest of the table, I studied Doc. Why hadn't he ever married? He was a handsome man, tall and slender, smart as anything, and more loyal than a body could rightly hope for. His limp was hardly noticeable most of the time, and he was one of the most well-off, honest men I knew. I saw him a few times on campus while I was at the same university. He'd been happy then. Of course, I barely lasted a year before I came home. I missed Sam too much. Maybe Doc had been lonely for the mountains, and that's why he'd come back too. That, and his daddy had retired to Texas and left him the clinic.

I scrubbed at the table like it was the answer to everything.

A gurgling signaled that Rosie's medicine was near gone, and I turned to take over her care. But Doc set the clay pot aside, showed Rosie his empty hand, then reached behind her ear and produced a penny mint from thin air. She clapped, then snatched the candy and popped it into her mouth. Just like magic.

As Rosie went back to playing with her doll, I poured a bit of hot water into the sink and shaved some soap from the bar before loading the breakfast dishes in. Rosie chattered to her dolly—pouring Rachel tea and taking Rachel dancing. Some days I wondered at why I let Rosie name her dolly after my dead mama. At first I thought it would help to remind me of happier times—waltzing in the parlor, rolling pie crust for Sunday potlucks. But other times hearing the name haunted me, dragging me under the wavering surface. Daddy coming home drunk, hollering. Mama forgot to sweep the stoop or someone had seen me cavorting at the park. Then the thuds, her begging him to stop, and—

I hummed quietly to myself to stop the memories. When I realized the tune, I dropped the pan I'd been scrubbing.

Handel's Water Music Suite no. 1.

My mind refused to sort out a different piece. The happy, bouncing notes reverberated in my head, a pounding dissonance to what the orchestral suite produced in me. Half a lifetime of musical training at Mama's knee, and that's the only collection of notes my mind could recollect? I scrubbed mercilessly at the dishes, scraping away the food along with the memory of coming into the empty cabin with the record on repeat, the regret of not setting out to search for Mama until the sun was low in the sky.

Mama never let the Victrola run on its own without somebody to enjoy it. She'd been telling me to come find her before it was too late. *Water Music.* It should have been obvious.

"I heard tell that the Judge got himself a new record player."

My fingers hovered above the sink, my mind scrambling to catch up with what Doc was talking about and where he was going. He had to know I didn't care what Daddy bought himself with his blood money.

"I could ask him for your mama's Victrola."

I grasped the edge of the counter, desperate to stay in control. Doc couldn't have seen the memories cascading through my mind. And he couldn't have guessed at them neither. He'd been away at school and didn't know about the music. It was Sam who was with me. Sam who cut away the weeds clinging to me and hauled me out of the water, me screaming, blood running down the gashes on my leg, merging with the water like it meant to stream out and save Mama. My warm life blood for hers.

"I don't think it'd be right to ask for it."

"You mean Sam wouldn't like it."

I bristled, anger sending steel down into my muscles. "I mean I don't want to be beholden to Daddy any more than I am now. You know what it's like as well as anybody, Doc." I swung round, and with fists dug into my hips, I must've been the spitting image of Mama. "What's gotten into you?"

"I didn't mean nothing, Annie." Doc maneuvered his twisted leg and stood, his face red from the exertion. "I want the best for you. Just like always. The Judge don't need the Victrola no more, and you always loved that thing near as much as your mama did."

He was right. Even after everything I finally understood about Daddy, about what he was, I'd let him keep the Victrola without even asking for it when I married. I'd regretted it ever since. Most of my good memories were tied to it, and, truthfully, Mama's death wasn't the Victrola's fault. It had tried to tell me, to warn me. It was me who'd failed.

Doc limped to stand behind me. I dropped the rag into the sink and rubbed at the ache in my head.

"I'm sorry, Doc. Don't know what's gotten into me."

"You don't need to worry about me. You got enough other things to concern yourself with." He nodded at the doorway as Sam helped his ma negotiate the opening.

Dovie May leaned heavily on him, but her grin said it all—she was thrilled to have her boys back and mostly in one piece. Especially considering how many others were already waiting in heaven.

But Sam . . . Emotions flitted across his face so fast it near broke my heart. For sure he was glad to be home, but there was sadness and fear there too. Three years ago his ma was spry as a twenty-year-old, commanding the garden and her home like a benevolent general. Now the apoplexy had near won the war, and despite her only being in her fifties, Dovie May's left half drooped and she was just able to shuffle forward at a sedate pace without somebody helping her. It had even stolen her color, leaving her skin as gray as the hair on her head.

"Land sakes, child." She shook off Sam's grasp on her arm. "I love you like nothing else, but I ain't dead yet."

Sam winced, and I couldn't help agreeing. It ain't wise to tempt the reaper.

But she winked at me and patted the wiry hair that sprang from her bun like little imps dancing around her. Wasn't nobody who couldn't be happy with my mother-in-law around.

"She's a mite more forthcoming with her words than she used to be." Doc pulled out a chair for Dovie May while I filled a bowl with mush, then set it in front of her.

"All this service reminds me of the time you two was hoping I'd forget you hitched up the team and pulled over Gerald Pitner's outhouse"—Dovie May snorted—"*while* he was in it."

"He did deserve it, Ma." Sam stood stiff like he might get another switch on the backside on account of it.

"Good Lord, that boy screamed like a stuck pig." Doc slapped Sam's back, grinning.

"Still can't believe you talked me into that one."

"I'd do it again if anyone gave our Annie trouble like he used to." Doc settled his hand on the small of my back and winked. Sam frowned, his eyes landing on Doc's arm.

"Ain't nobody who'd come after me with Sam here." I slipped out from Doc's touch with practiced grace and kissed Sam's cheek. "Ain't that right?" I hesitated 'til my husband met my eyes and smiled.

In the corner of the room, Doc took out his little silver case and popped another one of them white pills into his mouth. Seemed I was the cause of headaches for more than one man.

"Y'all okay while I go sweep the porch? I don't rightly know when I last had the chance to do it, and I saw spiderwebs out there last night."

I shivered at the memory as I reached for my garden hat. "Oh, and there was something out there for you, Doc."

"For me?" He caught the bottom edge of his vest and rubbed it, like it might have some kind of answer. Catching his nervous tick, he jumped a bit, then stepped around the table and followed me through the breezeway to the porch.

Bailey laid on the swing in a long patch of sunshine lazily cleaning himself. The swing otherwise empty.

"It was right here."

I pushed Bailey out of his spot. Had he somehow concealed the box? Nothing.

I searched next to the steps, in the bushes, across the bare yard, and then shook my head. Packages that size don't blow away, and they don't go walking away on their own neither.

"Maybe I was just seeing things," I said to myself as much as to Doc. The cat lifted his head and studied me as if confirming that I was a mite too close to going over the edge of sanity. But I'd held the box, opened it.

"More'n likely it was Peter's, and he took it to the cabin."

I nodded, again leaning over the railing to peer round the bushes. Doc shrugged and started to turn toward the kitchen. "But I can go ask him if you'd like." There was a gentle question in his voice, almost like he was sorry for me.

"Ain't no matter to me, I guess," I said, dismissing him. I straightened and swiped at a cobweb like the missing box didn't bother me one bit. But why did Peter need a box of medicine? He said it'd been months since he was done with the pain medicine on account of how peculiar it made him feel. But maybe the powder in that vial wasn't medicine at all.

I stopped my brooming. Oh fiddlesticks. I was on the farm, not in Daddy's house. There wasn't nothing or nobody here with secrets to hide.

I knocked down a web big enough to capture Bailey. The porch felt better already.

I pulled in a lungful of air, clearing out the tangle of my thoughts. Most times I was thankful for the farm. Thankful for the crooked peach trees pushing out fruit even with the little care I gave them while Sam was gone. Thankful for Sam rescuing me from the Judge's rule and the busybodies in town. Thankful for a husband who loved me. Thankful for all I had—especially Rosie.

Today I just needed to remind myself of that.

I let the sun bathe my face for a moment before tugging at the brim of my hat. Mama'd have a heart attack if she saw all my freckles. Somehow she'd spent a full year on the farm tucked away in the granny cabin and never once sprouted a blemish on her nose. But then she never left the house much at all, except the once. And there isn't a part of me that don't wish she'd stuck to sitting in the rocker on the porch.

A burst of laughter spilled from the kitchen, and I joined in even though I didn't know what they were laughing at. With all the extra help around today, I could finally get out to the strawberry patch and check if the blossoms had started producing early fruit. Maybe we could find enough to make a pie, though I didn't have enough flour for both that and more bread. I leaned on the broom, mind a-whirring for a solution. The leftover corn mush. I could use it for a makeshift cobbler. Another blessing. The good Lord knew we'd be able to use that mush later.

The sun had climbed high overhead, heating the world to near boiling. I arched my back against the strain of stooping over the strawberry rows. Still, I had to near pinch myself to make sure I wasn't dreaming. Hours ago, Peter had found Sam, and the two had traipsed into the woods where the steady whooshing of the saw told me they'd found a rhythm and would soon have a set of trees felled and prepped for a new fence line.

Doc had left for his clinic, promising us dinner in town tomorrow—his treat. And although Dovie May had been watching my Rosie, now she was dozing in the shade of the oak tree, peaceful as you please. I let her go right on sleeping. She needed the rest. Rosie's little head bobbed in the strawberry rows as she chased Bailey this way and that. Sure as the sun was hot, I knew more than a few strawberries fell victim to their pouncing and rolling. But I couldn't find it in myself to be angry.

My cheeks grew hot. My mama tried growing strawberries only the one time. I was about Rosie's age, and I was so proud that I picked all them strawberries.

I could still feel the fear welling inside me at the fury on Mama's face when she'd spied the white berries in my basket. It's awful ironic that Daddy was the one that'd stopped her from thrashing my backside. She was usually the one who sent me skittering to my closet so's Daddy wouldn't find me. In fact, Mama never hit me. But strawberries were Daddy's favorite, and he was expecting them to last all season.

Daddy might've stopped them that time, but the devils still got into her—one way or the other.

A curl of hair tickled my cheek, and I shoved it back under my hat, pushing away the complicated memory as well. Why in heaven's name was Mama haunting me again? My throat ached, and I walked down the hill for a drink, telling myself it was just on account of being thirsty.

I filled a bucket at the pump and dipped the ladle in, shattering the image of my face on the surface of the water. A tiny web of ripples sprang back from the edge of the bucket, and I touched them, causing more confusion and chaos.

The pond had been so smooth when they came to get Mama, despite the storm that'd ripped through the mountains the night before. It would have made more sense if it had been chaotic, out of order. But her hair lay out on top of the water, quiet, slowly shifting like it belonged there as much as the seaweed.

Water dripped off the ladle onto my foot, and I jumped, spilling half of it.

Rosie stood at the end of the strawberry row, watching me, head tilted like she was listening for the world to tell her what to do, her little legs already dirt streaked. Seeing as Daddy always expected his world neat and tidy, Mama would've been horrified. But Sam would say a slightly dirty child was the sign of a happy child . . . long as they washed up before dinner. I raised the ladle in her direction, question drawing my eyebrows up. She rubbed her hand down her dress, feeling for reality just like me.

I don't rightly know where the devils came from, but I prayed they weren't catching. I'd made a promise long ago that they wouldn't get me or my girl. I rubbed the bruising on my shoulder.

Used to be Sam out here laughing and working with me and making me believe I could keep that promise.

Used to be.

And that's where everything had gotten stuck—in the used-to-be's.

Used to be an educated woman, used to be the biggest prize this side of the Ouachita Mountains, used to be expecting my first baby with my husband at my side, excited about starting a family and reviving the Mattas Peach Orchard. Used to be . . .

And that's when I realized I'd never thought to pray for Sam to escape the devils. He'd always been the white knight who saved us. What if . . .

A hawk shrieked high above me, laughing at my smallness there on the ground.

I poured water into a couple of jars, then directed my girl into the house. I wasn't listening to that fool hawk. There wasn't no way I was going to let them devils in.

— S A M —

By the time I'd settled Ma outside and finished hauling a day's supply of wood for the stoves, Peter had already marked a few tall, straight trees and dragged the gear out to the site before coming to find me. Hours later the sun was high over the mountain, full and hot, baking my head, drawing sweat despite the shade of my straw hat. I'd forgotten how much work a farm was. Not that piloting a little amphibious boat through ocean swells under fire was easy, mind. It's just that sawing trees and digging holes made use of muscles the navy had let rest far too long.

I stood and wiped my face with my kerchief. A few hours ago it'd been clean and smelled like Annie. Now it needed a bath near as much as I did. At least Peter had a pair of spare trousers I could borrow, allowing Ma to work on cleaning my two sets of dirty uniforms. She said she wanted to do it, though I wondered if she had the strength to be hauling wet laundry.

Down near the house, Annie bent over a row of sweet peas, picking them for our supper. Her skirts swished around her, and I wondered how she managed to keep neat and clean despite working in the garden.

Truth told, I could near taste the strawberry cobbler she'd promised to make. We didn't get much fresh on the ship. And if Peter could be believed, my Annie'd learned to take near nothing and make something downright tasty. The crusty bread this morning was sure a welcome change to the bricks she used to manage. Don't rightly know how Annie had learned herself a lifetime of farm wife necessities from Ma in a few years' time.

Ma would say it was on account of the fact that Annie listened for more than half a second—a not-so-subtle hint that her son could stand to learn something from his wife. "But," I'd say, "standing still ain't near as much fun." I'd surely earn a grumbling smack on the arm, but Ma had learned from *her* husband that sometimes a body just needs to wander round a bit 'til he got himself facing the right way again.

Annie scanned the mountain, no doubt wondering at the quiet. The breeze lifted the brim of her hat. Lord Almighty. I grinned and waved, all while wishing we had less of an audience . . . and less responsibility.

"You know"—Peter's voice made me jump—"you were younger than I am now when you married her."

"You already that old?"

"You're a lucky cuss. You know that. Right?"

I nodded, watching my brother stare at my family, feeling the loneliness in his observation. "Your time's a-coming. There's all kinds of gals down in town who—"

"Ain't no woman wants half a man who has to check in at the hospital down the mountain near every week."

"You ain't half a—"

"I am, and bending yourself backward to convince me of something different ain't a kindness." Peter kicked at the newest fence post, but there wasn't anger in his voice. More like resignation.

I studied both my hands, opening and closing my fingers. I still don't know what I would've done if I'd lost one.

"Well, I sure do appreciate the help. I know Annie does too."

"If you're done being all sappy, we best get back to work, or we'll never get this thing done."

I laughed. Same old Peter. I turned with him, but as I did I caught sight of the fence line leading up to the sorting shed and sighed. Broken.

"Hey, Peter."

He set down his hammer.

"We got enough fencing to fix that up there too?"

Peter squinted into the sun, shaking his head like he didn't know what I was talking about.

"The fence running up the west side." I pointed. "By the sorting shed. I'd hoped to let the sows out there tomorrow to clean up the fallen peaches before they mold. The pigs could use the extra feed, and if'n they eat most of the rot, we won't have to pick it all up."

Peter studied the garden fence line, then the posts we'd cut, then the far fence. "I suppose. If we use some haywire too." He seemed to be calculating. "But won't the sows damage the trees?"

"Not if'n there's enough peaches on the ground. 'Sides, we can keep an eye on them while we're doing morning chores. They probably won't finish everything by the time we have to leave for town, but some is better than none, I reckon."

"You sure that's all you want to do up there?"

I frowned. What in heaven's name was he—

"Doc told me about that time on the bluff when you were a mite younger than me, smarting because Annie'd been sent away to college. He'd come home from school for a visit, and he said you—"

I threw a hasty arm over my brother's shoulders, sheepish as a youngster caught stealing a cookie. "Ain't no reason to recollect on that."

"You got drunker than a skunk."

"And threw up for what felt like days straight."

Peter pulled a flask out of the jacket he'd thrown over the fence and held it out to me. "Seems this might be another time when you might need to . . ." He let me fill in the blank for myself. And I have to admit it was tempting to pour alcohol into all them blank places.

"I don't do that no more."

"You're a better man than me. When I first got home, it was the only thing that helped me sleep on account of the pain . . . and the dreams." He sipped a bit and pulled air through his teeth with a grimace. "It was medicinal. And it's a sight better than the things I've seen other veterans taking. Better than what the docs wanted me taking, even."

He took another drink, then held out the flask to me. "You sure you don't want none?"

The biting smell of alcohol sent a rattle through my body, remembering. Ma never abided liquor in our house, but Pa was known to have a drink or two with the other men from town. Ma said it got worse after he came home from the Great War. Desire swelled inside me. A longing to let the alcohol fight the nightmares that strung themselves together from sunset to daybreak. But I hadn't had a single nightmare in my own bed. That was something. Wasn't it? And I knew Annie's fears and how they walked hand in hand with drink.

"I'm all right." My smile felt strangled, but Peter didn't seem to notice. I tapped a cigarette out of the package tucked into my shirt and lit it, drawing in the warm, steady smoke before releasing it into the air.

Peter shook his head at my offer of a cigarette, then screwed the lid onto the flask and stowed it in his jacket. He picked up the hammer, weighing it in his hand before he held a nail in place with the blunt pinchers of his hook, then drove it into a post. "Sometimes you gotta just survive 'til you can get to the other side. Ain't nothin' wrong with that. And Sam, don't shut nobody out. Talkin', as hard as it is, helps."

Peter tugged on the chicken wire, then hooked it on the nail and drove the nail bending around the fencing. The slam of the hammer echoed in the quiet.

"Long as you don't get yourself stuck there," I said.

Peter missed the nail with his next hit.

"I was talking to myself. Not preaching at you." I always did make a mess of things with my brother.

He slapped his hook on his thigh like he was brushing off the remnants of dirt. "You do make a horrible preacher man. But for the record, I ain't stuck." He drove in another nail, then grinned so's I knew we were okay. "You gonna help? Or just watch your little brother do everything like usual?"

"Like usual, huh?" I hefted the chicken wire and set off up the incline. "See if'n you can keep up whilst I fix the fence over yonder."

———————

I sat against a fence post in the newly enlarged garden, head leaning against the warmth of the last rays of sunshine held in by the wood. It was well past the time I should've been back at the house for supper, but it was quiet here, and my entire body ached like the hammer'd been used on me all day instead of on the fencing. Everything that still needed fixin', haulin', or doin' sat behind me somewhere. If I couldn't see it, it could wait. Ma was forever saying we needed to take a bit of time here and there just to rest, and out here a body could breathe. Lord, I'd missed this. You'd think the ocean would be one big mess of quiet, but with the motor and the men, the comings and goings, wasn't a quiet place to be found.

Least both the fences were done. Tomorrow we'd release the pigs under the peach trees, have one nasty chore done, and be able to put off finding more feed for a day or two. I called that a victory even though it had taken me the better part of the day to fix the fence up by the sorting shed. Now to win the war. The cuts in the fencing and prints on the ground told me someone had destroyed the spans on purpose so's they could walk horses up the mountain without going round on the road. Peter told me those drifters he'd seen on the road had actually caused some trouble, but he'd sent them on their way a good space back.

Made me a mite nervous to know men had been up by the sorting shed at some point, that my fears had been right. Folks were taking advantage of Annie. If they knew I was home, would that stop them from coming back? I didn't like the idea of strange men coming and going this close to my family . . . especially with all the nonsense that happened in Hot Springs.

Night was coming on hard now, and I pushed to my feet. Wouldn't do to get myself injured navigating out here without the benefit of light. Peter and Doc would sure get a kick out of me explaining how's I broke my leg tripping over a tree root.

A white furball shot out from behind the fence and twined in my legs. I laughed and leaned down to gather up Rosie's kitten. Bailey bristled and hissed, his tail fluffed out against an unseen enemy.

"It's okay there, fella. It's just your papa. Something out there got you spooked?"

The cat growled, turning again to the ridge, and the hairs on my arms pricked. Any mountain man knows to trust the animals round him. I scanned the area for the telltale glow of nighttime eyes. A light flickered on and off again in the direction of the sorting shed. That weren't no animal up there . . . at least not the four-legged kind.

Squatting, I rubbed the cat's back. "What's that, do you think?"

He twitched and bolted through the trees back home—where I should go.

Behind me, the outline of the road curved away from the light now glowing steadily just at the crest. Far enough up that Annie would never be able to see it from the house. The glow disappeared, and I squinted. Who was up there?

I closed my eyes and sighed. It was real. Right?

I slapped my cheeks a few times and opened my eyes.

The light blinked on, then off.

I stood there dumb. They best not have cut through my new fencing. I hefted the hammer from my belt and trudged up the incline. I'd tell them to move on.

About forty yards off, I caught the smell of cigarette smoke and stopped dead against the writhing shape of a peach tree. All I had with me was a hammer. What if there were more than a couple of men, and what if they'd brought more than a little tool as a weapon? Wouldn't put it past the sinister populace of Hot Springs to use a half-abandoned farm for something shady. I'd heard tell of more than a few drug deals and illegal liaisons in the hills. Heck, I'd been part of arranging some of them way back when. Then again, it might just be a drifter.

Fire from the sunset faded, dying behind the mountain. I closed my eyes and listened. The farm pulsed with the soft sounds of insects and animals. A bird fussed, moving from tree to tree behind me, chirp-ing to itself as it nestled in for the night. Everything as it should be.

I opened my eyes again and eased out of the tree line. Following my memory, I clambered over the fence and edged to where the source of the light had been. I knelt at the open door of the shed. A cigarette butt. Somebody had been here.

Rocks clattered down the mountain, and I twisted through the doorway into the safety of the shed, peering back into the orchard. A man-shape floated from that direction, and my heartbeat picked up pace. I hefted the hammer. Surprise would be my only advantage if'n this was one of the Judge's men. He moved easily like he'd been here a time or two in the dark.

Sweat trickled down my neck.

Rabbit and Jake half-scrambling, half-drowning because of their packs as they scrambled to the beach. Tripping over an empty boot. A glimpse over my shoulder, the water red as it sucked down our craft. *Run. Run. Run.*

I shook my head to dislodge the memory. Wasn't no sniper in the forest. Just one man. I settled my feet underneath me so's I could spring on him when he got close enough that my hammer could outmaneuver a gun.

The man flung a leg over the fence and whistled the opening to Beethoven's Fifth—high, high, high, then low and drawn out long.

Peter.

"What in tarnation are you doing up here?" I stomped out of the shed. Beethoven had been our signal ever since we'd been old enough to need a secret code to fool Ma into thinking we was innocent when we weren't.

"Apparently, I'm scaring you near to death."

"Few years back I'd have cuffed your ears."

Peter grinned, settling one foot behind him in a fighter's stance. "You can try."

"When'd you get to be such an ornery, mouth-flapping so-and-so?"

"I learned from the best."

Laughing made the fear in me melt away. There were two of us to take care of things now. I didn't have to do it all alone.

"Did you see anyone on your way up here?"

Peter frowned and pivoted round.

"There was a light up here, and—"

"A light?" His eyebrows lifted, looking so much like Ma when she suspected we had a fever that I flinched.

"I ain't dreaming it, Peter." I held out the still warm cigarette.

He plucked it from my fingers, examined it, then flicked it into the weeds. "Looks like the Camels I smoke. I was up here making sure all the gaps are closed."

When had he started smoking? I'd never quite kicked the habit, but Peter . . .

He stuffed his hand into his pocket, the wheels spinning in his mind so fast I could near hear them. "You know, when I came back from the Pacific, I sometimes saw—"

"I ain't crazy." Frustration snuck into my voice. "I know what I saw. There was a light. Somewhere up here."

"Sam." Peter touched my arm, and I shook off the metal hand. "Sam," he said again. "I know what it was like over there. I read your commendation for the Silver Star and put it together with what other folks was saying about what happened. It just takes the mind some space to heal. You gotta give yourself time."

"I said I ain't crazy." Now my voice was low and sounded so much like a predator it near scared me lifeless.

"Nobody's trying to lock you behind doors down at the hospital."

Panic ripped through me, my mind seizing. I stumbled backward until the rough edges of the fence pricked into my back. Last place anybody wanted to go was where they used electric shocking—or at least drugging that took all sense away. There wasn't no hope there, just suffocation. My breath came in snatches and burning heaves. "I ain't—"

"Sam?" Peter touched my arm again, and I jumped away.

"Sam." He didn't try to touch me this time, but he made sure he was clear in my sights. "You're safe. I shouldn't have said nothing. Let's look around. Real careful-like. It'll put your mind at ease."

Reaching into the shed, Peter lifted the lantern from its place, then lit it. As he walked round the outside of the building, the light flickered, then disappeared around the far side. Realizing that anybody could be hiding back there and attack my defenseless, one-handed brother, I raised my hammer and ran to the shed, nearly colliding with him as he came round the corner.

I stumbled back and pretended like I knew he'd be right fine, but I followed him through the door like he might never come back if'n I lost sight of him again. The tables and peach boxes were neatly stacked. Still. Quiet. Everything like it was supposed to be. No sign of vermin of any kind.

I peered over a table and behind some boxes. No blankets or parcels suggesting someone had stayed or was planning to come back.

"Well," Peter said, leaning against the empty table, "you find anything?"

I shook my head, rubbing my dustless fingers together, thinking. "Ain't nobody here." Least not right now. But if the shed hadn't been used since last harvest, why wasn't there no dust nowhere and no critters to be found? Something didn't sit right. I wished I'd walked round the shed with him to prove to myself everything was as it should be. It might just be drifters like Peter had said, but what if it was someone else? What if they were doing something illegal that no one wanted known? That'd be a whole other kettle of fish.

Peter held the lantern high and pondered on me. "How 'bout we take the lantern with us? I can return it tomorrow when I let the sows out."

"There's enough moonlight now." In truth, there was barely any, but I refused to be treated like a child afraid of the night.

Peter blew out the lantern's flame, and darkness closed around me again. Ain't nobody up here, I told myself. I shut my eyes against the silence. We're all safe . . . for now.

"Everybody's waiting supper on us." Peter's voice was quiet and careful like he knew how near panic I was. "Let's get on down the hill. It'll all be better once we get some food inside us. Least that's what Pa always said."

Took us more than a spell to make our way home. But the light from the house twinkled and lured me away from my fears 'til I near forgot everything but my whining stomach and the smell of fried collard greens and bacon.

Soon as I entered the kitchen, Rosie jumped from the table and flung herself into my arms, chattering away. "And Bailey caught a mouse, and Meemaw made a . . ." I lost track of what she was saying on account of not quite understanding her toddler version of English when she talked so fast. Well, that and because of the sheer relief crossing Annie's face.

I strode across the kitchen and cupped my hand around my wife's cheek. "You okay?"

Annie nodded. "We just didn't know where you were, and there're stories . . ." Her eyes flashed up to mine like she'd been caught, and then she shook her head. "Ain't nothing. There's water on the stove for you to wash up."

What I saw in her face wasn't nothing. I poured a bit of the hot water into the bucket of cold and scrubbed at the dirt under my nails with the brush. I guess I should've let them know where I was, but I'd never had to do that before. It was almost like . . . My head snapped up, watching Peter whisper to Annie. What was he hiding?

Annie caught my eye and smiled brightly.

"Peter was explaining that y'all thought you saw something by the sorting shed, and you went to check on it. I'm ever so grateful that you're watching out for us." She set a plate in front of me as I sat down. "I'm glad it was nothing at all."

I nodded. What was I supposed to say that wouldn't make me sound crazy or argumentative? There wasn't nothing but a spit-shined shed and a warm cigarette butt to prove something was off-kilter. As sure as if he'd poured a bucketful of water on a lit candle, Peter'd sabotaged any argument I could make.

Ma glowered at Peter, then me. I forced myself to smile like there wasn't nothing wrong, but she *mm-hmmed* like when she'd caught Peter lying about how all my underwear ended up in the pigsty.

Peter cleared his throat, the first one to break. Ma turned toward him and frowned, biting her top lip.

"Let's pray." Ma took a gander at me before bowing her head. "God, please bless this food. Bless the hands that made it." She paused, and I waited for her to pray for her boys to learn to tell the truth. Instead, she sniffled. "And thank You that both my boys are safe back home and working together to take care of their family. Tell their pa he'll have to wait a little longer to see them again. Amen."

Lord Almighty, she knew how to bring us all back in line. She was right. We needed to work together. Peter might be a thorn in my side, but he was my brother. The one who'd tailed me my entire life. Peter who built the tree fort with Pa and me, who helped me smooth over arguments with Mary and later Annie. He was the one who helped Ma and Mary in the house and kitchen after school when Pa got so sick and I was taking care of the farm the best I could. He'd never betray me. And why did I think he was up to no good? On account of his having a smoke and not noticing something I'd seen? I owed my brother an apology. That was for sure and for certain.

Ma tucked into her collard greens and declared them "the best thing I ever did taste."

Peter shoveled food in his mouth with his right hand, his left arm surrounding his plate like one of us might snatch it away.

Annie laughed and scooped another spoonful onto his plate. "I'll make sure your big brother won't steal your food." And then she smirked at me all full of innocence.

"If'n I remember right, it wasn't his brother that went stealing his food but his sister and her best friend." Ma grinned at my Annie. "And looking like sweet angels is what got y'all out of trouble."

"Nothing sweeter than Charlotte Anne." I grasped Annie's hand in mine, making mooning eyes at her. "'Cepting maybe that cobbler cooling on the stove."

"You eat all your vegetables, and then we'll see about that dessert."

I spooned the last of the garden's peas off my plate, then shoved them into my mouth all while grinning across the table at Annie, letting her see the rough-cut farm boy I used to be. "How 'bout now?"

My wife laughed, and the whole world brightened. No darkness anywhere in it.

"Maybe we can all go outside to eat dessert and find some of them fireflies Peter says y'all saw up on the ridge."

I stilled. Fireflies? Is that what Peter told her I saw?

The lines on Ma's forehead deepened. "Awful early for them things. Ain't it?"

"I'm just glad it wasn't them hobos again," Annie said, snatching my plate while I struggled to breathe, the walls shrinking in, the surface of the water getting farther and farther away. Annie smiled at me, all hope for the future, and I prayed to God she'd never lose the sight of goodness.

But there weren't no fireflies on the ridge, no more'n any were in our yard. It was more likely somebody signaling to somebody else. But I couldn't go saying that. No one would believe me now. Peter would never do anything to put me and Annie in harm's way, let alone Ma. That didn't mean he was right, though.

I straggled behind everyone and sank to the porch steps, barely tasting the cobbler. While Rosie skipped around playing in the dirt, the adults chatted about this and that, and my mind leapt ahead, planning. Testing ideas and discarding them 'til I had a plan ready. I'd get them all safely tucked away for the night, then keep an eye on things just in case.

CHAPTER
Eight

—ANNIE—

I woke to a scraping sound on the floorboards and groaned. Better not be Rosie. Wasn't even daylight. I rolled over to curl into Sam, remember the warmth, and know that his coming home wasn't a dream.

But the sheets were cold.

My sleep-slowed mind struggled to catch up. Had I dreamed his arm slung heavy over my belly?

I used one of our precious matches to light the lantern by my bed, then squinted into the room. Sam's military jacket still hung on a hook next to my work dress. Wasn't a dream, then. Maybe he'd got hungry and gone to the kitchen for a snack. He'd be back presently if that was the case. I patted his side of the bed intending to straighten it for him, but it was neat as a pin. Had Sam not come to bed last night? He'd gone out to check on the animals and, as exhausted as I was, I was falling asleep before I'd even fully laid down.

Silvered shadows of trees danced a peculiar beat under the lace bottom of my bedroom curtains. I hadn't washed the gingham before I cut it, and now I was paying the price of learning wifely skills by accident. If I'd had someone to teach me how to do it right, the outside world couldn't haunt my bedroom.

The barn door clattered, and the hairs on my arms stood. Wasn't the first time I wished we had ourselves a guard dog. I pulled on my robe and tugged it closed. Where was Sam? Carrying the lantern, I wandered to the sitting room hoping he'd be stretched out there. But it was empty. I told myself there wasn't nothing wrong. That he'd be in the kitchen or the barn and the noises outside had to be him.

Wasn't many folks who made their way through our orchard, but anyone who did at this hour wasn't likely up to any good. We couldn't afford to have nobody stealing from the pantry or barn. There wasn't enough as it was. I hesitated inside the door leading to the breezeway.

"Why are you lollygagging, Charlotte Anne?" I whispered to myself. It was more'n likely Sam out there. 'Sides, three years on this farm with only Dovie May and Rosie had taught me what to do.

There wasn't nothing inside the house that had caused the scratching that I could see. So I peeked through the door and scanned the breezeway and yard for whatever had woke me. The sky was a strange mix of predawn gray and pink that did nothing to help me see but lit up my white robe like a candle. A trace of a body skittered across the barnyard, and I stepped back into the protection of the doorway, feeling for the shotgun.

It was gone.

I blew out the lantern, then set it down and swallowed, holding myself as hushed as the night.

Footsteps sounded behind me, and I swung round, fists flying. The shadow caught my arms, smashing my face against him, smothering my scream in his chest. The smell of sweat and smoke and bitter fear made me gag, my body quivering, knowing what a man might do.

"It's me." Sam's voice was barely a sigh, and I sagged in relief.

"Somebody's out here."

I shifted to see where he was pointing. The oak tree stood a silent guard at the back side of the house, its branches barely moving in the gathering wind. It was nearly the same thing that'd spooked me earlier.

"I don't see—"

"Lock yourself inside the house." He nudged me toward the open doorway, then shifted 'til the gloom shrouded him. "And don't come out for nothing."

I barred the door behind me. My head rested against the wood, and I reminded myself how Sam had always been my rock. But if Doc was right, Sam was seeing ghosts without the good sense to know what was a ghost and what wasn't. Peter'd said they found fireflies and those were the flashing lights Sam saw. But the moment we went out to see them, I knew Peter had covered for his brother. There weren't no fireflies out in this cold.

I wanted to believe my husband now, but nobody was out there. *Come back to me, Sam.*

The door rattled in response to my prayer, a venomous breath sneaking in to join the figures on the wall next to me. My imagination tripped forward, seeing narrow devil fingers reaching down, down inside my chest.

The house sighed against the wind, whispering, "Charlotte Anne." I squeezed my eyes shut tight, hands over my ears, a little girl pretending the bad in the world wasn't there, that daddies weren't mobsters and mamas didn't choose to leave their little girls only to come back as ghosts.

"Charlotte Anne."

"No." The word ground out between my teeth. "Mama's gone." My fingers sought the cross Mama'd left me, now pinned to the wall. "I don't believe in ghosts." Thunder rolled in the distance, and I bit my knuckles. My false bravery shattered in sharp pieces. I may not believe in ghosts, but I did believe in devils. And sure as my heart was beating, one was out hunting tonight.

Yea, though I walk through the valley of the shadow of death . . . The prayer slipped into my mind, trickling into the sitting room. "I will fear no evil." Dovie May's antidote shriveled on my tongue, and I leapt away from the grasping devils, panting. Grasping for reality. The fingers were merely the crosspieces in the window. The breath simply the breeze coming down the mountain. I touched the door to remind myself of what was real.

A flash of light split the sky, engraving stark shadows into the house and sucking the light back a moment later. I stifled a scream, then stood shaking, barefoot on the other side of the door where I thought I was safe . . . where I *knew* I was safe despite the devils crawling up my skin.

A shot rang out, and I flung the bar up, then bolted through the door. Up in the hollow, there was no calling for help from anybody, but Sam surely needed it.

Lightning pulsed in the roiling clouds—a silent announcement that another storm was a-coming. The garden needed the water, but I didn't much relish a soaking. Sticking to the shadows, I trotted out to the oak tree and pulled myself into the branches. I'd climbed the tree enough times to know it would give me a view of the whole farm. 'Sides, I wasn't about to traipse through the field with an armed veteran on alert. Dovie May's stories told me that was a sure way to get a body shot. But if Sam was right and someone was on our farm, I couldn't leave my husband out there alone either.

The clouds above me churned, eating away at the sky. The flashes threw writhing patterns across the ground.

The silhouetted trees at the west edge of the orchard shifted, and I pressed into the tree trunk. There was a man there. Wasn't there? I squinted like that might separate the darkness into shapes.

Trees braced against the wind.

There.

There it was again. A shape separated, then stumbled into the clearing. A head coming, shoulders. Lightning flashed, and the man's face came clear.

Sam. It was just Sam.

My fingers relaxed on the branch, and I scrambled down the tree and out into the orchard.

"Sam!"

He lurched toward me, the shotgun dragging across the ground. The trail of it staggered back through our peach trees as far as I could see.

"I told you to stay inside, darlin'." He scanned the skies, then dragged me behind a tree, his steps erratic.

He was banged up right good and filthy from what had to have been a fall down the hill. A trickle of blood coursed down his cheek. I didn't see blood anywhere else, but Sam shook like the whole world was set on blowing him over.

What was out there? What happened to his head? I studied the blank hillside.

"We have to get inside." The shout burned in my throat but was still drowned in the noise of the rain as the clouds released a torrent on us.

Sam's eyes snapped to mine. "Annie?" Thunder rumbled, echoing against the mountains and blotting out the words his lips formed.

"You aren't safe here. Get below decks."

Decks?

He was stuck back on the Pacific. I cupped his cheek in my palm, directing his eyes to mine. "Easy now. You're safe." I was doing what he'd done for me more times than I could count.

Sam's wild eyes locked on mine. A puff of air escaped his lips. Relief warred with the fear in his eyes. A child waking from a nightmare.

The hairs on my arms stood on end, and Sam pulled me to the ground underneath him just as the earth shook. Lightning exploded a few yards away, and pebbles rained on my skin.

"We gotta get out of the fields." He grabbed my hand, and we ran pell-mell through the weird light, the peach tree branches distorting in the wind and flashes of light.

We stumbled into the living room, gasping and heaving as Sam shut the door and locked it tight. He stowed the gun, then stood watching me. I crossed my arms over my chest, wishing he'd say something. Water ran in rivulets through his hair and off the ends of his shirt. His lips lifted in a wry grin. And I stood wary, wondering which Sam was with me.

"We're a sight, ain't we?" The laughter in his voice dragged me back through time to him carrying me into Dovie May's kitchen all those years ago. It was worth all that fear—the ice cracking, the cold cramming itself into my mouth—just to have Sam haul me out like a hero from my storybooks and carry me all the way from the pond. This farm had always been the place where I was safe.

No, Sam had always been the place where I was safe.

My husband fumbled with the buttons on his shirt, water shimmering on his bare chest, the bandage wrapped around him.

Heat burst through my body, and I stared at my muddy toes as he let his shirt puddle on the floor. Don't rightly know why I felt like a naughty teenager spying on my best friend's older brother.

"Didn't mean to scare you." Sam lifted my shawl from the rocker, then wrapped it around me. I shrugged off my robe, then shimmied out of my wet nightgown, letting it drop. It fluttered down so's its sleeve touched Sam's discarded shirt. If only it were that easy to reach out and touch Sam himself.

Sam threw a blanket from the davenport over himself, then tossed another bit of wood in the stove and motioned for me to come closer. But something in me hung back. This time he'd recognized me, but what if he hadn't? Or he'd taken a moment too long to realize I was his wife and not the enemy? Or worse, what if it had been Rosie?

"Why were you out there, Sam?"

He ran a hand through his hair and sighed. I remembered the look—the one he had when he'd come into my closet at Daddy's house, convincing me that the Judge's anger had run its course and it was safe to come out.

"I slept on the porch to keep watch, and then I heard voices, so I followed them." He pulled the blanket closer, protecting himself from whatever was to come. "They went up to the shed, where I saw the light earlier. I don't know why Peter said we saw fireflies. The light I saw wasn't no bug, and Peter . . . He said he didn't see nothing, but we scouted around the shed anyway. I found a warm cigarette butt, and everything up there was too neat and tidy. But Peter explained everything away."

"I was up in the oak tree, Sam."

"I couldn't let it lie if'n it meant somebody might be hiding on the farm." Sam continued like he hadn't even heard me or didn't know what I'd meant. "There were men up there tonight, Annie. I followed them, and they were sorting boxes. I saw them clear as I can see you, but I wasn't close enough to hear what they were saying, see who they were or what was in them boxes. One took off on a horse and the others in their automobiles before—"

I had closed my eyes against the pleading in his expression.

"You don't believe me."

He'd only ever believed me. Couldn't I do the same for him?

"I . . . Sam, I've been up in the oak tree. You know I would've seen if there was someone up in the shed. I saw shadows, but then you came out from where I saw them, in the orchard. I . . . I didn't see nothing else." I would have seen something. Wouldn't I? I coiled the edges of my shawl in my fists, not daring to let him see my eyes. It was one thing to see lights that weren't there, but hearing voices? Seeing people? That was crazy. Wasn't it? Why did I not believe Sam? My Sam.

The door opened, then shut with a quiet click. When I opened my eyes, Sam was gone. I heard his footsteps drum down the porch steps. From the window I watched him stride out to the barn. The only sound left was the mournful tones of the wind chimes Sam made me for my birthday.

Seems the war had gotten hold of Sam like a terrier and wasn't letting go.

The thunderstorm trailed off the mountain, leaving wisps of cloud in the brightening sky and so many puddles in the yard that the house seemed to float atop a marsh. Good thing we'd run out of time to plant the new seeds yesterday. They would've been halfway to Malvern on account of the gulley washer.

After I dressed, I stoked the stove in the kitchen and started some potatoes in the oven for breakfast. I stared into the flames, warming myself, picturing Sam throwing hay in his soggy britches and bare chest. Part of me wanted to go out and tell him I would believe the mountain was the ocean just because he told me so. But I knew good and well it wouldn't help if I didn't actually believe it. I snatched the broom from the corner and attacked the kitchen floor like it was responsible for all the wrongs in the world.

The swishing was so loud that I didn't even hear Dovie May come in 'til she cleared her throat. "I don't rightly think that floor done anything to you." She hobbled over to me, her hand outstretched, and I handed her the broom.

Dovie May's head barely reached my shoulders, but there ain't nobody who don't obey her.

"Where's Peter?"

"Out in the barn." Dovie May studied me. "What's eating at you, sweet girl?"

I brushed at my apron and blinked back tears. *Ladies do not blubber, weep, or cry. They carry themselves above all the cares of the world.* But how could I tell her I was afraid her son was seeing what wasn't there?

"Don't you go closing yourself off to me." Dovie May stepped closer and cupped my chin in her gnarled hand so I couldn't move away while she brushed away a tear with her thumb. "Your mama was one of the best women I ever knew, but there was a whole heaping lot she got wrong. You think holding herself apart from everyone else helped her?"

There was only one answer to that question, so Dovie May didn't even wait for it before she settled me into a chair and eased into the seat next to me.

"I told you about when my Herbert came home from the Great War." Dovie May looped my arm into the crook of hers. "Lord, I missed him something fierce, and I expected everything to end up happy like they do in the storybooks. Was I ever in for a surprise. We think everything eventually goes back to what we want it be. That everything'll be happy and familiar, the good winning. We never want to travel beyond the point where everybody's happy. But life's everything after, and the question is, what are you going to do with the truth life drops in your lap?"

She patted my knee and groaned as she pushed herself out of her chair. "I ain't ever known Sam to be wrong about nothing. Have you?"

I thought about all the times Sam showed up at just the right moment—reaching through the ice after me, catching Gerald Pitner's fist from the air as he flung it at me, diving into the pond when I'd gone in after Mama and gotten stuck myself. He even knew how to get Daddy to let me go when all Sam's friends said he was asking for a death sentence. Maybe there was something up the mountain I'd missed. That even Peter had missed.

"You go on out and tell my sons to hurry up with the chores so's we can get done with breakfast and go into town. Doc promised us dinner in a real restaurant, and I ain't gonna miss it on account of them lazing about." She grinned as she lifted the percolator from the stove and poured two mugs of coffee. "I'll finish in here and watch out for your baby girl."

Dovie May was right. We'd had our fairy tale. Sam was back, and it was up to me to figure out what I was going to do from here. Guess I'd make things best as I could and trust that the good Lord and Sam would figure out the rest.

The mugs warmed my hands as I tiptoed between pools of water out to the barn. If the days got any warmer, we'd be swarmed with skeeters right quick.

I eased through the crack between the barn doors, then froze. Peter was up in the loft pitching hay down into the stalls like the devil himself might be in the hay mound, and Sam was in a stall shoveling out the muck in much the same way. What should have been a silent, coordinated display was a raging battle scene.

"I'm just trying to do right by my family. Provide for them and protect them." Sam's voice rose in frustration, flinging horse dung into the waiting wheelbarrow with such force that the impact echoed in the barn.

"You think Charlotte Anne felt safe last night?" Peter slashed at the air with the pitchfork.

"You ain't her husband, and you ain't got no right to—"

"She's my sister. Same as Mary is. I got every right to stand between her and anybody who puts her in danger, even if that person's you!"

Sam straightened, his fists clenching and unclenching. "You . . ."

He dropped his shovel to the barn floor. "Ain't gotta listen to no interloping, uncommitted, jacka—" He stopped cold when he saw me.

I glanced at Peter like he'd know what to do. He glowered at me, shook his head, and then abandoned me to my angry husband.

"Dovie May sent me out with coffee for y'all." The brew sloshed out of the mugs as I lifted them like a peace offering. "She said you best hurry with chores so's we can have breakfast."

I passed Sam his mug and rubbed the coffee from my hand.

"How much of that'd you hear?" He frowned at me, his eyebrows knit together.

"Enough," I said, and set down the second mug before lifting my voice so's Peter could hear. "Y'all don't have to worry 'bout me none."

Peter stabbed his pitchfork into the mound of hay, then stomped down the ladder. I scrambled backward, away from what was likely a keg of dynamite waiting to explode.

"I do gotta worry 'bout you." Peter gave me a brittle smile, tapping my arm with his hook before turning on his brother. "You gonna tell her what you done? You gonna tell Ma?"

Sam shrugged like he was ashamed.

"I don't understand." Was this about last night?

"He bought ammonium nitrate pellets!" Peter was shouting like Sam had bought enough opium to supply the entire town.

"Ammonium what?"

"It's a fertilizer." Sam rolled his eyes at his brother.

Now I knew I was missing something.

Peter huffed. "Fertilizer that's been known to blow up entire trains. If you ain't willing to tell her the whole truth, there's part of you that knows this ain't a good idea."

"I did the reading. I know how to store it, how to handle it, how to spread it." Sam ticked it all off on his fingers before turning to me. "It'll make the garden produce twice as much and strengthen the peach trees. And it was inexpensive and available."

"On account of the fact that the government don't need it for bombs no more!"

"Bombs?" I gasped, my hand flying out to take hold of the stall door. I wanted to trust Sam; he'd never steered me wrong before. But bombs?

Sam ran a hand through his hair. "We'll put it up in the sorting shed. It's far enough away from the house that even if something happens, it won't affect us none."

"A bomb going off won't affect—"

"There was a salesman at the naval station. He gave all us farmers a special deal."

"You already paid for it?" My lungs deflated, and I wasn't sure how to breathe no more. "But there ain't nothing in our account. How did you—" And then I realized Sam had mortgaged the farm. I sank to the floor of the stall. We'd never been mortgaged before. If this didn't work . . . "Lord Almighty, Sam."

"It gets worse. They're delivering it Monday." Peter's ire echoed around the barn.

"Monday?" The word slipped from my throat, and I snapped my mouth closed around it. That was two days from now. They were delivering something that could explode in two days. I inhaled slow and deep like Doc had taught me, then exhaled, realization seeping in with each breath. This was why Sam was obsessed with the sorting shed. He had some bizarre fear of what he was planning to do, and that drove him to seeing people doing things that ought not be done up there. Except it was *him* doing the shady dealing.

Peter took another step toward Sam, his brutal verbal attack leaving my hero in tatters and me flayed and exposed.

"And if there's drifters in and out of there, the shed ain't a safe place to store the durned stuff. So what are we going to do with it, Sam? Where are we going to put a load like that in two days' time?"

"When I bought it I didn't know—"

"No. You're right. You didn't know. You didn't even think." Peter poked the curve of his hook into Sam's shoulder. "You haven't been home in three years." Poke. "Hadn't taken a gander at the fields to know if they even needed extra fertilizing." Poke. "Or at the buildings to know if there was a safe place to store it." Poke. "Didn't take into account how Ma or Annie might feel. You didn't—"

Sam snatched Peter's hook and held it mid-air. "We can put a lock on the durn shed. What is your—"

"That will be quite enough." Dovie May stood framed in the doorway like an avenging angel. "Your brother was doing what he thought best at the time. He was coming home not knowing you'd be here. More'n likely, Annie and I would never have known what kind of fertilizer Sam bought until we saw the return on investment. But"—she pulled herself up as tall as her tiny frame allowed—"we do need to find a safe place to store it. So I suggest you two put your heads together and figure it out in a manner fittin' how your pa and I raised you. Now, y'all finish out here, wash up, and get your sorry selves inside afore I tan the lot of you."

I leaned against the worn slats of wood and nibbled on a ripped nail, tasting blood. I dropped my hand, Mama's voice echoing in my head. *A lady does not bite at her fingers.* What would Mama think of me now? Ragged clothes, ragged nails, and afraid of my own husband.

Dovie May hobbled to where I hid and settled next to me with a groan.

"He's a good man and smart as anything."

I nodded, not knowing what to say. Just because a body was good or smart didn't mean they escaped the bad in the world. And it certainly didn't mean Sam wasn't seeing things that weren't there.

"He'll be all right." She patted my knee. "*We'll* be all right."

"I know." But truth be told, I didn't, and the arch of Dovie May's eyebrow said she knew I didn't believe it.

I served everybody breakfast, but I don't remember a thing about it other than it was quick. Peter and Sam must've made some kind of peace, because they left the table together to let the pigs out in the orchard and finish chores. Still, it didn't surprise me none when Peter said he was staying behind to take care of the livestock while we went into town. He'd ride in on his bicycle tomorrow and meet us at the church.

I loaded food and clothes, half tempted to leave our church things behind. But I pushed away the thoughts, forcing myself to work hard enough to silence my mind. Idle hands are the devil's workshop. If I didn't think, I couldn't feel, and nothing could make me afraid.

CHAPTER
Nine

— S A M —

I poured myself a third cup of coffee from my thermos, then gulped some of the brew and screeched like a stuck pig. I'd scorched my mouth good. And with the morning I'd had, all I wanted to do was fly into a tantrum reminiscent of my drill instructor.

I hadn't missed the looks between Peter and Annie. They thought I was crazy as a loon.

I set the mug on the porch rail to cool and then herded the pigs out to the orchard while Peter finished the mucking. Wasn't no arguing with him, but I couldn't hold my tongue no more.

Did I have proof of what I'd seen? No. But that didn't mean I was wrong. I knew what I saw, proof or not.

Last night I'd been half asleep on the porch swing when voices floated over the sound of the crickets, shushing and laughing like they was drunk. "Hush. You're gonna wake him up."

I hadn't moved right away. I wasn't sure if'n I was dreaming again. But when the chatter continued, I followed the men up the hill. There was some scraping in the shed, then quiet. The lanterns cast long ghost shadows through the open door. While one man sorted, another shoved little boxes into two bags, and the last man counted, making tallies in a notebook. What were they up to? It was one thing for drifters to use the shed as a place to rest but a whole other thing to be hiding away a secret in there.

Intending to throw the intruders out, I sprang up, but then I stopped right quick. I hadn't brought any kind of weapon with me. I cursed Peter. He'd had me so convinced I was wrong about the light that now I couldn't trust myself to think straight. Couldn't exactly confront these men without a way to "encourage" them to leave my family alone. I skittered home, where I grabbed the gun, near scaring Annie to death.

By the time I skedaddled back to the shed, the lightning had started flickering. And from there my memory got hazy, so's I couldn't rightly say what happened. I just knew I came to with my head hurting, Annie scared, and the rain washing down the mountain.

I kicked the porch step so hard I felt the ring of it in my ears. Ain't nothing good that comes from a thunderstorm.

I stopped cold.

Lord Almighty, I was starting to sound like Annie's mama, seeing devils in everything.

One thing's for certain. I don't rightly think I'll ever forget the fear and pity in Charlotte Anne's eyes when we got inside the house. It was the same look she gave her mama when Rachel had started jumping at anything that moved, thinking the Judge was after her.

It wasn't no secret that the war had twisted more than one man's mind. But why would I conjure up men sorting boxes on our farm? Didn't make no sense nohow.

I wanted to stay on the farm and find out what in blazes was going on, but we'd promised Doc we'd be down, and I needed to buy a padlock for the shed. Right or wrong, that fertilizer was being delivered on Monday, and I needed to be sure it was secure. Last thing I needed was some hobo to come dropping in and exploding himself.

Peter, Annie, and I finished the morning chores, skirting one another in a strange exercise of fear and anger and maybe a bit of regret. And through it all, my conversation with Peter rattled around in my head with bruising intensity.

All the chores, the rhythm of them, cleared my murky thoughts, and now I was certain. The light had been there, the voices and men too. Sure, I had nightmares, and sometimes I didn't know where they started or ended. But the imagined moments had always been on the ocean or in the jungle. I'd never dreamed about something happening on the farm. Not once.

It was late morning when I hitched Buttercup to the wagon. Everybody loaded in near silence, and I clucked the horse on.

As we left the farm, Peter stood at the edge of the barnyard, a statue sure and strong in his convictions. He'd made it plain he was fine without a restaurant dinner and would join us at church tomorrow. He'd do morning chores, then bike down for church and ride back up with us.

But I wondered why Peter would choose cold leftovers over a hot restaurant meal. Guess I didn't blame him for not wanting to make the ride up and back down the mountain twice. But still, I mixed that question right in with the rest of my brewing thoughts until I was hot under the collar with everybody, even the ones who didn't deserve my burning tongue.

Annie sat next to me at the edge of the bench like she'd rather be in the wagon bed with Ma and Rosie, and I didn't blame her none. I'd hardly been back and I'd attacked my brother and my best friend, claimed to see men sorting boxes, and was apt to bite the head off anybody who dared to come near. Even with near fifteen years of knowing me, if I'd been her, I might not believe me either.

Somewhere along the switchbacks and an hour of clip-clopping horse hooves, I screwed up enough courage to apologize to everybody.

"Apology accepted," Ma snorted from the bed of the wagon. "But, son, you been doing an awful lot of apologizing in the last two days. Maybe you oughta think on not doing the sorts of things that need apologizing for before you go doing them."

Annie blanched like she'd been the one smacked with the words. "Dovie—"

"No. She's right. I been pricklier than a porcupine." I did my best impression of an ornery critter—all teeth and snarls until Annie giggled and Ma rolled her eyes. Fact is, I still needed to prove there was something sideways going on at the shed without making myself seem crazy in the process. And me being an ornery so-and-so wouldn't help my cause.

I inhaled the warm mountain air and Annie's scent that matched her lavender dress, then gently wrapped my arm around her. Somehow, someway, I needed to find the Sam Annie had married and figure out how to deal with the military Sam, even if it meant squeezing the life out of him.

The sun had crept past its peak when the trees cleared enough for me to see Hot Springs spreading out from the mountain roads. Steam floated from the spring water the earth's furnace kept at a nice, constant, hot-bath temperature. There was good reason folks back east called it the Valley of Vapors.

The ghostly mists floating above the waters made most everybody think the springs were responsible for a great many things. And the rumors of the miraculous brought all kinds searching for a rebirth of sorts. Everybody from Babe Ruth to Al Capone had escaped their cares to take a dip in one of the bathhouses lining Central Avenue.

If only the waters could seep into my mind and wash away the nightmares.

We passed the Arlington Hotel, the dual towers ruling over the V-shaped intersection of Fountain and Central. That meant we were nearly to Doc's clinic, which sat opposite the famous bathhouses and was squished between Mr. Farmer's grocery store and the drugstore. I'd spent half my life in that clinic trying to stay out of the elder Dr. Becker's way. My best friend's father had been a doctor in Hot Springs long before Doc had taken up that same mantle, but the older man didn't have Doc's gentleness. Just a German propensity for orderliness and quiet, something in short supply around two rowdy boys. But he'd been generous, taking care of Pa when he got sick without accepting payment, and then gifting Doc the clinic before he'd escaped to the relative ease of retired life in Texas.

Up on the third story, where Doc and I had played in the spare room, you could see the Army and Navy Hospital on the hill across the way. I used to sit up in that room, watching the men limping around in a stupor and wondering what had caused their glassy stares and odd outbursts.

Now I knew.

As I steered the wagon past the hospital, I glanced at the spire pointing to heaven and tore my eyes away from the men in wheelchairs, draped in blankets that dropped off too steep and sudden where their legs should have been. I couldn't let my mind wander toward the perilous what-ifs and the men behind the locked hospital doors where no one could hear their crazy screams.

I reined in Buttercup and waited at the intersection for a break in traffic. Most everyone drove automobiles in town, and the noise of it made me as skittery as a jackrabbit on ice.

A red Cadillac blared its horn as it shot around the wagon, sending our horse rearing forward in shock.

"Whoa there, girl." I hauled in the reins, heart pounding, desperate to keep control. Buttercup lurched into the busy intersection, scattering passersby and narrowly missing a gentleman in a linen three-piece suit. I aimed her for an alleyway and near ran her into the wall. Her hooves scraped for purchase on the slippery pavement, and I leapt from my seat and grasped the bridle. Both the horse and I panted with exertion, and she pranced backward, nearly stomping on my foot.

The commotion had jolted Rosie from her nap, and I heard her gasp. But a wheeze caught her up and set her to coughing so bad I handed the reins to Annie and clambered into the back to help Ma.

"What do we do?" Panic colored my voice, and I sat helpless as Ma banged a cupped hand over my girl's back over and over. I'd known Rosie had the asthma, but knowing and seeing are two different things.

Annie whipped the wagon through a side street hollering at folks to move. She swung round the last corner to Doc's place, then heaved the horse to a stop, pulled the brake, and leapt out of the seat in near one movement. She whipped the reins around the hitch and ran for the clinic.

"Doc!" Annie burst through the clinic's alley door, and I scrambled to cradle my girl and get out of the wagon without jarring her too much. Rosie's face was red, her eyes alternating between clenched and enormous, her open mouth scraping for air.

My girl clutched in my arms, I pushed through the door and stalked straight through to the back, bypassing my frantic wife. "Doc!"

My best friend lurched through the back door, his sleeves rolled up like he'd been in the middle of some procedure and might lop off somebody's head for interrupting him. He stopped mid-stride when he saw my Rosie. His face went white, and he motioned me to follow him into the exam room.

"Annie," Doc said calm as you please, "start the water. You know where everything is. Sam, undo her dress so's I can get a mustard pack on her."

I fumbled with the tiny buttons, my Rosie gasping and heaving under my fingers, her arms flailing. The slow clank of Doc riffling through bottles jarred my nerves. I clenched my teeth to keep from shouting.

While I bounced on my toes, Doc measured a powder into a bowl, then added some liquid and stirred. Skidding into the room, Annie shoved a steaming pot of water under Rosie's face, then spun, opened a cupboard, and pulled out a thin towel for Doc to slather with the mustard plaster. My wife and best friend moved in a co-ordinated skill that made me realize how often they'd done this. I near hyperventilated at the thought of Annie alone with Rosie at the house doing this by herself.

Doc laid the plaster on my girl's chest and eased her head over the steam. I kissed Rosie's forehead, and she leaned away, gasping, eyes rolling back.

"Slow down, my sweet. Slow down. Uncle Doc has you." Doc lifted my girl into his arms and stroked her hair. Relief trickled into Rosie's face, and Doc kissed her forehead.

Acid climbed my throat. Doc had saved her, but all I wanted to do was steal the look she'd given him. Rosemary was *my* daughter. I knew it wasn't fair for me to expect her to see me as her protector yet. I knew it like I knew summer followed spring. But it was my right. The war had stolen my daughter's trust from me and settled it on my best friend.

I slid out of the exam room and leaned against the office wall, breathing as if I wasn't capable of nothing else. I'd asked Doc to watch after my family, but the way Rosie had reacted to him . . . and the way Doc had moved with Annie—their arms touching, her leaning over him, her hair brushing his shoulder as he treated my daughter. It wasn't no secret that Doc had once loved Annie. Did he still? Had he expected something in return from her?

"Sam?" Annie's voice seemed awful far away, and her hand on my arm made me jump. The stone weighing heavy on my lungs shifted. She'd come for me.

"Rosie'll be okay. It's been a long time since she's had an attack this bad. Doc thinks it might be on account of all the flowers starting to bloom. We can give her more medicine, and that'll help."

What if it didn't help? What if she got worse? But I nodded, forcing away the what-ifs.

Ma hobbled into the office, concern creasing her face. "I put Buttercup in the stable out back and put in some grain and water. How's our girl?"

"She's okay." Annie tucked her hand into mine and squeezed it before we went back through the door together. Doc rubbed Rosie's back, and Annie peeked under the mustard plaster, telling me she had to make sure there wasn't no blistering. Doc and Annie spoke, but their voices made a low buzzing. They were a good team. Doc glanced up at me, his eyes bloodshot but clear.

"Thank the good Lord we was so close to the clinic."

I gaped at Ma.

The good Lord? He coulda cured my girl with one word. He coulda prevented the whole war, my nightmares. He coulda made it so's my own daughter would know me. But He hadn't. The good Lord indeed. The heat of my thoughts burned my chest hotter than a mustard pack, and I stormed out of the clinic's front door, desperate for fresh air.

The traffic surged in front of me, blurring and pulsing. Focusing on the bar across the street, I licked my lips, tasting the freedom.

Didn't see nobody moving about through the clinic windows. Ma had disappeared into the exam room with Doc and Annie. And I was horribly, terribly alone. I wanted something to fill the aching hole or at least numb it. Across the way, wedged between two bathhouses, a bell jingled merrily above a door marked Andy's Bar. I swallowed.

One drink couldn't hurt. Might even help tame the thoughts bouncing around my head.

Smoke hung in a haze suffocating the bar's electric lights and windows. I coughed and battled away thoughts of my daughter's rasping breath. But was this how I wanted her to think of me? The barkeep smiled and motioned to the stools in front of him. I glanced back toward the door. Wasn't no one coming out of the clinic doors to find me. I ambled to a seat, my mouth as dry as it would be after a five-mile march without water.

Was just a few hours past lunchtime, but more than a few men sat tucked here and there. I recognized two or three, and several of the others wore bits and pieces of military uniform cobbled together. A woman in the corner giggled and inspected me like a man might inspect a new horse or car. I tugged at my uniform pants, knowing the shame of not filling out my civilian clothes no more and yet not being able to afford new.

"Beer?" said the barkeep.

"Got anything stronger?" I needed to get back before Annie found me here.

"Rum work all right?"

I nodded, and the man poured two fingers of amber liquid from the jug into a glass. I dropped some coins on the counter, and he counted them into the till, each clink reminding me that I wasn't buying food or medicine for my daughter.

I twirled the liquid, seeing the reflection of light in the ridges, the deep rings in the valleys. My own reflection warped and spun—a dark-haired monster contained in a glass. I tipped the liquor into my throat, willing the sting to drown my thoughts. The barkeep poured me another. I drained it, and the soft edges of the bar overtook the cold shadow of the things I couldn't control—my baby girl gasping for air, the screech of metal against a coral head, the ping of bullets searching, the dull thud when they found their target . . .

There's no accounting for suffering. No accounting for who lives and who dies. For why the sun rises and sets. The sooner I got comfortable with that, the better.

CHAPTER
Ten

—ANNIE—

We finally found Sam wandering the street across from the clinic, stumbling a bit, searching round like he'd lost something. But he saw us and weaved his way to us. His unsteady gait was something I recognized all too well, and fear and anger sunk their teeth into my neck 'til it ached.

"I got us a padlock and . . . this for my brave girl." Sam brandished a penny candy for Rosie and gave me a lopsided grin, his eyes clear and bright. Maybe I'd been wrong, but then I smelled his breath. The candy didn't cover what was there.

Rosie snatched the candy, then stuffed it into her mouth before thrusting one hand into her daddy's and one into mine as she bounced down the sidewalk. Sam's chest puffed up, and I caught his sideways glance at Doc as he snugged Dovie May's hand into his other arm. It left Doc standing on his own to lead us through the streets like a tour guide rather than a friend.

I opened my mouth to say something to Sam but then snapped it closed. What could I say that didn't make it sound like I wanted to hold Doc's arm? But my heart still ached that Doc was shunted to the side . . . again.

Just as we reached the intersection at Central Avenue, the foot traffic halted. I stood on tiptoe to see what was happening and immediately wished I hadn't. Mayor McLaughlin was rolling down the street driving his matched bays, Scotch and Soda, waving to the folks on the sidewalks. Was something he did near every day. Hot Springs's very own one-float parade, complete with all the flamboyance of some Chicago mob boss.

"Surprised he don't force folks to salute as he drives by." Sam shouldered through the crowd.

But that wasn't the mayor's way. Leo McLaughlin walked round town with that carnation stuck in his lapel smiling at you like you were the best thing he'd seen all day long . . . lessen you didn't get with the program. Then your farm might get foreclosed on or someone'd find opium in your cabinet and you'd be accused of dealing. He didn't need no salutes, just a body's loyalty.

Daddy materialized in front of the mayor, his distinctive, green-banded fedora tipped against the sun's rays. Wishing we'd thought to avoid McLaughlin's late afternoon ramble, I pressed back into the crowd. But my motion caught Daddy's eye, and his smile slipped just enough that I knew he'd seen us. The reaction made my stomach twist. I'd rather be invisible.

Sam stood tall, glaring at Daddy, tucking Rosie and me behind him as though with one gesture he could protect us from everything that man had done.

Doc tipped his hat, and I acted like I hadn't seen. Doc lived in the city, where you had to pretend in order to survive. Still, Sam didn't need the reminder of what we might have done back home to make it through the war.

As the mayor disappeared around the corner, we crossed the street, then ducked under the white awning of Petit Paris. With a pretentious name like that, I wasn't sure I'd ever be allowed inside.

I stood in the entryway and fiddled with a curl that'd escaped my hat. I don't know the last time I'd eaten in a restaurant. Must've been with Daddy. His favorite place was a shady hole, accented in red, with smoke curling from the tables as if we'd descended into hell itself. Mama had always sat stiff against the sight of the waitresses, their uniforms cut too low to be proper. The women were always nice to us, but the men made my skin crawl the way they eyed Mama.

I shut my mind to that thought and stared at the light-blue drapes curved artfully over the bright windows. Waiters floated between tables, austere in their tailored suits and bow ties. I stood stiff, desperately wishing for something more crisp and less washed out than my lavender dress.

Sam leaned to my ear. "You're absolutely lovely. Like the most beautiful wildflower that blooms on the mountain."

"Wildflower?"

"Ain't no strength to a hothouse bloom." He tucked the curl behind my ear and gathered up our Rosie to follow Doc and the host to our table.

Doc pulled out a chair for me, and I sank into it, the cushion nestling me in. Lord Almighty, I'd missed the softness of upholstered dining chairs. Rosie, sitting between Dovie May and me, gawked about her, mouth wide as a waiter walked by with a flaming dessert. Why anyone felt the need to set bananas on fire and call it flambé was lost on me. Still . . .

"Close your mouth, sugar. Ain't polite to let it hang open." I cringed at how much I sounded like Mama when she was trying to appease Daddy. I hoped at least my voice was gentler than hers. There wasn't no Daddy to appease here.

"Mama, why's there so many forks?" Rosie's whisper was loud as fireworks on a quiet summer night.

I turned to Sam for reinforcements, but he wasn't sitting next to me anymore. Where'd he go?

I glanced around the restaurant and found poor Sam backed into a corner, over by the kitchen. Doc was talking to him, making calming gestures like he was dealing with a half-wild horse. But Sam shook his head like he was trying to shake something off, his body rocking and his stormy eyes darting to the front door like he might bolt. What had happened?

No one had seen him over there yet, but, Lord, the rumors would fly when someone did. Didn't rightly know that I could live with any more whispers. I stared at my fingers in my lap as they wrangled the fabric napkin. Did we have to do this here?

Dovie May caught my attention as she pushed herself out of her chair, then hobbled to Sam, daring anyone to judge an old woman and a broken sailor. Her soothing voice carried over the restaurant buzz, and Sam glanced from the door to her to me. His hands fluttered to his forehead to wipe at the sheen there. Dovie May patted his arm before tucking hers into the crook of his elbow. As they came back to the table, somehow she made it appear like he was helping her. But Sam was leaning so heavy on her, I knew that wasn't the case. Least Doc was trailing behind in case they needed him.

A woman cackled at the table next to us. Sam shied away, bumping into my chair, before he took a deep breath and eased into his seat.

"Sorry about that, y'all." His face was drained of color, and he took a sip of his water like it might drown whatever demon had chased him to the corner of the restaurant. "Nobody oughta bring fire that close to a body." A smile quirked the corner of his mouth, and his hand rubbed against the crease of his pant leg.

Fire?

Dovie May nodded to the man with the formerly flaming dessert and Rosie pivoted, gawking at the man. I righted Rosie and settled my other hand on Sam's long leg which bracketed mine. He stopped fidgeting but scanned the room like someone might jump out at us with a gun.

Doc mumbled something to Sam, but Sam ignored him, his entire body rigid, eyes wide and wary. I scanned the room for what was making him so agitated. A couple perched in the corner, the befeathered woman nattering about some silly adventure she'd had with the family dog. A man hunched over his steak reading a newspaper. Nothing I saw should be cause for alarm. Was there something here I'd missed? Or was my husband seeing danger when there wasn't nothing to be afraid of?

The dog-woman guffawed, and Sam stifled a flinch, confirming my fear.

Around me the muttered comments and hubbub grew stuffy, the world soft and wavering on the edges as if I were back under the pond staring through the ice to the surface. But there wasn't no one to save me this time. Somehow, I'd have to figure out how to save us both.

Don't rightly remember Doc ordering our food, but he must have because it arrived all steaming without any work on my part. It was so good my tongue couldn't find its way to talking. All it wanted to do was taste. Chicken with a gravy even Mama would have been jealous of, mashed potatoes, and peas near drowning in butter. I hadn't seen so much food in ever so long.

I was still picking round the chicken bones when Rosie started squirming in her seat.

"Doc." Dovie May set her cloth napkin on the table. "Would you be so kind as to escort Rosie and me out to take a gander at those adorable pups?" She pointed to an urchin across the street selling puppies out of a wooden box.

Doc frowned at me. "If you two will be all right?"

"Of course we'll be all right," I said, twisting the napkin in my lap again, my stomach suddenly overfull and queasy. What was wrong with me?

Doc handed Sam some money before giving Dovie May his arm. "It would be my honor."

"You two take your time. We'll make sure Rosie is settled for the night." Dovie May winked at us, then swished out of the room with my daughter in hand like she was a right proper lady. Doc glanced over his shoulder one last time before limping across the street. I could've sworn he was disappointed. In what, I wasn't sure.

An awkward silence stretched between Sam and me. Used to be we'd talk right through dinner without needing a distraction to break things up. And if there was silence, it used to be a comfortable place.

And there it was again. Stuck in used-to-be's.

Wasn't no way of going forward if you're stuck gaping backward. But I didn't know how to yank free . . . to yank my husband free. Didn't even know if he wanted to be free. Deep inside I knew Sam's reactions weren't really his fault, but I'd seen jealousy in how he watched Doc, and the anger rolled off him in waves when I least expected it. His defiance of Daddy wasn't nothing new, but Peter and Doc? Sam seemed so dead set on misunderstanding the smallest things and then pushing folks away. I knew he was trying, but a body didn't know what might set him off. Doc helping with Rosie's mustard pack and corn mush were mighty innocent. Why was everything so hard?

Sam rubbed the top of his glass, repeating the circle over and over again so much the lemonade was beginning to circle too. A shake started in his hand, and I reached across the table and twined my fingers through his, hoping to absorb some of whatever was snaking through him. But he dropped his other arm to his lap, where his leg took up the nervous beat.

A blush rose to my cheeks as I wondered what other folks saw when they saw us. A war-decorated sailor, trim and, after shaving off the beard, well-kept. A little jumpy perhaps, but darkly handsome. And me? What did they see when they studied on me? When they saw the straggly blond hair pulled tight under an old, creased hat, circles under my eyes. Once everyone said I was beautiful and strong. The war, the loneliness, the encroaching threats had all changed me as surely as it'd changed Sam. Dovie May was sure if we were left on our own, our love would spark and make everything shine bright again. It was obvious in her wink before she'd led Rosie out the restaurant door.

Was love enough to break through the murky fear and pain?

I supposed we should try. Wasn't worth living jittery and afraid of what was coming next.

I studied Sam from under my lashes as he straightened a fork and then straightened it again. He nodded at the woman talking about the stupid dog as she walked behind me. I took a sip of my water even though I wasn't thirsty, then set the glass on the table and watched the water swirl and settle.

How could I not think of a single thing to say to my husband?

Our waiter stepped to the table wondering if we needed anything else, and I wanted to hug him for breaking the silence. My Sam smiled at him, shook his head slightly, and took the bill. All manners and politeness. Then he laid out more dollar bills than I'd seen in a long time. He didn't so much as flinch, but I near choked on another sip of water.

Realization popped into my mind like that silly lightbulb in the comic strips. Sam had known how much this dinner would cost. He knew letting Doc pay for us would make him feel beholden to his best friend. And he brought us anyway. Sam was courting me. And if he was trying, couldn't I?

My mind scrambled to find a safe topic. "The fence line is real nice. The sows liked being on the hill in the sunshine."

Sam studied the table's surface, and I wished he'd look at me. I'd always been able to tell exactly what he was thinking by looking into his eyes.

"You did good, Sam."

His leg stopped jiggling.

It wasn't everything, but it was something. I was struck again with the desire to be free with him like we'd been before. What was it we used to talk about? The farm, our dreams. My hand drifted over my abdomen, remembering the feel of Sam's fingers on my belly hoping to feel the baby flutter. And the times we didn't need words at all.

My chest tightened, and I licked my lips. The clean haircut he'd given himself earlier in the day gave him a feel of seriousness that contrasted with the ever-present quirk to his lips. A line of worry creased between his brows, and I wondered what he was thinking. Was he frustrated with the way things were going on the farm? Was he disappointed in me? He'd always laughed at my crazy insecurities, my obsessive concern about what other people thought. But he'd always loved me anyway. Had that changed?

I smoothed the front of my dress, bumping along the tiny buttons. Years ago, when I'd sewed on each one, I'd been so proud they'd all matched. Now the dress was all frayed around them. Soon I'd cut the buttons free and put them on another dress. My fingers stopped. Was there a way to do that in a marriage? Take the things that were still good and tack them onto something new?

Sam finally finished inspecting the table and raised his eyes, catching me watching him, and he blinked, slowly. A half-smile joined the brazen lift of his eyebrow.

A flush crept up my neck. Oh heavens. My body was acting like a teenager caught wondering what it'd be like to kiss Sam's full lips.

His smile grew even as I studied my fingertips, trying to tame the heat sparking in my belly. It was silly to be embarrassed. He was my husband. I was certainly allowed to . . . well, to let my mind wander. My hand drifted to my forehead as if I could cover my thoughts.

"My lands, you are pretty." Sam lifted my chin, the back of his knuckles tracing down my shoulder and throwing gasoline on all them sparks. "All the boys in my unit were jealous. Said your image rivaled any of the girls they'd ever seen."

It'd been what everyone always said. But his schoolmates were also quick to wonder if he had a death wish. Me being the Judge's daughter and all.

He took a sip of his lemonade, and his Adam's apple dipped with the effort. When he set the glass on the table, the smile had disappeared.

"I'm sorry about the ruckus this morning. I'm supposed to protect you and—"

"Just a misunderstanding. It'll be fine."

"But what if it ain't fine?"

"We got that lock for the shed like you said, and that'll take care of it. Right?" My fingers fluttered around with a mind of their own, trying to convince the world not to make me go forward from here. To let me whirl around and go back to a few moments ago and never arrive back here with all the questions.

Sam shook his head, and my ears rang like Daddy'd just walloped my backside good. All I wanted to do was run. Run so fast that everything would blur and disappear. That was possible, wasn't it? Forget all the responsibility and just go? Not listen to what was coming?

"I ain't worried about the fertilizer." His voice was quiet, like it was coming from the other side of a locked door. "It's . . . what I saw . . .

the men . . . It isn't the same as the nightmares." He wasn't accusing folks of lying, more like he was apologizing for something he'd done wrong. And that's when I knew for sure.

"When did you start drinking again?"

"I'm not . . . I . . ."

"The candy didn't cover the smell of it on you earlier."

Sam sighed. "Today. I drank today. I was trying to keep the memories out."

Memories. Scrambling to my room when Daddy came home from drowning whatever haunted him in whiskey. Mama's screams while I hid in the safe embrace of a locked closet. The shattering glass, the silence broken only by my own muffled sobs.

Sam knew what alcohol meant to me, but he drank anyway. Would he be like Daddy, getting worse and worse over time? Needing more and more drink to banish his own devils? I could near feel the closet floor, and nothing in me wanted to be shoved back in there.

"Dovie May always told me that if I tried to shut the bad memories out, they'd just sneak in under the cracks and be locked in with me. Worse, it seems by locking the door I also locked out everybody who was willing to help." I winced as the anger in my voice singed my own heart.

My husband shook his head, the irony not lost on him. Folks always called me stone cold. Probably still did. I just didn't hang around long enough to hear it anymore. But Sam had always been different, open, and willing to be patient while I slowly cracked the door open for him. And the moment he struggled, I scorched him with my words.

Sorry. The word stuck in my throat.

"It's okay, Charlotte Anne."

The waiter reached in, clearing away our plates, the ravaged bones of our meal an appropriate picture of our dinner. I prayed that it wouldn't be for our marriage too.

Sam took my hand, holding it steady until I focused on his calm, dark eyes. "It's okay. You're right, and it won't happen again."

I couldn't move, couldn't find a way forward. I was frozen like some fool marble statue. Sam raised his eyebrow in question—*Don't believe me?* He leaned over, his breath heating my fingers a moment before his lips brushed my fingers. He winked like the old Sam when someone had given him a challenge.

He rose, then drew me up next to him and tucked my arm into his. Settled there, with his warmth against me like that, I believed we could do it. That we could take a veteran struggling with black nightmares, mix him with a stone-cold wife with fears near dripping off her, and start a new life, dazzling as a sunrise.

In the fading light of the day, we walked down Central Avenue, past the drugstore, its red awning hanging over the sidewalk. Sam let go of me to dig out a cigarette, surprising me a little. When had he started smoking again? He lifted the pack, asking if I was okay with it. I smiled, then sauntered back to the drugstore while he took out a match. Advertisements were taped neatly to the windows—Wonder Bread, Barbasol, Nehi Orange. All so normal, so American, and easy.

I stared at the smiling army officer pictured above the text for the soda. He held a glass bottle, his arms around his girl, who pressed her lips on his cheek. I traced that cheek, then my own lips. This is what I'd expected. Smiling, kisses, and happily ever after. It was so like me to want something and be too afraid to ask for it. Too timid to do something about it.

My eyes strayed to Sam leaning against the corner of the drugstore's brick wall. Smoke spun around him before swirling up into the light of the streetlamp. He caught me watching and waved his fingers at me, playful, before staring across the street at a group of uniformed veterans, the fit on them just as loose as it was on him. Apparently, our short walk had scared away the edgy, jumpy Sam who'd materialized at the restaurant.

I turned back to the advertisements. Nehi Orange was Sam's favorite. Before he'd shipped out, he had scraped together enough coins and bought us one right here. We sat on the bench outside and sipped from the same bottle. Afterward we hadn't even made it all the way home before the moonlight convinced me to lean into him.

My cheeks heated remembering how his lips tasted sweet as a summer's day. Would it ever feel like that again?

The group of veterans crossed the street, and Sam chatted with them like he'd known them his whole life. I smiled. The old Sam never knew a stranger. Snatches of their conversation floated to me.

"Can't believe it's still so corrupt . . ."

"There's a group doing something . . ."

"If we could just . . ."

Sam knew better than to outright oppose the mayor. He knew better than most what that could lead to. Lawyer Sid McMath and his band of veterans could talk all they wanted. Wasn't nothing changing in Hot Springs even if McMath won the prosecutor's seat in November. One man couldn't do much against an entire army dug in for generations.

I shifted my weight, glancing into the brightly lit drugstore. Maybe I could scratch together enough to buy us a bottle of Nehi to share. Remind Sam of life before. I stepped through the door as I riffled through my pocketbook, praying for a stray coin or two. I unearthed two pennies from my tangled handkerchief.

Three more. Please.

It was as near to a prayer as I could find.

I stood in front of the Nehi display, my fingers tapping a rhythm against my leg. I didn't even have anything to trade. I would have to come back later. I turned, dragging my feet.

"Need something, Charlotte Anne?"

I stiffened. Angus Martin, one of Daddy's men, stood so close I smelled the onions he'd had for dinner. He towered over me, his bulky suit puckering where he likely concealed a pistol.

Fear climbed my throat, suffocating any answer. Gus looped a finger around another escaped curl, then trailed it down my arm. I snapped my pocketbook closed and shook my head, pulling the curl away from his reach.

"If you need a drink, I know where you could get one." His enormous hand closed around my arm, and I jerked away, nearly toppling into the display.

"Ain't no need."

"Maybe *you* ain't got a need." He stepped closer to me, his tongue flicking across his lips.

Stars filled my vision, and my fingers shook against the leather of my pocketbook. "I ain't got no business with you. So . . . so I'll ask you to move." My voice quavered, and I hated myself for it. But Gus had hunted me ever since I was thirteen—the one time I tried to run away and really meant it. I'd done something to anger Daddy, and he took it out on Mama. The dull pounding sounds of his fists left my soul bleeding and broken and convinced Mama would be better off without me making life harder for her. So I packed a little suitcase and ran into the streets. I guess I'd intended to find my way to Dovie May, but I didn't really have much of a plan.

Didn't take Gus much time to find me. He wasn't but a year or two older than Sam, but he was already mean as a bobcat. Mama said it was because he'd been raised without parents. But it didn't matter much to me. Gus had snatched me off the street, his arm wrapped around my waist, laughing at my hollering until he dropped me on a stool at the casino's bar—a place Daddy'd never let me come. His heavy hand on my knee so's I couldn't go nowhere.

"You're lucky your daddy's the Judge, sugar. Otherwise you might find yourself upstairs with the other girls who run away from home." His unshaven chin burned against my cheek, and he reeked of staleness, cigarettes, and power. When he had leaned back, he nodded up the stairs, where a girl about my age sat on the lap of a man older than Daddy, letting him run his fingers up her thigh.

"I think you best leave the lady alone, Gus." Sam filled the doorway of the drugstore, and I'd never been so grateful to see my husband. I elbowed past the goon, and Sam pulled me into a hug, his eyes never leaving his opponent—a bull ready to charge at the slightest provocation. But I didn't belong to Daddy no more, and neither did

Sam. Nobody would stop Gus if he dragged Sam out back, shot him dead, and hauled me away.

"It's okay, Sam. He didn't mean anything." I laid a hand on his chest, pleading, tugging on his arm 'til he turned with me.

Once outside, I glanced back. Gus was watching us, his hulking frame outlined against the bright light of the store. My stomach screwed up tight, and I knew we'd not seen the last of him.

— S A M —

Annie walked next to me, her fingers hovering in the crook of my arm but not touching it. Didn't blame her none. My whole body was numb from holding myself together. And she wasn't nobody's fool. I'd have liked nothing better than to plunge my fist through Gus's nose. The fact that he'd clearly had a pistol was the only thing that held me back. Well, that and knowing full well I didn't have the Judge's protection no more. And all that provided ample opportunity for the Judge's right-hand man to—

Annie fingers tightened on my arm, and I stopped, realizing how fast I'd been walking, attempting to run away from the problems I'd thought I'd left behind.

"Sorry, Annie."

"What are you sorry about?" She peered up at me, concern making her eyes soft.

"Everything. I wasted three years."

"Samuel Robert Mattas, you ain't never wasted anything in your life." Annie tugged me back into motion, her skirt brushing against my pant leg.

I studied the line of sidewalk cement as it dove over the curb into the cracked asphalt street. "I went to war, fought to protect my family, and come home to the law still snuggled up next to perverts, drug dealers, and mobsters. I feel like them oaks." I gestured to the trees in the parkway. "All strength and purpose being slowly choked out by a kudzu vine. Drifters doing who knows what up on the farm. And I couldn't even protect you from the likes of Angus Martin. What kind of hero am I?"

"He didn't drag me away, did he?"

"He tried, and—"

A cry shot through the street. Everybody round us kept moving like there wasn't nothing wrong, and I ground my teeth, knowing they were just toeing the line.

I took a step toward the sound, but Annie snatched at my arm.

"Sam. No. Nothing good's going on over—"

Blurred figures jumped about in the alleyway across the street. A couple of men held up another, dragging him across the trash-littered pavement, their shadows morphing and billowing like ghosts on the brick walls.

I squinted against the glare of light between them and me, hoping to pull out details. The goons threw the man to the ground, and one kicked him hard enough his body jumped. Groaning, the man flopped over, and light flashed on his medals and distinctive white belt.

"That's a marine, Annie. Am I just supposed to let them beat him to death?"

"What are you going to do? You ain't got a gun."

"I didn't go to war to come back to this." The words ground through my teeth.

"But—"

"Stay here."

I untucked Annie's hand from my arm and ran across the street. A quaking snaked through my body, and I glanced back at Annie standing on the sidewalk, wringing her hands like she could wash away my intentions.

I bounced on my toes a moment, thoughts crashing around in my head. I wasn't a fighter like Peter. Annie was with me. But it was two against one, and the man was a veteran.

A hulking man joined the mob and waved off the crew, leaving only the giant and the beaten man in the alley. The big man circled round into the light for an instant before he turned his back on the street again. But it had been enough for me to see who it was. Gus.

White-hot anger burned through me, and I pounced, landing a blow from behind to his kidneys before throwing myself on his back, my arm wrapped around his neck. I would reverse the tables. I would choke out everything wrong in Hot Springs.

Gus arched his back, and his cry echoed hollow. He stumbled, then recovered and rammed me backward into the wall. But I didn't release him. This was not the first time I'd fought for the life of a marine. It would not be the first time I'd won either.

My injured shoulder screamed as I pulled my arm tighter against his throat, leaning my head back, using my weight as a weapon. Gus scratched at me, but the scarred skin under my shirtsleeves didn't much care.

He shook his head like a bulldog about to reengage in a fight, then reached his right arm across his body.

The pistol.

I swore and hammered my knee under his ribs. He fell sideways a moment before he again recovered and twisted, stabbing his one hand back into my face while he grabbed for his gun with the other. The move threw me off his back, and I ducked my head as I skidded across the garbage-slicked alley. There wasn't no weapon here that could defeat a gun at this range.

I was going to die.

A scream ripped through the streets, and I braced myself for the shot. But instead, a crack and thump. I peered back to see Annie standing over a crumpled Gus. She tossed a split plank of wood to the ground as if it were a snake.

Her hand covered her mouth as she stumbled backward to the wall, as far from me as she could get. "I didn't . . . What did I . . ."

My whole body shook. What had we done? I kicked away the gun, then leaned over Gus and checked for a pulse. We hadn't killed him, but if Gus even guessed who'd attacked him, there wasn't nothing and no one to protect us. Thank the good Lord that I'd attacked from behind and the alley was black as the belly of a whale. It wasn't likely Gus would know I'd been the one to jump him.

The marine stumbled to his feet, then saluted me and hobbled from the alley.

Annie slid to the ground, rubbing a thumb across the palm of her other hand as if trying to erase the street grime from her white gloves. The weight of what I'd done near drove me to my knees. I'd attacked one of the Judge's men. Wouldn't matter that I was Annie's husband. They'd come after me all the same. And then what would happen to my girls?

My stomach heaved. I'd die before I allowed the Judge to take them back to that house with him. And he might just oblige me.

"Annie?" I approached her like I might an injured animal. "Annie, we gotta go afore he wakes up."

She stared across the alley, eyes blank, tears trailing down her cheeks, her fingers continuing the attack on her gloves.

I squatted so's she could see my face clear as day, but she didn't respond. She'd only ever been like this when her daddy was in a drunken stupor. In those moments, I'd have to sneak past him to spirit her away. Only this time all this was on account of me. Some white knight I was.

I stuffed my panic underneath my training. First thing: *Get yourself and your people out of immediate danger.*

"I'm gonna pick you up. All right?" I looped my arms behind Annie's back and under her knees and picked her up like she was a child. Her pocketbook slid off her arm and made a *thunk* on the ground, contents rolling this way and that. I stifled a curse as I scrambled after her handkerchief and tube of lipstick, then groaned to standing again. My body was already shaking from the strain on my shoulder and the new scuff marks running the length of my body. But I forced myself forward. We had to get out of there before Gus came to.

As if he'd heard my thoughts, Gus murmured, and my mind scrambled for the next step in the emergency plan. Second step: *Blend in and return to the safety of friendly territory.*

Now, that was going to be harder. I slipped out onto the sidewalk. Blood trickled down my cheek like a neon sign declaring I was an enemy. I didn't dare run, so I hugged the edges of the sidewalk with my hat tipped over our faces. Annie's gaze trailed over my shoulder, and I kissed her forehead wishing I was Snow White's prince.

By the time we reached Doc's clinic, sweat beaded my forehead despite the cool mountain breeze. The metal alley door creaked as I opened it, and we slipped back into the little square breezeway. A square of light slid through the glass pane, and I shivered in the half-light. I settled Annie on her feet and slammed the bar home, locking out the rest of Hot Springs . . . least for now.

"We're safe." I brushed a bit of dirt from her cheek.

Annie shuddered and gaped up into the yawning darkness of Doc's stairwell. I wiped my face with my kerchief and then sheltered her hand in mine as we stumbled up the narrow steps and through the door into Doc's apartment on the second floor. Ma stood at the stove on the far side of the room warming her milk before bed. I'd never been so happy to see her. I stood quiet, soaking in her peace. Every motion was calm, sure. She knew where she belonged, and that sent her roots deep into the ground, able to weather whatever life threw at her.

But I was only half-formed. Stunted so many times by life's storms that my innards were all tangled and my roots groped wide for a foothold on the rocky mountainside.

Ma turned then and caught me watching from the depths of the stairwell. She smiled, creating neatly furrowed rows across her cheeks. She'd been beautiful enough to be the catch of the town once, but this way, soft and slow, she was more beautiful than the sunset over the mountains.

Annie eased around me into the light of the kitchen, and Ma's smile dropped.

"What happened?" Ma sounded like she was near ready to tan my hide with the spoon she shook at me.

"I—"

She grasped my chin in her hand and swung my face so's she could see all the scrapes. "You haven't been in town more than a few hours and you're already fighting? I swear you're aiming to cut years off my life."

"It wasn't my fault, Ma."

She raised an eyebrow, cutting off my excuse like she knew I'd been the one to barrel down the alleyway without thinking. Properly chastised, I studied the peeling corner of brown linoleum. Ma huffed in victory, then hobbled with Annie to the davenport. The two women eased into it, and Annie stared out the alley window like she was made of wax. Solid and yet infinitely fragile.

"Get her some tea, son."

I rattled round in Doc's kitchen and found the teapot, then filled it with water and put it on the stove. What in tarnation had I been thinking? I slammed a teacup onto its saucer with enough force it should've shattered. I wanted to break something, make something crumble under the force of my anger. 'Cept if I did, it'd be Annie that paid. I clenched my fists and took a breath. Then another. Just like Doc had taught me all those years ago.

"Gus Martin and his goons jumped a marine in the alley," I said before Ma asked again.

"And you decided to be the rescuing cavalry all by your lonesome." The way Ma said it told me she knew me for the fool I was.

"But you weren't alone." Doc stood in the hallway that led to the bedrooms and staircase going up to the third floor. Anger sparked off him like he might go and catch fire. "You dragged Annie into the fight, and by extension that little girl back there sleeping innocent as you please."

Ma rubbed Annie's back, soothing my wife. "Lord, I raised you to stand up for everybody. But, son—"

"I was an idiot. Okay? Is that what you want to hear? I am a lowdown, no good—"

The clinic buzzer sounded, and I clattered to a stop, my wheezing breath rattling loud in the quiet. The buzzer sounded again, and Annie's whimper near undid me.

"I'll go take care of whoever's down there. You stay up here." Doc stared pointedly at me. "And don't make a sound." If it could've, the heat in Doc's voice would have burned me to a crisp.

His uneven gait pounded down the stairs, and the door at the bottom squeaked before his steps continued through the office.

When Doc opened the clinic's front door, the bell dinged merrily, and the lamp by the davenport flickered as if a ghost had swept inside and breezed right by us all. My fingers tightened into fists. It wasn't no ghost in the clinic.

Frantic voices. Low and hard. Footsteps centering under us in the treatment room.

"What in heaven's name happened, Gus?" Seemed Doc emphasized the last word. Was he warning us to run?

I shot a wide-eyed look at Ma, and she shook her head, signaling me to be still.

"We'd never outrun them." Her voice was a hair above a whisper. "And where would y'all go anyhow? You have to trust Doc."

She was right, but . . .

"He got jumped in the alley." Lord Almighty. The Judge, the devil right beneath us. Fear burned my fingertips. I'd always been able to outsmart him and Gus. But now we were cornered rabbits. Doc wouldn't be able to do much if'n they'd come to attack us.

"Know who did it?" Doc's voice was calm and inquisitive without a hint of panic. Don't know how he kept his head.

Metal clinked.

"Some vigilante attacked me from behind." Gus cursed. "Those veterans are causing more trouble than they're worth. Mark my words, they're gonna keep coming at us 'til we silence them permanent."

"Serves you right for peddling that—" The Judge was cut off by a cry of pain and a growl from Gus.

"Sorry 'bout that." Doc chuckled, easy as you please. "You'll have a new scar for your collection, but my doctoring is good as you'll get anywhere else, I reckon."

The voices moved away through the office, and the bell on the clinic door jingled merrily. I sank into an armchair and stared at my bouncing knee. I'd near choked the life outta another man and then led him right back to my family. What was wrong with me?

Ma's arm was still around Annie, but she was studying me, measuring. I jumped to my feet. I couldn't stay. Couldn't subject Annie to anymore. This wasn't no fairy tale where our love would save everybody.

"Sit down, son. Ain't nobody coming after us, and Annie needs you more than you need to run right now."

Doc came in and sighed, running a hand through his hair and making it stand on end like he'd been electrified.

"They don't know nothing. You'll be safe for now. But, Sam"— Doc's jaw clenched—"you gotta figure out how to control yourself."

"So I just let them get away with all this—the illegal gambling, using town money for improving the brothels instead of the orphanage, folks running scared of Mayor McLaughlin and the likes of Angus Martin?"

"If you can't let it go for you, then let it go for your family. You know as well as I do what those men are like."

Just walk away and pretend it didn't happen . . . for Annie.

Doc poured a cup of tea, then put in a bit of milk, a spoonful of sugar—the way Annie liked it—and added a few drops of liquid from an amber bottle before extending the cup to her.

"Drink up. I added some laudanum to help you sleep." Doc sat next to my wife, rubbing small circles on her back and talking quietly.

I sank back into the chair. Annie would be better off without me. Rosie too. Doc would never attack a man and force Annie to protect him, and I suspect Peter wouldn't neither. I stood, figuring on watching over Annie while she slept and then leaving in the night. Doc and Peter would take care of everybody.

The war had destroyed whatever I'd been, and there wasn't no going back.

Doc's apartment was silent as a winter night, but muffled voices from the street harmonized with the clock ticking in the main room. I reckoned it was twenty minutes since that clock had struck four. Sitting in the hardback chair by the window in the guest bedroom, my feet had gone numb, but I refused to shift and relieve the pain. I should've left long ago. Everybody'd be rising with the sun in about an hour or so, and I needed to put distance between us.

The moon hung above the city, a hazy smudge in the night sky, its light not able to get through enough to help a body navigate much of anything.

Annie sighed and rolled over, her face slack in easy sleep. The laudanum Doc gave her was doing its job. The few freckles sprinkled across her nose made me near believe she'd sprung out of a picture book—a pixie girl come to spread joy and goodness.

My fingernails bit into my palm, and I turned away to watch the clouds swirl over the moon. I'd given up everything to do what my country asked of me. I'd done what I thought I was supposed to do. And now I was wandering round, fighting against evil all over again. Ma would say God was out there ready to help, but maybe He wasn't no better than the moon. The smoldering light hovered above me, but it didn't seem strong enough to make no difference at all.

I pushed to my feet, then hoisted my bag and settled the note I'd written on the nightstand. Annie didn't need my darkness putting out the light she had.

Closing the door behind me, I tiptoed through the sitting room to open the door to the stairwell.

"Where you going?" Ma's sleep-cracked voice leapt through the quiet apartment, and I spun, heart pounding. I'd forgot she was sleeping out here rather than risk waking Rosie to join her in the extra room.

"I—"

"You best be sleepwalking, 'cause I know my son ain't walking out on his kin."

"They're better without me."

"How you figure that?" She swung her legs off the davenport. "You come sit and talk to me 'bout it."

"I ain't got the words, Ma."

"Sometimes there ain't no words. But that don't mean we don't try." She patted the cushion next to her.

I clutched the doorknob, sensing escape on the other side, but I ain't ever walked away from Ma without paying the consequence. I walked back to her, hovering for a moment like a guilty child before sitting next to her.

Ma wrapped her arm around me and squeezed tight. "Sometimes we need another language for what's happening inside us. I think that's why the good Lord gave us touch. A hug says comfort more than any ole words ever could."

"Ain't nothing that can make the darkness go away, Ma." I appreciated her help, but homespun wisdom wasn't no cure for what the war had done to me . . . for what I'd become.

"Good gracious. It hasn't even been a week. 'Sides, there ain't no growth without darkness. You know that better'n most. If you throw a seed atop the soil, it'll get snatched away by the wind or the birds. You gotta bury it in the good, rich soil, and then it's gotta split open afore it can grow. And, son, we were all made to grow and stretch into the sunlight."

"What if I'm planted too far down? Everybody thinks I'm crazy. That I'm seeing things that ain't there. Panicking in a restaurant and attacking folks on the street." I scrubbed a hand through my hair. "Don't think I have the strength to climb out."

"Your pa used to say, 'The best place for miracles is where we don't fully believe. Where our believing has run out.' And he would know. I say if you're still breathing, there's still time for a miracle."

A miracle. Problem was I wasn't no seed and wasn't likely to sprout roots.

"You go on back to bed. Your pa struggled something fierce too. But you got more than a little of his light inside you, and there's more than a few folks who will help us through. We'll figure out what's next in the morning."

Ma struggled out of the bed she'd made on the davenport and dragged me up with her. "You need me to tuck you back in? Or can you do it all by your lonesome?"

I shook my head, a grin sneaking out despite myself. "Thanks, Ma."

"You got yourself some fine girls, but Doc and Peter ain't their hero. And truth told, neither are you. You're a man. A good man, but a man. You think on that some."

"Yes, ma'am."

I snuck back into the bedroom, dropped the note in the trash, then set my hat and shoes near my bag and slipped into bed. Annie shifted, her arm wrapping around me like she might pull me up into the sunshine. I forced myself to relax and close my eyes against the night. Maybe I'd find some answers at God's house in the morning— and discover a way to get back to the man Ma thought I still was.

CHAPTER
Twelve

—ANNIE—

I woke to Sam's feet twitching in the tangle of our blankets. Don't rightly know when he came to bed. He'd sat and watched me long after I'd crawled under the covers, hollow and jumpy as a puppet on a string. Half of me took his worrying as the protection of a guardian angel, and the other half was downright bristly toward him. He knew good and well how hard I worked to keep Daddy at arm's length. And we were already beholden to him for the supplies. Why Sam couldn't turn a blind eye just this once . . .

I rolled over to the window, and a streak of sunshine trickled across the wood floor, splitting into tiny rainbows as it passed through drops of rain—God's promise stretched and scattered. There wasn't much about Sam's coming home that I'd expected. But he was still here and still standing up for folks who needed help. Maybe less had changed than I thought—'cepting the fact that I had never in all my years hit a body. But, truth told, I'd wanted to knock Gus in the teeth more than a time or two.

The aroma of sizzling bacon made me grin and enticed me out of my cocoon. If there was anything holy, it just might be a crispy slab of bacon, almost burned but not quite. And a body could get used to someone else waking early and making breakfast for you.

I patted my head, sure my hair was as mussed as my mind felt. I put on my robe, grabbed my clothes and shoes, and then sneaked to the bathroom out in the hall, thankful it was unoccupied. I also thanked God for the invention of indoor plumbing and the opportunity to use it. I still didn't know how Doc had plumbed the old building, but I wouldn't complain about the water closet or the luxury of using it. Maybe someday we'd have running water out at the orchard.

I flicked on the light and gaped at my reflection in the mirror. I looked like I'd had a run-in with Daddy's boys after getting caught in tornado winds. Guess it was silly to expect different after a day like yesterday. After hanging my nightgown on a hook on the door, then dressing and cleaning my teeth, I splashed water on my cheeks and ran damp fingers through my hair, working it into a frizzy bun at the nape of my neck.

Now I was the spitting image of a frazzled schoolmarm, a style I'd adopted more than once since Sam had been gone. Somehow it made me feel like I was respectable—or at least a shade better than a lost cause. Sam had always preferred my tresses loose and free to run his fingers through. And it had always made me feel a smidgen free as well.

But there wasn't nothing that could save the nest that was my hair today. I dropped my hands to the sink and stared at my eyes in the mirror, lines starting a path around the dark circles. Wasn't no reason my mind had to be knotted up and trapped on account of my hair. That was as silly as expecting Sam to come home and rescue me from all life's difficulties.

You can do this, Charlotte Anne.

I could be the woman Sam needed 'til he got things straight.

A knock whispered against the wooden door. "Got you coffee," Doc said through it. He'd been waiting for me . . . again. But he always knew what I needed. It was still a wonder to me some woman hadn't snapped him up. I shook away the thought and eased open the door to take his offering.

Doc was dressed in a tailored dark suit and bow tie—his Sunday best. My heart fell. I'd nearly forgotten. It was Sunday, and I didn't know if I could face all the biddies at church with their fake smiles and concern covering venomous curiosity and gossip.

"You gonna argue with Dovie May again?" Doc must have seen the distaste in my expression, and he knew it wasn't on account of his coffee.

"No." I managed to sound offended, like I hadn't tried to argue my way out of church more than once.

Doc's eyes twinkled, but he held his laughter. "Finally wised up and accepted you ain't never gonna win?"

I rolled my eyes and turned to the mirror to tuck an imaginary hair behind my ear. I was okay with God . . . at least most times. Just not with the fork-tongued folks who darkened the door of His so-called house. Like a duck shedding water, Doc let the gossip roll right off his back, but I always left that place feeling like a drowned rat. And if any of the biddies caught sight of Sam's panic or the bruises still fading on my arms . . . But there wasn't much to do about that. I lifted my chin, then walked down the steps behind Doc like I was carrying Mama's books on my head. Even Daddy'd be proud.

Rosie, miraculously transformed into a churchgoing princess, was seated at the kitchen table, an emptied plate in front of her. Excitement rippled off her in pealing laughter, and her feet bounced to the music on Doc's radio. Church to my girl meant dressing up and being plied with a church mint or two from her meemaw and uncle Doc. I used to feel that way—excited to listen to Mama's piano playing and eat brownies at the church potlucks.

All my determination crumbled, and I halted, not quite ready to admit it was time to take the next step into the day. If only I could go back in time.

Maybe I could slip back to the bedroom and hide.

Dovie May placed a tray of bacon on the table, then noticed me hovering in the doorway. She hobbled over to me, my moment to run gone.

"You need to trust your man, Annie. He's always been a good boy. Still is, even if'n he's a little lost at the moment . . . same as you."

Two lost parents didn't make for much of a proper home. I pressed a hand over my heart willing it to slow as I watched my daughter's seated dance. How in heaven's name was I going to contain her in church? Folks would take a gander at us and know how adrift we were.

"Your girl reminds me so much of you when you was young." Dovie May ruffled Rosie's hair. "Sitting at my table proper as you please, singing away, talking to your paper dolls and grinning something fierce. I ain't saying life's easy, mind. Only that you maybe oughta go find that girl again."

I watched my Rosie happily chattering to Doc, and my whole body ached with the swell of tears building up inside me. I wanted what she had. I wanted to wake up from this nightmare and be twelve again—blissfully unaware, playing tea with Mama's real china because she trusted me to be careful while Daddy was gone. I'd even take Mama's scolding to be a proper young lady if it meant she'd never leave me. If it meant Sam would never go away and be shattered by the war. *God, please.* I closed my eyes against my own pleading, the crumbling hope.

"Maybe let's start with your hair, darlin'." Dovie May's voice was gentle, like she knew where I'd gone.

I blinked, trying to pull myself out from under the memories.

My mother-in-law nudged me into a kitchen chair, pulled out my schoolmarm bun, and brushed through my waves like she had when I was a girl. Back then, I would never have believed that someone needed to tell me to have more fun. Where was the girl who'd snuck out to skate on the ice? The girl who rolled down the back hill in her white pinafore and laid out on the dew-dampened ground to watch the stars? Mama had near torn her hair out at my unladylike behavior. Of course, she cared more on Daddy's account than her own. He had his expectations.

Lands, I'd been happier then. Maybe Dovie May was right. Maybe I needed to find that girl again.

Dovie May pushed my hair into finger waves, holding them in place with a few discreet pins. How she ever learned to do hair like that I'd never know, but she was a wonder to be sure.

I relaxed under Dovie May's ministrations as Rosie and Doc jigged along with the Andrews Sisters singing 'bout the boogie woogie bugle boy. Wasn't often that I wished for much in the way of modern things, but I did miss the music. After Mama and me fled Daddy's house, waltzing along with her Victrola in the Mattas cabin was one of the few times Mama ever smiled. Maybe I should let Doc retrieve it from Daddy.

The music slowed, and as the voice of Harry Sam flowed out of the radio, I imagined my Sam whispering, "I'll get by as long as I have you." It wasn't that long ago that I was dressed in pale pink, spinning on the dance floor in Sam's arms, Benny Goodman accompanying us.

The church cronies would have dropped in a fit of vapors if they'd seen us back then. I smiled at the thought of their bony fingers covering their mouths as one of their number slid to the floor in a faint of horror.

I heard footsteps in the hall, and Sam came in, smiling like the Lord Himself had called him forth. His dress blues set off his mahogany hair right fine, and I couldn't find no hint of the erratic man who'd taken over last night.

Rosie squealed like she'd just won the biggest doll in the world. And when she launched herself into Sam's arms, he swung her up 'til she touched the ceiling. When he lowered her, Rosie wrapped her arms around his neck and planted a wet kiss on his cheek. Was like she'd always known her daddy.

Sam kissed the top of her head, careful not to mess her hair, but his eyes searched 'til they landed on me, hungry. My mind scrambled, debating what I should do, what I wanted to do. What would be right? What wouldn't be?

But Sam didn't hesitate one bit. With one arm holding our girl, he pulled me up with the other and twirled me into him. His hand traveled up my back and eased me closer, his eyes never leaving mine 'til I was inhaling his exhale. *The two shall become one.* He hesitated, and I watched the gold in his iris darken. I closed the gap, my lips on his. A groan rumbled in his chest. The taste of his tooth powder lingered even after we pulled apart.

Doc cleared his throat, and my skin blazed as I snapped round. Sam captured my arm and drew me back under the protection of his side.

"That bacon smells like it comes from heaven itself." Sam guided me into a chair between him and Rosie, then grabbed a piece.

"It's the last bit from your hogs." Doc grinned at Sam and handed him a cup of coffee. "You always did know how to choose the best stock."

"I don't know as I can take credit for this one since I wasn't here." Sam sipped at his coffee. "Y'all did a mighty fine job of keeping up the farm. Thank you for all you done, Doc."

Doc sniffed like something didn't smell quite right, and I squirmed in my seat right alongside my daughter. What was going on between these two? On the surface, they seemed like their old selves, but everything beneath was shifting like the muck on the far side of the pond. If we weren't careful, we'd all get pulled under.

Sam opened his mouth to say something more, but I popped out of my seat, my smile so big it hurt my cheeks.

"Anybody want some of those canned peaches we brought? They'd be mighty fine with the—"

Doc stood. "I know you ain't really eaten, Sam, but we need to head out to church so's not to be late."

I dropped into my seat like Mama had snatched me back. I'd near forgotten about church again. What if Daddy was there? What if Gus saw us in town and put everything together? What if—

"We'll make it together," Sam said in my ear. "'Sides, Ma told me there's a new preacher, a Pastor Marshall. Maybe this one'll be more to your liking." He touched my elbow, then lifted Rosie and twirled her around before snuggling her in his arms.

"You finish getting ready." Dovie May nudged my elbow, a reminder to listen for the girl inside me. "I'll clean up here."

I swallowed. I didn't know if I could make myself walk through the street let alone do it like Rosie. Sam set her on my lap, and she threw her arms around me before smacking a kiss on my cheek.

"You bootiful, Mama."

Lord, who could resist that? I would do this for Rosie. I set her down, then ran to the bedroom to pull on my church gloves and hat and tuck my purse under my arm. Ready to pass the inspection of the gossiping biddies.

"Race y'all!"

Rosie's shout jolted me from the hallway, and I bolted down the stairs after her, laughing at the sound of everybody scrambling behind us, even Dovie May. I crashed through the door to the alley, giggling in spite of myself, immediately slowing to a sedate pace as if I was the most elegant lady in all of Arkansas.

Sam crashed into my back, and I stumbled, but he caught me round the waist. His crooked grin made me think I might just survive the ladies at church.

"Fast as ever." Sam wiped a trickle of sweat from his forehead. "There's a reason you always won all them foot races at school. Remind me not to challenge you."

He dropped his cap on his head, then held my hand 'til Doc and Dovie May caught up. He swept Rosie up in a piggyback ride, and I tucked my hand into the crook of his arm. I felt like nothing could destroy this family.

We walked away from Central Avenue and the illegal activities oozing from the casinos and bars. When we turned the corner, the laughter drained out of me, swirling down into the murky sewers beneath the street. The church steeple pierced through the bright-blue sky, a few clouds skimming past. I wished to escape to the heavens and race away with them.

Dovie May held Doc's arm like he was her son, and they limped together in the sunshine that bathed the street. Sam set little Rosie down, and she pranced next to me, her curls brushed into soft waves and her white bow tied perfectly behind her. Her dress still fit, but only on account of the lace trim I'd added. Before long she'd need a new one. Maybe I could stop at the mercantile while I was in town and get some new fabric cheap, or at least order some for whenever the government graced us with an allotment. But my coupons were back at the farm, and it was Sunday. I chewed my lip thinking on how to make it work.

Doc's soft cough brought me back to the sidewalk in front of the church. He'd shifted to block my view, but his slim body couldn't obscure Daddy standing in front of the church, his floozy's arm looped through his. He looked so much like a Luciano mobster that any decent lawman would arrest him on the spot.

Julia, I'd heard her name was, was so tiny and her hat so full of feathers I thought it might take flight all on its own. The thought of it flapping away with her still attached gave me enough to smile about that I was almost polite to Daddy and her, nodding back when they nodded at me. But my hand tightened in the crook of Sam's arm. I did believe that she might be younger than me.

Behind me one of the old ladies tsked and slid past us, shaking her head.

I ignored the sweat from my armpits surely staining my dress and straightened my spine. This had been Mama's church, where she played the piano every Sunday. But not a one of these folks had stood up for her when she left Daddy. Nor for her motherless daughter once she was dead. Didn't matter this was the church I grew up in; I didn't really belong here. The people, they didn't want me entering their doors or bathing in the sunshine colored by their lifeless stained-glass window.

Now I realized I had *never* been one of them, and after her parents died, Mama wasn't neither. The church used her for their Sunday music, and the Judge's "respectable" presence was tolerated. It's a wonder what money can buy. Now they treated me like I was nothing, making up stories about Doc and me while Sam was away.

I didn't know what gave them such cause to treat me like they did. Maybe it was on account of Mama committing an unpardonable sin, or maybe them thinking I was uppity with my year of college education, or maybe it was a backhanded way of showing Daddy they disapproved of his work. It didn't matter none. I didn't want anything to do with their dead beliefs that had nothing to do with the God I'd seen in Dovie May.

We stood in the aisle waiting to be seated whilst a withered woman banged away at some hymn caught in a polka's oompah-pah rhythm. I resisted the urge to protect my poor ears from the offense. Least they could do was tune the darned instrument. I'd even do it for them. Mama'd taught me how when I was knee-high to a grasshopper. But they'd never let me touch the thing unless I repented of whatever it was they felt was wrong with me.

Just as I turned to flee out the bright church doors, Peter stepped in front of me and caught my elbow.

"I don't believe the service is even started yet. It'd be a shame if'n I came all this way to sit with my family and y'all left without me."

Peter slid my hand into my husband's elbow and winked at his big brother, whatever had gotten between them forgiven.

I looked from my family to the gaping maw of the church. In the end, it was Rosie's squeal of pure delight that propelled me down that aisle. 'Sides, there wasn't nobody or nothing that could make me want to disappoint Dovie May again. And I do believe both she and Peter knew that.

Dovie May settled us into her pew—middle of the church, far left side—right next to Doc's slender frame. Perfect view of the piano where Mama used to sit, even though she hadn't sat there in seven long years. I'd only been sixteen.

Out of the corner of my eye, I saw Peter greeting a few folks, even returning Julia's tiny wave. "She's one of my nurses at the hospital," he said in response to the lift of my eyebrow. "She's all right."

"If you want to cross Daddy, that's your business," I said, leaning into him so's he could hear the skepticism in my voice. When I straightened, the whispering started behind me.

"It's been awhile since we've seen her."

"She appears rather peaked. Don't you think?"

"Don't think any of them's been sleeping. I wonder what they've been doing up there. Shouldn't be bringing more children into the world if they can't even keep the one they've got well."

"What do you think she does up there with three men and nothing but an old cripple as chaperone? Think they're doing more than chopping wood?"

I stared straight ahead, pretending I couldn't hear while the ladies snickered. But Sam's fingers clenched on the pew in front of us. I held my chin high and prayed he'd be still. Doc slowly turned red clear down his neck. But I refused to react. Wasn't going to give them any satisfaction whatsoever. They could go right on whispering at the back of my perfectly proper head.

"Wasn't her ma not much older than her when . . ."

Though she was wrong about Mama's age when she died—just into her forties—the words against her still stabbed me between my ribs, and I gasped for air. Sam shifted uncomfortably, rubbing his arm like it'd gone to sleep, and Dovie May just stared ahead like always, keeping her peace. *Don't give them no more fodder, Annie,* she'd say.

But the woman in front of us turned and glared behind us hard enough that even St. Peter himself would've cowered.

Well, the ladies behind me couldn't stand it, 'cause the whispering quieted. While I didn't think I knew her from nobody, everybody else treated her like she might just up and walk on water.

My benefactor had soft wrinkles above her eyebrows like she was permanently surprised. I'd guess her to be about how old Mama would've been now, but she was half a step out of season with her white hat announcing she didn't care a whit about when a body could wear certain colors. And I liked her all the more because of it. My girl swung her polished shoes in and out, and the woman near melted in front of me.

She rustled around in her pocketbook, then returned her smiling gaze on my Rosie. In her hand was a penny candy. Wasn't a better friend in the world than that. Rosie stared at the woman like she wasn't sure whether to take the treat.

"It's yours, sugar," the woman said.

When Rosie reverently took the candy, tears crept into my eyes. It took so little to make a body feel welcome. The woman caught the attention of the ladies behind me, then winked and made a show of presenting Doc, Dovie May, and me a candy too. She dug a minute more for a candy for Sam as well. Well, if I didn't need a hanky before, I did now. It'd been ever so long since I'd tasted a candy.

"Thank you." It was all I managed.

I unwrapped the white candy pinstriped red and green. The minty smell reached my nose, and I thought of Christmas. Of laughter. Of all those times I sat on the floor in Mama's sitting room listening to Chopin ripple out of her piano. The sweetness near shocked my tongue. It tasted like happiness and a time when all was right in the world.

"Don't expect you'd remember seein' me here. I'm Leah Belle Barker. I used to listen to your mama play that piano up there, usually from the back row, though. You're about the same age my girl would be if she were still alive. She passed on not long after your mama did."

I near choked but managed to smile since Leah Belle still was. She blinked once like she might have been clearing out memories, then offered her hand—a common courtesy seeming to be lacking in Hot Springs.

"Doc told me y'all don't make it down often, so I was glad to hear you were comin' today. Y'all are welcome anytime. I been gone a long while, and it's good to see friendly faces. Well, I'm assuming we'll be friendly. I'd like that very much." She nodded at Dovie May, then made a show of glaring at the biddies behind me again, and, Lord, was I ever grateful to have someone like her watching over us. "My second husband, God rest his soul, took me away from town and from the memories of my girl. But after he passed, I wanted nothing more than to be home in Hot Springs. Though sometimes folks round here just don't know what it means to be kind to the newcomer.

"And, oh!" Leah Belle fluttered a crisp handkerchief in front of her like she might fly right to heaven with her thought. "If it ain't too forward, I'd like to come up your way sometime. Just to visit. Though I wouldn't mind picking up some peaches when they're ripe neither. My mama always raved about Mattas peaches. She said they tasted just like a little slice of heaven."

I couldn't do nothing but nod. Dovie May had been a member of this church all her life, and I don't know that anyone from there had ever visited the farm after she married except to buy peaches. Didn't approve of fresh air and clean dirt, I guess . . . even though the good Lord made it beautiful.

Miss Leah Belle turned back round, and I near floated above that pew, already dreaming on what I'd serve for my very first visiting friend. Dovie May shifted like her backside was uncomfortable, then slipped her mint into her pocketbook. Saving it for Rosie more'n likely. And I was almighty thankful for the folks watching out for me.

I don't know what Pastor Marshall preached on, but Leah Belle had preached a better sermon than anybody'd ever preached before.

CHAPTER
Thirteen

— SAM —

The heat of the sunshine was awful nice after the chill of the marble sanctuary. Leah Belle had thawed Annie's fear right quick. Don't know that the woman even recognized what she'd done, but Annie was likely to follow her to the ends of the earth. I offered Ma my arm and laid my other one across Annie's waist as we followed a skipping Rosie down the church steps. Maybe there was some good in the world after all.

At the bottom, we crossed into the shadow of the spire, and I shivered like someone had walked over my grave. Annie stiffened, and I knew she noticed it too. I followed her gaze back to the church door and just caught sight of Gus's pasty head as he sauntered down the church steps and bumped hard into the Judge before strutting past us like a rooster.

Strange.

"I really don't like that man." Annie's eyes followed Gus, and I glanced at her, a little fear creeping up that she'd spoken the words loud enough for him to hear. But she'd kept her shoulders turned so's her voice was blocked by my body.

"Ain't seen him in church before neither." Nor showing blatant disrespect for the Judge. What was he doing here?

"Daddy won't let him do anything." Annie sounded far more confident than I felt, especially when I caught Gus ogling Annie and licking his lips. He even had the nerve to catch my eye afterward and not look the least ashamed.

"I'm not as worried about the Judge as other folks." I clamped my lips shut, sorry I'd let the words escape. If'n Gus was up to something behind the Judge's back, that put us all in a heap of trouble. The last thing I wanted was to be in the middle of a battle between the two.

I blinked. Was that what was happening up at the shed? Some kind of plan to overthrow the Judge? It'd make sense to use our land to hide shady dealings from him. There wasn't any place in Hot Springs he wasn't less welcome. And yet the Judge wouldn't do nothing to put Annie and Rosie in harm's way even if he wanted to rain fire on the head of a young buck challenging his authority.

But from what I knew of him, Gus didn't have the brains for that.

"What's going on?" Annie touched my hand, reminding me of everything I stood to lose.

I kissed Rosie's cheek and set her next to Dovie May, who was sitting on a bench catching her breath. Would the Judge tell me what was happening if I asked? What would I do if he asked for my help? I'd left that life a long time ago, and I didn't want to go back nohow.

My brother was talking with the woman the Judge had with him—Julia, Peter'd said. He seemed to be giving his full attention to her, maybe even standing a bit too close. But I could tell he'd witnessed the commotion on the steps and was shifting his weight so's he could act if'n there was trouble.

Peter worked for the Judge far longer than I did. Would he know what was happening? When his eyes flicked to mine and then to the Judge, I couldn't help but wonder if he might be scheming. Was that why he was so cozy with the Judge's gal?

"Sam?" Annie gripped my hand, tugging my attention to her.

The Judge watched Gus stop to smoke, then studied me like he was deciding something. When he started trudging toward my family, my body tensed, terrified that the white marble steps of the church were about to become some kind of altar—blood spilled and all.

"Come on, y'all. It's time we get going." I herded my family in front of me, glancing around for Doc only to see him slink out of the alley behind Gus, hand the man an envelope, and lean forward to whisper a few words. What in tarnation? It'd be one thing for Gus to be giving Doc something, a payment for yesterday's services or the like. But . . .

Had Doc just sold us out, told Gus who'd attacked him? I stopped dead, thinking on the men I'd seen up at the shed. Had one of them been moving like he'd had a limp? I still couldn't remember everything from Friday night, but would Doc actually work for the mob?

I turned my family up the next street to avoid walking past the pair. I'd depended on Doc to keep my family safe. My whole body shook, and I cursed myself for not bringing my shotgun, a knife, anything.

We needed to get to the wagon and out of Hot Springs. At least on the farm we could find a defensible position. I waved my girls and Ma in front of me and drove them forward, picking up Rosie when she fell behind. I had no idea where Peter was now, but even if we left before he did, my brother knew not to dawdle in town . . . and he had his bicycle. That'd be two of us to protect everybody. And Annie was as good a shot as me.

"Sam, dear." Ma turned, her face red and sweat beading on her upper lip despite the enormous brim of her hat. "You might be in the kind of shape for a forced march"—she gasped, her head twitching drastically to the side—"but the rest of us ain't."

Clenching my fists, I bit back the frustration. But there wasn't no use in running my family so hard they died on the street. So much for heading home to where it was safe. I forced a hand through my hair, forgetting it was Brylcreem-slicked. I needed a plan . . . and fast.

The Judge.

I didn't want no business with the mob, but I knew the Judge would protect my family even if he sacrificed me to Gus to buy their protection. And it didn't seem like I had much choice. Sometimes you got to make your own miracles.

"Sorry, Ma. You know me. I'm starved like I've never eaten before. Why don't you all rest on that bench over there? I'll be back in a jiffy. I think the Judge had a question for me."

Annie's head snapped back like I'd slapped her good.

"It'll be all right." I pulled her in and kissed her forehead, wishing with everything in me that I could pause the moment and never move past it. "You keep an eye on these two, but ain't nothing anybody's going to do this close to the church steps." At least I hoped not.

Pasting a smile on my face, I waved and trotted down the street, head swiveling, alert to any sign of Doc or Gus.

"There you are." Doc popped out of an alley, and my heart near stopped. I edged toward the church, drawing him away from my family.

"Where y'all going in such a hurry?"

"Ma thought she forgot to set the oven proper for the roast. Didn't want the durn thing to burn." I laughed and took another step away from my family.

Doc frowned and pointed behind him. "The clinic's that way."

"Ma's taking a rest while I go find—"

"Sorry to hold y'all up." Peter turned the corner, and my breath escaped loud enough to spook a bird from one of the trees lining the street. He must've seen us turn down this street.

"I was having this strange pain, and the Judge's Julia gave me a . . ." Peter trailed off lamely when he saw Doc.

Doc shoved his hands into his pockets and raised his eyebrow at my brother. "What are y'all really doing?"

"Peter, why don't you take Ma and the girls back to the farm? I'll be up presently on your bicycle."

"But—"

"I got a question for Doc, and Rosie's going to need a place to nap before we're done." I silently pleaded with Peter to take our family away, and he knew me well enough to know something was wrong. He scratched his arm with his hook, studying me and then Doc, seeming to beg us both to be calm.

The entire time Peter ambled to the bench, I frantically thought through and discarded scenarios—knock Doc out cold and run? But Gus would come after us for sure. I could outrun Doc to the Judge, but then Doc could just go after my family.

Doc cleared his throat, then stared at me, head cocked to the side like he was hearing my mind whirring. "Are you going to tell me why you're acting so crazy?"

His question slammed into me. Stars filled my vision, and I consciously relaxed my clenched fists.

"I ain't crazy."

"Didn't mean you *are* crazy, just that you're acting a mite more nervous than usual." Doc leaned against the brick wall, his weight on his good leg, and I was reminded of all the things polio had stolen from him. But he hadn't let it hold him back. He'd always dreamed of becoming a respected doctor. And he'd done it. He'd overcome all the pain, the disabilities, and did what no one but his father and me thought was possible. Would he let himself be beholden to the mob?

"You saw me with Gus, didn't you?" He laughed and wiped his handkerchief across his forehead like he was suddenly relieved. "I was giving him more pain meds. It isn't exactly legal for me to give them out, but the pharmacy's closed, and Annie beaned him good. I didn't want to let him go all weekend without something."

I opened my mouth and then clamped it shut. Was he telling the truth? And why'd he use what Annie did like a threat?

"Sam, if he hurts, he'll be more ornery and out to make trouble for whoever jumped him."

"Jumped him?" Lord Almighty. Doc made it sound like *I'd* been the problem. "He was—"

He raised a hand. "I know you two don't get on, but he's still a patient. And I got responsibility for him just like I do for you."

One thing I knew for certain was that Doc always took his doctor's oath serious. But really? "Just like for me?"

"You know what I mean." He shook his head like he was my pa and disappointed.

"No. I don't know what you mean. I thought we were friends. But you're off in back alleys distributing opiates to a known mobster, you're putting your arm around *my* wife whenever you get the chance, and you're treating me like I'm some crazy loon who oughta be locked away somewhere." I kept my voice steady so's no one had reason to say I'd proved the last bit with my tirade, but my words still echoed off the buildings like the devil was whispering the accusations over and over into eternity.

Doc stuffed the handkerchief into his coat pocket and frowned at me. "You were the one who asked me to take care of Annie." He pushed away from the wall and turned toward the clinic. "And that's all I done."

The dejection in his voice pierced through my fear, and my reckless anger crumpled. Doc was my best friend. I'd taken the sight of drifters on the farm and added it to Doc's taking care of a patient to somehow equal him constructing a complicated plot against me and mine. I slammed my palm against the brick. I'd made a mess of things again.

I swung round. "Doc, I'm so—"

"Sam? Sam!" Annie's panicked voice rose like she'd encountered the gates of hell themselves. Near the bench where I'd left her, Annie knelt over a twitching mound of . . .

"Ma!" I charged down the street past Doc, ears ringing, gulping air, the world tilting, tilting, waves crashing over the side like the sidewalk might swallow me whole. I collapsed next to Ma's convulsing form. Doc arrived and rolled her to her side, and I stripped off my jacket to tuck it under her head.

Ma's eyes were rolled up in her head, mouth agape in a silent scream as her head slammed against the pavement again and again, her legs stiff like electric shocks shot through her. My hands fluttered over her, useless. No, worse than useless. I had let my imagination run away and drove Ma so hard that . . .

Doc yanked a wooden depressor out of his pocket and thrust it into Ma's mouth, holding her tongue. Annie pressed Rosie's head into her chest as they sobbed into each other. Sidewalk pebbles dug into my knees, and I welcomed the pain 'cause there wasn't nothing I could do.

God, Ma was dying, and there wasn't nothing I could do.

CHAPTER
Fourteen

—ANNIE—

Dovie May shuddered once more, then a sigh escaped her and floated into the air. My eyes snapped open, hands frantic, fingers climbing her arm.

"Dovie May? No. No. No." I touched her cheek, still warm but gray, slack, motionless. After the apoplexy, her other attacks had barely been a blip in the day. Nothing like this. "Dovie May? Please." My voice cracked against the fear. She couldn't be gone.

Please, God.

The street was quiet, sun shining warm on the chirping birds and Doc as he scrambled around Dovie May. I wanted to scream at it all.

Rosie whimpered, and I pulled her in tighter. What would we do now?

Sweat had beaded on Dovie May's forehead, marring her slackened face. I dug round my pocketbook for my hanky, but before I found it, Peter knelt beside me and gently wiped the beads away with his. He looked so much like the sheriff closing Mama's eyes that the world set to trembling.

Sadness piled up inside me like the spring thaw slamming against the mountain dams. Once you let yourself start feeling, it all breaks loose. I clenched my teeth together, fighting the rushing sound in my ears. I wanted Sam near me, but he stood, hands pressed against a wall, head leaning on his fingers. He seemed barely able to keep upright. I couldn't ask him to help me bear my load too. So I leaned into Peter, borrowing his strength and feeling ashamed for it 'til he wrapped his arm around my shoulders. His hook dug into my flesh, reminding me of all the things life takes away without a backward glance. If we didn't stick together, we'd all wash away.

Footsteps rushed up behind me, and I turned to see Leah Belle and Julia racing toward us, completely disregarding everything proper. I didn't have the energy to stand, but Leah Belle dropped to her knees, collecting me from Peter and rubbing my back so's he was free to bend over Dovie May with Doc and Julia.

Julia clasped Dovie May's wrist, her expression serious and professional, reminding me that she was a nurse, after all. Perhaps I'd misjudged her attentions with Peter. Doc's face was grave as he leaned his ear against Dovie May's chest, and I near dropped Rosie on her backside when he smiled.

"Her heartbeat's strong and steady. Let's give her a minute."

Fear and thanksgiving poured through me in equal measure, making my eyes drip tears something fierce.

Like she'd heard Doc telling everybody they'd have to wait on her, Dovie May groaned and rolled to her back, then struggled to sit. Ain't nobody who liked being coddled less than Dovie May.

"Ma?" In one motion, Sam turned, dropped to his knees, and hefted his mother's back 'til she was upright.

Dovie May swatted at Sam. "I ain't broke. Just a little banged up."

Sam sat back on his heels, his whole body shaking. "I thought you were . . . You aren't . . ."

I laid a hand on Sam's shoulder, and he shied away, panting, the whites of his eyes showing like a caught wild horse.

I straightened Dovie May's skirt and pretended there wasn't nothing wrong.

"It's just the shock." Julia quieted my shaking hands, and I thought about Sam in the restaurant not being able to stop himself from twitching. Was this what he'd been feeling—the panic, all the emotions too big to be named let alone felt without exploding?

"Sam?" Peter slid past me and took hold of Sam's arms. He dipped his head so his face would fill my husband's vision, and Sam's attention snapped to Peter, spinning a moment before focusing on his brother.

"You got to pull it together, Sam. Ma needs you to carry her to Doc's. You hear?"

Dovie May shook out her handkerchief, then huffed while she patted her forehead and then her bosom in a way Mama would've called common. "I don't need nobody to carry me. I'll be right as rain if'n y'all . . ." She took a shuddering breath. "If'n ya'll would just let a body catch her breath."

Sam flinched, but Peter held him firm, letting him know he wasn't alone, certainly wasn't responsible, and there wasn't nobody here who'd let him run.

Dovie May's hand trembled a little when she stuffed her hanky back into her pocketbook, but when Doc tried to check her pulse, she near knocked his head clean off. "Stop your frettin'. I got overheated, is all."

Doc shifted, then frowned like he did when he was about to lecture somebody. "Dovie May, I'm a—"

"And you don't got to remind me you're a doctor, young man. I ain't senile. And as you can see"—using my shoulder as leverage, Dovie May pushed herself to a wobbly stance—"I can stand on my own two feet just fine."

I stood next to the swaying woman, clutching her waist as color returned to her cheeks and she adjusted her hat.

"But I would like to go home if'n that's all right with everybody."

We all turned to Doc, 'cepting Dovie May, who didn't need nobody's permission and was already rambling toward the clinic with Rosie's little hand tight in hers.

"Tough as the mountain is tall. Ain't she?" Leah Belle slipped an arm through mine.

Doc frowned at her and shook his head. "She had another seizure, but I do believe she'll be fine. Tired, but fine. Y'all keep a close eye on her for a few days, and if it happens again, hog-tie her and bring her to see me."

Julia trotted ahead and took up walking next to Dovie May. To my surprise, Dovie May accepted the presence of Daddy's floozy and even smiled at her. Julia reached up, then plucked a magnolia from a tree and tucked it into Dovie May's hair, and I had to grudgingly admit that maybe she wasn't so bad after all.

Leah Belle insisted on coming to help as well, and while I felt a mite guilty breaking up whatever her Sunday plans had been, I was grateful for the help. She put together roast sandwiches for everybody to eat on the way back up the mountain while I shoved our meager clothes into our bags before Dovie May, Leah Belle, and Rosie and me all tramped down the stairs. Sam and Peter had already hitched Buttercup, and Julia was in the wagon bed fluffing the hay and spreading out our blankets—apparently not caring one whit that she'd snagged her nylon stockings. Of course the Judge would still have his black market contacts, so she could just bat her lashes and he'd buy her more of the scarce, newfangled things while the rest of us had to make do with pen lines up our calves.

Sam handed Dovie May up into the back of the wagon, where Julia settled her in next to Rosie in a right fine little nest. Peter clambered in and then hauled in his bicycle before he helped Julia jump out. Peter'd watch over his ma and my girl as well as I could. And that left me to climb onto the bench with Sam and pray that this day would soon end.

Doc pressed a packet into my hand. "Aspirin." He glanced across me to Sam, some kind of apology passing between them. "Dovie May might come down with a fierce headache."

And what he left unsaid told me everything. For all Doc was able to do, all his kindness to us, watching over us, he was as powerless as any of us against whatever'd attacked Dovie May.

Before Doc could latch the wagon bed shut, Leah Belle rushed out of the clinic with Rosie's doll swinging out in front of her. "Don't forget this."

"Oh Lordy, don't know what we would've done without that." I'd leave my head behind if it weren't attached.

Despite her tight skirt and high-heeled shoes, Leah Belle got herself into the wagon and snuggled the dolly into Rosie's arms. "I know what being a mother is like. It's a wonder my children didn't get left behind on a regular basis." Leah Belle's voice didn't quite match the smile on her face, but she hopped out of the wagon with a skip and kissed my cheek like she didn't have a care in the world. What would I do if I ever lost my Rosie?

Doc secured the wagon bed, then stepped free of the wagon.

"I'll be up to check on y'all tomorrow," Leah Belle said. "If'n Doc would be so kind as to give me a ride."

Doc blanched when she hooked her arm through his, but then he nodded. "I can rearrange my schedule tomorrow."

"Walk on." Sam clucked to Buttercup, and our horse leaned into the harness and broke into a neat trot, clip-clopping through the streets. As we turned up the trail to the mountain, Buttercup slowed with the strain, and I turned and watched as the trees closed in around the city. And good riddance. What was supposed to have been a relaxing change of pace had become a nightmare.

In the wagon bed, Rosie'd already fallen asleep next to Dovie May, whose snores competed with Peter's heavy breathing.

"They're all napping already." I studied Sam's profile, and his eyes briefly drifted closed before snapping open again. "You all right?" I shifted closer to him.

"I'll just be glad when we're home."

I don't think he meant to make it sound like some accusation— like the disasters in Hot Springs had been my idea or my fault—but his words had bite like a snapping turtle. I opened my mouth to say something but then clamped it closed. Wasn't no words that'd make it any better. Sam had always been as steady as they come, but now . . .

He squinted at the road in front of him like the familiar route was turned all topsy-turvy.

I leaned against his side, not wanting to acknowledge what I was beginning to realize was true—no matter how much I tried, I might not be able to save us all.

The sun hovered above the tips of the mountains as Sam pulled Buttercup to a stop in front of the barn. Last night's rain made the ride up a sloppy mess of mud and washed-out logs. It took near forever to get home, and I was grateful Leah Belle had packed extra sandwiches as we was all hungry as a family of bears. Her kindness made pushing the wagon out of ruts a good deal easier to endure.

I hopped out and helped Dovie May and Rosie out of the wagon. My mother-in-law stood panting and holding the edge while Peter jumped out. When his ma swayed a bit, he looped an arm around her waist and hollered, "You got the horse okay?"

Sam nodded, and I bustled Rosie over to Dovie May's cabin, helping Peter steady his ma up the steps and then settle her on the bed.

When Rosie aimed to hop up next to Dovie May to play, Peter leaned over my girl and whispered like he might be telling her a forbidden secret. "Rosie, how 'bout we go help your daddy with the horse? And I think I got a bit of roast left over for that kitten of yours."

I bit my lip to stop from laughing at how serious she got. Uncle Peter knew exactly how to intrigue the naughty side of my child into doing something good without realizing she was.

She leapt onto his back, and he cantered away like he was the white horse for a shining princess.

I sat on the edge of the bed with a sigh. It felt ever so good to be home.

"That boy growed up more than a little while he was gone." It didn't take much understanding to hear the pride in Dovie May's voice. And it was deserved. Peter was a good man.

"What's eatin' on you, sugar?" Dovie May touched my shoulder, then slid her fingers down my arm until her gnarled hand cradled my own. It gave me full view of my cracked fingers and nails rough chewed down past the skin.

"Your mama used to do the same thing. Despite her fancy groomin' otherwise, she worried on her fingers when worry was chewin' on her mind." She placed my hand on my lap, then patted my fingers, a call for peace. A bit of my responsibility fell away with each touch.

"How do you do it? How do you hold it all and not burst?" I shook my head like that might rattle everything into some semblance of normal. Just a few hours ago I was determined to save my husband. But back here, I was reminded of what we still had ahead and how little I knew how to fix it. Fear clawed into my mind, tangling with memory. When Mama thought nobody was listening, Rachmaninoff poured from our piano. Twisting, angry runs, the bass chords climbing, pounding, arguing with the treble, running but never quite escaping, smashing into each other, the treble crying out, trembling until it gasped its last. I'd only heard it a few times, but I knew clear as anything who the bass notes were and who was the treble. Thing is, no one else ever knew she had anything but church music in her— stately hymns, sleepy Mozart, and when she was feeling mighty fancy, Bach . . . 'cepting Sam. He knew.

"It's a strange thing, living in sadness and fear. I wasn't sure I could run this place after Herbert . . ." She sighed. "But then you and your ma came to stay in this cabin, and later Sam finally came to his senses, left the Judge, and married you. And when you had little Rosie, you needed me. You girls . . . You reminded me that, somehow, someway, you gots to choose joy. You'd think holding joy right up against sadness would shatter a body. But it don't. Joy . . . it sneaks in all around where things is broke, sticks it all together, and finds a way to make you whole. It's where things is broke that the joy shows through."

I laid my head on her shoulder, now curled down from sickness and worries. This woman had been strong my whole life. Standing up to my daddy, holding me together when Mama died, standing strong when her boys left for war. Even the apoplexy and seizures hadn't stopped her. But then all this . . .

"Dovie May," I said, shifting so I could ease her against her pillows, "I feel like I'm becoming bitter as chicory coffee."

"Don't think you could be anything other than sweet as sugar. It's just your way."

My laugh was soggy. "I don't see joy in any of this."

"It's always been interesting to me how folks see the same exact thing and see it so different. Take a morning rain for example. A body can stand by a window and see the rain quiet, tumbling from the sky, a tinkling patter refreshing and wetting the earth. And another body, maybe even standing next to the first, sees dismal, boiling clouds spewing cold drops onto an already soaked world."

"But what if all you see is a flood rushing down and your ark's sprung a leak?" I hated the whine in my voice, but Dovie May grinned like I'd got the answer right.

"Sometimes you gots to choose what you see. And sometimes God uses broken things to save us." She fluffed her pillow a bit and wriggled deeper under the blankets. "Ain't no light that can get through something solid. It sneaks through the broken places. Give our Sam a chance to show you, and I'll bet you'll like what you see."

"I already do."

Dovie May raised an eyebrow. "Do you, now?"

I wasn't sure what my mother-in-law was getting at, but I nodded all the same.

"Course I do." I forced myself not to look away from her. "Folks don't throw something away on account of it being a mite broke unless they've tried mighty hard to fix it first."

"Maybe Sam don't need fixin'."

I smiled, trying to reassure her that he and I were fine, but she captured my hand in hers, the pressure strong and sure.

"I don't mean that things might not change," she said. "I'm just sayin' that sometimes there ain't nothing a body can do to fix somebody else. And meddling only makes it worse."

Believe it or not, Dovie May was the only one who'd been cautious about me and Sam getting married. She sat me at the kitchen table and told me she needed to talk with me about the wedding. Seein' as she was the closest thing I had to a mama, I thought at first she intended to talk about our wedding night, and I'm sure I never blushed so hard in all my life. Then soon as she realized why I was turning pink, Dovie May blushed too, saying that wasn't what she had in mind. Once she recovered, she told me marriage wasn't all a walk in the park and escaping into some fairy tale ending like all them books I read.

"Happily ever after don't happen lessen each person in a marriage works. It's like a team of horses," she'd said. "They both have to carry their own load."

I shook my head, dislodging the memory, more confused than ever. That was what I was trying to do. Wasn't it? Carry my husband's load? But it wasn't working out all that well for anybody.

While I hummed a lullaby, Dovie May fell asleep in no time, her body relaxed and trouble free. I slipped out of the cabin into the yard, feeling the pull of my pillow. But the evening chores needed doing, and somebody needed to see to Rosie and feed everyone a bit more afore bed. I heaved the barn doors open and wondered at the abandoned expanse. Where were Sam and Peter?

Elsie calmly chewed her cud, and the sows were snout deep in feed. Buttercup lifted her head from her haystack, then nickered and went back to her grain. Wasn't a better present than chores already done, and I skipped across the yard and up the porch steps hunting Rosie. But I near collided with Peter coming out of the living side.

"How's Ma?"

"She fell asleep right quick. Still full of spit and vinegar, mind, but more than a spoonful of sugar mixed into the lot. I think she'll be all right."

"Sounds like a little miss I know."

"My girl has you wrapped round her pinky, don't she?"

Peter grinned like he was right proud of his position as beloved uncle. "I fed her a bit of bread and cheese, and she's already in bed. But she made me promise I'd send you in for a last good-night kiss from her mama."

"Y'all are gonna spoil me for sure."

"Nah. Just the brothers' turn to take care of things for a bit. Consider it payback for leaving you here so long to do our jobs for us."

I blinked back tears. I hadn't cried so much in a day since I was pregnant, and there wasn't no way I could be pregnant now. Sam and I hadn't even . . .

"It was Sam's idea. He wouldn't say so, but I'm guessing he wouldn't mind some appreciation." Peter wiggled his eyebrows, teasing me like he used to tease Mary. He elbowed me and whispered, "He's in the kitchen." I blushed clear to my toes and waited 'til Peter's footsteps disappeared before opening the door to go see Rosie.

For sure and for certain Sam was trying, and I was grateful. But deep down I wondered if choosing to see the good was enough to save us. If the last few days had taught me anything it was that the bad kept hunting me no matter who was out there trying to help.

—SAM—

I stacked the last dish from yesterday's hurried breakfast in the cupboard. The moment we'd moved in here, Annie had assigned everything a place, and now everything was put away in that place. Neat and tidy. It felt good to be useful again, or at least not causing more trouble.

As I wiped at the kitchen counter, Annie was talking to Peter in the breezeway. Something about Ma, and vibrations of fear pounded against me. I gripped the edge of the counter, leaning into my arms. Doc had helped throw Gus off our trail, tended to Ma when none of us knew what to do, and I'd all but accused him of being in league with the mob. There wasn't nothing to be afraid of here.

I rubbed at a sticky stain on the table, grateful that the maddeningly repetitive work somehow calmed my mind. At least I could find a measure of rest somewhere.

The door to the living side opened, and I dropped the rag, then trailed after Annie as she ducked into Rosie's room. I leaned against the doorframe while my wife tucked in Rosie's blankets and hummed over her until our daughter's little eyes drifted closed. Was like God Himself came and settled an angel in our house.

"You're a good ma to her."

Annie raised a finger to her lips before kissing our girl's forehead and then ducking under my arm. I followed her to the porch, where she curled into the swing and settled her skirts over her knees. Was that an invitation?

When we were first married, we'd sit out there and gaze at the stars, talking about getting old together. More often than not one thing would lead to another. I grasped my hands behind my back, forbidding them to follow old patterns. I hadn't earned the right to be her husband that way yet.

"Annie?" She jumped at the nearness of my voice. If I hadn't known her, I would've missed the flash of real fear before she buried it down deep. But I'd seen it clear as the stars above us. I'd given her more than one reason to worry. Lord, I needed one of those miracles about now.

I sank next to her on the swing, desperate to give my wife comfort, if nothing else. The ropes creaked as we rocked, giving a rhythm to the music of the nighttime woods.

Annie's foot jiggled, and she picked at her fingers, shivering in the cool air. I draped my arm across her shoulders, the familiar position settling me, but her stiffness stole my words. I'd lost the ability to talk to her.

I leaned back into the swing and watched a star streak across the sky, its tail burning itself out. Rather like my wife—beautiful and covering all kinds of ground, yet threatening to burn out awful quick.

"I don't know how you did it, Annie."

Her eyes reflected a bit of the starlight. "What do you mean?"

"You were up here, mostly alone for all that time, giving birth, taking care of an infant and the farm and Ma." The thought made my heart race in near panic. "I don't think I could've done it. And it makes me wonder . . . well, it makes me wonder if y'all made it fine, do you still need me?" Her half-crazy husband who might snap at any time.

I took her hand in mine, and when my thumb slid over her knuckles, her eyes flicked to mine like she wasn't sure neither.

"I guess I just don't know how to do this." The admission stuck in my craw. I wasn't any kind of man if I didn't know how to help my own family.

Annie chuckled. "I don't think there's an instruction booklet for coming home from war. Leastways there isn't one I've seen that makes a lick of sense."

"I just . . . I know this hasn't gone like you planned, like you hoped for. Peter says I gotta talk about it, but . . ." I stared out to the barnyard like the answer might float by on a moonbeam. "With all you been through, you didn't let that darkness inside you. But all I seen and done? I can't bring all that here and dump it on you."

"I ain't gonna break, Sam."

"Why'd you choose me, Charlotte Anne? You never really needed me." My laugh was brittle around the edges, breaking down to my vulnerable middle. "Except maybe that first time."

She slipped her fingers around mine, my new blisters and calluses kissing her old ones.

"Sam, I . . ." She trailed off, blinked at me and then stared up into the sky streaked with twilight color.

I gawked up there too, hoping for something that would tell us we'd be all right. But there wasn't no more shooting stars, just the plain old expanse, hovering distant and quiet.

"I suppose I chose you on account of the fact that you dared loved me," she said, and in her voice, I heard hope blossoming mixed with wonder at my forgetfulness. "And then"—she squeezed my fingers like she did when she was making sure I was listening good—"you loved me no matter what. Dripping wet from the pond or sobbing, always drowning in things I couldn't control. You were my hero."

"And what now? I'm broken." Shame leaked into me, but she clung tight to my fingers, refusing to let go.

"You think because the war changed you I don't love you anymore?" She leaned forward so's her face blotted out the rest of the world. "What kind of person do you think I'd be if I pushed you away when you needed me most? 'Sides, I didn't choose you because you *saved* me. It's that you saw everything and stood by me anyway. Nobody ever stood up to Daddy before you. Whenever I got turned around and needed someone to be there, *you* were there. Maybe it's time for me to return the favor."

"Maybe. But you don't know what I done."

"You went to war to protect me and Rosie and your ma. Whatever you done, that's the why of it." Annie stood and held out her hand to me, watching.

I let her pull me to her chest. Our noses touched, and we sat, breathing the same air, hesitating, testing.

"After what I seen over there, I didn't think there was anything good left."

"I think we can find some."

Annie closed her eyes and pressed her lips against mine. Lord Almighty. Her shaking fingers clutched my shirt, and then she swept me through the house into our bedroom.

She pulled my shirt over my head, and I kissed her forehead, slowing her, making sure she had the space she needed. That this was what she truly wanted. Blue eyes snapped to mine and wandered down. A frown scrunched her eyebrows together as her fingers strayed to the wound on my shoulder. Wasn't no bandage to cover it no more.

The world held its breath as if a hunter had entered the room. Everything in me wanted to hide, to prevent her from seeing the things that had broken me.

"Oh, Sam." She kissed the puckered skin around where the bullet went in, and then her hands trailed down my chest, finding other scars that had rolled over wounds and memories. When she walked round me so's she could see my back, I near whimpered, knowing what she'd find. Knowing the questions it would raise.

But she whispered a kiss on each wound as if her lips were a potion to remove the pain.

Her fingers explored the twisting of pink on my hip, the burn a testament to my failure to save a single member of my crew or the final load of marines assigned to my care. I stared at my fingers, the instrument of death.

Lord, forgive me.

As she stepped round to face me again, I figured I'd see horror taking root in her. The fact that I would do it all again to protect her didn't mean she'd choose to stay with a man who had such reminders of violence.

"Sam." She held my chin. "Sam, I'm so sorry. I had no idea."

I sank to the bed, sobbing against her waist, my hands clenching her dress. Crying for the engine fire I'd missed so's we had to put in to shore. For missing the sniper that shot Rabbit clean through instead of me. For the empty boots in the sand, separated from the bodies of the marines I was charged with landing safely. The blood-red water sucking at the rancid beach sand—in and out, in and out. For waiting a moment too long to check on Jake. The retribution and self-protection with the crunch of the enemy's bones . . . another man's throat under my hands.

"It wasn't supposed to be that way." My words broke at the edges, plunging off the cliff into the chasm with me.

She held me tight against her, rubbing my back, the slow rhythm settling me 'til I took a shuddering breath and let it out long and deep.

Annie's hands left my shoulders, and I scrambled to keep hold of her, fear sneaking out of me in a desperate moan. But she leaned down and kissed my forehead. One of her tears splashed on my knee, and I sniffed.

"I didn't mean to make you cry." It's the last thing I wanted. "I'm supposed to be your hero, but—"

"It's okay, Sam." Annie knelt in front of me, holding my hands to her lips. "Marriage takes two. We'll figure this out."

"It'd take a miracle."

"Well, the only way you see a miracle is if you believe in them first."

And with Annie curled up next to me, I decided I might just believe in the miraculous after all.

———

Don't rightly remember falling asleep, but I woke to a knock on the living room door and sunshine through the window. I scrambled out of bed, then yanked on pants and pulled a shirt over my head before running my fingers through my hair, hoping it wouldn't look like I'd near slept through the day.

"Doc. Leah Belle!" Annie blocked the living side doorway, and I coughed so's she'd know she didn't need to protect me none. She glanced over her shoulder at me, then winked and opened the door wide. The fact that she remembered the signal from our early days made me happier than any man alive.

Doc stepped back into the breezeway. "I'll go check on Dovie May, then I got something for you, Annie." Doc spun and left me wondering on what we'd do with company on a day when we needed to plow the garden and get the shed ready for the fertilizer delivery.

Leah Belle grasped Annie's arms and studied her. "Charlotte Anne. You're such the spitting image of your ma, I don't even know what to do with myself." She wrapped Annie into a hug so big you might think they'd been lifelong friends held apart by circumstance far too long. My wife hesitated a moment before wrapping her arms around the other woman. It gave me a mind to dance a jig. I knew how lonely Annie must be, and if that meant I'd have one less body helping with chores, I'd figure a way to make do.

"Would you care for some coffee?" Leading us into the kitchen, Annie shifted into her hostess role so smoothly her mama would've been proud for sure.

"I wouldn't mind a cup, but then I hear tell y'all have more than a little work to do." Leah Belle wrapped one of Annie's aprons round herself. "And I aim to help."

"But—"

Leah Belle tsked and waved away Annie's protest. "I grew up on a farm. I know what's what and how to get things done that need doing. 'Sides, your Rosie is so much like my daughter at that age that y'all feel like family. And family watches out for each other no matter what. Now, if your man will fire up the stove so's you can rustle up that coffee"—she winked at me—"I can cook him the breakfast he still needs."

Maybe the good Lord was already providing a miracle.

I scarfed down two slices of toast and a couple of eggs. Then Ma stepped in, saying she and Peter had eaten over at the cabin. She looked better than she had yesterday, and by the look on her face, she didn't take too kindly to Doc showing up at the farm to check up on her, even though he said he would. I wasn't sure how she felt about Leah Belle comin' along, but the woman had come in a blue work dress and flat shoes instead of what she wore to church. Right sensible and ready to help. That had to account for something.

Doc squeezed past me hefting a crate as I headed out to join Peter. Part of me wanted to linger and hear what stories Leah Belle had to tell, but we needed that hill plowed and the shed secured. We were already behind in planting. And I wanted to be sure that if'n anybody came back to use the shed, they'd have to make enough ruckus that it would prove I wasn't just seeing things.

I found my brother in the barn sharpening the blade of Pa's old plow. And that was another miraculous bright spot. If'n Peter hadn't decided to come home, I'd be in a world of hurt.

I offered him the mug of coffee I carried.

"You always were the thoughtful one."

I shrugged. Didn't take a genius to notice he liked to sip at a second cup as he started work. Also didn't take much to know it was the small stuff that repaired things between folks.

Peter took the mug and sighed in pleasure. "I can't say as I miss the chicory Annie was passing off as coffee before. Tasted burnt as a stove."

I lifted my mug in agreement. "Something else to be thankful for. Speaking of the fresh coffee, Doc is here already. He brought Mrs. Barker from church with him."

"Yeah. I heard him drive up. The dead in their graves could've heard that automobile comin'."

I couldn't imagine hardly nobody but mobsters paying cash for doctoring right now. How many of them did Doc have to treat to afford that thing? I set my mug on a shelf, then searched for a brush in the horse tack box. Ma would remind me that even mobsters needed caring. But did Doc have to be the one to do it? It wasn't like he was the only doctor in Hot Springs.

I grabbed the stiff dandy brush and groomed Buttercup before fitting her with the harness. Peter slid the bridle over the horse's nose, and she jangled the bit in her mouth before letting it settle in her cheeks.

We hadn't used the plow for a long while, but Peter and I dragged it behind Buttercup and attached it to the harness like we'd never stopped.

"Peter," I started, not knowing quite where I wanted to go, "how long has Doc had that auto?"

"Least as long as I've been home." He shrugged and buckled the harness traces. "I heard tell he traded for it. However he finagled it, that auto comes in handy for him to come check on Ma and bring more medicine for Rosie. Don't suppose he'd have time to come up a couple times a week otherwise, 'sides Sundays."

That often? "Are Ma and Rosie that bad? Annie said Ma's spell in town was the worst one in a long time and Rosie hasn't had an attack in forever."

"Overall they're doing well now, but Ma said it wasn't always so, and you saw what their attacks are like. My guess is Doc don't mind exchanging house visits for a home-cooked meal and a bit of company." Peter snapped his mouth shut, eyes a hair wider than strictly necessary. "I mean keeping Ma company. You know how well they get on."

And they did, but the fact that Peter felt he had to clarify what he said meant he wasn't so sure it was Ma's company Doc'd been seeking. Which meant I hadn't imagined the desire in his eyes as his looks lingered on my wife. My best friend might not be entirely happy to have me home.

"We're all happy to have you home, Sam."

I raised an eyebrow at Peter, wondering how he'd read my mind again.

"You're my brother, and I happen to know more than a little of what you're likely thinking." He passed me the plow lines. "And I also know you're thinking you want to get started plowing while I install the padlock on the shed and double-check its roof for leaks."

"Sure. You take the easy job, baby brother." When he winced, I bumped his shoulder to let him know I was just ribbing him. "I'm glad you're home too. And I'm sorry I didn't keep up with you enough to know what was happening."

Peter rubbed a finger over the blunt tip of his hook before he grasped Buttercup's bridle. "It takes two to communicate. I owe you an apology too."

I wasn't sure if'n he was sorry about not letting me know he was injured or 'bout coming home or 'bout the fertilizer or even 'bout not believing me, but the thoughts got all tangled up, and Peter turned away from me before I got it all straight. In the end, I figured it all rolled into the same thing. Peter was minding things for me just the same as I'd always done for him. We might be a little more broad-shouldered and banged up than when we was kids, but family was family.

At the flat top of the first hill, I stopped and watched Peter amble the rest of the way to the shed, wishing I'd gone with him to prove to myself once and for all whether I'd seen men hiding things in that shed. I near tied the horse to a post to do just that, but more than a little part of me was afraid I wouldn't find nothing.

'Sides, I needed to plow so we could plant the corn and I could feed my family this winter without more handouts from the Judge— especially since I already had to figure out how to pay him back as well as the bank. Another problem for another day.

"Giddyup." I forced the point of the plow into the hard earth, its handles biting into my blisters. At the end of the row, I lifted the plow and clucked at the horse as I eased back on the lead reins to turn the corner. Lord knows we could use a tractor or a farm truck, but there wasn't no getting enough gasoline let alone finding a vehicle we could afford.

"Haw!" I called to Buttercup as I drew in the slack of the left rein.

Down at the house, I saw Doc drag Ma's rocker down the cabin steps and round to the shade of the house, followed by Annie, Leah Belle, and Ma. I laughed as she collapsed onto the chair, then shooed everyone away like they were a cloud of pesky flies. Rosie plopped onto the ground next to her, and though I couldn't hear her words, my daughter's motions told me she was telling her meemaw a story while Ma darned socks. Doc waved at me, then lent Leah Belle his elbow to help her 'cross the little berm at the base of the garden. I lifted a hand, careful not to allow the plow to jump or pitch. Maybe I'd read everything about Doc's attention to Annie wrong. He seemed as attentive to Leah Belle and Ma as he was to my wife.

Doc and Leah Belle bent over the rows of beets, pulling up the roots. Beets weren't my favorite on account of how many I'd eaten in my lifetime, but there was good reason to grow them. Everything from the greens down to the tip of the root was useable, food for the family as well as good feed for the animals. And I knew Doc had helped plant them. I should be thankful that he'd been available and willing, but it still soured my stomach to think he'd been here instead of me working side by side with my Annie and watching Rosie grow.

I lifted the plow again shouting "Gee!" at Buttercup, then turned right for the next pass and then left for the next, then right again, the turns blurring together. I rolled my shoulder against the growing ache.

Another turn and another and a countless series of turns while the sun tipped over the midway point of the sky.

I peered down the hill and near collapsed in frustration. Not even halfway through the field, and I was already paining. I sighed and stared over the horse's ears at the trees, hoping the rows furling out from the plow were straight and true.

Reaching the end of another row, I turned Buttercup round and near jumped out of my skin when Doc appeared.

"Didn't mean to scare you none. I brought you water and lunch." He set down a bag, then lifted out two jugs of water, a sandwich, and a thermos. "And Leah Belle sent up coffee. I know y'all have had a couple long days."

"Mighty kind." I drank more than a bit of the coffee, then took a jug and drank all the water in it. Doc chatted about Rosie and the garden, but I only managed a grunt or two in acknowledgment. I just didn't have nothing left to navigate talking to another person I didn't quite know how to navigate no more.

"Actually"—Doc dug the toe of one boot into the loosened soil—"coming up here was an excuse to have a word with you. I know you been gone awhile and might not realize it's—"

I lifted my hat from my head, wiped sweat from my brow, and estimated how much ground I had to plow yet and how long it would take. The gently sloping field wavered in the heat, and I blinked, focusing my vision. It was warm, but certainly not that warm, especially compared to the Pacific.

"I know you're her husband and all, but . . ."

My attention snapped back to Doc. What was he accusing me of?

"I'm doing the best I—" I leaned against a fence post, heaving in air.

Doc tilted his head, watching me like the doctor in the field hospital. "You okay, Sam?"

I nodded, feeling my innards bouncing round. "I don't mean to be rude or nothin', but what exactly are you saying, Doc?"

"That crate I brought has a present in it for Annie's birthday."

"Birthday?" I echoed.

"It's today. I got the Victrola from the Judge. I figured you might not have had a chance to get to the store and you might want to give her the records, or—" He stepped closer. "Are you sure you're okay?"

I nodded but then slid to the ground, knees akimbo and jutting up to the sky.

"What's the date today?" Doc towered over me, seeming to grow tall as the trees.

I dropped my head into my elbow, trying to keep my mind from flying to pieces.

"What's going on?" Peter's voice rang in the haze.

Why was it murky? And why was Peter so upset?

"He just all of a sudden got light-headed."

I opened my eyes, and Peter peered at me, his face melted into an awful sharp-toothed maw, his fingers grown into talons waiting to slash me to bits.

"The devil!" My shout slammed through my head, bruising my mind and sending me scrambling backward into a crater, where I sank. Hands reached from the ground, grabbing at my ankle. I pointed to warn Doc, but the words wouldn't come. Buttercup skittered sideways, and Doc grabbed at her reins, fear and concern lifting his brows.

"Sam?" Peter's muffled voice came through the devil mouth, but the swirling slowed as I matched the sound with the bits of Peter's face I recognized.

Doc poured the second jug of water over my head, and I jerked at the shock of it, swiping away the droplets as Peter's eyes and mouth settled into place. I panted, leaning over, gulping air so's I wouldn't vomit.

Lord Almighty, I was going crazy for sure and for certain. What would I do now?

Peter slung his damaged arm underneath me, cradling me with the warm wood until the world settled back into place.

Don't reckon I know how I talked Peter and Doc into letting me finish the plowing. Maybe Peter figured he could keep a better eye on me while he and Doc loaded the ammonium nitrate pellets from the delivery truck into the shed. He sure didn't want me handling bags of unstable fertilizer in my state. Maybe he was right, but I knew I needed to drive my body to exhaustion, punish my mind, bury the thought that the nightmares might be taking over reality and there wasn't nothing I could do about it.

CHAPTER
Sixteen

—ANNIE—

After we'd finished crop thinning the bottom portion of the peach trees, Leah Belle shooed me out of the kitchen, saying I couldn't make my own birthday dinner and I "couldn't help neither." Doc had told her today was the day, and she'd been pleased as a peacock that she was helping give me a party. Dovie May frowned like she wasn't sure about a second-rate substitute for my mama invading her kitchen, but Leah Belle looped her arm through Dovie May's and declared she was desperate to learn how to make her famous Karo nut pie.

"Folks been after that recipe since I was a girl. Ain't nobody learning it just 'cause they asked." Dovie May stomped through the breezeway the best she could, still grumbling. "But I guess you can be some help by shelling them pecans."

Dovie May's grousing made me giggle like a schoolgirl. She hated shelling pecans, but there wasn't no way she'd let Leah Belle know that.

Outside, I taught Rosie to snap her fingers and skip, and then we took turns chasing Bailey and playing marbles 'til she decided it was teatime. Rosie tugged me into the garden where she'd fashioned herself a fort from the teepee trellises, and I ducked into her playroom.

Late-afternoon light pressed striped highlights into the new branches of Dovie May's trellised sweet pea vines, their tendrils curling, twisting, striving for purchase. Each stem unfurled dainty veined pink flowers. Dovie May's authoritative voice drifted from the kitchen, followed by Leah Belle's laughter, and I settled on the ground, wishing Sam could sit with me. Then it would be a perfect day.

Rosie picked up the teapot I'd created out of a rock and some leftover wire and pretended to pour into a leaf cup cradled on her lap. She started to hand me the cup but stopped so abruptly that the leaf twirled to the ground. Her little nose lifted into the air sniffing, so much like Bailey's. I laughed and then sniffed the air myself. Whatever Leah Belle and Dovie May were baking smelled mighty fine.

"Your daddy and uncles best come soon or my drooling might get to embarrassing levels." I slurped more than a little like Bailey hunting for scraps.

Rosie scrambled to her feet, no doubt getting ready to call in the menfolk when the jingle of Buttercup's harness announced them coming round the corner.

Rosie ran to her uncle Peter and leapt into his arms. He caught her, but just barely, and the grin he gave her didn't come anywhere near his eyes.

I could near feel the tension crackling between the three men. And Sam, trailing the others, was pale enough to be mistaken for a ghost.

"Y'all all right?" I trotted to my husband and laced my fingers through his. He stiffened, and I watched the fear drape over him, snuffing out all the light.

"He just had a bit of heatstroke," Doc answered for Sam. Peter ducked his head and led the horse to the barn. It gave me mind of a guilty child hoping to get away with stealing cookies from the cookie jar . . . or not getting his brother in trouble.

What had happened? Doc shook his head, shooting a subtle glance at Sam.

"I'll get y'all some water." I dropped Sam's hand and ran to the well in the side yard. I worked the pump filling a bucket, then dipped out a ladle full of water and brought it back to my husband, who'd trailed me partway.

He gulped it all in near one swallow. "Thanks, Annie." He passed me the ladle without so much as glancing at me.

"You okay?"

He nodded, scratching under his hat like he was trying to remember something. "But I forgot your birthday."

Was that all this was? Heatstroke and a forgotten birthday?

"You ain't never forgot my birthday, and you didn't forget this year neither." I cupped his cheek, the bristles on his cheek scratching at my palm. "You got yourself home just in time to give us all an excuse to put on an even bigger celebration. And I expect you to sing for me and sweep me off my feet with some kind of dance. That'll be present enough."

Something still haunted the edges of him, but it seemed to be floating away, and he kissed my forehead. "I don't deserve you."

"Yes you do. You were born you, and that's enough for me." I wrapped my arm through his. "What do you say we go in and tell your ma and Leah Belle we're famished?"

"Ma'd smack my backside so hard I wouldn't be able to sit for a week. But you? You can near get away with anything. So I'll follow you in."

"Sacrifice me, will you?" I nudged his hip with mine, and Sam chuckled with me. Felt awful good to be able to settle him.

After we ate our fill of stew and fluffy bread without so much as a hint of sawdust, Rosie near danced over to a small stack of presents.

"Guess we best open those, long as it's okay with you, Rosie." I opened my arms to my daughter, and she bounced into my lap. "Think it'd be all right if you helped your mama open her presents?"

"Best open mine first." Doc slid the huge wooden crate in front of me, then stood grinning like he'd gone and dug up a chest full of Spanish gold.

I felt the warmth of him standing next to me, and I wished he'd step back a mite, but I smiled at my husband's best friend anyway. "You didn't need to go getting me something. Your help has been more than enough."

Sam tipped back in his chair, arms across his chest, the look in his eyes assessing and unsure. I swallowed, wondering what I was supposed to do. But Rosie saved me the pondering by wrenching open the lid before I could do much more than have a hair's breadth of worry.

"Hang on there, darlin'." Doc gently nudged Rosie away. "How 'bout if I help you?"

He leaned over the crate, popping the side off with a crowbar to reveal a Victrola.

If I didn't know what to say before, now the world had come and sucked all the air from the room. Mama's Victrola.

Sam let the legs of his chair settle back on the floor, his jaw working like he couldn't find the air to breathe either. Don't think Doc was trying to upstage Sam, but he'd done it all the same.

Peter jumped up, then hefted a small box from the counter and set it in front of me. "Your daddy sent these for you too. Said your mama intended you to have all this anyway." His words tumbled over each other as he glanced at his brother. "We all know how much Annie likes music. Why don't we put on a record? We can all work off that almighty good dinner before we have some of Ma's pie."

I caught Peter's vision right off, and I reached into the box and yanked out a record without paying attention to what it was. *Swan Lake.*

Rosie clambered into my chair and clapped. Peter pulled the record from the sleeve and waited for my direction.

"The waltz side," I whispered, fingers shaking, then praying that Sam and I wouldn't end like the ballet—Odette and Siegfried, running from the evil sorcerer into the open arms of a watery grave. I would've picked different if I'd thought it through.

But Peter had already fit the record, turned the crank, and was lowering the arm. Doc stepped back and smiled at Sam. Least he knew a waltz with me wasn't his place. Sam hesitated like he wasn't sure quite what was expected of him, but when the scratches and the tick, tick, tick of the album filled the kitchen, he bowed over me, asking me for the dance.

The pizzicato violins rained down their short notes, and Sam pulled me into his arms as the strings swelled into the swaying melody. Peter swung Rosie into the air with the crescendo of the kettledrums, her giggles overtaking the woodwinds while her uncle pranced round to the music. Doc bowed to Leah Belle, and she allowed him to move her slowly through the kitchen. She glowered more than a little, but I figured she was just used to a better dance partner. And when she saw I was watching, she smiled so's I knew it was okay.

All of us danced away while Dovie May clapped, and a smile slowly crept onto Sam's face, growing bigger until the final decisive chords finished ringing out and we all dropped to our chairs panting.

Sam leaned across the table and pulled the record box toward him, mumbling to himself as he thumbed through the records. "Aha!" He wiggled his eyebrows at me and set the record. "I did promise you a romantic dance."

I waited, wondering what record he'd found. Taking my hand, Sam spun me into his chest, then dipped me low. A piano arpeggio rippled up, and I slipped back in time to a place where life had been so much easier. Nat King Cole's satin voice reached out to us.

I smiled. "I Love You for Sentimental Reasons."

"It's perfect."

Sam sang with Mr. Cole, his deep voice vibrating against my chest, lulling me into his rhythm. It wasn't just the words telling me Sam was mine and asking me to love him back; it was his steady embrace promising that he'd never leave and that we'd find a way through the hard times no matter what.

The piano and guitar unwound over us. Dovie May and Peter sat swaying with the rhythm, their smiles big as the Ouachita Mountains. I was pretty sure mine was about the same, and I refused to let it slip even when I saw Doc and Leah Belle leaning against the wall, watching us like they was missing out. Doc, I understood, but Leah Belle . . . she'd said she'd lost two husbands. Maybe she was just thinking on that.

The waterfall of notes at the end gave Sam an excuse to twirl me out and back into his arms.

His lips brushed mine. "You have my heart, Charlotte Anne."

And he had mine.

Rosie giggled, and Peter changed the record to "Sing, Sing, Sing," saying Dovie May had found this one. And we skipped and danced to Gene Krupa's drumbeats. Even though Leah Belle sat out, Rosie somehow convinced Dovie May and Peter to stomp to the sound of the horns too, weaving in and out of Sam's and my feet, with ole Benny Goodman on his clarinet.

In all, Peter and Dovie May had rustled up five whole disks of swing, and Daddy had sent at least a good portion of Mama's classical collection.

We danced until we all dropped in chairs around the table, panting like we'd been to war against the devil himself and won.

Dovie May jumped up. "I near forgot!" She hobbled into the pantry, then rattled around as her voice called from far away, "I near forgot the pie." She came out balancing the biggest pie I'd seen since rationing had started *and* a bowl of whipped cream. "Don't ask me where I got the sugar. I've been squirreling it away for nearly a year so's I didn't even touch the Judge's stash."

She set it on the table with a spin to show off the perfect spiral of pecans.

"And I still didn't get the recipe." Leah Belle mock-sighed with a wicked smile.

Dovie May raised an eyebrow at the woman. A body couldn't miss the annoyance in the look, but I smiled so big it hurt my cheeks. Dovie May was back to her recipe-hoarding self.

Sam held out his fingers like he was framing my face. "Wish I had film to capture this, darlin'. I don't ever want to forget how beautiful you are at this moment."

"You know well and good I look like some kind of maid." I patted the scarf tied around my head, felt the dust there.

"Naw." He pecked my lips. "No woman'd be fool enough to hire such a pretty maid. You'd be too tempting for the men of the house."

Doc gasped, and my cheeks heated.

Sam frowned, shoving back from the table. "Gosh darn. I went and did it. Sorry, ladies. I'm still getting used to being in the company of the fairer sex." He swept low into a bow to accompany his awful attempt at a British accent. "Pray let me atone for my slovenly ways with another dance, and then we shall feast on pie."

Well, how could I refuse such an offer?

It must've been after nine when Rosie near dropped right where she was. At his ma's suggestion, Peter carried my daughter to bed over in the granny cabin, Dovie May tucking her in while Sam and I kept swaying in the kitchen. Doc chatted with Leah Belle while she made another round of coffee, but when she finished, she handed Sam and me each a mug and then shooed Doc toward the door. "We done our damage here. Best leave these two to themselves."

"Thank you, Leah Belle," I told her.

"Thanks for everything, Doc." Sam smiled from the table. Doc nodded and shuffled to the door, his shoulders sagging like he'd lost some internal war. Alone was a hard place to be.

I traced my finger on the edge of my mug. From outside I heard Dovie May's and Peter's voices saying goodbye to our guests, then the engine start to Doc's car, and last the symphony of frogs and other nighttime critters taking up their chorus.

Sam sipped at his coffee and winked at me. We were alone and settled for the first time since he'd come home. I leaned into his right side, his chest cradling my shoulder. He shifted and trailed his fingertips up my arm 'til goose pimples broke out. He tipped my chin toward him and leaned over me, tears glistening in his eyes.

"What's wrong, Sam?"

"I love you more than anything, Charlotte Anne Mattas."

Before I could ask what that had to do with his tears, his lips pressed hungry against mine, weaving a delicious enchantment that made me forget everything that'd gone wrong since he'd been home. He slid me onto his lap, drawing me in, the warmth of him burning through my cotton dress to the skin of my legs, my chest, his stubbled cheek setting my lips afire. My hands tangled in his hair, my body declaring all the things I'd wanted to tell him but couldn't find words for. His hands engulfed my hips, sliding with painstaking care up my waist, my back, shocking the tender bare skin of the nape of my neck, my scarf slipping back and down even as he stood, lifting me effortless in his strong arms before allowing me to skim down his body and settle my bare toes on the floorboards. My dress swirled between us, still dancing with joy, and one side of Sam's lips lifted, teasing me with an impish grin.

But I had no inclination for games. With a practice born of repetition and desperation, I towed him out of the kitchen, hoping the good Lord could take two and make them one once again.

CHAPTER
Seventeen

—ANNIE—

I startled awake. A low growl rumbled in the room like a mongrel dog fighting over a bone. My bedroom was held in the eclipse of a tight fist, and I blinked, disoriented. I was flailed out on my back, arm flung above my head.

I was sweaty to be sure, but I didn't have the hot of a fever. I frowned thinking I must not have been asleep long to still be so warm. The dog growled again, sounding like it might be inside. I shifted slowly to my elbows, trying to find its location as I shrunk away from the sound toward Sam, praying I was wrong.

Suddenly it leapt onto me, and a blanket flapped at my face, trapping my legs, pressed down by a . . . a . . . oh God, not a dog. I flailed again. Someone had gotten in. His hands, wide and strong surrounded my throat, squeezing, suffocating me.

I clawed at the hands circling my neck. Where was Sam? My mouth opened, the scream strangled. I flung a fist forward, cracking it against what had to be a jaw, and again, but the fingers on my throat didn't budge, and stars sparked in my vision. Finally remembering what Sam had taught me, I plunged my thumb into the man's eye socket. His holler thundered throughout the room, and I scrambled away, picking up a boot on my way, flinging it back at the bed as I tumbled off balance to the floor.

A thud followed clearly by a man's "Ow" brought me back to reality.

Sam was rubbing his chin where the boot had connected, frowning. I crab-crawled backward, putting me in mind of Daddy's beaten dog. But this dog wasn't going to bend down nohow.

When Sam pushed himself off the bed, I bolted to the living

room and snatched the gun, then turned on him, cocking it in one smooth motion.

Sam's hand raised in front of him, a placating gesture like I was the one who'd gone mad.

"I suggest you stop coming toward me."

His feet stopped, and I risked peeking into his eyes. Soft, compassionate, confused. The one swelled red and streamed with tears.

"Charlotte Anne, you gotta believe me."

"I don't got to believe anything other than you're getting worse. You had your hands round my neck."

"I was dreaming. It was . . ." Sam crumpled to the floor, knees to his chest, rocking himself like a mama might a newborn baby.

The tip of the gun dipped, but I fought the compassion bubbling in my belly. "Fact is you don't got control of it. What if I'd been Rosie? You would've killed her."

A sob seeped out of Sam. "I didn't mean to. It was . . . like I was back. And Jake . . . He was the last of my crew left. We hid in a cave by the water hoping someone would come for us. He was late coming back from watch while I slept. I went to go check on him and . . . and he was in a pool of his own blood, a Jap soldier leaning over him. I caught the soldier by surprise, but he got a shot off before I could draw my gun. I . . . I . . ." Sam's hands spread like they might be around a body's neck.

Understanding slammed into me. Sam had strangled that man to death. He'd been an enemy soldier, but . . .

I took a step back, and Sam rolled up to his knees, pleading like I was an executioner with the power to pardon him. "He was set on killing me, and I had to get home to you and Rosie . . . and now . . ." Sam shook his head, no doubt trying to loose the demons from his mind. "I'll sleep in the barn from now on. Y'all need me for the farm, but I can't risk . . . I don't want to . . . I don't want to hurt you or Rosie. I couldn't live with myself if I did."

I thought of the men down the mountain at the hospital. The ones locked behind doors, their screams reaching all the way to the street.

An owl hooted outside, and I jumped, shaking my head. Knowledge of what stifling place we were condemned to yawned wide beneath my feet, drowning out any words I might've found.

Sam's hand clenched onto my wrist, and I tried to snatch it back, but he held tight. "Don't let anybody lock me up. You hear?"

I nodded, fear rippling through me, my mind circling back to Mama lying on Dovie May's davenport. *I should've run before, Charlotte Anne. Should've run.* If she had, maybe she'd still be here.

But this was different. Wasn't it? Daddy'd made a choice to be what he was. Sam hadn't chosen to be drafted. Hadn't chosen to kill or be killed. I'd read enough about combat fatigue to know it struck randomly. I'd promised for better or worse. Right?

My mind flitted back to the first time we'd slept in this old house. I have no idea where Sam found his unending reserves of patience. Every bump, noise, and creak had me sitting bolt upright, convinced there was a bear clawing at the door . . . or worse, that Daddy'd changed his mind and come after me.

I remembered feeling the heat of Sam's leg on mine, his whisper on my cheek, the curve of his bare shoulders when he climbed out of bed to check for me, again.

But this time it was Sam who'd fallen down some hole and dragged me with him. What happens when the devil got to you and there wasn't no one left to pull you out of the never-ending depths?

CHAPTER
Eighteen

—SAM—

For a moment last night, I'd thought I might escape paying penance for all I'd done and hadn't done in the war and while working for the Judge. Annie pressed against me, the warmth, the realness nearly convinced me I was free.

What a fool I was. There ain't no rest for a wicked soul.

The whispers of all those I'd failed called to me, and as I sat on a hay bale, I clutched a glass with a shot of amber liquid swirling in the bottom. I'd found relief there more than once, and I licked my lips remembering the taste. The oblivion.

The barn walls creaked in the wind, and Buttercup shifted like she was trying to escape the ghosts as much as I was. I set the glass on a ledge, then pressed the heels of my hands into my eyes until I saw stars. I thought of Annie and me lyin' out in the fields, watching the stars crawl across the sky. Back before I left, we'd dreamed of our life together, of growing old.

Rosie's Bailey cat meowed and curled his tail around my arm like he was Ma asking me to pay attention to her words. But I wasn't exactly sure what he was trying to say.

"I don't rightly know what's wrong with me."

Other than I was talking to a cat.

Bailey gazed at me, his tail hanging in a question mark above his back.

"You're right. I gotta find a way to control this."

Bailey rubbed against me like he'd understood what I'd said and was confirming what I needed to do. He'd seen them men on the mountain same as me.

I poured the liquid back into the bottle Peter had stashed in the equipment stall. I didn't need oblivion; I needed proof. I needed to know, really know, I wasn't crazy. If I proved it to myself, maybe I'd be able to control the images, channel them somehow. I snatched the key to the shed's padlock from the hidden alcove behind the tack box and lifted the lit lantern from the wall.

As I snuck into the barnyard, the scuffle of night animals quieted, preparing to make way for the daytime, leaving a wake of eerie blankness. Shivers crept up my spine as I tiptoed round to the back of the house. The devil himself had slunk down the mountain and breathed a cloud over everything. Ghostly mist spun wild and free across my little farm, breaking in front of me, trailing me 'til I nearly sprinted up the newly plowed field.

At the top, I bent over, gasping for air to fill my lungs. I surveyed the hilltop in the creeping light. I'd been lower on the hill when the fertilizer delivery come. It had taken Peter and Doc all afternoon to load the bags into the shed, arrange them neat, then lock up the place. I twisted the key, its teeth biting my palm. I should've helped them and searched for clues despite my spell. It hadn't done me any good to avoid the place.

I knew well and good that the thought was ridiculous. What was I hoping to find underneath all them bags that neither my best friend nor my brother had seen? But if I ever wanted to sleep, I had to try. I unfastened the padlock, then flipped open the slotted tongue and hung the lock back on the eyelet. The white bags were piled up about waist high, but there was a walkway so's we could retrieve bags from the entire length of the shed. I held the lantern high, being careful not to get it too close to the bags. Wouldn't do to set it all on fire.

I hung the lantern on a hook by the door and pictured exactly where the three men had stood. Edging toward the west side of the structure, I realized I could squeeze back toward where they'd been. Along the back wall, Peter and Doc had left another walkway, and I turned. The smallest of the strangers had leaned over, retrieving things from the floor. I walked the length, pondering the semi-darkness at my feet, then stopped. I backed up, and sure as shooting the floor there made a different sound. Spinning, I dropped to my knees and pulled at the floorboards. A short expanse lifted. My fingers pricked, and I near danced with joy. Inside was a ledger and a burlap bag.

I'd been right. Something was happening on my farm.

And if'n it was on the up-and-up, they wouldn't be hiding. I didn't care if it was Gus or the Judge; I'd be darned if I'd let it continue.

I shook out the bag, and a small package dropped into my palm. It was an awful lot like one of Rosie's medicine boxes. I turned it over and opened the lid. Nestled inside was a bottle. I squinted at the label but couldn't make out the words in the poor light.

I dropped the box and ledger into the bag and stood, holding the bottle to the light.

Opium.

The word screamed that Samuel Mattas wasn't crazy, and he had proof.

As I shimmied out from behind the fertilizer, I clutched the bag like my life depended on it. I would have to get into town and call the law.

I halted, my joy spilling away. The law? More'n likely the law in Hot Springs was awful cozy with whoever ran this operation. I couldn't call the sheriff.

Then who? Sid McMath and the rest of the GI Revolt might be willing to help, but they didn't have any real power. At least not yet. But when I had a smoke with those men in town, one of them mentioned a newspaper article about Mr. Hoover and his G-men. I'd read it too. And word was they were investigating the mayor.

So, the FBI, then. I'd have to call over to Little Rock and hope they would help.

I lifted the lantern from the wall, then locked up and started toward home. I'd leave Annie a note and head to town before everyone woke.

Wasn't more than a dozen steps from the shed when I realized the fields were entirely silent. With the sky brightening, the birds should've started up their chirping. My skin pricked, and I lowered the lantern to the ground, spreading my legs to prepare for a quicker escape. A light shimmered at the edges of my vision, but when I turned, it was gone.

Was it just a deer eating breakfast that had made me so jumpy?

I laughed and bent to pick up the lantern, then a shadow launched itself from behind the trees, its unnaturally long arm swinging. I leaned away, but the arm cracked against my skull, and I was falling, rolling, the grasses shrouding me.

"Payback hurts. Don't it?"

Had someone really spoken? Or were my own regrets echoing in my mind?

"Should've left it alone." A voice for sure that time . . . a different one.

I blinked. The stars disappeared, reappeared, then darkness.

———

Why was I cold? I lifted my head, but I couldn't summon the energy to locate my pack.

A soft crackling nearby made me smile. Someone had lit a fire in the fire pit to keep me warm. They'd keep the night watch. The grass was mighty fine cushion too. Now I could close my eyes for just a minute . . .

CHAPTER
Nineteen

—ANNIE—

It was still night when I rolled over and sat up on the edge of the bed. I didn't have no more tears to cry, and the day would come regardless of my longing to get back under the covers and pretend. But pretend what? There wasn't nowhere I could go back to that didn't lead right up to this point.

I tugged on a work dress and wrapped a scarf around my neck. It would be hotter than blazes under it, but what else could I do? I peered into the mirror and pulled the edges of it higher, hoping to hide the evidence of the bruises blooming awful colors against my pale skin. I dropped my hands. Even if I kept the scarf there all day, daytime was bound to expose everything. And there wasn't no way to explain fingerprints around your neck. Ain't no falling that causes that.

In the kitchen, I yanked open the stove door, the ashes puffing out at me like a fire-breathing dragon. I jumped back, wanting to throw a temper tantrum worthy of a toddler. But there wasn't no way to start a fire when you flail at it. I took a deep breath, gently blowing on the coals and feeding it bits of wood 'til it caught. I slammed the door shut. It seemed I was back to doing everything all by my lonesome.

Except one thing was different. Back then I'd had hope. Hope that when Sam came home, we'd be all right. I lifted my soot-covered hands and snorted. All I had now was ashes.

I brushed the black off on my apron and stuffed my feet into my work boots, not bothering to tie the frayed laces. Animals still needed feeding, Elsie needed milking, and we'd need the eggs from the chickens. A farm don't stop for nobody, and there wasn't nothing else I could do to make a living. Playing piano down at the Quapaw

Bathhouse wouldn't make ends meet . . . even if they'd hire me again. With all their crystal and marble, they were far too highfalutin for a farm wife with broken nails. They only hired the crème de la crème.

I trudged out to the barn like I was heading toward a firing squad or turning myself in to Wonderland's Queen of Hearts for my very own beheading. Sam was out there, and I didn't rightly know what I was going to say . . . what I was going to do.

I heaved the barn doors open and wondered at the dead quiet. Sam should be awake by now.

Buttercup nickered nervous and stomped her foot. Hairs rose on my arms, and I backed out of the barn, closing the doors.

"Sam?" The purple dawn swallowed my voice, and I swung around shouting for him again. The smell of woodsmoke reached me, and I sighed in relief. Maybe Sam had slept on a bedroll in the cabin. I trotted up the steps and cracked open the door. It was cold as a tomb, and Peter wasn't asleep on the couch. I backed out, not wanting to wake Dovie May.

Chewing on a nail, I stumbled back to the house, then snatched the shotgun off the wall in the living room and made my way through the breezeway, swallowing the fear and begging my hands to steady.

The sound of crackling drew my attention to the ridge below the sorting shed, and I gasped. Flames leapt from the mountain, streaking toward the sky, gobbling air and dirt, making its way to the fence line, the shed . . . the house. In an awful moment, I realized Sam had been right. Someone was up there, and I hadn't believed my own husband.

They must've taken Sam and Peter. Wasn't no way either of them would let a body start a fire that close to the fertilizer pellets otherwise.

I raced up the mountain, pleading with the good Lord to save my husband and his brother from whoever had taken them. *Please, God, don't let my own stupid distrust be the end of us.*

Skirting the wide-open garden, I found refuge against the edge of the woods. Branches reached out and slashed at my skin, but I dared not break free from the protection of the trees. I didn't know much about stalking nobody, but I knew enough to stay hidden. As I crested the hill, flames shot from a pile of debris, and a man threw bits in, feeding the hungry blaze.

I squinted against the light, wondering where he had stashed Sam and Peter. I hesitated, logic piercing through my panic. How in the world did one man subdue two warriors?

A tiny blur of white streaked across the garden, a miniature angel in its wake.

"Rosie," I whispered.

Oh God, if You've ever listened to one of my prayers . . .

A scream burst from my throat, startling the man and causing another shadow to tear through the garden toward the flames.

I ran pell-mell through the no-man's-land field, shouting like my voice might be enough to destroy the enemy or at least distract him from my daughter wandering toward the raging flames.

The man stepped from the far side of the fire, dark hair disheveled, stubble of a beard creeping across his chin.

"Sam?" The shotgun dropped to the ground, and I backed away just as the second man appeared in the ring of light. Peter, holding Rosie safe in his arms. I near collapsed from relief.

"It ain't what it seems, Annie." Sam's voice echoed from far away.

"And what's that, Sam?" I couldn't even look at him. I knew I wouldn't see the madness. I'd see the cool, calm eyes—lakes I'd get lost in, forgetting exactly what I'd seen.

"I didn't—"

"It's one thing when you put yourself in danger. I could maybe . . . maybe have forgiven you for that. Even what you did to . . ." My fingers touched the scarf strangling my neck. "But . . ." I stumbled, caught myself on a tree, my burning lungs gasping for air.

"You got to believe me." Sam tipped my face up. "I would never—"

"Never get drunk?"

Sam sucked in a breath as if the heat of my words scorched his skin.

I shook him away, my ears ringing.

"Never near kill a man with your fist? Never hurt me?" I stepped toward him, my own fists begging to fly, but it wouldn't do no good. My Sam was gone. Some monster had swallowed him whole and come back in his stead. "Truth is, I don't know what you would and wouldn't do no more."

"Annie, why would I—"

"Maybe you thought it'd make us believe you'd really seen something up here. Maybe you thought you saw something and were trying to do right. I don't know why. But I saw you feeding them flames."

"It wasn't me that started it, and I was trying to put it out. There was a man—" Sam grabbed my arm with one hand and pointed to the forest with the other.

"I told you to leave it alone. You need help, Sam. You believe me yet?" Peter's voice cracked.

"It wasn't me." Sam's voice broke too as he glanced back at Peter, hoping someone would believe him.

But my belief was all used up.

"Who else, Sam? Who else coulda started the fire?"

Peter set Rosie aside and started throwing dirt onto the blaze, using his hook to break up the clumps before tossing in pitiful handfuls.

"Annie." Sam took a step toward me but stopped when I near growled.

"Ain't no more sorries you can say that make a difference." I pressed Rosie into my skirts, my hands covering her ears so she maybe wouldn't hear. "I think you need to leave. I won't let the law take you, but you . . . you need to leave." Fear, anger . . . it all tumbled together, raging inside me, screaming, *It ain't fair!*

"At least let me help put it out." Sam had turned to Peter, pleading with him now.

"Annie," Peter said, appealing to me too. "Truth told, we can't do it on our own."

I nodded but then turned my back on the two men frantically throwing dirt on the flames. Sounds swirled around me, but I couldn't make much sense of them. The frantic calling. The pounding of Peter's feet running down the hill, then him struggling back past me with shovels. My own footsteps striking Dovie May's wooden steps, her voice asking me what was wrong as I set Rosie on the davenport. My nonsensical response.

God had ignored my prayers, and the devils had come to destroy us all.

— SAM —

I hadn't done it.

Had I?

Please, God.

The fire heaved and collapsed in response to my prayer, a perverse being allying itself with the trees encircling me. The gnarled shadows reached down, down inside my chest. I was trapped, stabbed in place by the darkness, nostrils flaring like the two-year-old horses at the races across town.

Annie's screams echoed in my head, and I threw another shovelful of dirt onto the fire.

When thou walkest through the fire, thou shalt not be burned.

The verse slipped into my mind, quieting the smoldering but doing nothing to dull the ache drumming through my whole body.

My shovel bit into the ground again, breaking rhythm with Peter's only to wipe the blood trickling into my eyes.

Blood? Again? I touched the wound on my head, and memory flashed. He'd hit me. The other man. He'd been there sure as I was alive. I stilled, forcing myself to remember, hoping to jar something free, a detail I'd missed or forgotten.

Unnaturally long arm. He'd had a branch or something and cracked me over the head. His voice. I shook my head as I tried to force the pieces in my brain to drop into place. And then I remembered the voice. *Payback.* Only person I knew round here that might want payback was Gus.

"But why was he up here?"

Peter's shovel stopped. "Why was who up here?"

"Tell you when we get this blasted fire out." I returned to suffocating the last of the coals before Peter asked more, and it wasn't long 'til the flames had burned themselves out.

"We're lucky we got so much rain." I squinted behind me at the shed, knowing now why Peter'd been so jumpy about putting the fertilizer so near the house. We'd use it up this year and then find something safer for next.

"What's going on, Sam?" Peter's question startled me, and I swung round, nearly knocking into my brother. "Why in heaven's name would you start this fire?" His face was near as red as the glowing coals.

I stepped back, shock burning my words to ash.

"Look," Peter said, scrubbing his hand through his hair. "I know you're having a hard time of things, but this ain't the way."

"I . . ." What could I say to convince him? I'd had the proof. A whole bagful. I could near feel the smooth of the amber bottle and the roughness of the burlap. What had happened to it all? I scuffed a foot at the embers and the wire binding of a notebook rolled free. I dropped to my knees, then shook my head in wonder as I used my handkerchief to pick up the curling metal.

"What are you—" Peter grabbed at my shirt.

"Proof." I held up the wire and cackled like I really had gone crazy. "Peter, I came up to check on things in the shed. I found a loose board, and underneath somebody'd hid a bottle of opium and a ledger. I think they're running a drug operation up here. Likely using the shed as a meeting place to transfer it."

Peter studied me, then at the wire in my hands, then me again, his eyebrows warring with each other. "Why are you doing this, Sam?"

"Doing what?" The burn from the hot metal reached my fingers, and I yelped, dropping the bit to the ground.

Peter stood over me while I scrambled in the dirt.

"Are you going to help me find it?" I squinted at him, but he just shook his head.

"It's a piece of the chicken wire we used the other day to mend the fence." He said the words careful like I was an angry bear, and my heart dropped.

My own brother didn't believe me.

Peter squatted in front of me and lifted the wire. It curled perfectly even like a spiral.

"It's too thick to be chicken wire," I said weakly.

"Sam, you gotta stop. It ain't safe to keep doing this." He pushed the wire into my hand, then pivoted toward the house, shuffling down the hill, never once glancing back.

I turned the wire in my fingers. Dagnabbit. I didn't have enough proof for nobody to believe me. But that didn't mean I couldn't tell Gus I knew what was happening and to stay away from my family.

Shoving the wire into my pants pocket, I stomped to the barn and yanked open the doors. The protest in my muscles felt glorious. I near saddled Buttercup, but I glanced at the house, remembering they might need her for the fields. 'Sides, taking Peter's bicycle would be faster. After I returned the shed key to its hiding place, I pushed the bicycle outside, then swung my leg over it, wobbling a bit as I pedaled up the hill out of the holler. Then I turned south down the mountain, the tireless rims clacking against the stones in the road as my mind twisted with the road.

Not 'til I was halfway to town did I think about the fact that if'n I was confronting the devil in his lair, I might not ever come back.

—ANNIE—

Peter shut the cabin door behind him and sank into the davenport next to me. His head hung in his good hand, the hook sitting uneasy on his leg.

Outside, Rosie laughed and Dovie May sang some silly song. Life as it should be.

"Where's Sam?" I sniffled, and the burn of the smoke smoldered in my chest. I coughed, wishing I had the strength to pull it all together so's my fear and sadness wouldn't drip out of me no more.

"Fire's out."

A queasy feeling filled the bottom of my belly. Everything Peter wasn't saying said volumes.

"What'd he see this time?"

Peter leaned back against the cushions and sighed. "Said he found opium and a ledger under a loose floorboard in the shed."

"Opium?" Panic sent my voice climbing. Daddy'd tell me I should've made Sam stay working for him. He would've protected him from the war, and I wouldn't have been sitting in my mother-in-law's cabin afraid to walk into my own house on account of the fact that my husband had gone plumb crazy.

I loosened the scarf at my neck, desperate to get a little more air. "What am I going to do, Peter? You won't stay here forever."

"Still don't have nowheres to go at the moment." A lazy smile lifted one side of his mouth.

I saw the old Sam there, and I near choked.

"Oh, Annie." Peter reached to pull me into a sideways hug, but then he stopped, his fingers straying to my neck.

I plucked at the scarf as shame scorched my cheeks. "He didn't mean—"

"Didn't mean to wrap his hands around your neck? Those are fingerprints. That don't happen by accident."

"He was dreaming." The answer was lame in my own ears, and Peter cocked his head like he might've heard me wrong.

Through the window, I watched a bright-yellow warbler as he hopped on a branch, happily chattering to his mate. Part of me wished it would storm on the happy bird's head, and the other part wished to turn into the swan from *Swan Lake* and fly away with the warbler. If only it were that easy.

"This is my fault." Peter's voice sounded hollow from behind his hand scrubbing his face, and I almost missed the words.

"What?" I leaned forward so's I could see him clearly. "How is this your fault?"

"I knew what was happening, and I didn't stop it." He groaned and struggled to his feet. "We gotta go find Sam."

I followed in Peter's wake, trying to figure out what he had planned. But Peter always held himself in. It was one of the many ways he wasn't like his brother.

Dovie May watched us as we passed her in the yard.

"You seen Sam?" I asked. I was somehow glad when she shook her head.

Peter stomped away, nothing deterring his mission. What would he do when he found his brother? What would I do?

"Sam?" Peter shouted into the yard loud enough to wake any critter that might be napping on a sunny morning.

Dovie May grunted as she levered herself off the ground. I shook my head, and she corralled Rosie into her cabin. The fact that she didn't ask why near broke my heart. Even Sam's ma knew something wasn't right, and we hadn't told her nothing.

While I turned into my house, Peter broke off to search the barn. I opened the door to the kitchen, where the forbidding darkness spilled into me. A body can hide where the light is closed out, but the devils can hide there just as easy.

"Sam?" My voice echoed in the room. As I tiptoed to the pantry, my fingers trailed over the Victrola. If only we could turn back time. Was Peter right that all this was our fault? Could we have stopped Sam's nightmares? Stopped him from setting that fire?

Unease pulsed through me, and I bolted into the breezeway, closing the thoughts in behind me. I near ran through the living side of our house and even checked the outhouse before I allowed myself to seek out my brother-in-law.

In the barn, I found Peter hitching Buttercup to the wagon. "He took my bicycle. My guess is he took his suspicions to town and is hunting trouble."

My hands wound in my skirt. I didn't know what to do with Sam, but if he went to town accusing folks, they wouldn't care that his mind was tangled up. "Peter, they'll kill him."

Peter's mouth flattened to a grim line. He knew it just as well as me.

———

The ride to town never felt like it took so long. I was grateful Dovie May had stayed home with Rosie and offered to do what chores couldn't wait the best she could. But I could've used the distraction of entertaining my girl. As the trees crawled past, I tried to play the game Dovie May taught me when I was a child, hunting for and naming animals or cloud formations or pretty leaves. But all I saw was the black stripe shadows of the trees looking for all the world like prison bars. And after that, nothing took my mind off the fact that we were racing to save my husband.

Before we even turned onto Central Avenue, the sound of traffic and crowds and busyness invaded my ears, breaking me. There were people everywhere.

"How are we going to find him?"

"We'll start with Doc," Peter said, confident as if he had it all planned. "We can use his telephone to cover more ground more quickly."

In front of us, an automobile screeched to a halt, and Peter cursed, yanking on the reins. His hook slipped on the leather, the reins leaping away like they were happy to be free. I gripped the rails bracing for a collision, but Peter snagged the limp line and whipped away from the crowd milling on the sidewalks without so much as breathing heavy.

I was still gasping when Peter shouted, then leapt up and waved. Doc, head down, strode around the corner, his speed causing him to hop on his good leg to catch up with himself. Peter dropped to the bench and yanked on poor Buttercup again so's she near sat on her haunches in an effort to turn the wagon. He snatched the edge of my sleeve, righting me while still managing to navigate the turn and ignore the automobiles blaring their horns. If we weren't in such a panic, I'd say Peter might've been enjoying himself just a hair too much.

At the sound of the horse bearing down on him, Doc bolted to the side, one hand holding his bowler hat firmly, the other shaking a fist at us 'til he saw who it was.

"Thank the Lord. I need all y'all's help. The Judge called."

I scooted over on the bench, adjusting the scarf around my neck while Doc hauled himself into the seat next to me, still talking and blessedly not noticing. "Sam's gone over the edge. He's at city hall."

Peter cursed again and urged the horse around the streets. Doc patted my knee and smiled at me like he was trying to be brave but couldn't quite do it. His hands twitched, and he clasped his fingers together in his lap, his mouth moving like he might be praying. I didn't think it was a bad idea, but I didn't know what to say to God no more. He'd do what He thought was best more'n likely . . . and I might not like it so very much.

Prayer done, Doc pulled out his pill case, then selected the last white circle with shaking fingers and popped it into his mouth. A headache of my own bloomed behind my eyes, and I wished Doc had another aspirin for me.

When Peter turned the last corner, the squat government building appeared, and I near cried from relief.

Sam was on the steps, alive for now. But he was hollering at Gus and Daddy so loud I heard him already. "You stay off my land, ya hear?"

Traffic clogged the street, and as soon as Peter slowed Buttercup to a stop, Doc slid from the wagon. I scrambled after him, tripping over my skirt. No way I was going to wait for the agonizingly slow traffic to crawl up to the hitching post.

"Sam!" My voice cracked from the strain. I lifted my skirts and ran fast as I could, not caring that I'd left Doc behind or who saw my knees. Storefronts flew by, and I knocked into folks, not even bothering to apologize. Whatever they were saying behind their hands likely wasn't good, but I didn't stop.

Surely Gus wouldn't do nothing serious. Not without Daddy's blessing, and I couldn't believe Daddy would allow it. Least not in front of me. If I could only get there.

"Officer?" At Gus's word, a deputy shoved himself off the city hall wall and sauntered down the steps like a mountain lion stalking his prey.

I flew up to Sam, then yanked him back and thrust myself between him and the other men. "You leave him be."

Gus licked his lips, sneering at me. "You gonna protect him all by your lonesome, sweetheart?"

Sam's grip tightened on my arm, but I stretched as tall as I could. I'd knock Gus 'cross the head again if I had to. Didn't rightly know what I was going to do with Sam myself, but wasn't nobody locking my husband up, especially the likes of Angus Martin.

Gus took a step toward me like he would challenge me then and there.

"That'll be enough, Gus." Daddy's voice was quiet, low, and

carried a hint of deference I'd never heard from him. Least not for Gus.

Doc huffed up the steps behind me, followed by Peter, who placed a steadying hand on his brother.

"Good night, Charlotte Anne." Daddy pulled off his fedora and wiped at his balding head with his kerchief. "Did you gather up everybody you knew and bring them?"

"I know what I'm up against, and I ain't backing down from this. You leave my family be." My voice was ragged with panic, causing Gus to chuckle.

"I ain't after you." Daddy shooed the officer away and glared at Gus. "Leastways not to lock nobody up."

"You just stay away from us." Sam's muscles bulged under his shirt, and I clung to him praying that we could still head off a war none of us would survive.

"Wasn't me that come storming to town with a cockamamie story." Gus reached 'cross his body to his waistband, and Sam angled me behind him.

"Let me take care of this, Angus." Daddy laid a shaking hand on Gus.

My mouth went dry. Don't think I'd ever seen Daddy tremble. It could only mean one thing—he wasn't in charge anymore.

Sam held me tight, standing tall and not letting me back away. Hunters always went for the kill when someone turned tail and ran. And while Sam never played the prey, there was no guarantee Gus wouldn't attack anyhow. *Come on, let it go.*

Gus hesitated, his fingers tracing a gold chain across his spreading middle before he nodded and walked a few paces up the steps like he was some kind of god holding court over all of us mere mortals.

Sweat trickled down my back, and I shook it away. What I wouldn't do for the shotgun full of buckshot about now. "We'll be leaving, then."

I turned to go, but Daddy snagged my arm.

"Doc," he said while keeping his eyes trained on me. "You make sure he don't come back this way. I gotta talk to my family in private."

Doc's glance shifted from Daddy to me, but I smiled, granting permission. I could hold my own against Daddy out here. He dragged me down the steps a mite, Sam trailing.

"You gotta back off, Sam." Daddy glanced around him like someone might be listening from behind the straggling bush. "You don't know who you're messing with here, and I don't know if I can protect y'all."

"We don't need protecting." Sam growled and stomped down the steps. Peter followed Sam, snatching the bicycle, then trotting to catch up. The two brothers walked side by side, dark heads tilted together. Maybe Peter could talk some sense into my husband.

"I don't understand. Why's the mayor care what Sam thinks about Gus?"

"It ain't the mayor I'm worried about. You just keep your husband out of Hot Springs for now. You hear?"

I blinked at Daddy, not understanding but nodding all the same. Who other than the mayor and his goon Owney could scare Daddy? Whoever it was had to be near powerful as the devil himself. I scrambled after Sam, leaving Doc to hobble after me, the click of his leg brace stabbing into my thoughts.

I caught up to Sam and slipped my arm through his. My head held high, I pretended we were out for a stroll like everybody else. But my heart pounded, and I expected to see the sheriff following with his gun and handcuffs.

Ladies do not let anyone see them sweat.

But Mama, even you'd be sweating this time.

Sam yanked at Buttercup's reins to untie them, then clambered into the wagon seat, not even offering to hand me up with him. I turned and waited for Peter to stow the bicycle, then for Doc as he shoved through the pressing crowd. When he looked up, I near fainted; his face was pale as a ghost, and his eyes were wide with fright.

Doc stumbled to a halt in front of me, grasping Peter for support. "They're gonna come after Sam. The Judge left, and Gus sent the deputy to try for a warrant."

Peter swore, then swore again for emphasis. "You hear that, Sam? You let your fool temper get away from you, and now they're coming after you."

The heat from the sidewalk rose up and scorched my skin. Hell itself reaching to pull us in. I leaned against the wagon, not trusting myself to stay upright no more. Would this nightmare never end? Peter lifted me into the wagon seat, and I scooted over, my leg bumping Sam's. I leaned away.

"Annie?"

"Don't, Sam. Not right now."

Peter climbed in. "Doc, do what you can to stall them. We'll take care of things up on the farm."

Doc nodded and hobbled back toward the government building. Sam clucked to Buttercup, and she eased into the traffic.

"You do know they won't hesitate to throw you in jail or worse." Peter slammed his hook against the bench, leaving a groove in the wood.

"I ain't afraid of the Judge, little brother."

"Well, maybe it ain't him you oughta be worried about. You forget who runs this town? You ain't been gone that long."

"They're dangerous," Sam said like he was pointing out something we didn't know.

"Of course they're dangerous." I felt near on exploding. "So why are you poking at them?"

"I didn't go to war, didn't go through what I went through, to come home to this."

"This?" My voice rose, and I dug my fingers into my legs, fighting for control. "*This* is me and your daughter and your ma. That's your responsibility. Taking care of us, not—"

"What do you think I was—"

"You willing to throw us away for something that may or may not have happened?"

Sam flinched, and I wished I could snatch the words back, tell him I didn't mean it. But lies never helped nobody.

"You know I love you more than anything." Sam touched my leg, and for all its irrelevance, the kindness sent tears spilling down my cheeks.

"You think you can win if you fight them direct? This ain't the war. There's different rules here."

"Good Book says it ain't never right to let nobody get taken advantage of." My husband's righteous spouting made about as much sense as purple dirt, but he wasn't going to hear none of it.

Peter cleared his throat. "Bible also says more than a little about being wise. There's better ways than all-out war, Sam. You know that as well as I do. And what you did today was declare war on folks who don't have issue with killing women and children."

CHAPTER Twenty-One

—ANNIE—

They were coming after Sam. My shaking limbs collapsed at the porch steps, and I couldn't summon enough strength to stand, let alone pack food and blankets and clothes for Sam to go hide somewhere.

I nibbled on my nail while I watched light dance through the trees. Following the stretches of limbs into the sunshine, the blue extended to eternity. What would it be like to live up there? Forever seen and known. Looked forward to. Loved. Protected.

"If'n you keep doing that, you ain't going to have any fingers left." Dovie May's teasing wiped the dream from my mind.

"How can you joke at a time like this?" I hid the bleeding cuticles in the folds of my skirt. I'd nearly lost myself in thought, forgetting someone here read me well.

Dovie May wrapped her arm around me. I sat stiff against her, trying to figure out how to move forward.

"I feel like Goldilocks. I found a life that was just right only to discover there's bears after it."

"You might just find those bears is friendly. I know it ain't easy, but you used to trust Sam. Why'd you stop?"

And that was the question everybody was asking. But there wasn't anybody with an answer. Before the war, I followed my husband without question. But now . . . now the man couldn't even walk outta the house without me questioning it. Problem was I never knew what he was going to do or say. As if flying into Hot Springs and riling the entire mob wasn't enough, on the way home he'd told me stories that must have been dreamed up by the devils themselves—mysterious men hiding opium under loose panels in the shed. As if the mob needed our shed to do their dirty work. 'Sides, Peter had already searched the shed, and Doc had too.

"You think on that, darlin'." Dovie May groaned, hauling herself up with the railing. "In the meantime, we gots to hide Sam."

I set Rosie to hulling peas on the porch so she could use the husks to make a bed for her dolly. It would keep her busy while I figured out what all needed doing.

"I'll gather some blankets and a change of clothes." Dovie May shuffled into the living side of the house while I trudged into the kitchen.

I lit the lantern and took it to the pantry. What could Sam eat that didn't need cooking? I tied some jerky together with a string, grabbed the last jar of peaches, and took some of the beet greens and settled it all in a bag.

Lord, the navy probably gave him better rations than this. What else could I give him?

I turned a slow circle and spied the remainder of Dovie May's Karo nut pie. I lifted the towel, and the decadent smell of caramelized sugar slammed into me. Just yesterday I'd cut through the pecans glistening in the sugary filling, and we'd laughed and danced and . . .

Sure as corn kernels grow corn, I wished today had never come. But since that dream carried no more weight than a dandelion seed, I'd send Sam with memories of us that he couldn't ignore so's he'd remember what was at stake. I snatched a knife and empty canning jar, then cut a piece of the pie, dropped it in the jar, and sealed it with a feeble prayer.

Come back to me, Sam.

Wiping my fingers on a towel, I peeked out the door to check on Rosie. My fingers bit into the doorframe to keep me from collapsing. Daddy was sitting on the porch laughing with my little girl.

He tossed his fedora into the air, letting it spin 'til it landed square on Rosie's head and dropped down to her nose. Fear trickled along my arms like a winter's rain. I wanted to hide in the kitchen and storm the porch in equal measure. Daddy'd only come to the farm one other time—the day after Rosie was born, when Dovie May had run for provisions and I was alone and weak as a newborn kitten.

Just like then, I smelled the storm coming, burning the air before the clouds billowed over the bulrushes. Don't know why he'd come now. Maybe he thought stepping between us and the law might change things between him and me. But he couldn't say anything that would change what I'd told him when Rosie was born. I wasn't leaving Mattas Peach Orchard, and he'd have no chance to pollute his granddaughter.

Rosie spun a circle, her little-girl dress and pinafore lifting, dancing with her. I cringed at the dirt on her knees, the stain from breakfast and ragged hem of her dress. Daddy'd see all the things left undone but miss everything important. Rosie was fed, loved, and safe. Wasn't nobody going to hurt her here.

I glared at the man sitting on the stoop like he belonged there. My shadow covered him, and he glanced up, happy as you please, like he'd gone and saved the world.

I smiled at my girl, trying to hide the anger and fear crackling through my body. "Darlin', why don't you see if you can find Bailey. I bet the Judge here would love to see the best barn kitty in the world."

Rosie stopped mid-spin, then clapped her hands to her mouth, absolutely in love with the idea, and went skipping off in search of her favorite playmate.

"Ain't many friends up here for a little girl."

"I don't have time for you right now, Daddy." I clenched the towel in front of me like it was a weapon, and I turned back into the kitchen, where I proceeded to clean, frantically hiding dirty dishes and bric-a-brac that build up from life with a child. Daddy's presence crowded the room, pinning me to the counter.

"I don't want anything. Doc and I just came to warn you that the sheriff's coming for Sam. He'll be here soon."

"Why you coming to warn us when you could've just stopped him?" And why'd Doc go get Daddy? Next time I saw Sam's best friend, I'd give the man a tongue-lashing he wouldn't soon forget.

"There's some things I don't have control of no more. I just want to help."

"We don't need your kind of help." I turned on Daddy, giving him my best attempt at intimidation.

He sighed, easing into the chair at the head of the table—Sam's rightful place. When he picked up Sam's picture from the table, I turned my back.

"I'm family." His voice held more than a smidgen of pleading, but I slammed down the pity.

"You gave up the right to call yourself that a long time ago."

"Like it or not, I'm the only one around here that can help you. They'll lock him up, Charlotte Anne."

"Is that a threat?" The shotgun rested next to the door, and I wondered if Daddy would stop talking if I aimed it at him. I don't think I'd actually shoot him. But if he didn't stop, I just might. Sam was stronger than the war, stronger than whatever devils preyed on his mind. We could survive anything . . . even this.

Daddy's hands splayed out on the table, watching me stare at that gun. "You got a place to hide him?"

My teeth ached from the strain of clenching them. I slammed a fist on the counter.

"I have had enough, Daddy. Enough! You come in here acting like there ain't nothing that happened between us, acting like you want what's best. You never once said anything about Mama. You know I found her. You know I watched as they pulled her out, mouth all screwed up in a scream, gray as old barn wood, blue lips, blotches on her cheeks from no air, pockets full of rocks. And you said nothing. Nothing at all. You just brought me home from Dovie May's and . . ."

Daddy sat unstirring, white as marble.

"Do you know I still have nightmares? Some nights I can't close my eyes without remembering Ma in that pond. You and your whoring, your drinking and gambling. You think that's a better life? You think the life that killed Mama is what I want for Rosie? For me? Well, it ain't. We don't need you. We'll protect Sam and be just fine without the almighty Roswell Erwin Layfette."

Daddy sat head down, watching his fingers spin that godforsaken hat of his, not saying nothing. Wrinkles etched into his forehead, the gray winning the battle against the black still on his head.

"Well?" Why wasn't he saying nothing? Why wouldn't he look at me?

"You're right. I wasn't there when you needed me. And I should've been."

I took a step backward, instinctively gauging the distance to the door. There was no such thing as a quiet, calm Daddy, and now I was a mama bear ready to protect her cub just like my mama had tried to protect me.

I edged toward the door, sneaking a kitchen knife behind my back, wrapped in a towel. Where was Rosie? She should've been back by now.

"Doc says Dovie May's not doing so well."

My eyes snapped back to Daddy, trying to cipher what was behind the flat expression on his face.

"What's that got to do with anything?"

Daddy stared at his toes. His shoes, usually bright and shiny as a summer day, were mud splashed—even had a small footprint across the toes.

Right then I knew. They wouldn't be content just coming for Sam; they'd come for all of us. To squash us all like bugs without a second thought. And I hated Daddy even more for knowing. For being the one to tell me.

He stood, shaking his head. "There was a time when you were my little girl. You remember that? You'd put on dance shows just for me. Take me out to moving picture shows and a soda after. Certainly wouldn't have felt the need to sneak a knife behind your back." His lips smirked, but his eyes were hangdog long. He rubbed the edge of the table with a thumb, smiling at the smooth, perfect corner Sam had made.

"Your Sam is a good man. He found a way to train himself better than I would've been able to. He'll find his way back."

I tightened my grip on the knife, but Daddy held up a palm.

"I'm just asking you to let me help you until he does."

If it were just me, I'd tell Daddy where to take his offer. But it wasn't. I had Rosie to think about. Dovie May too. I found myself nodding all while wishing I wasn't making myself beholden to this man again.

"It's settled, then. You get Sam hidden, and I'll do what I can when the sheriff comes."

He started toward me, but I turned my back on him, the man I used to run to when I cried. The last one I would go to now.

I set the knife down and braced myself on the countertop, knowing it was solid. The knife tangled in the cloth blurred wavy behind the water in my eyes. They were coming for us. Seemed there was nobody who'd escape my curse. Who would save my daughter?

"Papaw! Papaw!" My Rosie staggered into the breezeway, arms tight around Bailey's front legs and chin.

I wiped my face with my apron, then pasted on a smile. "Oh sweet girl, you got to be careful with the kitty."

Daddy grinned like he'd beat the odds in every single horse race across the country and squatted on the tips of his toes so the knees of his suit hovered over my unswept floor.

He rescued Bailey, tucking the cat's back legs up into my girl's arms. "There, now. What a big girl you are. Bet Bailey loves his mama as much as your mama loves you."

My girl lit up right proud.

"And with love like that, there ain't nothing bad that can hurt too much."

Slapping his fedora against his leg, he pushed himself to his feet. He ruffled Rosie's hair all while watching me try to calm the shaking of my hands in my dress pockets. Love helps whole heaps of things, but I wasn't so sure it would stop the bad entirely. Sometimes it just made things a whole lot worse.

Daddy stepped back out into the sunshine and disappeared round the corner of the house—as much of a ghost as ever.

CHAPTER
Twenty-Two

— S A M —

Sure as the sun rises in the east, I'd messed up good this time. Doc was scared enough he brung the Judge. And even the Judge paced the barnyard like Al Capone was aiming for him. Everything in me wanted to stay behind and protect my family. But Doc was right. It wasn't heroic to put folks in danger because I didn't want to look lily-livered. Sometimes the bravest thing to do is retreat and find another way round. And you best believe I was going to hunt down another way.

While Ma and Annie put together provisions, Peter, Doc, and I put together a plan. Doc had closed down the clinic and would stay at the farm for a few days to help make sure nothing happened. I would hole up like a coward at the old tree fort Pa built with Peter and me. It was a secret just between the Mattas boys and Annie, so Doc and even Ma didn't know where it was hidden out in the woods.

I was loitering in the barn, doing as many chores as I could to help and holding off leaving when the Judge came in. I finished brushing out Buttercup's leg and straightened so's I looked straight into my father-in-law's icy blue eyes. He'd been behaving mighty strange, and I knew better than to back down just because an enemy was acting peaceful.

The Judge nodded to me, then leaned against the doorframe, his eyes flitting back toward the house. Worry lines between his brows furrowed deeper. I peered through the dust floating in the bright sunshine, fully expecting a ghost to drift out of a hidden corner. I couldn't figure why he was so worried.

"I'll stay and help you out of this muddle best I can," he said. "But you need to hightail it out of here. They ain't likely to let this rest if they see hide or tail of you."

He wasn't angry, really. He was disappointed and resigned, and that fact threw me all out of whack. The unspoken agreement between us was that he'd leave us alone if'n I protected his daughter. It was a bargain we'd both kept until I'd gone and dumped Annie smack-dab in the middle of the biggest mess I'd ever seen.

But the fact that Annie was in danger at all made me all kinds of upside down. The Judge answered to the mayor, and the mayor didn't have no qualms with me . . . at least as far as I saw. I just didn't want Gus on my land no more. The only answer that made a lick of sense was that Gus didn't answer to the Judge.

I dropped the brush in the tack box with a *thunk*, the finality of the noise the perfect melody to my life. There wasn't nothing I could ask that the Judge was gonna answer. I knew that.

So I just said, "Yes, sir," then trudged across the yard and up the porch steps to the living side like a misbehaving teen. I yanked open the door, nearly colliding with Annie. The enormous navy bag on her shoulder threw my wife off-balance, and I caught her round the waist so's she wouldn't topple. She was soft under all her fierce strength, and emotions darted through her huge eyes like clouds across the sky.

"I'm sorry, Annie. It'd be easier for you if I wasn't here." I thought of the dancing, the laughter, all reduced to ash by the constant concern, the nightmares. The reality of it choked me. My own foolishness was driving me away.

Annie kissed my forehead, the sweet smell of my own fear slowly blown away by the mountain breeze. "Pretty sure it'd be easier for you if *I* wasn't here sometimes."

Fear slithered up my body like a rattler. "Ain't nothing easier without you here."

Ma peeked around the door with a smirk wide as the ocean. "Seems we're all exactly where we're supposed to be, doing exactly what the good Lord wants us to be doing. Helping each other."

"I'd rather not need the helping."

"My Herbert used to always say, 'The same God who made rainbows and sunshine also made the thunder and lightning.'" Dovie May wrapped one arm around me and one around Annie so we were all held together as tight as her strength would allow. "I have to believe He knows what He's doing."

Dovie May released us, then slid around me into the breezeway. "Rosie's taking her nap, and I'll let you say your goodbyes. But don't dawdle none. The Judge says the law ain't far behind him. And if'n he's worried, I'm doubly so."

Annie clutched the straps of my pack. "I just got you back."

I lifted the straps off her shoulder and eased her stiff body into my chest. "I'll be up in the old fort. Remember the one?"

Annie nodded into my chest. And I couldn't help wishing I were bringing her back up there again for a secret picnic. Instead, I'd be hiding all by my lonesome.

"It was stupid of me to go down there." The words tumbled out, piling onto my guilt like I hoped to bury it. "I'm just a crazy ole veteran who stepped on a bee's nest. They'll forget about me soon enough." I hoped my crooked smile reached all the way to my eyes so's she'd believe me even if I didn't believe myself. "And once their anger runs out, I'll be back." *I hope.*

Slinging the pack onto my back, I retreated through the breezeway. As I plodded up the path to the woods, I glanced back. Peter, Doc, and the Judge all stood at the bottom of the porch steps solemn as pallbearers at a funeral.

"I won't give up on you," Annie shouted, and I blew her a kiss before turning back up the mountain. Annie wouldn't give up on me, but who was going to save *her*?

Should've left it alone. The memory of the voice before the fire flickered through my mind. And whoever said that was right. I should've left it alone.

Please, God. Protect my family.

—ANNIE—

Sam hadn't been gone more than an hour when the sheriff's car stopped at the top of the lane. Gus lumbered out one side, and the sheriff popped out of the other like one of them hideous jack-in-the-boxes—gruesome smile and all.

Daddy emerged from the side of the house between me and them, and it felt like a Western shoot-out.

I knew good and well that predators were more likely to attack when they smelled fear, so I lifted my chin and stood on the porch steps in plain sight. But I still shifted Rosie behind me and wished my skirts were Western-movie wide so's they'd hide her.

"Angus." Daddy nodded at Gus. "Sheriff Watkins. What brings y'all up here?"

The sheriff blanched and near tripped over his own tiny feet, but Gus strode up to Daddy like *he* was the boss.

"You know what we're after, Ross."

I gripped the rail and wished—God forgive me—that I'd killed the man when I'd had the chance.

"Last I checked I wasn't no gypsy mind reader." Daddy glanced at me and winked like he was playing some kind of game.

The sheriff wrenched the barn doors open partway, then stopped when Daddy hollered after him. "Sheriff Watkins, I know you ain't got a warrant. You sure you want to choose this side?"

Watkins hesitated a moment, considering Daddy before he yanked his sidearm out of its holster.

Just as the sheriff turned back, Doc sidestepped through the barn doors with Peter behind him.

"Won't find nothing in there, Jim. But you're welcome to search it." Doc pushed the doors open wide so's the sunshine filled the barn. Buttercup nickered at the officer, and I heard the man search through the haymow, stabbing a pitchfork to the floorboards. The deep thud of it echoed again and again. If Sam had been in there . . .

I sucked in a breath, pressing my knuckles to my teeth to prevent me from crying out. Sheriff Watkins wasn't looking to find Sam; he was looking to kill him.

When the sheriff emerged from the barn, I near sighed in relief. It was ridiculous. I knew Sam wasn't there. But all the same, I was mighty glad that horrible man came away disappointed.

Gus, however, stomped up the porch steps, then pushed Dovie May out of the kitchen doorway. I cringed as I watched through the door, clutching my mother-in-law while the bull of a man slammed through the pantry and my cupboards. Just as the crash of a jar shattered the quiet, Daddy came from behind us and marched into the room.

"Angus, you best move on, now. You won't help your cause by destroying my family's food stores, and you know it."

His cause? What did Daddy mean? Dovie May grasped my shaking hands as Gus shouldered past us and barged toward the living side. The idea of him pawing through my underthings near made me lose what little I'd eaten.

Sheriff Watkins climbed the steps and tipped his hat to Dovie May and me. "Sorry about all this, folks. Just doing my job."

"Fiddlesticks." Dovie May raised a thin eyebrow at him like he was a naughty schoolboy making excuses for tugging the dog's tail. "This ain't upholding the law, and you know it as well as I do."

When Gus stormed back through the living room door cussing up a blue streak, the sheriff scuttled backward.

"There's a shed up on the hill." Gus pointed, leering at me like he knew something I didn't.

"I'll get the key," Peter said smooth as fresh-churned butter.

Doc followed me up the bottom part of the hill. From there we watched as the sheriff and the portly Gus struggled to keep up with Peter trotting up there.

My eyes strayed 'cross the way to the woods, praying that Sam was well out of range. "What's Gus hoping to find in the shed?"

"Don't rightly know." Doc popped two of his pills into his mouth. I frowned as Peter stepped back from the shed door. That place had been nothing but trouble since the veterans started coming home. Soon as we finished with that fertilizer, I might just burn it to the ground.

Gus yanked open the door and swept his hand for the sheriff to do his duty. He came out shaking his head and pointed Peter toward the house.

Peter's raised voice rattled throughout the orchard, but I could only start making out what he said as they drew closer.

"Fool sheriff don't know fertilizer when he sees it." He turned to holler at the men trailing him. "Ain't explosives no more. The government's the one that sold it to us."

"It ain't safe for a youngster." Gus's voice boomed over whatever Watkins was saying.

Sweat prickled on my scalp, and I snatched at Doc's arm. We turned, and I bounded up the porch steps and into the living room, pulling Dovie May with me. I slammed the door and barred us inside.

"Ain't nobody taking my daughter from me," I hollered.

Dovie May's head snapped up, and she hustled to Rosie's bedroom, slamming windows shut as she went. She couldn't know exactly what was going on, but I was glad she knew what to do anyhow.

Now the men were all shouting at one another, but Daddy's voice cut through them all. "You might have bought yourself the mayor's ear, but without me, you don't have the loyalty of everybody else. You keep pursuing this, and you'll have a fight on your hands."

There was silence.

Then in the distance an automobile engine started, and I slumped against the door shaking. Everything was starting to make a little more sense. Daddy wasn't in charge no more, and that meant we were in a whole heap of trouble, especially since it seemed Gus didn't view my husband as a harmless buzzy bee.

"Charlotte Anne?" Daddy's voice filtered through the door.

"Daddy?" My voice cracked.

"They're gone for now, darlin'." I hadn't heard him sound so tired in all my days. "Doc is following them in my Hudson to be sure they're gone. You come on out so's we can talk."

Dovie May peeked out of the bedroom door and nodded her agreement.

Using the table as leverage, I struggled to my feet and stood blinking away stars before I lifted the bolt and opened the door. Peter stood behind Daddy, and frustration, worry, anger, and something I couldn't name warred across my brother-in-law's face.

"Can they really take her?"

Daddy studied his feet, and I knew it was a stupid question. The law in Hot Springs did whatever they pleased, which meant we had to figure a way out on our own. And the fact that they were so set on finding Sam meant they had something to hide. He might not have been right about everything, but I was convinced Sam had seen something he wasn't supposed to see.

Lord, were we ever in a tangled mess.

"I'll sleep out in the barn tonight, Peter in the cabin so's we cover both places," Daddy said. He flashed a bright smile at Dovie May. "Hope you don't mind sleeping with Charlotte Anne and Rosemary. If we do have any trouble, you'd be safest there."

But someone had to go to the shed to figure out what Gus was hiding, and I didn't trust no one 'cept me to do it.

CHAPTER
Twenty-Three

—— S A M ——

In the midst of the forest, I sat hunkered down in my childhood tree fort that barely clung to a maple branch. With the leaves all furled out, I had a speckled view of everything from the starry sky to the shed just across the way and down to the roof of my house—tiny as a toy all that way down the mountain. I saw everything, but there wasn't much I could do without making this whole situation worse.

Even with three surplus blankets wrapped around me, I shivered. But truth be told, it probably wasn't on account of the nighttime chill. Down the mountain, my family was exposed. Open to Gus's attack.

Should've left it alone.

The words hammered on me, shifting and morphing. Even though I felt like I should have been able to place the voice, the answer dodged around just outside my reach. Maybe because it'd been said so soft. One thing was certain—the voice didn't belong to Gus. The man had sounded sorry, like he'd wished things could be different. But the laughter afterward—the one that had belonged to a second man—that had been Gus. The certainty of it had hardened when I watched him with the sheriff at the shed.

Gus was a brute to be sure.

I bit off some jerky and chewed it slow with my thoughts.

But that's all he was, a brute. He didn't have the knowledge or finesse to start an opium racket, let alone usurp the Judge's place. Roswell Layfette was sharp as a bayonet and just as deadly. Yet someone had gone and dethroned him. But who?

Ignoring the desire to go hunt out the answer myself, I snuggled into the blankets. I needed to hold the course. All my sleuthing had done was put my family in the crosshairs. Rosie had Annie, and Annie had the Judge, Peter, and Doc all there to protect her. Ma too. Wasn't no one going to get through all of them unless I mucked up the plan.

I inhaled, forcing myself to relax, using the techniques I'd learned in the navy to drop off to sleep even when my body and mind were flitting around like a bee without a nest.

Don't think I'd been asleep long when I snapped awake.

A thread of silver moonlight snuck through the roof of the tree fort, near blinding me. I breathed a prayer of thanks that it wasn't a storm and followed that with a prayer that it wouldn't start to raining neither. Just as I rolled over so's the light wouldn't wake me again, the barest whisper of sound reached me.

Opening the crooked door, I peered out across the fields, squinting down at the house. It was foolishness to think I would have heard something coming from there, but something in me thought if'n I could see the house, I could protect my family.

A shadow flitted from the woods away from the house and up the hill. Who in the world? The figure paused behind a tree, hesitated, and then floated the rest of the way to the shed.

Wind stirred through the trees, shushing, pleading with the world to be quiet, to ignore the shifting shadows. Just as the person reached the shed, a breeze ruffled across the hill, and a white dress fluttered out behind. Annie.

Another shadow detached itself from the far woods, and the world froze in front of me, an odd haze of ice filming the surface. I didn't dare move, didn't dare show where I was vulnerable. Annie could so easily slip through the surface. The devil only takes what matters most.

—ANNIE—

A gentle wind tugged at my skirt, making it float like a lady's ball gown. It had been simple to lift the padlock key from the barn during chores, but now, under the gaze of the cold moon, I wished I would've asked Peter to come with me to the shed after all. I hesitated, retying the knot in my shawl and mustering up my courage. I was here now, and I might as well take a gander. I groped around the shed wall until I found the lantern. Using a match from my pocket, I lit the wick, then closed the door against the night.

I lifted the lamp high, and the light magnified the shake in my body. All the fertilizer was so close to the flames. Probably should've brought a flashlight instead. I eased around the bags of fertilizer, holding the lantern as far back from them as my arm could reach. Sam claimed to have found a loose board somewhere back here. I stomped around, not exactly sure what I was searching for and feeling mighty foolish when I reached the end of the shed without finding anything. The flame flickered as I stared at the place where the empty floor met the empty wall. Now what? I thought back to what Sam told me in the wagon on the ride home. He'd walked the length and didn't find anything on the first pass either. I whirled round, determined to listen more careful this time.

When I'd almost reached the other side, a clunk sounded outside the door. In my scramble to blow out the lantern, I near dropped the durn thing. The door creaked open, and I huddled against the back wall, my heart thundering like it might just gallop away.

Footsteps shuffled to one side of the shed, and I sidled to the other. A shifting filled the shed like someone was tiptoeing behind the fertilizer. A little further and I could run for the door. If I made it to the woods I might be able to . . .

"Mama?"

I dropped the lantern, the glass shattering at my feet, and I stifled a screech. Lord Almighty, I was glad I'd worn my boots. "Don't move, darlin'. There's sharp pieces on the floor."

Feeling my way in the darkness, I edged back round, then swung my girl into my arms. "Rosie girl, what're you doing out of bed?" I raked through her tangles, trying to calm her as much as myself. How did she get past Dovie May?

"I following you." She shoved her fingers into her mouth, and I exhaled.

"What do you say we get back to bed?"

Rosie nodded, then snuggled her head into my neck. I'd just come back tomorrow, and we'd tear down that shed until we found enough proof so that the Feds would listen and stop whatever was going on. I didn't like to think on what was still a real possibility—that Sam had been wrong.

I closed the shed door and set the lock, but I couldn't get the key from my pocket with Rosie's backside planted over my hip. As I shifted her to the other side, I went to kiss her forehead, then stopped. She was gaping behind me, like she saw the devil himself.

I whipped around, my scream strangled by an enormous hand engulfing my mouth. I reared back, clutching Rosie to my chest. Wasn't nobody taking her from me, but whoever held me easily lifted me from the ground. I thrashed uselessly, a whimper escaping my throat as a needle pricked my arm.

My arm went numb, tingling. *God, protect Rosie.* She slid from my grasp, and I folded over struggling to catch her, falling, my head slamming into the rocks, the moonlight on the grass growing dimmer. But Rosie smiling? *God . . .*

CHAPTER
Twenty-Four

—SAM—

When the shadow stalking Annie proved to be a giant of a man, I threw the rope ladder out and didn't wait for the rungs to settle against the tree before I flew down it. I had no weapon other than anger and fear. But they were powerful, and I prayed they'd be enough.

Dashing through the trees and underbrush, I aimed for just downhill from the shed. More'n likely whoever had Annie had parked at the top of the lane, and that meant I'd have to cross the open ground of the garden before the trees in the orchard would hide me. Better to be behind the kidnappers until the trees protected my movements.

I hesitated at the edge of the woods, squinting at the shed for any flicker of motion. I near panicked when I didn't see nothing. But then two shadows sauntered in the distance—the giant and another, shorter figure, stumbling awkwardly through the peach trees. Maybe the giant was Peter and he'd joined Annie. Maybe I didn't have nothing to fear.

Then the taller one turned a bit toward the shorter, and I realized his hunchback wasn't actually a hunchback. Lord Almighty, the giant had my wife slung over a shoulder. There wasn't no way I could think on that without losing my mind for real.

So I pushed my body—sprinting across the open ground, my feet twisting and turning in the freshly plowed soil, the rise and fall of my breaths ragged and dragging on the bullet in my shoulder. But I was gaining ground . . . too fast. The realization slammed against me like I'd run aground. The two intruders were walking like there wasn't nobody to catch them.

But they hadn't counted on me.

I forced myself to slow down and think. If these were the men I'd seen before, there was another man unaccounted for. I scanned the area for a sign of him, but there wasn't no one else around. Maybe they'd left him in town? I padded forward, my head swiveling to keep a lookout for the missing accomplice, wishing Peter or the Judge would show up.

If I could get to the orchard just behind these two, I should be able to make up time and pass them without getting caught. I'd disable the car that must have brought them . . . or find something I could use as a weapon.

Being alone in enemy territory had taught me a thing or two. If only I could control my gasping. I wasn't ever much of a runner and fear swallowed up my breath. I peered through the darkness to track my progress, and a little head poked above the shoulder of the shorter man.

All the air exploded out of me.

Rosie.

Her head disappeared again, and I heard the murmur of voices, an exclamation. In her innocence Rosie must've said something about them being followed. Any second they'd turn and see me. With one last burst, I dove into the orchard and scurried behind a tree trunk. I didn't dare peek up the hill and expose the stark white of my face to the moonlight.

Footsteps rustled toward me, and I kept my panting as shallow and quiet as I could. A bird startled behind me and went flapping into the sky. The steps stopped, and little Bailey sauntered up the mountain.

Stay away, little kitty.

Bailey watched me for a minute and then trotted toward the voices. My body relaxed.

"Dagblamed cat." The voice cursed again before the man trudged back to his partner, who grunted like he was vexed at being disturbed by the critter. Then the footsteps resumed toward the road.

I held still a moment more and then ran, bent over, to speed past them. They'd turn downhill any minute, and I needed to be well past their line of vision before then.

Plunging into the heavier forest on the far side of the orchard, I clambered over fallen trees, where underbrush snagged at me like devil fingers. But I shook off the image. Wasn't no nightmare or trick of the moon going to stop me from saving my girls. Soon as I broke free from the forest, I scanned the road trailing further into the hills, just in case. There wasn't nothing between me and the footpath leading out into the meadow and the fork in the road leading across to the old Howell place, so I scrambled down the hill and round the bend.

There sat a 1940 soft top Lincoln-Zephyr Continental. I let out a quiet whistle. Only a few hundred of those had been made, and they didn't come cheap. Who in heaven's name was I up against?

Shuffling came from nearby, and I dove into the roadside ditch. Wasn't no time to disable the automobile. So I scrambled around on the ground to find a stick or anything sturdy enough to attack with. I couldn't risk hitting either Annie or Rosie, but if I took the men out at their legs . . . I hefted a sturdy branch, then squatted in the ditch and listened as their footsteps grew closer. Sweat pooled in my armpits, and my vision narrowed. I would not fail Annie. I couldn't fail her.

An enormous explosion ripped through the night, and I leapt to my feet, ears ringing, heart thrumming so hard I was sure it'd explode too. The entire night sky was lit from the top of the hill. Mesmerized, I watched pieces of the shed drift all the way down onto the plowed field. It was so quiet it might've been snow. They'd set the blasted shed on fire and exploded the fertilizer. Lord Almighty, what was I going to do now?

I near missed glimpsing the pair of shoes moving past, and I launched myself, slightly off-kilter, hollering at the top of my lungs while I chopped at the man's shins. He tripped, scrambling to keep upright, and my little Rosie let out a screech before she slipped out of his grip and crashed to the ground. The giant loomed over me. Though the moon behind him obscured his face, I knew it was Gus. I swung the branch again, but he jumped back, surprisingly agile for his bulk.

"You think taking me down would be that easy? Even the Judge can't stop me, and you ain't the Judge." He shifted an unconscious Annie on his shoulder and lifted his hand, the light catching on the barrel of his pistol. I scrambled away, tripping over the man on the ground and throwing myself into the deep ditch on the far side just as a crack echoed across the farm. My back slammed into the ground, my breath burst from my lungs, and I gasped, trying to get the air to refill my lungs.

Gus shot blindly into the forest, cursing. "That'll teach you to get in my way."

Gus holstered his gun, then pushed his accomplice in front of him to the car quick enough I didn't get a good look. Rosie peered to where I'd disappeared, shifting like she might leave her mama and bolt to me.

Run, Rosie girl. I'll save you.

But Gus snatched her and threw her into the car, dropping Annie on the back seat so Rosie couldn't escape. Rosie's voice lifted in a wail. Her little face peered over her mama's body, tangled and fearful. Surely her daddy would save her.

The other man pitched into the front passenger seat. Gus slammed the back door shut, cutting off the sound of my daughter and severing her from me. He scanned the ditch, hand on his holster, waiting for me to appear. My military training warred with my instincts. I wouldn't do nobody any good dead, but I wouldn't do nobody any good if I didn't do something. I pounded a fist onto the ground, then bounded out of the trench. But the war cry on my lips was stolen by another wail coming from down the hill. Gus pivoted and threw himself behind the wheel.

Peter burst into the lane on the far side of the car, and hope jumped in me.

Please.

As I reached the end of the lane, my brother dove for the handle, and the car ground to a start, my feet pounding, closer, closer, hopelessly far away. How could this be happening? Rosie's fists beating the window as Peter reached one arm inside the open door. The tires spit gravel, and the power of the car slammed the door on my brother's arm with a sickening crunch. Gus smirking as he passed, the growl of the car engine drowning my desperate yells and Peter's screams,

Rosie's tear-stained face in the back window, her arms reaching for me, the thud of my footsteps becoming louder and louder as the roar of the engine evaporated.

"No!" My scream burned my throat raw. Useless. Powerless. Falling, the gravel burning through my pant legs, scraping away my skin, my hope.

I knelt in the road, dust still flying round me, finding its way into my lungs, burying itself there. Don't rightly know how the ground didn't swallow me whole. I wished it would. I'd come home and brought the war with me.

My brother's moans slowly clawed through the ringing chaos, and the memory of the crunch snapped me into motion. *Oh, please, no.* Peter writhed on the ground, his body curled against the pain, his legs pumping like they might carry him away if they only tried hard enough.

I stumbled to his side, and my hands flitted over his body, coming away with sticky blood, history repeating. A jagged bone pierced through the skin of his good arm, his scarred stump cradling it, the hook dangling useless while blood seeped into the dirt around him.

I couldn't breathe. Why couldn't I breathe?

Peter opened his eyes and near lunged at me, crying out at the pain of the grating bone as he tried to latch onto the front of my shirt. "I'm sorry." He clutched at his arm, gasping with effort. "I'm sorry."

His eyes fluttered shut. Sorry? What in tarnation?

"Peter?" I touched his clammy cheek.

His eyes snapped open. "Get me down to the hospital, and I'll take care of everything. Hear? And find Julia."

"Julia?"

"The Judge's Julia." A breath rattled in his chest, and his head lolled back.

"Peter?" I shook him, but there wasn't no waking him.

My hands clenched into fists, and I wanted to break something . . . break *everything*. I slammed my hands onto the ground and screamed at the sky. "Why'd You let me live and come back if'n You was going to take it all anyhow?"

I wrested off my coat and balled it under Peter's head, hoping to make him more comfortable while every single bit of first aid training fled from my mind. Did I leave the bone sticking out? Snap it back in?

The hospital. Peter's words jerked me into action. I had to get my brother down there before the bleeding stole him. First I needed to staunch the flow. I ripped off my shirt and gently tied the rough fabric round his wound, but blood still gushed from his arm. Tourniquet. He needed a tourniquet. I tugged off my belt and wrapped it round Peter's upper arm. My sticky hands slipped on the leather as I wrenched it tight. When Peter didn't even flinch, I scrambled to my feet and sprinted toward the barn.

The pounding of my footsteps focused my thoughts. I'd get Peter to the hospital, then call someone to help me find Annie and Rosie. Don't rightly know who, but there had to be some lawman outside of Hot Springs who'd listen to a man who saw his wife and child stolen out from under his protection. Didn't make no sense to drag Julia into this neither.

I rounded the corner to the house, and Ma stood in the doorway of the barn in her robe with Buttercup bridled and the horse collar already on. God bless her.

"Couldn't finish hitching by my lonesome, but with Annie and Rosie outta their beds and that explosion and the shots, I knowed you'd need her more'n likely. Thank the good Lord He made sure the Judge was here too."

To prove her words, my father-in-law staggered out of the barn dragging the wagon behind him. I was torn between grateful and furious. The beginning of what to tell them escaped me completely, and all I could do was nod.

"Is that Peter's?" Ma's voice quaked as she pointed at me.

I held my hands spread out in front of me like I was giving something to her. The red had darkened and pooled in the creases of my palms. "Gus took Annie and—" My voice refused to admit that he'd taken my daughter, my angel.

Ma pulled me into her arms, and part of the weight lifted.

"Lord Almighty. Peter okay?" The Judge's voice was all flinty and dangerous.

"Gotta take him to the hospital. I think . . ." I forced my mind away from the image of his two useless arms. "I think he'll be okay." Last thing I needed was Ma's fear and the Judge's temper making things worse. I was struggling to hold mine back as it was. I yanked at the hitching straps instead of giving full rein to the dangerous mix of anger and fear burning in my belly. If'n the Judge had done something to stop this madness, ain't none of us would be in this mess in the first place.

Ma shuffled to the house in search of a clean shirt.

"We're lucky," the Judge said, flipping the harness round to me. "The fire the other night burned everything round the shed, and those clouds mean rain."

Took me a minute, but I realized what he meant. The burned field would mean the fire wouldn't spread. Lord, I hadn't even thought about that. *Please, let it rain.* Least the breeze was blowing away from the house and up toward the rocky peaks. Ma'd be safe until I could send help. The pressure of everything tore at me, hands shaking as I tried to fit the clasps around Buttercup's flanks.

"It'll be okay, son. You ain't alone in this," the Judge said as he finished hitching up the wagon.

Ma lumbered down the porch steps, my shirt waving in the wind. "What are you gonna do about our girls?"

My fingers shook as I buttoned the clean shirt she'd brought me, my joints cracking now with Peter's dried blood. I tried not to think on Rosie, her fear and confusion as to why her daddy didn't save her. And Annie. She'd had blood on her face. *Please, God.*

"Don't rightly know what I'm gonna do."

"I'll do what needs doing," the Judge answered for me. "It's past time somebody reined Gus in."

I didn't want to argue with him, but it was too late to be thinking on reining in one rabid dog he'd let loose. The whole lying, cheating enterprise needed to be put down for good. "It'll be okay, Ma." My voice broke at the knowing that there wasn't nobody in Hot Springs who could really help me. I didn't trust the Judge to do nothing but dump my brother at the hospital, then start a war that'd end up with my girls in the crossfire.

Ma held the reins while the Judge and I clambered into the wagon. "Well, here's what *we're* gonna to do." The bossiness in Ma's voice steadied me, and I'd never been so grateful for her telling what's what. "I'll do the chores that absolutely needs doing and keep an eye on the livestock and that fire. You get Peter help, then you call someone who ain't in Hot Springs."

Once I took hold of the reins, Ma stepped around to me and laid a hand on my leg. "But you listen good to your ma. None of this is your fault. You hear? You're the only one that saw what was happening. Ain't your fault none of us listened." She patted my leg and shot a glare at the Judge but continued talking to me. "Now, you go take care of your brother. And I'll worry about asking for help from Somebody who got the whole thing figured out already."

I knew exactly who she meant. Fact was God might already have it figured out, but it seemed to me like He might have gone and figured it wrong. Could I trust Him to straighten it out?

Ma hesitated a minute like she knew what I was thinking, but she didn't say nothing. When she stepped back, I clucked to Buttercup, and we raced to collect Peter.

Despite the fact I didn't want to be nowheres near the Judge, he proved helpful in hefting my brother into the wagon and snuggling him into a mound of blankets. Blood was already seeping through the edges of the shirt tied around his arm. Leaping into the driver seat, I drove Buttercup down the mountain, slipping, sliding, praying the wagon wouldn't fly over the edge of a cliff but also not willing to slow. I was grateful the Judge was back there keeping tight hold on my brother. There was just enough scrap of moon to light the path, and there wasn't nobody but us to get help.

CHAPTER Twenty-Five

—ANNIE—

I was cold, then hot. My head hurt. Strong arms cradled me into a firm chest. He smelled of a man—sweat, sawdust. What was Sam doing home? He should be hiding. Shouldn't he? And why was he so unsteady?

I wrapped my arms around his neck and snuggled in deep, only to have him pull away. Just like he'd done the first time we met. That time it was on account of me being soaking wet. But he'd listened to my pleas and took me to dry out at his farmhouse. As sure as I'm alive, it'd saved me from the worst scolding from Mama. Everything had been perfect. Warm, soft, just right.

Even though I'd been only nine, there was something safe about being in Sam's arms way back then. I found every excuse to go back to the Mattas house, and Mama miraculously let me. Maybe she knew how much I needed a hair of freedom. But it was probably on account of how very proper Mary Rose was.

Wait. Mary Rose. Rosemary.

There was something about a Rosemary.

Sam shifted my weight to walk through a rickety door, and I grasped onto his neck pulling him in closer, waiting for him to comfort me with a kiss, desperate to find something for my sluggish brain to latch onto. I squinted into the darkness trying to figure out where we were, but the world swam around me, and I couldn't focus. Had I hit my head?

"Annie." The voice was too smooth to belong to Sam. I leveraged my body round, sure I'd find the answer behind the wool coat holding me.

"Be still. I can't hold you when you're wiggling."

I quieted. That voice. My mind snapped back. It couldn't be Sam holding me. I opened my eyes with a start, flailing for balance. Good gracious, I'd nearly kissed Doc.

I leapt from his arms, apologizing profusely while he turned every shade of red I was sure I was turning too.

"Don't need to apologize." He sounded angry, but I couldn't puzzle out why.

Gulping back nausea, I sank to the floor, head between my knees. Where was Sam?

Doc knelt next to me, gently dabbing at the back of my head with a handkerchief. I touched my hair and gaped at my fingers coated in blood. Fear crawled up my legs like a host of fire ants.

"Doc?" Had he taken me someplace to treat the crack to my skull?

I turned, taking in the room—a kitchen. A mound of dirty dishes sat in the sink, but at least the wood floor seemed like it'd had a good brooming not too long ago. This wasn't no hospital or clinic, though. The room seemed to swim, and I hugged my knees to my chest to stop the shaking. What was happening?

Footsteps stomped up behind me, and I leaned into Doc despite myself.

"You just stay steady. You hear?" Doc's breath tickled my ear. "Everything's going to be all right if you just do what they want."

A pair of men's shoes appeared in front of me.

"The girl's asleep in the other room."

My fingers tightened around my ankles. Rosemary. Doc rubbed my shoulder like he was protecting me. He wouldn't let nothing happen to my girl. Would he?

The man squatted in front of me. Then his fingers clenched into my jaw and jerked my face up so's I was forced to look at him.

Gus.

Bile rushed up my throat. This must be his place. Good Lord, why had Doc brought me to Gus?

Gus reached to brush my hair out of my eyes, and I cringed away. He squeezed down on my arm. "You will do as you're told."

I nodded, hating that all my imagined strength had drained away.

Gus released me, then stood and sauntered away, the conquering tyrant, with Doc trailing.

"What in the world are we going to do now?" Doc's voice drifted away with his footsteps.

Please, God.

The words stalled in my throat. I knew there was some things God didn't stop. And there was some things you never came back from. My teeth bit into my lip, holding the fear at bay, the devil's whispers trickling up my arms.

Using the wall as leverage, I pushed to my feet. The floor beneath me seemed to tilt, and I rubbed at my forehead, willing my body to settle, for the world to stop wavering, for me to figure out what I was supposed to do. I brushed a twig off my skirt and a brittle leaf from my sleeve, flinching at the ache in my arm. The memory flooded back. The shed. The prick. Two voices. *Two* men.

Rosie smiling.

My knees buckled, threatening to spill me back to the floor.

Rosie'd been smiling because she saw Doc.

Doc had drugged me! He hadn't just come in after the fact. He'd been there the whole time. If I thought on it too hard, I might just curl up in a corner and never get up again. I gulped in a breath. There wasn't no question now. I had to get Rosie and me out before Gus decided what he was going to do with us. Wasn't nobody Rosie and I could trust but me.

A haze of light filtered in around the closed door where Doc and Gus had disappeared, along with the sound of a radio. The music covered their voices so's I couldn't make out what they were saying, but the light gave me just enough illumination to see. The sink was on the far wall, and a table and chairs commanded the center of the room. And there, on one side of the lit doorway, was another door. Is that where they'd put my girl? Swallowing, I edged toward the door, my hand trailing the wall.

"You said we wasn't going to hurt them." Doc's voice rose, and I froze.

"You were supposed to keep them away."

Doc's answer was muddled behind the radio.

"Nobody wants your excuses. We got to get rid of all the evidence . . . all of it."

A door slammed, and I jumped, eyes flashing round for a weapon. I dashed to the sink, digging through the dishes. No knife.

"Annie." Doc's voice slammed into me, my mind sinking down, down. "Please don't do something you'll regret."

There's something folks don't know about being trapped under the water. Sure it's cold and disorienting, but something about it slows your heart rate and focuses your mind. Sharp to a merciless point.

My fingers curled around a plate, and I whipped round, hurling it at Doc's head. The dish shattered on the wall, but Doc barely flinched. He bent over and picked up the pieces before he dropped them into a waste bin. Calm as you please.

He hesitated near the doorway. "You ain't gonna throw another one, are you?"

I wanted to throw every plate in the house at him, but it'd only bring Gus. A sob erupted from my throat. "Why, Doc?"

He dropped into one of the chairs at the table.

"Trying to pin down the cost of your choices is more than a little like figuring the height of your shadow. It changes depending on all kinds of things. One minute I think I've made the right choice, maybe even saved somebody's life. And the next, I know I've only made things worse and a whole lot of people are paying for the choice I made."

"You lied to us. There ain't nothing right about that. You were Sam's best friend. You were *my* friend. Why would you help Gus, of all people?"

He shook his head real slow like he couldn't believe I didn't know. "Dovie May always told me you have to crave something to be dishonest."

"What does that—"

"There isn't anything I ever wanted more than you."

I gripped the edge of the counter so's I wouldn't fall over. Somehow, I'd always known it. Why I'd been so skittish round Doc while Sam was away. But to hear it . . .

Had he been hoping Sam wouldn't come home?

"I needed the opium to control the pain so's I could help you. The sheriff caught me neat as a spiderweb, and the spider gave me a choice. In exchange for Gus continuing to provide the drugs for me, I could start distributing for his boss. Who'd question the local doc giving meds to folks?" A sad smile spread on his face, and he shrugged. "The alternative was jail. It would've destroyed my career and taken me away from you, but it also meant I'd have to admit to you how weak I was . . . how weak I *am*."

All those little pills he'd been taking weren't aspirin. I choked with a helpless fear coursing through me as it snarled with the anger and sorrow in one big, knotted mess.

"Oh, Doc . . ."

"I can't let him hurt you and Rosie, though."

"Then let us go."

"He'd only come after you, and I can't let that happen." Doc's wide eyes shifted toward the door before rubbing his hands across his thighs. "I'm leaving Hot Springs. I'd already decided that before tonight. Only way I can protect you is for you to come with me. You and Rosie. Gus won't follow us. I'm not important enough to him. And—"

"I can't leave Sam, Doc." I knelt in front of him, my knees protesting the hard floor, my stomach recoiling from being so near the man who'd sold us all for opium. "They'll kill him."

"If we don't leave now, Gus will torture you to get to Sam. He'll kill *you*." Doc's fingers wrenched on my arm, yanking me up and in close so I couldn't miss the fear, the anger scrambling through his face.

"Then you have to tell everyone the truth."

"What truth?" Doc shoved me, and I stumbled back. "That I sold drugs? All that'll do is get me thrown in jail. They won't touch Gus. You know what the law is like in Hot Springs."

"We'll call the FBI then, and—"

"And what? Make a deal? Gus protected his boss. I don't even know who it is. There's more here than you know. Besides, who'd believe an addict?"

"You're going to let them get away with all this?"

"I think you got me mixed up with Sam. I ain't no hero."

Lord Almighty, he sounded like a whiny child. I stretched tall, my eyebrow arching in full fury. "Then you don't got any notion of what love really is."

"Annie." Doc took my hand in his. He was shaking like the world might come to an end.

The door behind me opened, and I hefted another plate and sprang into a corner. Wasn't nobody going to do something without me fighting back.

A woman stepped through the door, the light glowing round her light-colored hat, and I near dropped the plate. It was Leah Belle.

"What in tarnation are you all doing here?"

I set the plate on the counter and burst into tears.

"Honey child." She pulled me into her arms and patted my back like I always wished Mama would. "You poor thing must be scared out of your wits. You go get your girl and we'll get out of here."

I had no idea how she'd found me or where Gus was, but she didn't have to ask me twice.

A chair scraped across the floor, and Doc stepped behind me like he was going to follow.

"You just give her some space. I'll take care of everything." Leah Belle snatched my arm.

With her near pushing me from the room, I stumbled a bit and caught myself on the doorframe. As I righted myself, I glanced back at Doc. With his eyebrows scrunched together and the tiny shake of his head, my heart near bounded out of my chest. Only time I ever saw him look like that was when Gerald Pitner was following me to the outhouse.

CHAPTER
Twenty-Six

—SAM—

By the time we skidded into the hospital drive, Buttercup was lathered, and the horizon was just turning a lighter shade of blue. The Judge hadn't said a word on the trip down, and my thoughts were all held tight behind a dam of control.

An attendant trotted out to help us lift Peter from the wagon bed. That done, the Judge said he'd be back after checking on Doc and taking care of "some other business." What business, I didn't dare ask, and I didn't have time to argue. But I did manage a "Don't do nothing stupid." The Judge nodded, then stalked away—a man on a mission.

Lord help us all, but I had Peter to attend to before I found my girls. I'd hunt down Gus come hell or high water. Mark my words.

The attendant and I hefted Peter into the blinding white of the hospital while the man peppered me with questions. I was so busy answering that I near missed the small, brunette woman standing guard behind the welcome desk. Julia. I took in her white dress and cap and remembered she worked here. I'd forgotten the Judge's gal was a nurse. No wonder Peter'd asked for her.

"Peter?" Without waiting for an answer, Julia scrambled round the desk and crashed through some swinging doors, yelling for a doctor. How such a tiny thing produced such a racket, I had no idea. But I'd never been more grateful in my life.

The attendant eased Peter onto a gurney. "Julia'll make sure he gets good care. I think she's more than a little sweet on him."

The Judge's girl sweet on Peter? And he'd been checking in at the hospital every week. The thought made me squirm more than a plateful of Ma's pickled beets.

Before I could even pretend to process that bit, Julia came back through the doors with a white-haired man in tow. The doctor peeked under the makeshift bandage, and I focused on Peter's face.

"You can fix it. Right?"

The doctor didn't do nothing to answer my question, and fear spiraled pictures through my head. What could a man do without the use of either of his hands? I clutched the edge of the gurney 'til the doctor caught sight of me and squeezed my arm.

"We'll take good care of him." Then he, Julia, and the attendant all disappeared through the doors with Peter. The doors swung back and forth and gave me glimpses of my brother retreating, smaller and smaller until I stood alone in the empty waiting room, thoughts crashing around the sterile walls, battering me with their force.

Now what?

Annie and Rosie. I scrubbed my face. Who do you call to report a kidnapping when you know the sheriff was involved with the ones that done the snatching?

Like Ma said, somebody outside of Hot Springs. The FBI was the only folks I could think of, but how's a body call them? I leaned over the desk, then hefted the telephone and dialed the operator. As soon as I asked for the FBI office, I knew she would let someone over at the mayor's office know somebody was snitching. But I didn't know another option.

Just as the operator connected me to the Little Rock office, the doors flapped open and Julia emerged, her eyes puffy with tears. I covered the mouthpiece and asked for privacy a moment. She frowned but stepped into a hallway around a corner.

Don't know what I expected from the FBI when a stranger calls and tells them a gangster kidnapped his wife and child, but I didn't expect them to just take a message. And when I told the person what I thought of that notion, she hung up on me.

I slammed the receiver into the cradle so hard that the bell rang in protest. I picked it up and slammed it down again. Julia came round the corner so fast I figured she'd been listening . . . either that or she didn't want her phone broke in two.

"Doctor Wilson will take care of your brother. He'll set that arm and Peter will be right as rain. Why don't you go for a bit of a walk? Maybe take some water to that horse of yours I see outside. We'll take care of things here."

"Ain't just Peter I'm worried about!" My voice echoed around the room, shouting back at me. "Gus took my girls, there might still be a fire up in the orchard, and—"

"Sam," Julia said calm as you please. "Did Peter tell you about me?"

"He said to come find you. You're a nurse."

"You think your brother was worried about himself when Rosie and Annie were in trouble?" She stopped, her eyes, wise and intent, said she knew more than she could tell me. When I opened my mouth to ask what she planned to do, she lifted her palm like a crossing guard. "You ain't the only one who can help. I'll send someone up to the farm, and we'll get Annie and Rosie taken care of too."

"Who's 'we'?"

But she just lifted the phone to her ear and motioned for me to leave.

I stomped out the thick glass doors, letting them slam behind me. You can plan your life, figure out how to handle every twist and turn, and still be thrown over the edge by an unsuspected breeze. And a hurricane just blew into my life.

———————

Outside, I found someone had tied Buttercup to a post. She was still puffing, and I was grateful Julia'd shooed me out. Taking care of the horse gave me something to keep busy with while my mind worked on what to do. All these folks told me they'd take care of things, but wasn't one of them I trusted. Not the Judge, not Julia, not a one. But I had no one else.

I rubbed the horse's nose a bit to thank her for being so sure-footed as we raced to town earlier. She nickered at me, saying *You're welcome.*

I was still cold despite the rising sun, so I put on the coat I'd used to cradle my brother's head. Then I unhooked the wagon and shoved it round out of Buttercup's way. After hefting a bucket of feed from the wagon as well as a water bucket, I staggered back to her. Exhaustion was coming on hard, but my girls, including my horse, needed me, and I wouldn't let no one or nothing else down. I loosened the mare's girth and bellyband, then switched out her bridle for the halter and set out the feed before going to find the water pump.

A man dressed in a white uniform pointed me to the side of the hospital. I found the pump and leaned my head against the cool of the brick while the tap spit water into the bucket.

"Sam?" I near jumped out of my skin when the Judge appeared at my side.

He bent and turned off the spigot. The morning light was harsh across the wrinkles burrowed across his face, matching the wrinkles in his suit.

"I should've gotten out long before now."

I grunted as I lifted the bucket. Water sloshed out and soaked the Judge's shiny black shoes.

"I tried before, but . . ." He closed his eyes like he could make the past disappear. "Anyway, didn't mean for any of this to happen."

I loosened the lead rope on Buttercup so's she could reach the water, then walked back to the wagon and grabbed the dandy brush, the Judge trailing me the whole time like a lost puppy. An unwanted puppy. I rubbed at Buttercup's sweat a bit harder than strictly neces-sary, and she glared back at me with a slight reprimand in the arch of her eyebrow. I patted her withers in apology, lightening the strokes, hoping the Judge would just go away.

"I just wanted to provide for my family better'n my pop did. Scrapin' by, eatin' whatever a body scrounged up in the woods. It ain't no way to live." The Judge shook his head.

His judgment of an honest life as a farmer and the shame of taking his help singed me deep. "There's places between starving and doing what you done."

"Don't get me wrong." He continued like I hadn't said a word.

"I missed Charlotte Anne's shenanigans and her ma. It started as a way to make ends meet, and then it just spiraled from there. I didn't mean for it to change me. I never thought I'd be the kind of person to do what I done, let alone lay a hand on a woman I loved. I didn't mean for any of it to happen." He sank to the edge of the sidewalk. "I tried to get out, but . . . After everything I done to protect her, I just can't believe I let them take Annie. Just so's you know, I just made sure they can't do it no more."

I stopped mid-stroke, trying to find words to all the questions that flooded my mind. But I was interrupted by Julia crashing through the hospital doors. That woman sure did make a racket wherever she went.

"Peter's awake and asking for y'all."

The Judge shot to his feet, and I glared at him for presuming my brother wanted to talk to the likes of him. Julia grabbed the both of us and shoved us through the doors.

"Peter is gonna need both of you if you're going to help Annie and Rosie." Julia'd transformed from the flighty tart on the Judge's arm to a no-nonsense drill sergeant. She stopped, considering me like she was judging whether I could handle what was about to happen. "There's things you don't know, Sam, but it's best if you keep your questions locked up for now and do as you're told."

CHAPTER
Twenty-Seven

—ANNIE—

Screams echoed in my ears, and I jerked awake.

I gasped in the gray light. Was it me who screamed? Was morning coming on already? All I wanted to do was sleep for the next month . . . or maybe a year. A door slammed, shaking the floor under me, and an automobile engine chugged away far in the distance.

The scream came again from nearby. Mama? How'd Daddy get in again?

My mind buzzed, and the world tilted, swirling away. I leaned against the wall, praying I wouldn't collapse. *Breathe. Just breathe.*

My knuckles burned white as the handkerchief in my hand as I clung to what was left of my sanity. I felt the floor stretching out beneath my legs before I realized I was sitting and I wasn't in Daddy's house. There was a rumpled bed in the corner, a door on the far side of the room.

And then I remembered. Before I could react to Doc's concern, Leah Belle had jammed a needle in my arm, shoved me into this room, and locked the door behind me.

"Sometimes the child pays for the sins of the father," she'd said.

My hankie fluttered to the floor, and I blinked back the memory of coming home from the pond, still dripping wet, the image of Mama's blue lips haunting. And there, stuck in the rose brambles was Mama's nightgown. How it got off the clothesline I'd never know. But there it was, tugging against a perfect red bud, trying to get away. As if the beauty in one bud might hold back the darkness and despair of a person's soul. Mama'd walked down from the farm, out to the pond, pockets full of rocks, and found a way to escape. But her freedom had only sucked me deep into an abyss, the ripples of her choosing to die spreading out from my core. I was paying for Mama's and Daddy's choices. The sins of the father . . .

Heart thundering in my ears like the dissonant chords of Debussy, my fingers pounded out the C-major scale on my leg, a maddening race to the top of the keyboard in a desperate attempt to set things right, to make my life fit the happy tones of the music.

I wanted to scream, run, fly anywhere. But more, I wanted to be strong. I wanted to escape. The scream reached my ears again. It wasn't mine. Rosie. Rosie was on the bed in the corner.

"I'm coming, darlin'. Mama's here."

Heaving air into my lungs, I stood on my drug-wobbled legs and shuffled across the room, only to trip over my dress that snarled between my legs and crack my knee on the hardwood floor.

I laughed a hoarse, desperate laugh like I'd lost all my good humor in a muck bucket. But I'd dig through anything if it meant getting Rosie outta here.

Limping to the bed, I scooped my daughter to my chest and hummed into her hair, rubbing her back in rhythmic circles. "Everything's all right. Mama won't ever leave you." Not ever. Take that, devils. My Rosie had me captured by the corner and tethered me to the earth.

My girl's tears wet my cheek, but her solid body told me what was real and what wasn't. I carried her to the window, and when it refused to open, I stared out across the vast emptiness. The evergreens piercing through the lightening sky told me we were on the southern face of the mountain—the only place the pines grow well. If we could just get out and make it to the woods, we'd keep the rising sun behind us, head west toward the national park, and we should hit one of the roads that'd lead to Hot Springs. We stood a chance.

Rosie let out a whimper, giving voice to my own fear. I had to be strong. For my girl.

"I'm hungry, Mama."

"I know, sweet girl. We went and got locked in this room. Think we can figure a way out?"

I set her on the bed, then bent to search under it for anything I could use to break the window. Nothing but dust rolling around.

I rested my forehead on the floor, wondering if praying made any difference at all.

The trilling beat of a self-obsessed whip-poor-will cut through the katydids repeating their names. Rosie repeated the call, and I sat back on my heels.

What were we going to do? I sat and untied my boot, hefting it. Would it break the window? Rosie climbed into my lap, and the weight of her forced me to stretch my legs out in front of me. I stared out the window at the tree line in the distance. Wasn't no way I could make it there while carrying my daughter.

A white bird flew into the sunrise—like an angel. There must be tremendous effort in being an angel, being forever in the light. It would be such a relief to surrender to the darkness.

I hugged Rosie to my chest. My angel.

Footsteps thudded across the floor, and a key scraped in the lock. I scrambled to my feet, my boot still clutched in my fist. Maybe if I threw it . . .

"Annie?" Doc's voice barely carried to me. "I'm coming in." He peeked around the door. "You ain't planning on hurling that, are you?"

When I tipped my elbow back to throw real hard like he'd taught me when we were kids, he shrunk back a bit. "I got a plan, but you gotta let me in."

I lowered my arm, but I didn't drop the boot. He tiptoed into the room like he was sneaking up on me. Made me want to throw the boot just watching him.

He reached out to take Rosie from me, but I held her in tight. "So what's your plan?"

"Leah Belle left Gus here to take care of things, but I got him drunk, and he's passed out on the couch. She took the car, but we can walk to Hot Springs. If we cut through the woods, we'll be there right quick. Then you can go to the Judge. He'll know how to help. Least that'll give you a chance."

"Mama?" Rosie whined, and I smoothed her hair.

"You got anything to eat? She's awful hungry."

Doc grinned and held out a bag. "Biscuits are a bit stale, but we can eat them as we walk." He handed Rosie one and me the bag before I put my boot back on and followed him through the house. At the very least, he'd get us out. After that, I'd figure out what to do. One step at a time.

Gus was spread out on the davenport, legs dangling off one end, head tilted back. He snored so heavy I thought for sure he'd choke on whatever alcohol he'd drunk.

Doc tugged on the front door 'til it popped open with a loud groan. I whipped round expecting Gus to spring up and kill me then and there, but he snorted, then rubbed his nose and went back to his steady breathing.

I wanted to run across the expanse and hide in the trees, but Doc's shuffle down the porch steps wouldn't allow speed, and I didn't know for sure which direction Hot Springs was.

Took us near forever to reach the tree line, and I glanced behind me at the house. The horizon had brightened off to the right of it. My stomach twisted a little. We were walking south, not west like I thought we'd need to.

"Doc?"

He motioned for me to at least enter the protection of the woods. "Just 'cause he's sleeping it off don't mean he won't have some nightmare and wake up. He's got plenty of guns locked up in there and enough wherewithal to use 'em."

The thought of Gus waking up sent me skittering into the pines, their branches closing behind me like the door of a crypt. I at least trusted Doc over Gus. A breeze lifted the edge of my skirt and set the trees to whispering their secrets to one another. Would they protect me? Or just soak up the blood, ignoring the goings-on of the humans in their midst like the people in Hot Springs did?

Doc glanced over his shoulder again, and I wondered what had him nervous—the thought of Gus catching us running or knowing he'd have to watch while the man killed me.

"Annie, we gotta keep moving. I know you got no reason to trust me, but I've been protecting y'all for three years. I ain't gonna stop now. Rosie's near as I'm ever going to get to my own child."

"If we get caught—"

"Then we best stop talking and get walking."

I looped my shawl round Rosie's backside and tied it behind my neck so's my arms wouldn't give out. The shawl was flimsy protection against the mountain chill anyhow, and this way, with her belly full, Rosie might fall back asleep and I wouldn't need to entertain her or keep her quiet.

Doc waited 'til I was next to him to start out again. His arm brushed mine, and I yanked it away. Just 'cause he was helping me now didn't mean I forgave him.

He sighed and stepped a measure ahead of me. We walked in silence 'til we reached a path even more broke than the road to the farm.

"We'll make faster progress if we use this part of the road, but I don't know when Leah Belle will be back."

I flinched at the woman's name. I'd thought she was a friend. I'd thought *Doc* was a friend. I'd questioned my own husband's sanity because of them. Lord Almighty, I was a mess.

"Once we get to Hot Springs," Doc said, "you gotta go find your daddy."

"Why would I go and do that?"

"Things ain't what they seem, Charlotte Anne. You shoulda figured that out by now."

I near felt the slap of his rebuke.

"What's there to figure out? Leah Belle somehow ousted Daddy and put Gus in charge. And the pair of them snookered you into helping them with the dirty work."

Doc whipped round on me, nearly stumbling. "I know everything's upside down and inside out right now, but it don't help to go flapping your mouth about things you don't know nothing about."

I resisted the urge to retreat, but my lips were cemented shut. Doc never yelled at nobody.

"Eight years ago Leah Belle's husband got caught skimming profits, and that meant he had to be eliminated. So the Judge walked into the man's shop, pulled the trigger, turned to walk out, and near knocked over a witness—the man's daughter who coulda been your twin sister. Every code the mob has says he shoulda killed her too, but instead he warned her to never tell no one, not even her ma and brother."

I suddenly remembered the gorgeous blue-velvet dress Daddy'd brought home yet hid away in the attic. He'd never wanted me to wear the thing. Never would say where it came from—

"Course, the mayor found out, and he thought the Judge was going soft. So Owney Madden bought some insurance. Everybody knew your mama was a little off . . ."

Doc clenched his jaw, daring me to guess at what he was talking about. When I couldn't formulate an answer, he stomped up to me close enough I felt the heat of his breath burning hot on my face.

"Your mama didn't kill herself. Owney murdered her to keep your daddy in line. Make sure he cleaned up his mess. Sent him that Christmas dress like the ones you used to wear as a reminder of what the Judge had to do or . . ."

I staggered under the weight of his words, the road wavering, the world going hollow, the smell of rotting pond water hauling me under.

"No." Mama's hair on the surface of the water, tangling there with the seaweed like it belonged. My diving in after her, getting caught there with her, thrashing against the invisible hands holding me, my leg slashing against the buried logs again and again to no purpose. Sam hacking away at the debris holding me fast.

"To make sure they didn't come after you next, the Judge followed orders and took care of the girl."

I clapped my hands over my ears, trying to keep out the truth, but Doc kept going, forcing me to hear, forcing me to see, to know. "Your daddy murdered Leah Belle's daughter to protect you. Leah Belle didn't know the Judge was the one that pulled the trigger both times; she was kept in the dark same as you. But she was encouraged to remarry an associate of the mayor's—Barker—and move away, leaving her sorrow behind. The mayor had long ago taken her son, Gus, under his wing, literally into his own home. With the senior Martin's okay, he raised him up to be one of the Judge's thugs."

Gus was raised without parents, Dovie May had said. Did that make it all true? I wanted Doc to stop talking. Why wouldn't he stop? But he rushed on, like he had to get it all out or he'd suffocate in the muck of it.

"Then a year or so ago, Gus found out your daddy had been the one to kill his daddy and sister, and he wrote to tell his mama 'cause he near worships the ground she walks on. The two of them couldn't let it go. When Barker died, Leah Belle came back to Hot Springs aiming to take over from the Judge, hiding out in the Howell place and biding her time as she worked on her plan to destroy him. The mayor don't care who runs the day-to-day things as long as his hands stay clean. She was smart enough to arrange it slow like, even making her acquaintance with me, most likely to get close to you, the Judge's daughter. She never let on that Gus was her son, and Gus never told me neither."

Doc turned away from me. "Your daddy might be a hard man, might've let the alcohol talk too much. Not that it makes his hollering and whoring okay, but he never stopped loving your mama. And he never laid an abusive hand on you. He's got his lines he don't cross. You think your ma ran away to Dovie May's, but your daddy *sent* y'all out there to protect you while he tried to get out. Lotta good that did him." Doc scuffed his foot against the ground. "Don't know why I didn't think Leah Belle'd be the one in charge. Gus don't have the brains for something like this, and there ain't a mama alive who could forgive somebody for murdering her daughter in cold blood. I'd have come back for vengeance if anyone had done that to you."

I collapsed on the side of the road, head draped on my arms, gulping in air. Daddy'd killed a girl to protect *me*. Doc had tried to protect me. Sam was trying to protect me.

Everything came back to me.

The devils came from me.

I was poison.

A growling crawled up the mountain, and I heard Doc stumble back up the hill, but I couldn't find it in myself to care. Let a cougar come and eat us all. It'd save the world the trouble.

Doc yanked at my arm, but I settled my head back into it.

"That's a car, Annie. It's Leah Belle coming back to make sure I done my job knocking you around and taking pictures. She's as vicious as they come. When she's done with you she'll take Rosie and torture her until Sam, the Judge, and everyone you care about bows down to the almighty Leah Belle."

I brushed him off.

"You really this weak?" he said.

"Ain't got nothing to do with weak." My words blurred together, drunk with shock.

"If you don't care about you, think about Rosie."

I started unstrapping my sleeping daughter. "You take her."

"Annie, I can't run. You're Rosie's only hope." He limped into the center of the road. "Soon as she gets up to the house, she'll know we're gone. But if I tell her I saw you run across the road, you got a chance. You go back into the trees on the other side. This road leads to Hot Springs. Go to the army hospital. Julia works there, and she'll know where to find the Judge."

"You can't—"

"This is *my* fault. I'm the one that told them to use the farm. I'm the one that told them it was a more direct route than going out of their way up the logging road to this place. I'm the one who told them that having the exchange in the shed would keep the Judge out of things. I thought it would protect you. I've never been so foolish in my life. For once let me fix something for you."

His words pierced the fog, and as the revving car engine grew louder, I scrambled into the trees.

"And don't trust Peter," Doc shouted as the car rounded the bend.

Don't trust Peter?

Gus, Doc, and . . . My feet stumbled, but there wasn't time to ask. So I ran into the woods from where we came, forcing myself to not glance back. On the road, the engine slowed, and I stopped my pell-mell escape, turning parallel to the road as I stepped carefully through the woods.

Doc's voice carried quiet desperation, but Leah Belle's shouts could've woke the dead.

"Good night! I knew I was right coming back up here. You're soft on the girl."

"I ain't—"

A smack cracked through the quiet, and I knew Leah Belle had slapped Doc.

"I own you, boy. Go get Gus. I'll take care of her."

A shotgun cocked, and I near choked at the sound of feet stomping down the road right toward where I cowered.

CHAPTER
Twenty-Eight

—— S A M ——

Don't rightly know what I expected when I entered Peter's hospital room. But I surely didn't expect to see my brother surrounded by three men in severe suits with badges and guns, all taking notes on what he was saying. The FBI? How did they get here already? I hadn't left a message but an hour ago. I counted back through time, and things just didn't add up. There wasn't no way they could've gotten here from Little Rock that quick.

And what were they doing interrogating my brother when he was injured and I was the one who saw everything?

Julia left me gawking at the door and shoved into the midst of the men, elbowing her way through to the bed. The three grunted but parted like the Red Sea in front of Moses leading the Israelites to the promised land.

She sorted through the bags on the IV pole, ducked under the lines that held Peter's right arm above him, and then lifted the stump of his left arm, studying her watch while she counted his heartbeats. Peter ignored her and talked to the agents like he knew exactly what they needed to know.

"When they set fire to the fertilizer, I knew we were in trouble. I'd hoped Sam could save Annie and Rosie, but then Gus pulled a pistol on him, and I had to try to save them. I didn't know another—"

Julia shushed Peter like she expected him to listen, then leaned over his bed to place a stethoscope under his hospital gown. He took a sharp inhale, blushing like a shy teenager. As she moved the stethoscope around, Peter's breath stirred a loose curl. She was taking her good, sweet time, and I shifted my feet, pleading with her to hurry. Peter seemed to be fine, and we needed to save my girls.

Julia straightened, looking satisfied.

"You'll be right as rain in no time. But y'all"—she turned on the dark-suited men—"y'all need to stop taking your notes and go save that gal and her baby. You wasted enough time lollygagging about when you knew she was in danger. We warned you, and y'all didn't listen. The good news is Peter thought ahead and took me to the house not more than a week ago, just in case. And Sam knows the old Howell place as good as Peter. We can take you. But you best get suited up quick, because I'm going with or without you, and you can try explaining that to our Mr. Hoover."

The G-men all snapped to attention, and I don't think my jaw could've dropped more if'n I tried. *Our* Mr. Hoover? "Julia's a—"

The Judge leaned against the doorframe like he thought Julia capable of saving the whole durned world. "She is, indeed. I've been wanting to get out for a long time. Even a man like me has lines they ain't willing to cross, at least not a second time. Gus getting so uppity a year or two ago made me more than a mite nervous. Soon as I got wind of what he was doing at the sorting shed, I visited Little Rock and offered my assistance. Fool boy made a serious misjudgment in using Charlotte Anne as a shield. Ain't no one going to put my daughter in danger. They set Julia up as my girl who also worked as a nurse. This hospital didn't blink twice at hiring somebody with experience on the front lines in the war. Truth told, I don't think she would've let them say no. She ain't afraid of nothing or nobody, so she's the perfect go-between since they already had Peter set up."

Wait. What?

"Peter?" My hand clamped around the doorframe so hard I was surprised it didn't buckle under the pressure.

No doubt hearing me, Julia wove back through the men and laid a hand on my chest, her perfume wafting up and near choking me. I was still trying to get my head round things when she turned her blazing smile on me.

"Why are you surprised? We've been after Mayor McLaughlin and the syndicates here for years. And your brother is brilliant, a marine, and motivated to oust the ruling party in Hot Springs. When Peter came to us with concerns about y'all's family's safety, Mr. Hoover fell all over himself to recruit him."

While all that could be true . . . "Why didn't he tell me?"

"We didn't give him no choice to tell you, Sam."

"There's always a choice." I'd never wanted to slug my brother more. Peter knew all along what was going on and let me believe I was going crazy.

My brother tried to push himself to sitting so's he could see around the other men, but Julia hollered. "You done enough, Peter. Let the rest of us do our jobs now."

Julia swung back to me without making sure Peter obeyed her. "He didn't have a choice," she said again like I was hard of hearing. "Gus is small potatoes next to whoever's in charge of this ring. Not even the Judge knows who it is. He's powerful enough that he's got the ear of the mayor and probably the governor all while backing the Judge into a tight corner. It was Peter's job to keep you safe and unawares while he figured out what was what.

"Now"—she smoothed my shirt where her hand had rested—"best stop acting like a guppy outta water if you want to come with us. I figure you might have some pull with Doc to convince him to help us." She said this as much to me as the agents behind her, but my mind spun as I tried to take everything in.

"Doc?" The world tilted again, and I was sure I'd fallen off right into the pit of hell itself. "*Doc* took my wife and daughter?"

"From what Peter told me, Angus snatched them, but Doc was probably the man holding Rosie. He's in this up to his eyeballs, addicted to opium too. And both men think Peter is in it with them. Course, now that he tried to stop them from taking Annie and Rosie, let alone keep Gus from killing you . . ." She laid her hand on my arm, but even though I saw it there, I didn't feel nothing.

The Judge pulled a chair round, and I sank into it. I'd invited Doc into my home. Asked him to take care of my family. My God, what had I done?

Julia slipped past me, and I could see her sashaying down the hall, talking to another agent while pulling off her nurse's cap. The first three agents filed out of the room like they weren't in no hurry to save an innocent woman and her child from the criminals at the old Howell place. I had half a mind to snatch a gun from one of them and storm the mountain myself.

The Judge clucked and shook his head, watching Julia. "Who'd expect a little ole nurse of being capable of coordinating all this? Don't rightly know why everyone so easily believed she'd choose me. But if I was a few years younger . . . Peter'd be a fool to let her go."

I gaped like the guppy Julia'd accused me of being. How could he think of things like that when his daughter, my wife, was suffering who knows what at the hands of Angus Martin?

I shoved off the chair, itching for a fight.

"Sam?" Peter's voice spun me round, but I refused to look at him, afraid of what might come out if I did. Could I be arrested for cold-cocking an injured G-man?

"I really am sorry, Sam. I—"

But I'd heard enough of Peter's apologies to last a lifetime. It was one thing to apologize for stealing my slingshot when we were kids; it was quite another to try apologizing for putting my family in danger and then making me out to be a crazy monster.

—ANNIE—

Leah Belle was so close that I heard the whisper of air passing through her lips. I shrank into the underbrush, wrapping my arms tight around Rosie and ignoring the pokes of the prickers. As Leah Belle moved, I caught sight here and there of her cream-colored skirt. Least my lavender dress was faded near the color of dirt.

She stepped further down the road, and behind her I saw the road zigzagging away and a broken-down old purple cabin peeking through the crook of a split. I sucked in a breath, hope resurrecting.

I knew where we were. This was the cabin near the meadow where we collected chicory and wildflowers. It was up the mountain a ways off the main road running from Hot Springs, past our farm, and on north toward Missouri, and it shared a decrepit logging road with the old Howell place. I'd always thought that house had been haunted. Now I knew different. It was where Leah Belle had been hiding out when she was in town so's Daddy wouldn't figure out who she was and what she was up to.

The bad news is that it was a long way to Hot Springs on foot, but I knew the way, and I knew the hunting traps Peter had placed. If I could get down there and do it just right, I might be able to lead Leah Belle and Gus into the snares and have a fighting chance . . . or at least hope to hold them off long enough for someone to come find me. It wasn't much of a chance. I knew the slim possibility of surviving a kidnapping. But this little housewife wasn't giving up easy nohow.

"You've always been such a princess," Leah Belle called out to me. "Everybody doing everything they can to save poor little Charlotte Anne. By killing my daughter, your daddy sold his soul to protect you. Of course, he tried to get out from under the mob, but when that didn't work, he sent you to Sam."

She took a few slow steps forward, scanning the underbrush like I might be fool enough to bolt while she was watching.

My legs shook from holding a half-crouched position, and I dug what little fingernails I had left into my palms.

"That boy bent himself backward to do right by you." Leah Belle's voice carried despite her distance. "But you didn't even believe him when he told you what he saw. Granted, he's a little fragile, and I did help him along a bit, but still . . ."

Help him along?

Leah Belle stopped like she'd heard my question. "Coffee is especially tasty when laced with opium. Didn't Sam tell you what happened to him out in your field Monday? That thermos I sent up came back empty, and I put enough in there to mess him up good."

Gravel trickled into the irrigation ditch as Leah Belle pivoted, studying the other side of the road. "Coffee and opium. Makes for a fine cocktail to tip a vulnerable man right over the edge."

I stopped cold. Lord Almighty, she'd drugged Sam! And worse, I'd believed the lie she'd encouraged over the truth of my own husband.

Rosie sighed in her sleep, and I shook myself awake from my horrified stupor. It was up to me to get us to Hot Springs and tell everybody the truth. Holding Rosie tight to my chest, I crept through the underbrush, following a game trail, thanking the good Lord that Rosie was so small and I wasn't wearing one of Mama's layered dresses. Even Mama couldn't disagree with me this time.

The automobile started again, and I quickened my pace, taking advantage of the noise to put space between me and the Howell place. When the sound of the car faded, I darted across the road and dove into the forest on the other side. A branch reached out and smacked my arm right good, catching Rosie's back as well.

Rosie squeaked, her eyes popping open, indignant that somebody'd wake her in such a rude fashion. I shushed her.

"We're playing hide-and-seek with Uncle Doc, sweet girl. We gotta be real quiet. Okay?" She nodded, but her scowl told me she wasn't sure she should go along with her mama's fool plan. I didn't have much space for error without causing a toddler temper tantrum.

A flock of birds burst from the bushes, and I hesitated mid-step like a deer sensing danger.

Please be Doc. Please.

Thundering footsteps came from above me, and I screamed. Gus was barreling down the hill right toward Rosie and me.

I wove through the trees, ducking into small places I hoped Gus wouldn't be able to follow. But he was mad as a hornet, and I swear he tore right through grown trees. All the headlong running made Rosie whimper, her tears keeping time with my feet and my panting breath. I burst into the open road, which had curled back on itself, and Doc hollered, followed by the sound of a car engine.

But I wouldn't stop. Rocks skidded from under my feet, careening down the steep incline with me. I needed to find some kind of weapon, something to slow Gus down. He was built like a bear and proving to be just as fast and strong as one. There wasn't no way I'd outrun him.

I lurched around a boulder, snagging at a tree limb as I passed, digging my heels in to hold it back. I shushed Rosie and listened for Gus's footsteps. My breath echoed loud in the quiet.

Please.

Gunfire erupted from above the cliff, and I dove to the ground, letting the limb snap back in place. A branch wasn't no weapon against a tommy gun. A series of bullets stitched across the boulder, and I cowered over Rosie. Bits of rock exploded and bit into my back.

"Good heavens, Gus. Your ma don't want her dead!" Doc's voice rose loud enough that I knew he meant me to hear. Sure as I'd known him my whole life, I knew he'd figured out where I was headed and was telling me to run.

I launched myself out from the rock, half tumbling, half running straight down the incline, my feet struggling to keep up with my body. Off to my left, snatches of purple peeked through the trees.

Not far now. The snares were just past the cabin on the far side of the meadow.

I scrambled around the maple standing guard over the crick, then leapt across the water and burst into the meadow, skirting along the tree line. Even though straight across was the most direct, I didn't much want to run in the open. Just because Leah Belle didn't want me dead didn't mean Gus still wouldn't take a shot. That man had never known restraint.

The sound of footsteps exploded from in front of me, and I shied away. How had Gus gotten so far ahead of me so fast? I'd never make Peter's trap line. I veered hard left across the open expanse. Maybe if I made it to the cabin . . . If nothing else, it would buy time.

The meadow stretched before me, forever long. My legs shook from exertion, and for the first time in my life I wished the meadow were smaller.

Just as I dove back into the tree line, a shot rang out from above the purple cabin. If Gus was up the hill, who was across the meadow? I whipped round, my breath coming in heaves, Rosie rising and falling in her sling against my chest, blessedly quiet.

A series of forms moved through the forest, and I bounced on my toes. How had Leah Belle called in more goons? And why? It was just little ole me.

"Mama?" Rosie's voice bounced off the trees, and I slapped a hand over her mouth.

"Uncle Doc's on the hill," I whispered in her ear. "We'll hide in the cabin over there. Okay?" And to my great relief, she nodded, a devious grin spreading on her face—looking so much like Mary I near cried.

Up on the mountain, Gus cursed, followed by the sound of him crashing through the trees, rolling down the hill all helter-skelter. I yelped and ran off toward the cabin, telling myself to keep things together. If I didn't stay on one course, I'd be caught in the open like a snared rabbit. I stumbled round a collection of lichen-covered rocks and stifled a shout of joy. The cabin was just up ahead.

With a last glance over my shoulder, I ran, bent over like I thought I maybe should. If I ever got out of this, I'd ask Sam how to protect myself better. Surely I should know more than I did.

Footsteps pounded behind me matching the frantic rhythm of my feet, and I increased my speed, my boots thumping against the ground with alarming noise. If I could get to the cabin, I could probably bar us in. And then what? Then what? There wasn't no cavalry coming, no way to call for help.

I tightened my grip on Rosie, and she whimpered against me. My hairpins had long ago ripped free, and my hair stretched out behind me like it was trying to fly. The footsteps behind me were closing in, and I was afraid my hair would be a convenient leash for the rest of me.

Where was Sam?

And then I was rushing past the side of the cabin, pivoting around the corner, throwing myself through the door. We'd made—

A hand struck out and slapped against the door, the impact vibrating to my core, shaking loose any delusion I'd had of surviving. I clawed at the wrist, screaming, desperate to keep him outside.

The hand disappeared amongst a ruckus of shouts, and I slammed the door shut, ramming the lock home. It was quiet a moment. I leaned over, hands on my knees, my ragged breaths filling the space until I was drowning in it, the world shimmering and tenuous.

Round, sharp pounding sent me skittering back across the open room. Did they think I'd just open the door?

"Mama?" Rosie squirmed in her sling, and I kissed her forehead, a tear sliding off my chin and nestling itself in her hair.

"Mama, why we running from—"

The knock came again. I unstrapped Rosie and tucked her inside the stone fireplace. "You hide here until Uncle Doc comes and gets you." Least she'd be protected from gunfire.

"But, Mama—"

I raised an eyebrow in my best impression of *my* mama, and Rosie squatted in the back corner, a pout sprouting on her lips. I turned a circle. There wasn't nothing in the cabin that could be any kind of weapon.

"Dagnabbit, Annie. It's me."

I froze in the middle of the room, positive somebody out there was trying to fool me again. That couldn't be Sam.

Rosie squeaked in indignation. "We lost. Daddy found us." Before I unraveled myself, she stomped across the room and tried to open the door. When it refused to open, she kicked it, then plopped to the floor, wailing.

Her piercing cry freed me, and I hoisted her up, shushing. Was it really Sam?

"Annie?"

Nobody else could sound like that—soft and frustrated all at the same time. I'd heard it more than a time or two when Sam had come to find me after Daddy'd wore himself out in a tirade. I fumbled with the lock, my fingers not working the way they should, until the door swung open.

Sam stood a shocked moment framed in the doorway, electricity passing through us both. My Sam.

I threw myself into his chest, his breath exploding as I finally caught mine, his arms wrapping around me a moment later. His shoulders melted into me, cradling me as I clutched his shirt. It had been Sam on the far side of the meadow. He'd come for me.

"You squishing me!" Rosie said, but I held tight. I never thought I'd find myself in my husband's arms again, and I wasn't ever letting go.

Sam's laughter reverberated against my ear, deep and familiar.

Another man stepped behind Sam, and I tensed. But Sam shifted, unconcerned, toward the dark-haired figure in black who tipped his hat to me with a quick, "Ma'am." He could have passed for a mobster himself, but the badge on his hip identified him as FBI.

"Angus Martin took off somewhere," the man said. "But someone else is holed up either in the Howell house or—"

"It's Leah Belle. She's the one in charge." The words ripped from my lips, the reality of them burning. "And Doc too."

Sam reached for me, but I stepped back needing to unburden it all.

"She drugged you, Sam. I'm so sorry. And I think Peter's involved and . . ." Lord, it was hard to admit all the things I'd assumed I had right and that I wished I'd listened to Dovie May and believed in Sam.

"Peter's on our side, and the rest ain't your fault, darlin'." Sam's rumbling voice settled me down to the core, his fingers stroking down my hair, my cheek. "They had me fooled too."

"Including us." The FBI agent swore. "I know I don't have the right to ask . . ." His eyes flicked to Rosie, then to Sam, and my fingers tightened on Sam's arm as if I could hold back the expansive world crashing in against us. They needed a guide, and what better guide than a man who'd grown up on the mountains and then survived against the Japanese behind enemy lines.

I dropped my arm, my hand slapping against my thigh, numb and useless. I knew he would go. He couldn't do anything else. The hero turned monster turned hero again. I pushed up on my toes and kissed the stubble on his cheek.

"Go. Just be gentle with Doc. He's the one who saved us."

Sam's brows wrinkled, and I wished I hadn't come between the two best friends. If not for me, Sam wouldn't have asked Doc for help, and Doc wouldn't have gotten addicted to the opium.

"You'll stay with them?" Although Sam's words were a question to the agent, they carried the weight of statement. And when Sam pivoted and marched up the mountain, the man wedged his body into the doorframe.

The last glimpse I had of Sam was his broad shoulders turned sideways to lift a hand in farewell.

I stumbled backward like I'd been slapped. When he'd gone off to war, he'd refused to wave, refused to say goodbye, saying he would see me again soon. I tried to duck under the black-clad arm to make Sam take back his goodbye, but the man nudged me back into the cabin. "Mrs. Mattas, for your safety, I'll have to ask you to stay inside."

For your safety? For the love of . . . Sam was hunting a woman who'd drugged him and who'd snuggled up to me like my best friend. Not to mention her psychotic son toting a tommy gun. There wasn't nothing safe here.

But Sam had asked me to stay. So I eased back into the cabin.

Come back to me, Sam.

CHAPTER
Thirty

— S A M —

Nothing in me wanted to leave Annie back in that cabin. Last time I left her, I'd chosen the wrong protector, and now we were all paying the price. But Agent Jones was right. I knew the nooks and crannies of this hillside near as well as my own backyard. If'n my family was ever going to live without looking over our shoulders, I had to help track down Leah Belle and Gus.

One of the agents had taken Julia and the car down the road a piece where he thought he'd seen Gus running, and the third agent, Paulson, was flanking me on my left, helping me tighten the noose on Leah Belle.

But I was more than a little unprepared. Sure, the agent had told me to stay out of the way, but I didn't have a gun or even a clear idea of where Leah Belle was, and I'd seen enough deer and bear up here that I wasn't entirely convinced it was Gus the agent had seen. I scanned behind me to find a snatch of purple through the trees. Least I knew Annie and Rosie were safe.

Dried leaves crumbled under my boots, and I ducked into the game trails snaking up the hill. At the top of the ridge, the head of the road slung over the back of the mountain, heading away from the main road into the wild country. I stood just inside the tree cover, overlooking most of the area, hoping I'd be able to see something that told me where everybody was.

I took a deep breath, sending out my senses, listening for anything off, staring in front of me hoping to catch movement anywhere in my field of vision. There was a twitch to my left, and I turned, searching out the disturbance.

The undergrowth at the edge of the road swished, and Leah Belle stumbled out, yanking at her slender skirt and yelling at the sky. "I'm going to kill that little twit."

My fingers closed around a tree branch, and I forced myself not to launch my body at her. Despite the fact she probably wasn't used to the forest, she swung that shotgun round like she knew what she was doing. Wouldn't do to get myself killed.

I whistled the shrill repetitive call of a cardinal and then hunkered down as I'd promised Agent Paulson I would. But there wasn't a response. Where was the agent? I sidled across the hill in front of her, racking my brain for a plan.

Leah Belle stopped at the top of the hill and hollered. "Come on out, Charlotte Anne! Don't do anybody any good to traipse through this godforsaken forest. We'll find you sooner or later."

Not if I could help it.

Leah Belle paced the road, coming closer to where I hid. "Where's that fool son of mine?" She spun in a circle. "I'm going to kill the lot of these incompetent men."

Scuffling sounded down the road, and I squinted into the sunlight spilling over the trees. Doc emerged from the forest and then limped down the road away from Leah Belle. Where was he headed? I shifted, trying to figure out how I was going to contain the two of them *and* find help.

The chatter of an automatic gun exploded back toward the meadow, and I spun toward the sound. Annie.

"Ain't no one here to protect you no more, little girl." Gus's voice floated through the trees, and I ran not caring if Leah Belle or the whole world saw me. If'n Gus had killed the agent at the cabin, Annie was trapped with no one to help her and Rosie.

— ANNIE —

Silence gripped the whole world, and my entire body shook with the reverberations of the scream of the agent and the bullets as they thudded into the cabin. Gus had killed the man without a second thought and was outside the door, coming for us. No flimsy lock was going to keep him out long.

Rosie stared up at me, eyes swimming with fear.

"Ain't nothing, darlin'. Just sounds like Uncle Doc ain't *it* no more. The man out there is. You hear?" I spun frantically, pleading with my brain to think. To come up with a plan to save Rosie even if that meant sacrificing myself.

Rosie scrambled into the fireplace and huddled into the corner like the expert hide-and-seek player she was.

"Smart girl." I forced down the panic. First step, hide Rosie. I shifted a few logs of firewood in front of her and nodded. Nobody'd find her unless they were really searching.

"Don't come out for nobody other than Daddy or Doc," I whispered. But what if none of us made it back? *Oh, God, please.* "Or . . . or a man with a badge." *Let someone find her.* "Or . . . the Judge. Tell one of the folks who . . . who aren't it that I'm hiding in the maple trees."

"Annie, let me in, and I'll let you and that girl of yours live." The door shook under Gus's onslaught.

"You remember? Where's Mama hiding?"

"Maple trees."

"Who you going to tell?"

"Anybody but him." Her eyes grew wider still, and her voice shook a little.

God, please.

I kissed my girl's head, brushing back the curls from her forehead, then turned to the window. Let Gus work at the door. I'd escape out the side. I eased the window open but then stopped. I'd need Gus to believe I still had Rosie or he'd search her out and have me trapped good.

Come on. Think. The only thing in there was firewood. I smoothed down my makeshift sling and smiled, then snatched a piece. I winked at Rosie before I slung one leg out the window, and then the other, turning to ease myself to the ground.

Gus pounded on the door. The man had never been known for his patience, but there wasn't no way he was getting what he wanted.

I tiptoed across the lane of grass and behind the trunk of a tree. Just a little farther.

Gus swore and stomped round the cabin. I imagined him as Jack's giant bellowing, "Fee-fi-fo-fum."

I swallowed thinking about Jack scrambling for the beanstalk. I didn't have no beanstalk to chop down and kill my giant, but I was just as smart as little Jack.

I ducked into the game trail, a plan forming in my mind. This trail should still lead to the row of maples we used for syrup tapping. But Gus needed to follow me.

Was I crazy for thinking I might be able to outwit him? I could still run without him seeing. But then I pictured Rosie curled up in the fireplace, trusting her mama. If I didn't take care of this man, he'd go back to the cabin and find my girl.

The moment Gus saw the open window, he spun. Now or never. I shook a branch just enough to get it moving, then sprinted up the trail. A bullet cracked into a tree above my head, and I ducked, my legs churning underneath me—a rabbit in full flight. My ugly work boots dug into the mountain, propelling me like no ball slipper would've.

I barely hesitated at the road before I dashed across, making sure to stamp a foot in the soft dirt at the base of the hill before scurrying up to the line of maples. I grasped the bottom limb of the third and most easy tree to climb and pulled. I'd climbed the oak tree back at the house, but now my legs felt long and ungainly as my knees kept smacking into the wood strapped to my chest. My feet scrambled on the bark, marching my body upward until I wrapped my legs around a branch, my arms shaking as I grappled its topside.

The log in my sling shifted, and I snatched it just as it broke free. My skin ripped against the splinters, and my legs tightened and shook around the branch. I stuck the log back inside the sling, my whole body trembling. How did a rabbit outsmart a fox?

The top of Gus's hat emerged from the forest and he turned to study the road.

I threw myself into the second branch. I had to be out of his reach by the time he figured out where I was.

The bark bit into my palms as I tugged myself up another branch and another. Sweat broke out on my palms, my muscles screaming in protest, desperate for rest. But Gus must've seen my footprints, because he was stalking up the hill.

One more. I had to get up one more. *Come on.* My fingertips brushed the branch above my head, just out of reach. I stretched, wobbled, and tipped, sensing the tilt, waiting for the moment I would break through and the ground would rush up and declare this rabbit caught.

My forehead cracked against another branch, sending a searing pain through my skull and down my back, but it stopped my slide. I pushed against the limb that had saved me, blinking, my neck numb from the impact to my head.

I couldn't see Gus anymore. Couldn't hear nothing but my own strangled wheezing and the wind spiraling through the trees. I was out of time. This would have to do. I shoved myself out on the branch as far as I dared. It bent under my weight, quaking with my movement, the ground opening up beneath me.

Twisting my legs around the branch, I eased the log out of the sling and waited for Gus to find me.

— S A M —

I burst from the forest onto the ledge, peering over the meadow and cabin sitting peaceful as you please—unless you took into account the still shape of a body splayed by the door. Anybody who'd never seen war might take comfort in the quiet, but a soldier knows there ain't nothing in the world more terrifying than absolute silence. It means someone's either sneaking up on you or everybody's left you for dead in enemy territory. Either way, you're in a heap of trouble.

I inspected the woods surrounding me. I'd lost Leah Belle somewhere closer to the Howell place. As long as I kept one ear open, she wasn't likely to ambush me. Not in her ridiculous high-heeled shoes and tight skirt.

I had no idea where Agent Paulson was, but I could've used his help about now.

As if my thoughts conjured him, a black shape emerged into the meadow, stalking whatever was down there. Was Gus holed up in the cabin with Annie? The agent peeked in the window and dropped his weapon to his side. Wasn't no threat left there.

My throat tightened, making me see stars. Wasn't going to end up like last time. I wouldn't let nothing happen to Annie and Rosie. I sucked in a breath and then another. My training kicked in, clearing my head. I scanned the forest below me, using the zigzags in the road to section out the view.

Where'd you go, Gus?

I squinted at movement just below me at the line of maples. A flash of violet fluttered in the breeze, peeking out from inside the tree branches. Annie?

A shape snuck up under the tree.

"Annie!" My wife's name burst from my lips, and I threw myself over the ridge, my heels skidding over rocks, my backside banging against the incline, gravel digging into my elbows.

Gus stopped, then pointed his gun in my direction. I threw myself sideways.

A scream erupted from the maples, followed by a grunt. Gus staggered a moment, then crumpled to the ground. Had his gun misfired?

I collected my feet underneath me and hobbled down the hill.

Annie dropped out of the tree, her skirts drifting behind her like a flag. She kicked away a log, then poked a toe at Gus's belly. Like she wasn't quite satisfied, she lifted a shawl from round her neck and trussed Gus up like a pig. Annie'd dropped a log on him and knocked him out cold. I winced thinking of the headache that man would wake up with. Served him right, though.

"Rosie?" I asked her first thing.

"She's in the cabin hiding in the—"

A shot cracked in the air, and I jumped behind a tree trunk. Leah Belle stepped out from the trees at the top of the ridge just above me, and she was aiming down at Annie.

—ANNIE—

"No!"

I spun to face the shout behind me. Sam walked backward toward me, arms outstretched, pleading, surrendering.

What?

A figure stepped out from the trees. Leah Belle, her shotgun pointed at me.

My feet stuck to the ground, fear splintering my thoughts. Did I risk running? Or stay put? Shadows played across Sam's broad back like a signal code I couldn't read. Some animal stalked through the woods, and the trees shifted, the forest settling in to watch the human standoff like it was some moving picture. But I didn't dare turn.

"Leah Belle, you gotta think." Sam's voice was maddeningly calm as he slowly edged closer, angling to put himself between me and that gun. "You kill Annie, the Judge will hunt you down, and it ain't likely the mayor will stop him. He's too busy dealing with Sid McMath. 'Sides, what would you gain?"

"Retribution."

"You know that don't bring comfort."

The shotgun shifted a mite.

Keep going, Sam. She's listening.

"And I know you actually like Charlotte Anne. She's a victim of the Judge, same as you. But me. Me you don't like. I chose to follow the Judge, chose to come after you."

No, no, no. Stop!

Sam took a step toward her. "It's me you want, not her."

The gun whipped toward Sam and exploded just as a man burst

from the trees beside him, tackling Sam to the ground, the pair jerking with the impact of the bullet.

A scream blazed through my throat.

"Don't move." Leah Belle's command froze my feet.

"Sam." My God, she'd shot Sam.

Leah Belle sauntered to the far side of the ridge, taking the path to the maple grove, never letting that shotgun drop from me for a second. I was absolutely, completely, and utterly powerless. Sam and whoever had tried to protect him were dying, and I couldn't do nothing to save them.

— S A M —

A man's body sprawled on top of me, his arms draped on either side of me, his belly against mine, mashing my back into the gravel at the base of the ridge. I couldn't hardly breathe. Pain seared through my shoulder and head, and I stared at the sky. Maple leaves tugged against the branches trying to fly away with the clouds as they floated across the blue. I squeezed my eyes shut, then opened them, clearing away the dusty confusion.

I heaved in another breath and tried to shift the person on top of me. He groaned and managed to roll a bit. Warmth flowed out of him onto me. Lord Almighty, the man was bleeding. Leah Belle had shot at me, but . . .

Doc.

Doc had leapt out of the trees and taken the bullet for me.

I rolled him onto his back and pressed against the gaping wound in his belly, desperation running wild through me . . . Jake on the ground, already dead, his body still warm but the blood no longer flowing. But this wasn't Jake. It was happening again.

"Why'd you go and do that, Doc?"

Doc blinked at me with glassy eyes. "Just wanted to be the hero one time before I died." He coughed, and blood spattered across my arms and rained down on his face. "Silver case in my pocket. One opium pill left. Would you—" He winced in pain.

The movement of him pulling a little case from his pocket was so familiar in my memory that I knew exactly where it was. The pill stuck to the blood on my fingers, but Doc swallowed it without any trouble. How long had he been masking his pain with opium? How had I missed it?

The sound of a shotgun cocking brought me up short. My plan had been to give Leah Belle someone to avenge her daughter with— me—but Doc had interrupted. I spun around, and Annie was frozen, hands raised in surrender.

Leah Belle was close enough I could see the white of her knuckles gripping the gun trained on me. "I don't much like missing what I'm shooting at."

Wasn't no way she'd miss this time.

I closed my eyes, waiting for the bullet, praying that Annie and Rosie would be well taken care of. That Leah Belle would let them go.

— A N N I E —

"No!" I lurched away, refusing to allow my mind to record Sam's death.

But there wasn't ever anybody who listened to me, and a gunshot ripped through the mountain. Leah Belle may as well have shot me, it hurt so bad. My legs gave out, and I crashed to the ground, praying God would see fit to pull me under. The devils had won.

Leah Belle's snort of twisted laughter broke through my fog. That woman had brought the devils to my doorstep and let them in. God help me, I would never, ever forgive her.

I snatched the log from behind me, fully intending to launch it at the woman, kill her with my own hands. I swung round but stumbled to a stop. Leah Belle hadn't been laughing.

She staggered backward, tripping. One of her shoes fell off and

flopped over, and her eyes and mouth were wide open in gaping surprise. She gurgled something, then dropped to her knees and toppled
over.

The log slipped from my fingers.

Sam still held his hands outstretched in a silent plea, like Leah
Belle might yet spring up and shoot us. But Daddy stepped out from
behind a maple, his pistol aimed at Leah Belle.

Daddy? How had he known?

And then I realized the body lying so lifeless on Sam's lap was
Doc's. He'd gone and got Daddy to help, then sacrificed himself to
save Sam.

He'd only ever tried to love us the best he could. What was I
supposed do with that? Tears trickled down my cheeks, and my arms
hung limp. Doc had been a broken man who charged in and saved
us from the devil himself.

Dovie May was right. Sometimes God uses the most broken things
to save us.

Daddy edged toward Leah Belle's prone body, leaning over to hoist
the shotgun, then emptied the chamber on the ground and tossed the
thing past Sam. It clattered round on the gravel, settling like it wasn't
nothing more harmless than a tree branch.

"She's dead." Daddy's whole body slumped like Leah Belle's death
was the heaviest thing he'd ever carried.

Sam slipped out of his coat and draped it over Doc's body. Blood
smeared across my husband's face and bloomed at a ragged tear on
the edge of his shoulder.

"You okay, Sam?" Daddy stood above the two best friends.

"Bullet grazed me. If it hadn't been for—"

"Ain't worth dwelling on that. Doc was trying to make up for all
the things he'd done. It's something I'll be doing for the rest of my
life."

Voices clamored behind me, and two agents popped round a tree,
weapons drawn. I stepped between them and Daddy, mirroring Dad-

dy's stance—hands raised, palms out—making sure they couldn't get a clear shot at the man who'd spent my whole life trying to save me.

Daddy lowered his pistol to the ground, and the FBI agents charged the rest of the way. One poked at Gus and replaced my shawl with a set of cuffs but left him lying in the dirt, and the other approached Daddy like he might be the devil himself. I walked backward, keeping myself between the gun and Daddy.

"Ma'am, I'm gonna ask you to step aside." The agent's face was serious as Hoover, but he didn't know who he was dealing with.

"The Judge saved me and Sam. Leah Belle would've killed us both."

I stumbled over a tree root, and Daddy caught my arm. His gentle grip on my elbow steadied me, a protecting force that had been there all along, hidden under the darkness where I didn't know to search for it.

"It's going to be all right, darlin'. Agent Paulson's gotta do his job, and I aim to cooperate. Agent, I apologize for leaving the confines of your vehicle. But when Doc came running down the road, I knew something was wrong. He gave me the pistol and led me up here. I know I broke our agreement, but I do hope you'll trust me."

The agent muttered to one of the others like he was confirming Daddy's story, and Paulson relaxed a hair with the answer. But it didn't comfort me none. The gun was still locked on us, and I knew they were still planning to take Daddy.

He leaned over and kissed the top of my head like he'd done every morning 'til I left the house for good. Poor Daddy. "I knew what I signed up for." He gently set me off to the side and wiped his thumb across my damp cheeks. "Don't cry. It's the best day of my life. I finally got my daughter back."

"But I don't want to lose you."

"We have Rosie," Agent Paulson said as he approached, a hint of threat in his voice.

I whipped round. "Whether I let you past or not, you best go get my daughter and bring her here!"

Paulson took a step back, his hands raised like I was the one pointing a pistol at him. "Okay, okay. She's with Julia."

"Julia! How could you leave my daughter with Julia?"

Sam groaned and forced himself to his feet, stepping next to Daddy and chuckling at me. "It's all right, Annie. Julia's an agent."

"I don't care if she's one of God's angels. No one uses my daughter for leverage. You hear?"

"I'll take care of her," Sam said to heaven knows who.

"Don't you try to handle me, Samuel Mattas. You help me take care of Daddy too, and—"

"I know you'll take care of them, Sam," Daddy said. "You always have."

I wanted to strike out at both of them for being so gosh durned calm about all this.

My fingers clenched around Daddy's arm, and he raised his eyebrows at me like he couldn't decide if he was mildly disappointed or rather amused. But a man over there had a gun pointed at us.

I'd had quite enough guns pointed at me over the last two days.

Daddy rubbed the hand I gripped him with. "Annie, I been working with the agents for quite some time, and as extra insurance, I gave Sid McMath the evidence of the mayor's voter fraud when I found out they'd taken you. But I can't protect you unless I finish what I started. I gotta let the agents take me and then testify against Gus and the rest of them. You have to let me go."

Sam's arm wrapped around my waist, and I felt all the fear and confusion drain away. Daddy wasn't leaving me alone. He was leaving me with a man he trusted, who loved me. I turned to the agent ready to take Daddy.

"You'll protect . . . my father?" My voice sounded so weak, and I hated that it betrayed me.

"You have my word on that." He pulled out his handcuffs and ratcheted them around Daddy's thick wrists. The metallic clicks sent tremors down my spine. They sounded so final.

The agent stooped to retrieve Daddy's pistol and Leah Belle's shotgun, then touched Daddy's sleeve. It was obvious that he was being gentle with the notorious Judge, but I hated the glint of sunshine sparkling on Daddy's cuffs. As much as I wanted him to be held responsible for what he'd done to Mama and what he'd done in town, all I could think about was the spark of Daddy's laughter when he chased me round the yard when I was small. Looking back, it's obvious that working for the mayor had taken its toll on Daddy, the darkness consuming him more and more until Mama had . . . until she'd been murdered. I wish I would've understood what they were protecting me from. Poor Mama.

Sam encircled me with his arms, and I sunk into him, grateful his chest hid Doc's body from view. What would have happened if I had trusted Sam from the beginning? Could we have avoided all this?

"Ain't none of this your fault."

Leave it to Sam to know exactly what I was stewing on.

"All these folks made their choices, and you ended up bearing the consequences."

Leah Belle's words echoed in my mind. *Sometimes the child pays for the sins of the father.*

Paulson stood over Gus sprawled out with his bleeding nose askew. "This fella won't be hurting anybody else anytime soon." He studied the giant on the ground and then grinned at Daddy. "Remind me not to rile your daughter."

Heat rushed to my face, but Daddy just laughed. "She's one of the most courageous people I know."

Paulson and the other agent heaved Gus between them and staggered down the ridge behind Daddy, leaving room for Julia to clamber up. *Rosie!*

Rosie squirmed out of Julia's arms, and I rushed to my girl, gathering her in and swinging her round. She giggled and leaned back, her ash-streaked face sparkling in the sunlight. Sam kissed our daughter's nose and folded us into his strong arms. Wasn't no devils going to take us now.

CHAPTER
Thirty-One

"Ye are all the children of light, and the children of the day: we are not of the night, nor of darkness."

—The apostle Paul
in his first letter to the Thessalonians

— SAM —

There's this time in the mountains when the rest of the world has been bathed in sunlight for maybe an hour or more but the sun hasn't quite gotten round to sneaking into the mountain hollers. It ain't dark no more, but it ain't dawn yet neither. Don't rightly think anybody's got words to describe it. Though I'd say at that moment, it felt a bit like stepping into another world . . . especially since the frost glittered on every blade of grass and bare branch in sight.

Though I couldn't feel Annie's skin through our wool gloves, my hand was linked with hers. Our daily walks were something Ma had insisted on—"Can't take care of nothing lessen you take care of yourself first." Don't rightly know what we'd do without her.

At the top of the hill, Annie and I stood in the crater that had once been the sorting shed. The scorch marks burrowed deep and jagged into the rock. We'd lost more than a few nearby peach trees too, but given everything, we were lucky to have saved what we did. The first fire Gus and Doc set had burned enough of the underbrush to create a firebreak. Who'd have thought the thing meant to make me look undeniably guilty would actually save the farm? The ash-covered clearing meant the men Julia and the Judge sent up the mountain were able to put out the fire afore it spread too far. They both said it was the least they could do seeing as they kept Annie and me in the dark so long.

Lord Almighty, we'd come a long way.

It'd been near seven months since I'd come home from the war, six months since the FBI dismantled Leah Belle's opium ring, and a month or so since Sid McMath and the Veteran's Party had ousted Leo McLaughlin. Hot Springs was headed to a new start, and I couldn't help thinking we were too.

Wasn't like I was healed, mind. More like healing, and from what I've seen, there ain't ever a time when healing from hurts is done. Easier, but not done. The nightmares were still there, hovering at the edges—more than a little like the bullet stuck somewhere in my shoulder. And when they crept up on me more than they should, Peter and I would strike out to hunt for a day or so, not talking about much, sometimes walking fast like we was escaping the fear. Other times we'd walk slow like we was recovering the things we needed to move on. I was mighty thankful Annie understood and let us go. God certainly knew I needed her around as much as she needed me.

Annie puckered her lips and puffed her breath, creating little balls of cloud I poked holes in. She laughed and leaned against my side. When I think about how close we'd come to losing everything to the shadows, it near stopped my heart.

"I'm going down to visit Daddy today. That still okay with you?"

"Sure is. Peter hired a few veterans to rebuild the sorting shed. He'll drop you off on the way to pick them up, then bring you back."

I kicked a toe into the scar on the ridge.

"That'll be good. I don't think I can ride the bike back up that hill no more."

"Junior getting a little too big for his britches?"

She elbowed me in the gut as she rubbed her expanding belly. "He's too big for *my* britches. This child better come before we have to plant. I don't think I'll be able to bend by Christmas."

"And you'll be nothing but beautiful propped in a corner. Rosie'll have a grand time dressing you up like a Christmas tree."

I ducked her playful jab.

And as though she'd been summoned by her name, Rosie popped out from a corner of the house with Peter fast on her heels. Those two were peas in a pod and, with Peter swinging a rope from his healed hand, up to no good, more'n likely. Ma shuffled out to the yard shaking her spoon at the pair. I grinned. Just like when Peter and I were kids. Julia would have her hands full when she married my brother come spring, but she'd have an ally in my Annie. At least for as long as they stuck around. We'd miss them, sure, but as sure as the mountain was made of rock, the FBI had plans for those two.

"I'll go make sure Rosie has some breakfast before she and Peter get too far into their adventures."

Cold nipped at me when Annie lifted her hand from mine and waddled down the mountainside, her fist dug into her back like she needed the weight behind to keep from toppling over. With how big Annie'd grown, Julia wondered if'n there was twins in our future. I grinned again. Wouldn't that beat all?

I looked out over the farm, the fields, the orchard, the barn, listening to Rosie's shrieks skipping around my brother's laughter. This was the world I'd seen in my mind's eye back in the Pacific before the shadows fell over me.

For a while there, I thought all that I'd hoped for had been a fairy tale, something somebody'd write in a book but could never happen in real life. But here's the thing most everybody forgets. Heroes always have a mission, something impossible they have to go and do. And if you pop into the middle of the story, you might just mistake the hero for a failure—or worse, a villain. But it's the scrabbling out of trouble and finding the truth deep inside that transforms that hero into a champion of light and goodness.

I rubbed at the scars streaking across my arm and shoulder. We'd had a whole heaping lot of trouble, that's for sure and for certain. It'd certainly seemed like the devils had gotten me for more than a small space of time.

Just as Annie reached the bottom of the hill, the sun crested over the mountain, sending a ray of golden light across the bare peach tree branches, lying dormant, storing up energy inside them.

No, things ain't ever perfect, but I finally knew where I belonged, with my roots deep in the Mattas family orchard. And with my family as an anchor, I was just beginning to believe I didn't belong to the night or the shadows.

I lifted my fingers into the sunshine, capturing the gold in my palm before running headlong to the bottom of the hill, scooping up Rosie and flying her in a circle. She soared into the sky like a dove, and I knew that no matter what came our way, we'd find a way to be all right. Not perfect, mind. But all right.

—ACKNOWLEDGMENTS—

The birthing of a book is never an easy process, and this novel had an especially lengthy gestation. About halfway through writing the story, I set it aside to care for my critically ill daughter. Watching my child fight for her life over and over is by far the hardest thing I have ever done. My faith and my hope were nearly crushed by the experience. By the time I was ready to tiptoe back into writing, more than a year had passed. My brand-new agent at the time, the fabulous Rachel McMillan, encouraged me to tackle Sam and Annie's story again. And so I did.

But a book can never be properly brought to the world without a lengthy list of friends, allies, and wonderfully detailed editors to help deliver it. And all of that took another three years.

I think it's fair to start the thank-yous with my husband, Chris, who manned the house while I was away at writer's retreats or off playing with imaginary friends in my mind. And I would be remiss if I didn't mention my two kids, who were incredibly patient with me as I repeatedly held up a single forefinger—*just a minute*—in response to their requests for dinner or help with homework. And for the record, my mom is a wonder woman able to balance working and bailing me out in a single afternoon, while my mom-in-law is a sanctified and gracious workhorse.

Then there are the writing cohorts who made sure I kept moving and stayed sane. Thanks to my friends in the Quotidians (Rachel McDaniel, Janine Rosche, Amanda Wen, and the rest of the crew) and Her Novel Collective (Julie Cantrell, Susie Finkbeiner, and the other powerhouse writers). Most especially thanks to Sarah De Mey, my faithful friend of more than twenty years. These women have listened to my crazy rants, cries, and hair-brained ideas that eventually became this and other books. All y'all are an amazing support system. I don't know what I would have done without you. Thank you also to Wana Hughes, Sarah's mama, who checked my dialect and area facts and also fed me collard greens for the first time. I am forever in your debt.

As an editor myself, I thought I knew how important editing was.

I had no idea . . . until my team got hold of Sam, Annie, and their family. I am forever in the debt of the team at Kregel, including Steve Barclift, Sarah De Mey, Lindsay Danielson, and Catherine DeVries, freelance editor Jean Kavich Bloom, and freelance proofreader Jeanna Lichtenberg.

Then there are the designers, production team, marketing team (including Katherine Chappell and Brianne Kerr), salespeople, the *amazing* bookstores, and finally you.

You, my dear reader, are one of the biggest reasons I write. Together we get to explore the real truths—the hard ones—in the safe and rather entertaining space of story. Maybe, just maybe, we'll all learn a little something to help us be true heroes on the other side.

Thank you for coming along for the ride.

—AUTHOR NOTES—

When I was in college, Dr. Tom Jones, my U.S. History professor, assigned us the homework of talking to a relative about WWII and/or the Great Depression. I took the opportunity to visit two of my favorite people in the world—my grandparents—who were a short two-hour drive away. Of course, my grandfather, who was a liaison pilot in the European theatre, didn't speak much of the war when my mother was small. But for whatever reason, sitting on the front porch with their granddaughter, Grandma and Bobpa told their stories over glasses of cold lemonade. For months afterward, I called my grandma and asked her questions about her growing up and married life. Those moments are beyond precious to me and lit not only my passion for history but ultimately launched this novel.

Like many other stories, this one began as a question: How did they do it? Despite having been shot down over Germany, despite the fact that seven out of ten liaison pilots did not return alive, and despite my grandfather's struggles with war memories, my grandparents' marriage was enviably strong. How does a marriage survive the devastation of war? Though I have notebooks full of my grandparents' stories, it didn't occur to me to ask this question before they passed.

Fortunately for me, others had asked and answered the question. *Soldier from the War Returning* by Thomas Childers was one of the first books I read that detailed the battle men of the "Greatest Generation" had with what we now call post-traumatic stress disorder (PTSD). It should come as no surprise, really, but this aspect of WWII isn't necessarily widely discussed or acknowledged. Hardest for me was realizing how little help there was for men like my grandfather who fought for our country and bore life-changing scars no one could see. It's as if a thin veneer was all that was available to cover their pain. And, as I've learned from my own trauma, covering pain often only allows it to fester.

So I turned to Jane Stockinger, LMSW, who answered my endless questions about PTSD and how someone in the 1940s could heal enough from PTSD-induced nightmares to eventually become a functioning member of society. EMDR therapy—eye movement desensitization and reprocessing—fascinates me, and despite the fact that I've experienced its effects firsthand, I'm still boggled by how our bodies were created to not only signal emotional distress but also to have an active participation in the healing process. There's a reason the combination of talking and rhythmic walking are helpful and healing. And there's a reason wide-open spaces and hard work are good for a body's soul. All of which I gave to Sam to allow him the greatest chance at recovery.

For more information on the connection between mind and body and the healing process of EMDR and other modern techniques, see *The Body Keeps the Score* by Bessel van der Kolk, MD. Another great resource for understanding battle-specific psychological wounds is *Wounded Warrior, Wounded Home* by Marshéle Carter Waddell and Kelly K. Orr, PhD, ABPP. Reading the latter of these books made me immensely grateful for the men and women of our armed forces and their families. If you are one of these brave people, my thank-you could never be enough.

My uncle Tony, a career navy man, was instrumental in helping figure out the nuances to navy rankings and terminology for a Higgins boat pilot. These men who drove small boats loaded with soldiers into withering enemy fire had nerves of steel. And for the record, if I've made mistakes in these areas, they are solely my own.

As for historical accuracy, the city of Hot Springs is adjacent to Hot Springs National Park, one of the first national parks. It's home to beautiful waterways and hot springs that drew famous athletes, politicians, and Hollywood stars to Central Avenue's bathhouses. Unfortunately, Hot Springs in the 1940s was also a hotbed of illegal activity and was widely known as the largest illegal gambling site in the United States. Yet it was all operated with the blessing of the city mayor, Leo McLaughlin, the sheriff, and, by many accounts, the governor of Arkansas. Though the events depicted in the book are fictional, more than a few stories confirm the legal machine in Hot Springs used money from bribes, occasional raids, and the like to keep the city flush with cash. My story of McLaughlin's daily parade down Central Avenue is true right down to the detail of the carnation in his lapel and his horses, Scotch and Soda. With the help of widespread voter fraud, McLaughlin held power for decades until the military men came home, banded together, and gained two seats in the local government—Sid McMath as prosecuting attorney and J. O. Campbell as tax assessor. They used that position of power to conduct the GI Revolt and oust the ruling party.

If you'd like more information about Hot Springs during the 1940s, I recommend you read two books. *The Bookmaker's Daughter* by Shirley Abbott is a fascinating and brilliantly written memoir by a woman who grew up a loved yet confused daughter of one of the men employed by the gambling establishments. Despite the fact that the men did little to hide their activities, Shirley Abbott, like Annie and many children of the mob underlings, had no idea what her father did until she was older. For the flip-side view of Hot Springs in the 1940s, read Sid McMath's memoir, *Promises Kept*. It's the story of a man growing up in poverty, serving his country with distinction, and then holding the government to the promises they made to the world.

Al Capone's history in Hot Springs is also real. A plaque in the Arlington Resort signals that this was his favorite watering hole. Hot Springs was, in fact, a sort of gangster retreat, laying claim to regular visits from men like Charles "Lucky" Luciano, Benjamin "Bugsy" Siegel, and many more. In fact, Owney "The Killer" Madden, the famous Manhattan gangster and owner of the Cotton Club, actually retired to Hot Springs in 1935 after being released from Sing Sing Correctional Facility. Again, his actions in this book are fictionalized, but his influence on the illegal activity in the town was widely acknowledged. For a fun side escape and a dose of the mob, visit the Gangster Museum of America in downtown Hot Springs.

I also had the privilege of delving into the Hughes family history through a book they put together. Reading the book loaned to me by my friend Sarah led to my uncovering not only the history of Hot Springs but loaned me the name Dovie. The real Dovie married incredibly young and cared for a passel of stepchildren who were remarkably close to her own age. And she did it with care and beautiful love. Though I had to sacrifice her real story for the sake of this novel, I hope I have done her character justice. All of the events and background of this character are entirely fictionalized.

The fertilizer mentioned in the book was actually responsible for explosions at several train depots, but to my knowledge it was never liable for fires or explosions on individual farms. But given the fact that the nitrogen was indeed intended for bombmaking, the possibility was real enough that I took license to include it.

As portrayed by the book, electricity and running water didn't make their way into the Ouachita Mountains until the 1950s at the earliest. In fact, my friend Sarah has memories of visiting her great-grandmother in the mountains in the 1970s and there being no running water. And though it would have made Annie and Sam's life easier to have motorized vehicles, in 1946, few vehicles were available for those in poor, rural areas. The only tractors were purchased on the black market at exorbitant prices inaccessible to most farmers.

Oh, and if you're curious, Ouachita is pronounced WASH-i-tah. You're welcome.

I hope you enjoyed *Shadows in the Mind's Eye*, but I also hope you will carry Sam and Annie with you back to your family and your lives. That you will choose to be the hero of your story and not give up when shadows coming a-haunting.

If you'd like to get in touch with me, you can find me at www.janyretromp.com or pretty much any social media @janyretromp. I would love to see you there and chat about books and life while we hunt for beauty . . . even if it isn't pretty.

Blessings to you.

—DISCUSSION QUESTIONS—

1. Both Sam and Charlotte Anne expect life to go back to normal when he comes home from the war. In what ways is post-war life different from what they expect? How do the differences between their expectations and reality play into their difficulties?

2. Annie says, "Memory's a slippery thing. It changes and morphs, solidifying only at the insistence of the most powerful things. It gets so that no one's ever quite sure what actually happened." Do you agree with her statement? Why or why not?

3. When Sam comes home from the Pacific, he finds Hot Springs still a hotbed of mob activity. In what ways do you agree with how Sam reacts to the illegal activity? In what ways do you disagree?

4. Sam and Annie are part of what journalist and author Tom Brokaw called the "Greatest Generation." How is Sam's struggle with reliving his experiences in the war different from your understanding of that generation? How is it the same?

5. Which character do you most identify with? What was their approach to the inexplicably hard things in their life? How does that affect that person's interactions with others?

6. The novel includes a good deal of discussion about the nature of evil and the character of God. The characters acknowledge that God doesn't stop bad things from happening. How do they—particularly Dovie May—reconcile the hurt and pain in their lives with their concept of a loving God?

7. Dovie May says, "Sometimes God uses broken things to save us . . . Ain't no light that can get through something solid. It sneaks through the broken places." What do you think about this idea?

8. Annie asks, "Was love enough to break through the murky fear and pain?" How do you think she would answer that question by the end of the story? How would you answer it for your life?

9. Sam often sees himself as a monster throughout the book. Why? Does that change by the end? As the story ends, how do the characters view the nature of heroes and happily-ever-afters?

—ABOUT THE AUTHOR—

Janyre Tromp is a historical novelist who loves spinning tales that entertain even while they give readers a safe space to explore life's most difficult questions. She is the coauthor of *It's a Wonderful Christmas: A Film-Inspired Collection* and the author of *Wide Open: A Historical Suspense Novella*, as well as three children's titles—*That Sinking Feeling* and two board books in the All About God's Animals series. She lives in Grand Rapids, Michigan, with her family, two crazy cats, and a slightly eccentric Shetland sheepdog.